AF484911

# A PUMPKIN PATCH

## AND

# *A Fling*

A Juniper Ridge Novel

Book 1

## STARLA DEKRUYF

This book is a work of fiction. Names, characters, places, and incidents either are products of the author's imagination or are used fictitiously. Any resemblance to actual events or, places, living or dead, is entirely coincidental and not intended by the author.

A PUMPKIN PATCH AND A FLING

STARLA DEKRUYF

Copyright © 2023 by Starla DeKruyf

Editing: Jeanine Harrell of Indie Edits With Jeanine

Cover art: Jaidyn DeKruyf

All rights reserved. No part of this book may be reproduced, distributed, or transmitted in any form or by any means, including information storage and retrieval systems, without prior consent and written permission from the author, except for the use of brief quotations in a book review.

For information on subsidiary rights, please contact the author at www.starlawrites.com

Print Edition ISBN: 9798985626940

Digital ISBN: 9798985626957

A Juniper Ridge Novel

# A PUMPKIN PATCH
## AND
## A Fling

# STARLA DEKRUYF

*For Dad, continuing my author journey after losing you felt impossible. But writing is helping me through the grief. You gave me the heart of a dreamer. I will forever be grateful.*

# Content/Trigger Warnings

This book is intended for readers who are 17+. Please note that there may be content in this book that may be triggering for some readers. This list is not exclusive, so please proceed with caution.

- Mild language
- Alcohol usage
- Open door sexual content with mild descriptions
- Child abandonment
- Death and talk of death of a loved one, (past)
- Grief
- Talk of God/prayer, and the afterlife

# Chapter One

## LULA

MOM ALWAYS SAYS: LOVE STARTS WITH A SIMPLE, TINY pumpkin seed. The overused statement brought me comfort as a child. I'd watch my parents as they worked side by side, toiling away in the rich soil out on our family farm, and warmth would expand in my chest. I was lucky. I was blessed. I knew the love between my parents was a rarity. And even more so, their love for the pumpkin farm.

But the thing that brought me so much comfort as a child, is the same thing I've grown to despise the most as an adult—pumpkins. And everything related to them. Most importantly—the Coleman Family Farm.

As I sit propped on a black leather stool in a dimly lit fancy music studio in Seattle, Washington, with my band, manager, and publicist, I'm feeling the complete opposite of comfort. I twirl a black Sharpie between my fingers, and my jiggle my knee while I allow my long, dark brunette hair to fall around my face. We all stare at the large flatscreen TV mounted on the wall, one combined breath held as we wait for TMZ to play the footage of our train wreck performance from the night before.

With it being the biggest venue yet on this tour—the Tacoma Dome, opening for the band Vampire Weekend—there had already been a ton of pressure to perform well. We were scheduled to play solo tonight at the Moore Theatre and two more shows this weekend in Portland, Oregon; one at the Crystal Ballroom and our last one opening for Vampire Weekend and Bon Iver at the Moda Center—ending the tour on our home turf.

And now suddenly, the train wreck performance is playing —right before our eyes. We're halfway through *Seasons*, one of our fans' favorite songs, and my voice is at its purest, right before it strains and then finally cracks and breaks completely. My face is horror-stricken, and my bandmates hold expressions of confusion and concern. Davey, our drummer, has no idea if he should continue, and Jax, on lead guitar, watches me for directions, only I don't have any to give. Olive, our violinist and backup vocals, steps in front of me and finishes the song for me, acting as if we had this planned all along. Only, it's obvious to our fans, and clearly, TMZ, we had not.

But that appears to be the least of our problems. Following the footage, their reporters, *if you can even call them that*, are joking about me suddenly getting stage fright. Or cracking under pressure. They, of course, have done their homework. Though it's not too hard to dig up my past when my last name is Coleman, and not only is my family's farm the biggest in the state of Oregon, it's also the only pumpkin patch.

While the TV screen portrays photos of the old Coleman farmhouse and the budding pumpkin patch, the reporters throw out the name *Coleman Family Farm* like they know me, like they know my family.

One TMZ reporter says, "It's no wonder a small-town girl like Lula Coleman would crack under pressure after growing up on a secluded farm with the privileged lifestyle it brings. Guess the Coleman family has been too busy praying over their pumpkins rather than their daughter's singing career."

A few groans and sighs exhale around me while Leslie, our publicist, pops the nicotine gum in her mouth. Mick, our manager, points the remote at the TV and turns up the volume, as if I need my family's name dragged on Dolby Atmos through the surround sound speakers—*no thanks*. I sink further onto the stool, my shoulders folding in on my anxiety-filled chest. My black lensed sunglasses act as a force field, shielding my eyes from the rest of the room.

But I'd rather they shield my eyes from reality.

An old photo from the farm flashes on the TV screen; it's of my family posing on the front porch of the Coleman farmhouse. I recognize it instantly. It's the last family photo we took. Right before my brother Riley left on deployment with the marines and I left for Portland. That was nine years ago.

A TMZ reporter says, "How selfish is Lula Coleman? Well, for starters, not only did she turn her back on her family, sources tell us she hasn't even been home for nine years. When her brother was killed overseas while serving with the marines, she never even returned for his funeral." He shakes his head solemnly. "I don't know about you, folks, but I, for one, don't think Lula Coleman is someone we should be fangirling over. I mean, it feels as if the entire sweet, indie-rock, girl-next-door facade is all it is."

Heat amplifies in my core, expanding into my limbs. I spring to my feet and snatch the TV remote from Mick's hand. I punch the power button before chucking the remote across the room, nearly hitting Davey in the head. The room goes eerily silent. Leslie stares at me, heavily black-lined eyes wide and her mouth slack-jawed, her gum resting on her tongue. But everyone else skirts their attention away. I have no voice to apologize to Davey. I wince and mouth *sorry* before slumping back onto the padded stool.

Mick steps behind me and rubs my tense shoulders. I shrug off his touch. He's only trying to help, but he's making my anxiety worse. I feel him back away.

"Sorry," he mutters gruffly.

If he really wants to help, he'll find a way to get me my damn voice back. He'll hire the best vocal coach. Or find me some holistic crap or therapy or some magic potion or spell to speak over me. I *need* my voice back. Because who am I without my voice? What am I if I'm not the lead singer of The Broken Halos?

Tears prick the corners of my eyes.

Olive, who also happens to be my roommate, stands and snatches a sparkling water off the table. "Leslie, you're our publicist. It's your job to keep this trash"—she gestures at the now blank TV screen—"out of the media. I mean, how are we supposed to recover from something like this?"

Olive has a slight accent, her hometown being Raleigh, North Carolina. I met her in Portland, Oregon, a few years ago when Mick put out a call for a violinist to join our band.

Back when we first started, we were too heavy on the guitar side, having a total of three; Jax on lead guitar, Oscar on rhythm, and Cody on bass. Mick thought we needed a violinist to even us out. It had worked for Florence + The Machine so why not us?

Leslie pushes away from the doorway, wringing out her hands, and paces the length of the room. "I'm already on it."

"A little late," Jax mutters.

She shoots him a death glare, probably regretting her choice of trying to quit smoking right about now. "With today's technology, there's no way to keep everything out of the media anymore. The best we can do is try to recover. And we will."

She looks pointedly at me. I pick up the black Sharpie and yellow legal pad sitting in front of me on the table and scrawl out the word:

*How?*

I hold it up so Leslie can read it.

"My question exactly," Olive says, eyeing Leslie skeptically.

The gravelly sound of Mick clearing his throat calls all of our attention. He takes his position next to Leslie, who has finally stopped her annoying pacing. They stand like a unified team and vaguely remind me of my parents. I shudder, preparing myself for some off-the-wall antic the two of them have come up with.

"The doctor who examined Lula last night confirmed she's got vocal cord nodules," Mick begins. "She's gonna need surgery. Followed by voice therapy."

Cody twists open a beer and flings the cap across the room. "So, that's it then. The tour is over. And probably our careers along with it."

My throat thickens while tears burn my eyes. Cody has some nerve. He used to play a couple of gigs a month at dive bars in Portland. He was nothing before he signed with The Broken Halos.

The room is buzzing again, mumbles of the band's jeopardized future being tossed around like grenades on a battlefield.

Leslie shushes everyone. "Now, we know things don't look good, but we have a plan." She and Mick look at one another and exhale a joint sigh. "Lula can't sing right now. She isn't even supposed to talk. She'll have surgery and then need about two months to recover."

Olive stands and throws her hands up. "So that's it then,

Cody is right. Because I hope your brilliant plan isn't that I'll be the one taking over as lead vocalist for our last three shows. Y'all know my voice isn't strong enough for lead."

"It's stronger than Lula's right now," Cody sneers and has the nerve to let out a rough chuckle.

A fit of rage stirs in my gut, and even a bit of nausea, at the thought that I wasted a year of my life dating the guy.

"No, Olive. Just take a seat, please. We all need to keep our cool." Mick leans his back against the wall. "We're canceling the last three shows."

The room roars with groans and curses.

"We don't have a choice." Mick raises his voice. "It will be fine. Big-name artists do it all the time. Hell, even Justin Timberlake recently canceled several shows with some excuse of needing self-care. At least in Lula's case, it's a legit medical condition. The fans should have empathy for her."

"Besides the ones who think she's a self-centered princess," Oscar mumbles.

And I have to bite my cheek to keep from arguing with him. Like he'd understand anyway? His parents were supportive when he left Southern California to pursue his dreams. And their arms are open wide when he returns home for visits. He doesn't have painful memories waiting back there—like a big brother who died long before he should have.

"Mick is right. Our fans are loyal. They're gonna feel bad for Lula," Olive agrees, ignoring Oscar's words and flashing me a sympathetic smile.

"And that's where the rest of you come in." Leslie begins pacing again. Always with the pacing. Those high heels clicking against the dark hardwood floor. I wish she'd just light a cigarette already and put us all out of misery. "You all need to get on your social media accounts and profess your undying support and love for Lula. Then, you need to do the same with your fans. Thank them for their support, and tell them how much you appreciate them. I want you to go above and beyond. Spend every day and night on there if you have to." She bends, smacking both palms flat on the glossy tabletop. "Just make a connection. And for the love of God, make it believable, people."

"Yeah, okay. We can do that," Jax says.

He reaches out and pats my hand, and his familiar touch calms me. Out of anyone in this room, Jax is the only one who can imagine what I'm going through. We've been best friends since the fifth grade, and he knows all the Colemans.

"Because we do care, Lula. We aren't all selfish bastards." He glares over his shoulder at Cody.

"We really do. We've built something really special here, y'all. We're family." Olive stands and wraps her arms around my shoulders from behind me.

Family. It's an afflictive word. I grew up with an incredible family. We were close. We shared love and commitment. But that same love and commitment are what smothered me. I never asked to be raised on the Coleman Family Farm. I never wanted to be a farmer, to devote my life to the soil and the rain and wind. To worry if my livelihood would be swallowed up by bugs or mildew.

When I wanted out, that same loving and close family was the first to turn their backs on me. In the past nine years that I've been in Portland, Mom and Dad have never come to visit me. They've never even been to a single concert. Nearly the only connection I've had with my parents since leaving the farm is Mom's Sunday evening phone calls. My big sister Emmaline—forever loyal to the Coleman Family Farm and will probably work there until her last dying breath—has two kids I've never even met. And Mom says she's got another one on the way.

My little brother Garrison and I text regularly. He's visited a few times and has been to some of our shows. He threatens to leave the farm and become a hunting guide, but I honestly don't think he has the guts. Sometimes I think my big brother Riley got the easy way out. He joined the marines when he was eighteen and never made it home after his first deployment overseas. But every time I think that, I instantly feel guilty. There's no easy way out of a family.

"And what is Lula supposed to do during the two months?" Jax asks.

"For starters," Mick says, "she's gonna do the exact thing the rest of you are doing. She's gonna post her gut-wrenching story, including her terrible diagnosis, on Instagram and Facebook and Snapchat, and tweet about it on Twitter and whatever other social network has been created in the last twelve hours since all of this went down."

Mick's face is tired. Dark circles shadow his eyes, and the wrinkles around his mouth are somehow more defined than usual. I don't envy his position. But I can bet he'd rather be in his position than mine right now.

"Okay, then what?" Oscar asks, scooting to the edge of the black leather couch and resting his elbows on his knees. "I mean, the rest of the band can at least keep rehearsing, right? But what is Lula supposed to do?"

My question exactly. I can only post my sob story so many times on social media before my fans will become bored and move on to supporting the next upcoming indie band. Or they'll have the same opinion as the TMZ reporters, and it won't matter what I post—they'll think I'm selfish.

Besides, taking two to three months off is completely unheard of. Since I left Juniper Ridge at the age of eighteen and headed to Portland with Jax, I haven't once taken a break. I don't think I know how. I assume it's in my blood. Something I can thank the good ol' Coleman family for. Farmers don't get breaks.

"I'm glad you asked, Oscar." But Leslie glances at me.

For a moment, I think I see a hint of compassion revealed in her big brown eyes, but I'm sure I've imagined it. She's only worried about covering her own behind.

"The most important job Lula has is resting her vocals. That means, for The Broken Halos to have a future, Lula cannot sing. At all."

I knew this already. The doctor at the hospital told me this exact thing last night. But to hear the words again while my band members hear them for the first time, feels as if my gut is being hollowed out.

"Even her talking must be limited. Especially during the first few weeks after surgery. She'll stay in contact with all of you through email and texting. And of course"—Leslie gestures at the yellow legal pad I've been jotting words on—"paper."

Mick clears his throat.

I cringe. I had a feeling this little meeting would not end like this. Mick and Leslie have something else up their sleeves.

He says, "There's one more thing. As we said, canceling shows isn't a huge deal. For big artists. But The Broken Halos is just now on the rise. You're still building a fan base. While your shows on the *Seasons* tour did sell out, this was your first tour—for your third album release. Your first album, *Recollection of Hearts*, didn't even sell enough copies for us to send you out on tour."

"But that was four years ago," Oscar points out.

"And your second album, *Extraction*, barely sold enough to break even."

"That album dropped in the middle of a pandemic. You can't hold that against us. That's BS." Cody chugs his beer.

Jax climbs off the stool next to mine, shoving his fingers

through his light strawberry-blonde hair. "You said it yourself, Mick, we're up and coming. Our shows for the *Seasons* tour sold out."

"Just cut to the chase." Davey flops back onto a leather couch next to Oscar. "What are you trying to tell us?"

Mick's attention flicks to me, his eyes glazed with exhaustion, and I feel the heaviness in them. My shoulders slump in on themselves, and I await my sentence. He and Leslie have planned something big for me, I just know it. I can feel it deep in my bones. And the longer he holds it in, the bigger it feels.

I use the Sharpie again and scrawl on the legal pad:

*Just say it.*

"We need as much support as possible from your fans." He pauses to suck in a deep breath. "And we believe Lula and The Broken Halos will get more support if she were to return home and spend the duration of her recovery on the family farm."

Untamed panic rises in me, and I jump to my feet, causing the metal stool to fly backward and topple against the hardwood floor with a loud crash. My chest tightens, and I violently shake my head. I fight to catch my breath as a giant lump the size of Mount Everest forms in my throat.

"Calm down, Lula, calm down," Mick says, his voice soothing though I can hardly hear him over the pounding of blood in my ears.

"It's not the end of the world." Leslie rolls her eyes and cracks her gum. "You'll go there, make nice with your family, take a few candid photos of you helping out on the farm. It won't be that bad."

But Leslie doesn't know my family. She doesn't know the last words we exchanged with one another that summer morning when I left the farm. Or the horrendous breakup with

Kade. She'd never understand the unresolved pain that awaits me there.

"It's not a bad idea, Lula," Cody says.

I shoot a death glare at him—of course he'd say that. Ever since we broke up two years ago, he always disagrees with me.

"Don't give me that look," he mutters, glancing away. "It will be the best thing for the band right now, and you know it."

I hate that he knows me. That he knows my "looks" and their meanings.

Olive clears her throat. "I mean"—she winces, and I know what's coming, she's going to agree with Cody—"it's not a terrible idea. Lula, that press, the stuff they dug up about you and your family—you never going back for Riley's funeral—it doesn't look good for the band."

Late in the night, years ago, I told Olive all about Riley and losing him. And why I haven't been back home, not even for his funeral. My skin prickles with affliction. This feels like a betrayal. Even if deep, deep down, I know it's not.

Jax slings an arm over my shoulder. He's attempting playfulness, but it's coming across as mechanical. "We've worked so hard, you've worked so hard, Lu. I know you, you won't give up on your dream, or the band's. I think you know, you gotta do this."

My shoulders sulk, my chest caving in on itself, and as much as I want to argue and tell them that they can all go to hell, I know I have to do this. For the band, and for me.

# Chapter Two

## AXEL

I awake earlier than usual and tiptoe out to the small kitchen and flip on the coffee machine. Making the Thursday apple delivery to Sal's Grocers isn't typically my responsibility. But when you live in the small rental on your employer's property, you take whatever job you're given. This is the start of my third fall season as a hired hand on the Coleman Family Farm. But let's be honest, hired hand is just a glorified term for "farm boy."

I tug on a pair of worn jeans and button my flannel shirt while I wait for the coffee to brew. I brush my teeth and throw on a red baseball cap featuring the logo of a baseball farm team north of Seattle. I played on the team too many years ago to mention, it's embarrassing. But I suppose not enough to quit wearing the hat. When the coffee machine beeps, I fill a travel mug full and dump in a couple of teaspoons of sugar.

I worry I may not be back in time before Sadie leaves for school, so dad-guilt forces me to set out a box of Froot Loops on the small wooden pedestal table. To balance out her breakfast, I place a banana next to the cereal. I grab a banana for myself just as there's a light knock on the front door. When I swing it open, Emmaline Coleman stands on the stoop, wiping the sleep from her eyes and rubbing her already enormous pregnant belly.

"Morning," I greet.

"Yeah, morning," she mumbles.

"So, I should be back in about an hour."

"No rush. I got this," she says on a yawn. "Remember, I got two kids of my own? And they're thriving just fine."

I'd argue better than fine. Emmaline runs a tight ship over at the Coleman farmhouse situated across the pasture from this smaller house.

"Thanks for coming."

"And thank *you* for saving the farm once again." She shakes her head. "I could kill Garrison for leaving us high and dry."

"It's fine." I lie and back up toward the truck. "See you soon."

She waves and slips inside the house to wait for Sadie to wake up and get her ready for school for me.

The old Chevy's bed is packed full of boxes of apples ready to be delivered to Sal's, a small grocery store in the next town over. Garrison Coleman is the usual delivery boy on Thursdays, but since he's off on yet another hunting trip, I'm the second-best man for the job.

The truck sprays gravel underneath the tires as I pull away from the modest two-bedroom home on the Coleman Family Farm property. When I reach the main road, I fiddle with the radio, but it gives me nothing more than static. I drink my coffee and nearly burn my tongue with the bitter brew.

The sun is already rising since according to the calendar, it's still summer. I drive faster than I should considering the business name is plastered on both sides of the truck. But the goal is to make it back in time before Sadie wakes up. In case I don't, Emmaline has agreed to see her off to school. But I'd rather it be me.

The Colemans already do enough to help me out with Sadie as it is. And I don't like shoving my responsibilities onto them. Even though Sadie is a fairly easy-going kid, she's mine to take care of.

I reach Sal's Grocers just before seven a.m. Sal's son, Parker, greets me outside and makes his way to the back of the truck to unload the boxes of apples. Since that's not my job, I head inside Sal's and search for the miniature blueberry muffins Hostess makes that are Sadie's favorite.

"Hey there, Axel." Sal comes out from the storeroom when I'm rounding another aisle. "I haven't seen you in ages."

"Hello, Sal." I smile and make my way toward him, reaching out for a handshake. "It's been a few months. I usually only see Parker when I come by."

Sal glances over his shoulder, peering out at the parking lot. "Where's Garrison?"

"Oh, you know"—I rub at the back of my neck—"off on another hunting trip."

Sal chuckles, shaking his head. "Sounds about right."

I resist the urge to throw the guy under the bus. I mean, sure, Garrison has been nothing but nice to me. All of the Coleman family have been nothing but nice. Though picking up Garrison's slack around the farm is getting old, and it's wearing on me. He's invited me along numerous times on fishing and hunting trips, but being away from Sadie for even a day is too long.

Never mind overnight.

"Say, how's that sweet little girl of yours?"

"Sadie? She's good. Just turned five last week."

"No kidding? My, my, they do grow up fast."

The bell rings over the double glass doors as Parker enters

the store. "Dad? There's a bunch of news vans out front. People too. They've got cameras and microphones."

"Well, what in the Sam Hill is going on out there, I wonder." Sal shuffles toward the windows and peers out.

I don't much care for crowds, so I continue my search for the muffins. Down the aisle where I finally find them, I spot a woman perusing the magazine racks and blocking the display of muffins. Her dark hair peeks out from underneath a ball cap, and oversized dark sunglasses hide her eyes. The fitted black jeans, high heels, and loose black top, revealing one bare shoulder, are enough to make me do a double take.

Not only because she's a total knockout, but she sticks out like a sore thumb in a place like Sal's. I give her some space, resisting the urge to admire the view from behind her, but she either doesn't notice my presence or she doesn't care she's in my way.

When she doesn't move, my patience grows thin. I clear my throat. She still doesn't budge. I don't have time for this. I reach around her for the muffins, and she jumps.

"Sorry," I grumble, "didn't mean to scare you."

She shrinks back without speaking, which actually does make me feel a little bad. After I snatch the package of muffins and another for myself and turn around, she's gone. I check the time on my phone and hurry to the register to pay. The middle-aged woman working the cash register is distracted. Every few seconds, she stretches her neck to peer outside at the commotion in the parking lot.

After she rings me up, I decide I better hit the bathroom before the drive back to the farm and I leave my purchases on the counter. When I push through the bathroom door, I freeze. Suck in a breath, I take a step backward. The silent woman in the baseball cap is wedged in the open bathroom window. Her butt is propped against one side with her high-heeled boots against the other while she attempts to squeeze through it.

"What the hell?" I breathe out.

She whips her head in my direction and tears off her sunglasses. I'm momentarily blinded by the icy-blue eyes staring back at me. She puts her finger to her lips, and I spin around to check if anyone is in the hall behind me. There isn't. I turn to face her again, and terror glints in her pleading eyes.

What else can I do but allow her to finish her escape? This is none of my business. And she doesn't have any merchandise in her hands that I can see. She mouths *thank you* before slipping the rest of the way out the window. I jog over to it and peer out just in time to see her sneak around the side of the building.

I rub at my neck and shake my head.

And here I thought nothing could surprise me anymore after living in a small town for three years.

Once I finish my business in the bathroom, and walk back out into the store, there's a few people inside lurking around. I may be curious, but not enough to delay me from getting back to Sadie.

Snatching my bag of purchases off the counter, I nod to the cashier.

I pass Sal at the glass doors. "See ya later, Sal. Have a good one."

"Oh, yeah, you too, Axel. And hey, you be careful. Looks like a mob out there."

"Thanks for the warning."

I push out the door, and Parker was right; there's a commotion of reporters with microphones, video cameras, and news vans consuming the parking lot. I'm not sure what's going on. While this is unusual in a small town like this, it's not unusual in the city I grew up in, north of Seattle. So I ignore it and proceed to the truck, tugging the brim of my hat lower.

"Hey, hey," a woman calls, rushing toward me.

I turn, and she has a microphone in her hand, the letters of a local news station in bold caps plastered on it. A guy trails behind her, holding a video camera. This is the last thing I have time for. I assume this has something to do with the recent local forest fire. Or maybe it's about a missing person case. I suppose I did hear about an old man a few days ago, just walked right out of his memory care facility and never returned.

But the image of Sadie, eating her breakfast without me, tugs at my heart.

I turn around to face the woman, palms up. "Look, I don't know anything, and I don't have time for anything." I swing open the door of the truck and climb in.

"Wait! Wait! If you could just answer one question? Have you seen—"

I slam the truck's door and back out of the space before I even have my seatbelt buckled. About a dozen people chase after me but give up once I make it out onto the main road.

I shake my head and let out a whistle. "Now that was seriously weird," I say.

Over a quiet staticky version of Chris Stapleton's latest song, there's a rustling next to me. I jerk my attention to the passenger seat where a heap of burlap rests that we use to cover the boxes of apples. There's a stirring underneath the pile. A rush of adrenaline slides through me, and I yank the steering wheel, causing the truck to swerve off to the shoulder. I pump the brakes, and the truck skids through the loose gravel until it finally stops.

A face suddenly appears, popping out from underneath the burlap—terror shining in giant, familiar blue eyes.

"What the—"

The woman frantically waves her arms. Probably to calm me down, but all it's doing is making me more terrified.

"Wait," she says, hoarsely as she holds a finger in the air before fumbling for her phone in her back pocket. She taps on it before holding it out to me.

"What the hell are you doing in my truck?" I bark.

I just need a ride. To the farm.

"What?" I grunt.

Please.

I pinch my eyebrows together. I don't have time for this. "Why to the farm?"

She hesitates before typing again.

Looking for a job.

I'm struck with a moral dilemma. Drive this possibly deranged woman back to the farm where who knows what kind of trouble she'll cause, or force her out of my truck and leave her on the side of the road.

She taps on her phone screen again.

Please.

The same pleading flashes in her blue eyes as when she was wedged in the bathroom window at Sal's. I tear my attention away from her and groan, fidgeting with my hat on my head. If having Sadie has changed me in any way, it's that I now have a soft spot. Because this woman is someone's daughter. And since she's using her phone to have a conversation with me, she either can't speak or she's too afraid to speak to me.

Whatever the reason, I don't care. But leaving her on the side of the road isn't an option.

I take my hat off and scratch my fingers through my unruly hair before exhaling and returning my hat backwards onto my head.

"Fine," I grunt. "To the farm. But then that's it. You're no longer my problem. Got it?"

> Got it. Thank you!

I turn the radio up, but she shoots forward in her seat and switches it off. *Okay, so no music.* I offer her a mini muffin, but she scrunches her nose at it. *So she's not hungry either.* Guessing that means she's not homeless. I've seen plenty of homelessness in my day around Seattle, and any one of them would have been damn appreciative at the offering of a Hostess mini muffin.

I guess we're driving the rest of the way in silence.

When I finally turn down the road that leads to the Coleman Family Farm, the woman sinks into her seat. I park out in front of the small house I call home, and glance over at her. A bare shoulder peeks out of her loose, black shiny top. It distracts me momentarily. She's probably the prettiest woman I've ever seen on the farm.

"Well, we're here. I held up my end of the bargain, now if you could please be so kind as to hold up yours."

She presses her lips together and smiles at me before returning the sunglasses to her face. But the smile appears forced, and if I didn't know any better, she's frightened. She taps on her phone again and holds it out to me.

Her not speaking is odd, but I've learned a lot over the last few years during my time in Juniper Ridge—it's best not to judge the folks around here. Or get into their business.

"You're welcome," I grumble. "Now, I gotta—" but before I can finish, she opens the door and jumps out of the passenger seat. "Well, okay then. Guess that's that." I shake my head and climb out of the truck.

When I unlock the door to the house, I glance over my shoulder and see the woman still standing next to the truck. I hesitate, feeling conflicted. The gentlemanly thing to do would be asking if she needs anything else. But when I peer into the house and see Sadie peeling her banana at the table, my heart gives a squeeze.

I slip inside and close the door behind me without looking back.

"Daddy!" Sadie hops off the chair and runs toward me.

I swoop her into my arms and swing her around as if it's been years since I've seen her instead of only a few hours.

"Hey, baby girl. Look what I brought you." I hold up the bag of mini muffins, and she squeals in delight. "You ready for school?"

"Almost. Miss Emma came to help."

I turn around and see Emmaline stepping out of Sadie's room with a pair of Mary Janes between her fingers.

"Hey, Axel. You made good time."

"Thanks again for coming over. You're a lifesaver."

Her dark brunette hair is gathered into a ponytail like it always is. "You're the lifesaver."

"Nah." I wave her off and set Sadie back down on the old hardwood floor.

"No, I mean it. My parents lucked out when you came

strolling into the office that day looking for a job." She picks up Sadie and sets her on the chair, releasing a grunt. "Let's put your shoes on, little missy prissy."

Sadie giggles at the nickname, and I can't help but grin. She's happy here. Which takes a giant load off my dad-guilt. Because the day I strolled into the Coleman Family Farm office looking for a job, I was more than desperate. And I'm pretty sure the mention of being a single dad to a two-year-old—whose mother had just up and abandoned us—made me a shoo-in for the job.

"Miss Emma put my tights on," Sadie says with a mouth full of muffin.

"Well that was sure nice of her. But remember, no talking with your mouth full."

"There, all done," Emmaline says on an exhale while she stands. "Now, I gotta get going. Lots of work to do. Big day." She heads toward the front door.

I sort of hop and jog after her. "Big day?"

She waves me off. "Oh, you know? Every day leading up to pumpkin season is a big day around here."

True. The pumpkin season is huge for the Coleman Family Farm. They make most of their money on the fall season alone.

I rub at the back of my neck and hold the front door open for Emmaline. "Say, uh, you know all that talk about your parents loving how I just strolled in asking for a job?"

She turns to me and frowns, planting her hands on her hips. "Um, yeah. Why?"

"How would they feel if, say, someone else did that?"

"Axel, is one of your friends looking for a job? Because if they are, you know Mama and Daddy would hire them on the spot. Especially if you're referring them. And we need all the help we can get this season."

"No, no, not one of my friends. You see, there's this woman." I take off my baseball hat. "She's looking for a job."

"Ahh." She grins. "It's a female friend. I haven't heard about you dating anyone. I'm sure Garrison would've mentioned it."

"No," I blurt. "Not a girlfriend. Not *my* girlfriend. Just a woman, looking for a job is all."

A commotion of people and news vans across the pasture near the Coleman farmhouse catches our attention.

Emmaline's forehead wrinkles as she frowns. She exhales a deep sigh. "I gotta go."

"What's going on over there?" I'm briefly reminded of the crowd at Sal's Grocers and the mob of reporters who nearly chased down the farm truck.

"If you know someone looking for a job, whoever they are, point them in the direction of the office." She stomps off toward the house, exaggeration in each step.

Sadie wraps her small body around my leg. "C'mon, Daddy. Don't want to be late for school."

"Yeah, okay."

She unravels herself and says, "Who are all those people? Are they here for pumpkins?"

"I'm not sure, baby girl." I nudge her toward my truck, parked on the other side of our house.

We climb inside, and I wait for Sadie to buckle herself into her car seat. It's not completely unheard of to have the local news interview the Coleman family. But it's still a few more weeks until we officially enter pumpkin season. And that's a heck of a lot more reporters than what usually comes out to the farm.

An uneasy feeling snakes through me. I hope the stowaway I brought to the farm isn't related to why all those reporters are here.

# Chapter Three

## LULA

An overwhelming sense of dread along with panic swell in my chest as I step onto the soil of the Coleman Family Farm. I gaze out over the pumpkin field and at the cornstalks neatly planted in uniformed rows, and a melodic familiarity drums beneath my skin.

The old Coleman farmhouse sits at the edge of the property, appearing picturesque with your typical white paint and black trim. Back in 1944, when Granddad built this house and he and Nonna started the pumpkin farm, it was cheaper to get electricity if the house was closer to the main road.

Not much has changed in the nine years since I left. Which, in a way, makes me even more agitated. I haul my bag and two suitcases from the back of the old farm truck I stupidly assumed my brother, Garrison, would be driving. He's been the one making the deliveries every Thursday to Sal's Grocers since he was sixteen. Instead, I about scared the shit out of some rando dude that my parents must've hired to take his place.

I slide my phone from my back pocket and text Garrison.

Where are you?

How come you didn't make the delivery to Sal's?

You finally get the nerve to quit and forget to tell me?

I wait for a response, breathing in the scent of fresh hay and dry dirt and hating how a simple, familiar smell can bring all those memories flooding back to my soul. I hold up my phone and take a picture of the property and text it to Olive.

I am officially in hell.

OLIVE

Looks beautiful to me. Wanna trade? I'm stuck in rehearsal while Jax and Davey argue over the importance of our song Hopscotch Heart.

Good luck with that.

OLIVE

You too.

Without a response from Garrison, I return my phone to my pocket and trudge across the muddied grassy field, yanking the two rolling suitcases behind me that aren't rolling so well over such terrain. I dodge the reporters who appear to be held up near the back door of the farmhouse, and I head to the front instead. By the time I make it to the porch, there's an inch of mud corroding the rubber soles on my new Timberland boots as well as the wheels of my suitcases.

*Just great.*

I take a deep breath before releasing it slowly. When I turn the knob on the front door of the farmhouse, it squeaks open, and I'm instantly bombarded with more memories. When I was a teenager and attempted to sneak out of the house, if the fourth step on the staircase didn't give me away, this dumb creaky door would do the honors.

I step inside and plop my bags down while my gaze takes a trip around the farmhouse. I'm acutely aware of the fact that nothing inside the house has changed. I'm not sure what I was expecting. That Mom would've finally gotten rid of Nonna's thimble collection and the three inches of dust blanketing them, or that Granddad's stuffed elk heads wouldn't be hanging on the main wall in the living room anymore? The sight gives me a slight ache in my chest, like I haven't missed anything at all in the last nine years. But at the same time, like I've missed everything.

I leave my muddy suitcases by the door and wipe my boots on the floor mat. Tiptoeing through the entryway and into the living room, I glance over each shoulder. It's quiet in the farmhouse. Too quiet.

When I almost reach the kitchen, a creak followed by a squeal sounds out, and I whirl around. A small child comes stomping down the staircase. It's a little girl. She reaches the bottom of the stairs and freezes in front of me. Long brunette hair, fashioned in two braids, hangs over each shoulder while two big blue eyes blink up at me. I know this girl. Well, I don't know, know her. But she's the smallest version of Emmaline I've ever seen.

"Hello," the word barely croaks out in a hoarse whisper. I'm instantly reminded that I'm not supposed to speak. I'm also aware of just how bad my voice is, and the discovery is startling.

"Hello," the little girl repeats. She sticks out a tiny, pudgy hand. "I'm Ariel, what's your name?"

Her words and the handshake gesture are so proper that she can *only* be Emmaline's daughter. I shake her hand. But when I open my mouth to speak, I think about Mick and Leslie and the band and how they're all counting on me. I hold up a finger and retrieve my phone. I tap a message, hoping she's old enough to read.

She frowns at the screen, and my hope fizzles.

But then she says, "Lula is the name of Mama's sister."

I nod and smile.

"Are you Mama's sister?"

I nod again and type on my phone.

"Mama is helping Axel get Sadie ready for school."

I have no idea who Axel or Sadie are, and I wonder if my sister has left her husband, Jackson, for someone new. Or maybe my sister had another kid that I have somehow forgotten.

"Sadie is my best friend."

*Yeah, that still doesn't clear things up for me, kid.*

The sound of the backdoor swinging open is followed by footsteps, and the voices of my mother and Emmaline trickle into the kitchen. Their tone is not pleasant. They both enter the kitchen and freeze when they see me.

Mom presses a palm to her heart, and a genuine smile appears, revealing fresh wrinkles I've never seen before. "Oh, Lula. You're home."

She crosses the worn hardwood floor in a rush and draws me in for a tight hug.

For a moment, time stands still, and I'm a young girl again. I clutch her sweater in my fingers and breathe in her rosy scent. Her bristled dark-blonde hair tickles my nose, and I rear back, suddenly overcome by unexpected emotion, fighting back tears.

"Hey, Mom." Again, it's strained and sounds worse than when I greeted Ariel.

Concern smears across Mom's face, and she takes my hands in hers. "You sound awful, honey. Let me make you some tea." She drops my hands and goes into mom-mode, filling the kettle on the stove with water, opening the cupboard, and pulling out tea and honey. "How's chamomile? That okay with you? And I've got this local honey. You remember the Finleys?" She calls over her shoulder.

I blink at her.

*Is she kidding?* How could I forget? My body reacts with a tingling sensation running through it at the mere mention of the name. Kade Finley was my high school boyfriend. We were supposed to spend the rest of our lives together.

Though it's funny that you can almost forget someone completely when you don't think of them for so long. Almost. But the problem is, you don't forget someone like Kade Finley.

"Anyway, they're making honey now. It's the best there is."

Emmaline clears her throat. "There's a bunch of news vans and reporters outside. So, Lula, you might wanna lay low for a few hours." She gathers her long, brunette hair into a tighter ponytail before finally crossing the kitchen to greet me. "It's been a long time."

I nod, and we share one of the most awkward hugs ever, and not simply because there's a giant baby bump between us.

Ariel tugs on my sister's hand. "This is your sister?"

Emmaline smiles at her daughter. "Yes, that's right. This is your Aunt Lula."

Ariel frowns at me again, her little dark brows knitted together. "How come I've never met you?"

"Your Aunt Lula is a famous singer." She's smiling, though it appears forced. She holds Ariel's hand. "She's been too busy traveling around the country and making music to be bothered by us."

And there it is. Emmaline is even trying to get her daughter on the we-hate-Lula bandwagon. All because I had dreams outside these old farmhouse walls and away from the family farm.

I don't bother trying to correct Emmaline. Or stick up for myself. My voice doesn't work, and besides, what's the point anyway? Once someone has their mind made up about you, there's no sense in trying to change it.

Mom is too busy rambling about the Finleys to notice the awkwardness going on in the kitchen right before her very eyes. She removes a few mugs from the cupboard before glancing at the clock on the wall.

"Oh, Emma, it's getting late. You better hurry and get those kids off to school. You and your sister can catch up later."

"Yes, Mom. I know what time the kids go to school." Emmaline rolls her eyes. "I guess I'll see you later."

"Bye, Aunt Lula." Ariel waves and I wave back.

The usage of the title is odd and comforting, all wrapped up together.

After the two head out the back door, Mom presses her fists to her hips. "That one is gonna take a real liking to you, I can already tell."

I raise my eyebrows at her.

"Our little Ariel is a singer. She's been singing longer than she could talk."

Learning this small thing about my niece that will connect us causes my heart to give a small heave in my chest. Because I'm proud, but I also know the price she'll pay to pursue her dreams. Having Emmaline as a mother is probably a whole lot like having my mother as a mother.

Maybe even worse.

"Now, let's have some tea and we'll talk."

I want to remind her that this will be more of a one-sided conversation seeing as I can't talk, but something tells me she already knows that.

"We'll only have a few minutes. Caleb will be up soon, and then I'm on childcare duty until Emmaline returns. He's our sleeper. If you wake him up too early, he's a grouchy little man."

Mom sets two steaming mugs on the sturdy wood table and gestures with a sweep of her arm for me to join her.

I recognize the name Caleb as Emmaline's youngest child. At least until the baby arrives. I've lived a pretty hectic life the past four months touring around the Midwest and West Coast with the band, but things around here seem just as hectic. One person going here, the other going in another direction, and where is Garrison and Dad and Jackson in all of this?

Hesitantly, I slide onto the bench at the table and bring my phone along with me. This way, it won't be only Mom talking at me. I'll have at least a small fighting chance at sticking up for myself. A pang of sadness pinches in my chest for feeling this way.

"We're thrilled to have you home. Even if the circumstances are less than ideal. I mean, you with your vocal cord injury. It's just terrible. I wish you would've called. Or had Mick or Jax call. I would've come to Portland for your surgery."

Now I know that's not true. I don't doubt that Mom loves me. But she never leaves Juniper Ridge. She hardly ever leaves the farm, especially this close to pumpkin season. By my calculations, my vocal cord surgery three days ago puts us at about three weeks until pumpkin season.

"I just don't know why you have to be so difficult. Why you had to tell your mama you're coming home in a text is beyond me."

I tap a message on my phone and slide it over to her.

I can't talk. Remember?

She waves me off. "Right, I get that."

But something tells me she doesn't. She will hold this over my head the entire time I'm here. Maybe even longer.

"And am I sorry this happened to you? Yes, of course I am. We all feel just terrible. But do I believe everything happens for a reason? Yes, of course I do. The good Lord knew we needed help this season and our Lula was the only one for the job."

Anger seeps through me, drenching my veins. I tap vigorously on the phone screen.

Don't bring God into this.

"Oh, Lula. Turning your back on your family is one thing, but please tell me you haven't turned your back on Jesus?" She presses her hand to her heart. "Your daddy says you have a good head on your shoulders and we raised you right and you'd never go astray, but I just don't know anymore." She rubs her temples, and my blood boils beneath my skin. "You're out there traipsing around the country, riding in a tour bus with boys, and singing these songs."

I stand abruptly, my legs tremble, and I force out a strangled, "Stop."

She holds a palm up. "Okay, okay. I'm done. Your daddy warned me not to force it. So I'm done. And Mick reiterated how important it is that we don't let you strain your voice. I'm sorry." She takes a sip of her tea, and I slowly ease myself down on the bench. "Now, we're happy you're home, but this won't be a vacation for you. If you stay here, you'll be pitching in."

I roll my eyes.

She waggles her pointer finger at me. "Nu-uh. Don't you roll your eyes at me, young lady. Whether you like it or not, you're a Coleman. Which means you not only have responsibilities but a reputation to uphold as well."

Everything in me wants to argue. I want to bring up the

past and remind her that nine years ago, when I left, she told me if I did so, I was no longer a Coleman. But I don't.

"Grams!" Caleb, I presume, calls from upstairs.

Mom pushes off the table and stands. "Now, it's nearly pumpkin season. We've got a lot of work to do. I'll give you today to settle in. Thanks to Ariel, who's agreed to bunk with Caleb, I've set up your old bedroom for you. Supper is at six o'clock, as always. Don't be late." She leaves me alone at the table as she heads up the long, narrow wooden staircase.

If I had my voice, I'd call after her and ask how I could possibly be late for supper when I have nowhere else to go. I sip my tea and scroll through Twitter, first searching the hashtag with the band's name. Most of what I find is fans sharing their condolences and a speedy recovery after my surgery. There are a few negative tweets, but I ignore them and go to my personal account. I haven't posted since I arrived home, and I have a feeling Leslie will be texting soon to rectify that. I compose a tweet, thanking my fans for the prayers and the positive vibes, and tell them I can't wait to be singing for them again.

I shoot a text to Jax.

> I can't believe you wouldn't come home with me. Wuss.

JAX

Sorry. You know I would if I could. But if we wanna get back in the studio to make our fourth album we gotta practice.

> Sounds like a cop-out

JAX

I love you!

> Yeah, yeah love you too!

I decide to ignore Jax's text. The very last thing I plan to do is see Kade Finley.

When I finish my tea, I toss the teabag into the trash and load my mug into the dishwasher. It's as if I'm moving on autopilot, the old actions and tendencies taking over. I do the same with Mom's mug before I pick up my duffel bag, hike it over my shoulder, and head upstairs.

The walls in the hallway are familiar with worn, peeling wallpaper. The pictures hanging on them are too. Old school photos of us four kids reveal the awkward years of braces and glasses and pimples. The one of Riley dressed in his United States Marines uniform steals my breath, and my hand shoots to my chest to catch it. He had a handsome face, a square jawline like Dad, and kind, soft blue eyes like Mom. I swallow and keep my head down, unable to allow memory lane to take me on a depressing trip any longer, and I slip into my old bedroom.

My eyes are momentarily shocked by the lack of recognition. Ariel's little girl trinkets cover nearly every square inch of the room. But the faded, yellow wallpaper is the same. And it sends an odd, warm tingling through me. I drop my bag onto the pink, fluffy area rug and peer out the window overlooking the Coleman Family Farm pumpkin patch.

Depending on the soil, some years my window overlooks the cornfield and other years, the pumpkin field. We always rotate the two fields, giving the soil a chance to recover from the year before. I roll my eyes to myself, annoyed with the knowledge about soil and pumpkins that will forever be a part of me and embedded into my brain.

The only difference about today's view is the several news vans parked in the field and behind the farmhouse. Numerous reporters putter around. Though the sight that catches my attention and causes my gaze to freeze is a fine-looking backside in worn jeans sliding onto the seat of a John Deere tractor.

*Well hello, Farm Boy.*

But when I get a clear view of the face attached to the backside, I sigh. It's the grumpy guy from Sal's who gave me a ride to the farm this morning. I back away from the window and plop down on the bed. Just great. Not only does the guy have an attractive face but he has the body to match. And since when do I find guys dressed in worn blue jeans and flannels attractive?

I drop my face into my hands and groan. Even that is a struggle to release. My phone dings and I slide it out of my back pocket. The contact name on the screen reminds me of the last time I found a farm boy attractive. It's a blast from the past, and since I haven't seen it on my phone in years, I'm surprised I've still got him programmed.

KADE

Heard you were back in town. We should meet up.

# Chapter Four

## LULA

MOM HAS CLEARED THE DRAWERS OF MY CHILDHOOD dresser, and as much as I don't want to stay here that long, I have no choice. I'm stuck. For at least the next two months.

I unload the clothing from my suitcases, stacking jeans and joggers into the wood drawers that are broken and not aligned with the tracks. I try shoving one drawer shut, but it won't budge, so I bump it with my hip unsuccessfully.

Garrison pokes his head in through the open doorway. "Back home for less than a day and already breaking stuff I see," he teases.

I grin and blow the short hair out of my face.

He bounds into the room like a playful puppy dog and wraps his arms around me, picking me up in our embrace. "It's good to see you."

He squeezes me so tight I can hardly breathe. When he finally lets me go, I smack him in the chest.

"Hey, what was that for?" He rubs at his chest.

I snag my phone off the nightstand and tap out a message.

> For not being there when I needed you today.
> You've been the Thursday delivery boy
> forever. What's up?

"Sorry." He slumps down onto the bed. "My hunting trip went long."

> Yeah. Heard all about your hunting trip.

I move to the small closet and hang some of my dresses on the old wire hangers.

"So what happened? I mean, I know what happened with your voice and the surgery and everything. That seriously sucks, sis. I saw the meme of your voice cracking."

A deep dread fills my body, and I turn slowly from the closet to face him, narrowing my eyes.

> I don't want to hear about the memes or the
> GIFs or what they said on TMZ.

"It's true, you don't." He winces. "It's bad," he whispers.

I cross the room and smack him on the shoulder this time; he flinches too late and rubs his arm. I make a fist but relent and collapse onto the bed next to him.

"Why didn't you ask Mama or Daddy to pick you up at the airport? Or Emmaline?"

> I don't need their help.

"Well, obviously you do, or you wouldn't be here now."

Garrison and I have always gotten along. While we were growing up, we were more like friends than siblings. And we had more in common than we did with Emmaline and Riley. But this also means that Garrison not only knows me better than anyone else in my family, he knows how to push my buttons.

> Only for a few months. Just until my vocal cords heal. Then I'm back to Portland.

"Too bad. We've missed you around here." He leans back on his hands.

> Doubtful.

"Oh, c'mon now. Regardless of what happened all those years ago, you're family. You're a Coleman."

> 9 years is a long time to be gone. Pretty sure when I left I was told I was no longer a Coleman.

Garrison puts his arm around my shoulder and tucks me against him. "You know Mom didn't mean it. And if it's any consolation, *I'm* glad you're home."

I allow him to hold me close for a minute or two before I pat him on the leg and stand, returning to my task in the closet.

"Oh, so hey, how did you end up getting home?"

I chew on my lip, hesitating to tell him the truth. But I worry it may come out later anyway.

> Uber from the airport to Sal's. Snuck onto the delivery truck you were supposed to be driving. Gave a rando dude a small heart attack.

Garrison's dark-blue eyes go wide, and he chuckles into his fist. "So he found you in there? And he still agreed to give you a ride?"

I nod.

"I'm surprised."

Why?

"Axel"—he rubs his lips with his thumb and pointer finger —"he's a by-the-book kind of dude. What you see is what you get. He doesn't play around. How did you get him to agree?"

Gave him a pathetic look and told him I needed a job.

"Yeah, that would do it, I guess. Your pathetic look always works."

I narrow my eyes at him.

"Though, still pretty surprised he agreed. Why didn't you just tell him who you were? He wouldn't have hesitated to give you a ride."

You mean Lula Coleman—lead vocalist of The Broken Halos? Or Lula Coleman—member of the Coleman family?

"The second one." He answers it like a question though, scratching the scruff on his chin. "I'm just saying, he's loyal to the farm. Loyal to the Colemans. There isn't anything he wouldn't do for us. He's a pretty cool guy too. A good fisherman. He'd probably be a good hunter too, if I could just get him to finally come with me."

"Hey, Garrison?" Mom calls from downstairs.

Garrison launches off the bed and moves to the doorway. "I'll be right down, Mama!" he hollers.

Why no hunting? If he's such a butt-kisser— would think he'd gladly tag along.

"Hardy har har. I'm not saying he's a butt-kisser. All I

meant is he's loyal. Mama and Daddy have practically made him an honorary Coleman."

Something about his statement rubs me the wrong way. As if this Axel guy has somehow weaseled his way on to our farm and into my family. But it shouldn't bother me. I cut ties with this place long ago, and I don't plan on mending them.

"He's got a daughter. Sadie. And he won't leave her overnight. Maybe in a few years, when she's a bit older, I'll be able to convince him."

*So the farm boy is a single dad?* Having this new information about him makes him more appealing. The single dad trope in romance books is my favorite.

"Anyway, better go. It's good to see you, sis." He slips out the door, and his footsteps echo down the stairs.

*Better run, mama called.*

I roll my eyes and then tear all the dresses off the wire hangers and stuff them into a drawer. They're probably better off in the dresser getting wrinkled than draped off those rusty old hangers. Besides, where am I going to go while I'm here that I'm gonna need to wear a dress?

My phone dings with a new text.

OLIVE

You still alive? How bad is it?

"Lula!" Mom hollers from downstairs. "I could use your help down here."

I cringe.

You have no idea.

I take my time on the stairs, dreading what awaits me. My phone dings in my hand, and I jump.

KADE

How about 8:00?

Tonight?

KADE

Yeah tonight.

Fine. Where?

KADE

My place. The Finley farm.

You have got to be kidding me. Kade Finley still lives on the family farm? I'm instantly smacked with a memory, senior prom, lying on a blanket in a bed of hay in the horse barn at the Finley farm. Kade and I, with our naked body parts tangled together. That night I asked him the biggest question that would forever alter our relationship. I asked him to come with me and Jax to Portland.

He of course said no. Adding in a few other things, like I'd be sorry if I left. Kade broke my heart that night. But these are painful memories I don't like to recall often. When you plan on spending forever with someone, you don't expect it to end so abruptly. And terribly.

I take the remaining steps down the old wooden stairs slowly, surprised to find my cheeks damp with fresh tears. After that horrendous night all those years ago, I swore I wouldn't waste any more tears on Kade Finley. Interesting how being back inside the farmhouse for only a few hours has already changed me.

Dad stands when I reach the bottom of the stairs. Heat and warmth expand in my chest at the sight of him. I hadn't realized how much I'd missed him until this moment.

"Lula. It's good to have you home."

He hugs me, but it feels cold and robotic—not matching his

words at all. I pull away, and Mom is holding on to the shoulders of a small boy with dark-blond hair.

"I need you to keep an eye on Caleb for a bit. I gotta run into town to help your grandparents with something. Emmaline is busy with interviews in the office and Garrison is working with Daddy."

When I turn to plead with Garrison or Dad, they're already on their way toward the back door.

Dad pauses and glances over his shoulder. "Garrison is helping me get rid of all these reporters out here disturbing my livestock." He shoots me a look of annoyance before going out the door.

Panic rises in me, and my chest tightens. I have no clue what to do with a three-year-old. Especially now since I have no voice. I tap on my phone.

> What am I supposed to do with him? I can't even talk.

"You'll be fine. Here, I'll put on a movie for him, and he won't even know I'm gone." She strides into the living room and turns on the TV. "And if he gets hungry, give him some fish crackers and water." She presses a kiss to Caleb's rosy cheek. "Aunt Lula is gonna watch you for a bit. You sit and watch your movie, and I'll be right back. Don't cause her too much trouble."

I follow after her as she makes her way toward the back door, and tug on the sleeve of her sweater.

"Lula, you'll be fine. Now, I have to go."

"Wait," I croak, and place my hand over my throat.

But she's already gone. I turn around and find Caleb standing there, blinking up at me, so small and helpless.

I'm about to tap a message to him on my phone and then remember, he's only three and can't read yet. I rub at my temples. What was Mom thinking? And how am I supposed to know if he's hungry when I can't ask him? My heart thumps hard against my ribs, and I'm tempted to interrupt Emmaline's interview.

But he slips his small hand into mine and leads me back through the kitchen. "You're gonna luv the movie."

Surprisingly, my anxious thoughts ease at his touch and his invitation. Warmth expands in my chest when we sit on the couch, and he sets a fish cracker into my palm. I smile and give him a nod before tossing the cracker into my mouth and putting my hand out for another one. I twist my lips into fish-lips and Caleb giggles in response. I try not to think about how sad it is that he's the first person to make me feel welcome since returning to the farm.

And he's only three.

# Chapter Five

## AXEL

Work finishes for the day, and I walk toward the back of the Coleman farmhouse to pick up Sadie. Since the news vans have finally left, I figure they must've got their story. But I'm still not sure what that is.

Before I reach the back door, Sadie's giggle echoes near the chicken coop. One of her favorite things is to visit with the chickens and collect the eggs with Emmaline and Ariel.

But when I round the corner of the house in a hurry, I run smack into the dark-haired knockout from Sal's. We collide, and she bounces off my chest and lands on her backside in the dirt. She's wincing on the ground by the time I have enough sense to give her a hand and help her up.

"Sorry about that. Are you all right?"

For a brief moment she seems dazed but doesn't speak.

"Fine. So you're okay, then?"

She nods and brushes off her backside. I skirt my focus away, so I don't get caught up in how good she looks in her jeans. But I catch the glare in her eyes. Irritation builds in my chest.

Where does she get off being annoyed. She's the one who didn't look where she was going.

"So, it looks like the Colemans gave you a job after all?" I grumble.

But she only continues staring at me.

"Daddy!" Sadie runs to me, and I pick her up. I toss her in the air before hugging her close to my chest. "Miss Emma said I could say goodnight to the chickens before I went home."

"I'm sure they enjoyed that. Bet they don't usually get a proper tucking in."

Sadie giggles.

"So, who's your friend?" I gesture to the brunette, who still hasn't spoken a single word to me and it's downright beginning to piss me off.

"Her name is Lula." Sadie wiggles to get out of my arms.

I set her on her feet and stretch a hand out to officially introduce myself to the mystery woman. Even if I am hoping she's not going to be around much longer. She's the definition of trouble if I've ever seen it.

"I'm Axel James," I growl.

Lula accepts the handshake, but when she smiles, it's obvious it's forced.

I don't pay much attention to the zing of electricity that shoots through my body upon our skin-on-skin contact. And I try not to let myself dwell on the fact that it's been three years since I've been with a woman. Since I've felt the touch of a woman.

I tear my hand free from hers and clear my throat. "We should get going. C'mon, Sadie."

Sadie waves to the chicken coop as Lula locks the gate. "Night, night chicks. Don't let the bed bugs bite. Bye, Lula. See you tomorrow."

"C'mon. Let's race back to the house. Ready? Set? Go!" I

take off in a jog and allow Sadie to pick up her pace so we can run alongside each other before I slow completely, allowing her to win.

Sadie works on a coloring page while I shower. When I come out of the bathroom, she has the Go Fish cards ready, and she's waiting at the table for me.

"Okay, three games and then I make dinner, deal?"

"And then three games after dinner?"

"Only if you take a quick bath tonight."

She purses her adorable lips as if she's really considering this. "Okay, deal."

I chuckle and run a hand through my damp, wavy hair. I can't believe I'm bartering with a five-year-old. Sadie hands me the cards, and I take a seat at the table across from her. I shuffle the cards and start to deal.

"Hey, Sadie? Who was that woman with you? You know, with the chickens?" I fan out my cards in my grip.

"Lula."

"Yeah, you said that. But why were you with her?"

She's distracted and too busy studying the cards held in her tiny, chubby hands.

"Sadie? Hey, I asked you a question."

"Miss Emma said Lula could take me to say night night to the chickens. She had to get Ariel and Caleb ready for karate class." She squints at her cards. "Do you have any twos?"

I glance at the cards in my hand. "Go fish."

She groans but is all smiles after she chooses a card from the deck. She would make a terrible poker player.

Sadie's answer still doesn't explain why Emmaline would trust a stranger to watch my daughter. Emmaline knows how protective I am of Sadie. She's one of the few people—not blood related— aware of my situation. About Sadie's mom leaving us three years ago because she couldn't handle the role or title of *Mom*.

I wasn't even the one who wanted to move to Juniper Ridge. It had been a pit stop on the way from Seattle to Reno on a business trip. The medical supply business I began a few years before had really taken off. I had an opportunity to meet with an investor in Reno who was going to put in a substantial amount of money to become a silent partner.

Joanie wanted to tag along. We'd only been dating for two months. My relationship with her was the longest I'd had in my twenties. I figured, what was the harm? We could stop at a few places on the way, maybe have a little too much fun in Reno, sign the contract, and return home to Seattle.

But when we stopped in Juniper Ridge, the blue skies and mountainous landscape and the small-town vibes took Joanie's breath away. And admittedly, mine too. But we were both city people—born and raised. So while thinking about our time in Juniper Ridge transported us back to a nice memory of a slower-paced life and picture-perfect scenery, that's all it was— a memory.

A few weeks after we'd returned home, Joanie found out she was pregnant.

I never intended on staying with Joanie forever. She was a "for now" type of woman. She liked fancy restaurants and designer shoes and handbags. The busyness of the city made her feel alive.

So when she suggested we move to Juniper Ridge to give our child a better life, I more than resisted. I dug the heels of my oxfords into the wet pavement of Seattle and swore I wouldn't go. But Joanie was persistent. And she was having my baby. I might have been a bit self-centered back then, but I wasn't a complete jackass. I grew up with a father who worked too many hours and wasn't around much. I wasn't about to do the same to my kid.

We packed up and made the move. I could do most of my work remotely. Though my business would likely take a hit by not being able to meet face-to-face with my clients on a regular basis. Joanie wanted to be a stay-at-home mom. I told her she'd hate it and we could put the baby in daycare so she could get a job.

At first, it seemed like she was handling the role of stay-at-home mom like a pro. But right around the time Sadie turned one, Joanie got restless. While I had grown to appreciate the slower pace of life in Juniper Ridge, Joanie had grown to despise it. She started leaving for weekend getaways with her old friends from Seattle while I stayed back and took care of Sadie. Eventually, she just never came home.

Joanie called me one night from a hotel room in Vegas. Told me she was sorry, but she just wasn't cut out for being a mom. She said to tell Sadie she loved her and she was sorry. I told Joanie we'd work it out. That both Sadie and I needed her. My medical supply business was going under because I was trying to juggle that along with Sadie.

Joanie replied, "*You guys will be fine. You're a fixer, Axel. But unfortunately, you can't fix me. You can't make me want to be a mother. I'm just not cut out for it.*"

She hasn't been back since. Neither Sadie nor I have heard from her since that phone call. The best thing that came of Joanie leaving is I finally stopped making excuses for her. I could be honest with Sadie once and for all. But it didn't mean she stopped missing her or craving the love from a mother.

Some nights Sadie still dreams of her. She awakes the next morning and tells me how she and Joanie had a tea party together. Then she tells me that one day, when her mommy comes home, they'll have a tea party together for real.

And that's how I wound up here—on the Coleman Family Farm. In need of a job and a more affordable place to live. They took a chance when they hired me. I didn't have a lick of experience working on a farm. But soon, both Sadie and I found our way. And in the process, a new family.

# Chapter Six

## LULA

DINNER WITH MY FAMILY IS SURPRISINGLY UNEVENTFUL. Unless you count the shocking noise level of the two children, arguing and whining. Along with the absence of Emmaline's husband, Jackson. Since no one's offered up an explanation, I've kept quiet about it.

Dad has hardly said more than a few words to me. He glances at me even less. And since I can't speak, my chances of starting a conversation with him are slim.

I nudge some candied green beans through the gravy on my plate with my fork while my mind travels back to my encounter with Axel earlier. We touched for only a fraction of a second, but I swear my chest is still radiating with heat from the collision. The sound of his husky voice is still lingering in my ears, along with the touch of his rough hand when it clasped around mine.

My phone dings and Mama hisses a *tsk, tsk*. The rule of no phones at the dinner table apparently still exists. But I check it anyway.

KADE

Can you head over now?

Dad scrapes his plate and it jolts my attention as he scoops the very last bite of mashed potatoes and finally glances in my direction. "So, Lula, how long will you be staying with us?"

The question makes me feel like I'm the guest at a bed and breakfast rather than a daughter who has returned home.

"John, you know she can't speak. Mick told us in the email that she'd be staying about two months."

"Perfect. Just in time to help us through the pumpkin season," Dad says.

"She can take over my chores so I have more time for hunting? I see an Elk in my future." Garrison waggles his brows.

"I think you get enough time off for hunting, slacker," Emmaline scoffs.

"Agreed." Dad stands and goes into the kitchen.

I follow him to the sink with my plate, even though I barely touched my food. There's something about eating your mom's cooking that should be comforting but instead, I'm mostly annoyed.

I tap on my phone and hold it out to Dad.

Can I borrow a vehicle?

He frowns at me. "Where are you going?"

To see Kade.

"Really? I thought you hated the Finley boy."

Mom spins in her chair to face me. "Now, don't you go causing trouble, Lula."

I bite my lower lip and ignore her, and instead type another message for Dad.

> He asked if we could talk.

He sighs. "Take the keys off the hook with the apple keychain. That's for the delivery truck."

I wrap my arms around Dad from behind, giving him a hug and kiss his cheek.

"Just don't make me worry, hey?" he calls.

I nod and hold my phone out to Mom.

> Thanks for supper.

Emmaline clears her throat. "Lula? A lot has changed since you've been gone. Especially in the last year. There's something you should know."

But I don't want to listen to Emmaline's advice. I ignore her and rush to the key holder hanging on the wall inside the office. Freedom feels so close. I snatch the truck keys and push out the back door, gulping in the warm night air.

When I reach the Finley farm, it's almost dark, but I pass several more fields than I remember them having, including a cornfield. *Since when did they grow corn?*

> I'm here. Where are you?

KADE:

> In the horse barn. C'mon in.

The mention of the horse barn sends the memories washing over me, and a dull ache forms in the pit of my stomach. What is this, a sick joke? He invites me over and tells me to meet him in the exact spot our relationship ended? It's been over nine years since that day, but in this moment, it hits me hard that the wound in my heart has never fully healed.

Just forget it. I'm leaving.

I back up the truck just as Kade comes running out of the barn. He waves his hands in the air as he stands in the beams of the truck's headlights. I sigh and put the truck in park, turning off the ignition.

I'm going to regret this.

# Chapter Seven

## AXEL

I'M LOADING THE DINNER DISHES INTO THE DISHWASHER when the sound of crushed gravel outside. I pick up the dish-towel from the counter and dry my hands while I cross the living room to the window and peer through the blinds. The Coleman Family Farm delivery truck is sitting in front of the house.

I check the time on the clock hanging on the wall. It's a quarter past ten. Why is Garrison stopping by so late? If he wakes Sadie, I'm going to kill him.

I open the front door and prop myself in the doorway, crossing my arms while I wait for him to step out so I can unload on him. But when the truck door finally swings open, Lula climbs out. Only, she doesn't climb out, she stumbles and falls out.

"What the—" I race down the porch steps.

She's lying in the gravel and trying to push herself onto all fours when I reach her.

I take a hold of her arm. "Are you all right?"

With her hands pressed into the gravel, she lifts her chin to gaze at me. The moonlight catches in her blue eyes, darkening them. She smiles a wicked grin in my direction that causes my chest to tighten. She allows me to help her to her feet, but when her legs wobble, I grab a hold of her before she falls again.

"Whoa, easy there." With my arm wrapped around her waist, I'm close enough to smell the alcohol on her breath. "Have you been drinking?"

Lula's smile disappears, and she rearranges her expression so it's serious.

"Lula? Are you drunk?" I bark.

She shrugs.

"And you drove? In the company truck?" I drop my head back and groan. "This is your first day of work? What the hell were you thinking?"

With one hand, she slides her phone from her back pocket and taps a message for me.

Got upsetting news tonight.

"Did you steal the truck?"

She appears hurt by my accusation, but what else am I supposed to think?

She shakes her head.

I narrow my eyes at her. "You want me to believe the Colemans just let you take the truck for personal reasons? On your first day?"

Lula nods.

"BS." I drag her to the passenger side of the truck. "C'mon, get in. We're going to the farmhouse, and Mr. Coleman can tell me himself."

She digs her boots into the gravel and shoves me away.

"Hey, I'm not losing my job over you." I gesture back at the house. "I got a kid to support."

She holds out a finger to me, then types on her phone.

Please. I can't go to the farmhouse.

"I knew it." I stab my fingers through my unruly hair. "You stole the truck."

I don't want my parents to see me like this.

*Parents?* Confusion whirls through my mind while I try to grasp what her message means.

I'm a Coleman.

Now I know she's lying because I know the Colemans. All of them. "What are you, a cousin or something?"

The corners of her mouth droop, and her eyes appear heavy.

I wish. My parents probably wish too. I'm the prodigal child.

Her confession causes bits and pieces of conversations with Emmaline and Garrison to shift in my mind. Mentions of another sibling were hinted at on occasion. But I just assumed they were referring to Riley, the Coleman sibling who died. I never knew there was a fourth.

"So, you're Lula Coleman?" The name sounds familiar, but I can't quite put my finger on why.

She nods.

Can I crash at your place tonight?

"What? Are you crazy?" I whisper shout.

Please.

"I have a kid," I mutter, annoyance filling me that she's already forgotten.

I know. I won't be a problem. I Swear. Please.

My relationship with my parents is complicated. If I go to the farmhouse like this, they'll tell Mick.

She leans a hip against the side of the truck to keep herself from swaying.

I have no clue who this Mick guy is, but I assume it must be her boyfriend or husband. And maybe that's why I've never heard of her. Maybe she's been married to some controlling, abusive guy who has kept her away from her family.

Rubbing at my forehead, I glance at the Coleman farmhouse and then back at my own, feeling conflicted. Is protecting this woman worth the possibility of putting Sadie in danger?

Please.

The pleading in her eyes holds the same desperation in them as earlier in the day. Something about it is haunting and I can't seem to say no to it. Or to her.

Wrapping my arm around her waist, I sigh and lead her to my house. This is going to come back to bite me in the ass. But she's a Coleman and my loyalty to them, all of them, wins out in the end. I'm fairly certain this woman isn't a risk to Sadie. I just need to sober her up and get her back over to the farmhouse before anyone knows she was ever here.

I help Lula inside and ease her onto the sofa. "Sit here and don't move."

She presses a finger to her lips and giggles.

Tiptoeing down the hall, I peek into Sadie's bedroom and find her sleeping soundly. She's clutching Perry, her favorite stuffed polar bear. I pull her door closed softly before going into the kitchen. I put on a pot of coffee and bring Lula a glass of water and two aspirin.

"Here," I mutter, handing her both.

She smiles her thanks.

You trying to sober me up?

"That's the plan."

She chases the aspirin down with a few gulps of water.

Good plan.

"Better than your plan," I scoff. "Drinking and then driving."

Obviously it wasn't planned.

"No? Because usually, someone doesn't drink when they know they'll be driving."

I was upset. Got some news and wanted to confront my parents.

"Yeah? And what changed your mind?"

She studies me, her vision trailing from my eyes down the length of me. My body heats under her intense gaze and I lick my lips mindlessly.

You.

I lift my brows and swallow. "Me?"

If you hadn't come out, I would've gone to the farmhouse.

That would've been a bad idea.

The coffee maker beeps, interrupting my racing heartbeat. Heading into the kitchen, I can't help but wonder why Lula still isn't talking. The phone texting is getting damn annoying. I fix two cups how I like it, with several heaping teaspoons of sugar, and carry the mugs into the living room. I hand one to her, and our fingers touch, sending a volt of electricity shooting through me from the physical contact.

I wince and shake out my hand. I don't have time for women. I especially don't have the luxury of having feelings for women.

Thank you.

I grunt and nod before taking a sip of my coffee. "Just don't make me regret this."

She grimaces after a drink of her coffee.

No cream?

Her ungratefulness is downright irritating. "Just drink it," I grumble.

She's quiet again, sipping her coffee slowly. Her eyes are tired and heavy-lidded, but her lips don't stop smiling, and I should ignore them. Instead, I can't help but be mesmerized. She has a beautiful smile.

You gonna stay and keep watch over me all night?

"If that's what it takes."

Okay fine. Then tell me something about yourself.

I shrug. I'm not a man of many words. Most of the time, Sadie says enough for both of us. Living in Juniper Ridge, and on the Coleman property in particular, has given me a simpler life. I like the quiet and slower pace on the farm instead of the busy city life. I also like to keep my life private.

"How about you first? For starters, why can't you talk? And where've you been all these years? How come I've never seen you? Or met you?"

That's a lot of questions.

"Start with why you haven't spoken more than one word since I met you?"

Vocal cord injury.

I purse my lips and frown at her. "And where've you been all these years?"

She smiles and curls her fingers around the mug, her eyes considering.

LULA

Chasing my dreams.

"That's a vague answer."

Now you. How'd you end up here? In the
Coleman newlywed house?

I grimace. "Is that what it's called?" Learning the name of the small house Sadie and I have been calling home for the last three years rubs me the wrong way. "They should really consider changing the name. I'm far from being a newlywed."

What happened to your wife?

"Nu-uh. My turn. Where did your dreams lead you?" I prop my ankle across the opposite knee.

Portland.

I chuckle. "They didn't get you very far."
She glares at me.
"Okay, sorry." I try to recover because I do genuinely want to know. "Let me guess, you ran away with your high school sweetheart?" I tease.
She mocks a gasp, and her infectious smile regrettably creates warmth in my chest.

Wrong.

I snap my fingers. "Darn. Thought I was on a roll."

My turn. What happened to your wife? To
Sadie's mom?

My mind goes to the compartment in my brain where I always go to retrieve the answer to this question. But instead, I feel inclined to tell Lula something new. Something true. "I was never married to Sadie's mom. And I don't refer to her as that. Because to do that would mean she actually deserved and wanted the title."

Lula winces.

"Around here, we just call her Joanie."

She regards me for a long moment.

I didn't run away to Portland with my HS sweetheart. Because he wouldn't go with me.

I tilt my head and a pang of sadness hits me in the center of my chest. It's stupid to be feeling this way and subconsciously, I try to rub it away.

He chose loyalty to his family over loyalty to us And our dreams.

I must give her a confused look because she elaborates.

The Finley Farm.

And there it is. The pieces of information I've learned tonight move into place, forming a full picture.

"Kade Finley was your high school sweetheart." But I say it more as a statement rather than a question.

She nods and stretches her legs onto the coffee table, crossing her ankles.

"I'm sorry, but I can't stand that guy," I mutter.

That makes two of us.

"That's where you were tonight?" I don't even wait for an answer. "And why you actually made it home without getting pulled over. You took the backroad that adjoins the two farms."

Did you know about their farm expansion?
The pumpkin patch?

"Of course. Found out a while back when your parents did."

She sits up straighter.

So they know?

"Everyone working on the Coleman Farm has been worried about it, but your parents seem to think they'll be okay."

But they're wrong.

I lean forward and rest my elbows on my knees, gripping the mug in both hands. "How do you know?"

They're planning to have a themed corn
maze. Star Wars. Hayrides. Food trucks.
They're gonna bring in a ton of business.
Business that normally goes to the Colemans.

It seems the alcohol is having a reverse effect and is no longer numbing her anger but is now causing her to be more emotional. Her eyes water, and I worry she's gonna turn into one of those messy drunks. I don't have the patience for that. And I definitely can't have her breaking down and sobbing, and waking up Sadie.

"And so you thought the best way to deal with this news was getting drunk? With Kade Finley?"

She narrows her eyes at me and swipes her fingertips at the tears running down her cheeks.

Again, that wasn't part of the plan. I was
upset. Kade offered me a beer. One thing led
to another. Next thing I knew we were playing
darts and were a couple beers in. But I'm not
drunk.

"I can't believe he let you drive." My jaw ticks as I set my empty mug on the coffee table.

He didn't have a choice. He never had a say
in what I did when we dated and that hasn't
changed now. He knew I wouldn't listen
to him.

"He could've at least tried. Or called Garrison to come pick you up."

She wipes her nose with her shirt sleeve and gapes at me.

Garrison and Kade hate each other.

I've been aware of the ongoing feud between Garrison and Kade. But I've never questioned the *why* behind it. "Over this? The Finley Farm opening a pumpkin patch? Because I've never seen Garrison afraid of a little competition."

I get up and grab a fresh roll of toilet paper from the bathroom and hand it to her. She smiles and tears off a few squares, wadding them together and wiping at her cheeks and nose. Her chest heaves, and fresh tears fall. I'm not really sure how to handle this situation. It's been a long time since I've dealt with an emotional woman.

I hesitate but go against my better judgment and sit next to her on the sofa. She continues to wipe at her eyes. I set an uneasy hand on her back, and when she doesn't flinch at my touch, I rub it in slow, soft circles, just like I do for Sadie when she awakes from a nightmare. Only, the physical contact between us causes heat to travel south and wake up parts of me that have been long since dead.

Parts of me that need to remain dead. At least until Sadie is off to college.

Lula sets balls of wadded-up toilet paper onto the coffee table next to her empty mug and glances in my direction, giving me what looks like a grateful smile. She swipes her phone from the arm of the sofa and types a new message before holding it out to me.

> There are many reasons why Garrison hates Kade. He dumped me. He wouldn't go with me to Portland.

I read over her shoulder as she types vigorously.

> He said he loved me. He was my first. Then he just let me go. He chose the farm over starting a life with me. Now this. The Finley's opening a pumpkin patch.

My hands seem to have a mind of their own as they massage Lula's shoulders, kneading the tension they find there. I blow air out of my cheeks. "That's a lot."

She nods and leans into my touch.

"I always knew Kade Finley was a jackass."

She smiles through watery eyes and mouths *thanks*.

I want to comfort her for all she's been through. For having a guy treat her so badly. No woman should be treated like that. Even though I barely know her, I'm drawn to her. I should chalk it up to the fact that she's the first woman I've let my guard down with since Joanie. But whatever the reason, I give into the desire pulsing through my body.

I glide my hand up to her neck and press my fingers against her skin. Her quick intake of breath is audible. I draw her closer without fully thinking. Even still, she catches me off guard when she takes my face in her hands and leans forward, smashing her lips against mine. My hormones zing throughout my entire body, and my lips react before my brain can play catch up. I rest a hand on her thigh and tether my fingers in her hair, and I devour her mouth before I finally come to my senses and pull away.

I withdraw my hand from her hair and her thigh and scoot away from her on the sofa. "I'm sorry," I mumble, breathlessly. "I didn't, I shouldn't." I stand. "We shouldn't have done that." I dash back to the chair and sit, shoving my hands through my hair.

It's okay. Really. I'm sorry too.

"You shouldn't be sorry. You're the one who's been drinking." I stand again and pick up her mug. "More coffee?"

Lula rises and sets her hand on mine, stilling it around the mug. Her lips pull into a smile, and she shakes her head. Taking the empty mug from me, she returns it to the table before picking up her phone and sitting back down on the sofa.

We're okay. You're a good guy.

But I feel like an asshole.

She gives me a reassuring smile.

Sit back down and talk to me for a while longer.

I stand there feeling conflicted, not fully believing her words but she makes me want to.

"I'm gonna grab you a blanket."

I find a fleece blanket along with a quilt Emmaline made

for me last Christmas tucked in my closet. When I return, Lula has her dirty hiking boots tucked up on the sofa, and she's already asleep. I unlace her boots and slip them off her feet before covering her up with the blanket. I can only hope she was sober enough not to be sick tomorrow. And that I can sneak her out of here before Sadie wakes up.

I've never had to explain a woman sleeping over before. I don't intend on starting now.

# Chapter Eight

## LULA

Waking up with a slight headache and feeling a little dazed is much better than a full-blown hangover, which is exactly the state I should be in. But thanks to Axel and his aspirin and coffee, I'm up early and only have a mild hangover. Though, I'm slightly confused about why I'm waking up in his bed.

I sit up abruptly, and my head pounds in protest. *Okay, not feeling as great as I thought.* Leaning back against the headboard, I take in the space around me. The familiar old wood paneling walls, along with the natural hardwood floors, give me a sense of comfort. When I pat my hands down my arms and legs and realize I am fully clothed, my shoulders relax.

"Thank God," I whisper. It sounds a bit strangled, though not terrible.

I shove back the covers and tiptoe to the window, peeking through the curtain. The view from this window is the same that I have from my window in the farmhouse. Why have I never noticed this before?

"Morning, Lula!" a small voice says from behind me.

I spin around and find Sadie standing in the open doorway, barefoot with her dark hair disheveled, and I realize the irony here. We resemble one another in appearance, and it's comical. Though something tells me her dad wouldn't find the humor in it.

I suck my lower lip between my teeth and wave at the little girl with one hand while the other fidgets with the hem of my sweater. My first instinct is to bolt out of this room and the newlywed house. Axel should've made sure I was gone before Sadie woke up.

"Are you staying for breakfast? Daddy's making pancakes."

My body warms and I suck my lower lip between my teeth as my imagination runs wild. What I wouldn't give to be able to call him *Daddy*.

*Must focus.*

I spot my boots on the floor next to the bed, and the nervous swirling in my stomach eases. I stuff my feet into them with forced enthusiasm but realize Sadie is still wedged in the doorway, awaiting my response. I shake my head and squeeze past her, lightly brushing her arm on my way out. Keeping my chin tucked to my chest, I dart down the hall and turn at the end of it, making a beeline for the front door.

"So, no breakfast then?"

I freeze in the living room. *So close.* I turn, slowly.

"Sadie was up early today. Earlier than normal," he says by way of explanation.

We both stare at her. Sadie's expression is confused, and I feel like I should stay to help smooth this over. But I have no voice. And I don't know the first thing about kids or being a parent.

I shake my head and mouth the words *thank you* before turning and bolting out of the newlywed house. As awkward as the conversation may go with Sadie, I have my own waiting for me back at the farmhouse.

But by the time I make the long trek across the property and reach the back door, the worry over the awkwardness has subsided, and I'm hot with anger once again, just like I was last night. I don't think about the possibility of Ariel and Caleb still sleeping. Probably Emmaline and Garrison too. I swing open the back door with so much force it smacks against the old wood siding of the house. I stomp into the kitchen, desperate for someone to please make sense of what Kade told me.

Mom's in the kitchen, pouring coffee into two mugs. "Lula, what's all this commotion?" she hisses, glancing at the time on the oven clock. "It's almost six a.m. Are you just getting home from the Finley Farm now?"

I tap on my phone, ignoring her.

Where's Dad?

"Well, he was resting in his chair while I fix his coffee. But I'm sure he's wide awake now. I'm sure the entire house is wide awake now."

I shoulder past her and stomp into the living room where Dad is in the exact spot my mom said he would be. She's also right about another thing. He's wide awake.

"You have a nice visit with Kade Finley last night?" Dad teases.

I narrow my eyes and hold out the screen of my phone to him.

Why didn't you tell me?

He sighs. "Which part?"

All of it.

Mom comes in huffing and puffing, a coffee mug in each hand. "Lula, what is going on?"

"She knows, Judy."

I whip my head in my mom's direction, and her mouth falls open before she clamps it shut.

"Sit down," Dad instructs.

But I'm too amped up to sit. I don't feel like having a calm conversation about this. But then I realize I can't even use my voice. It's not like I can yell and scream, so I sit down on the sofa kitty-corner from Dad.

"We've known for over a year that the Finleys had expanded their farm. They assured us they didn't mean anything by it. But their farm wasn't thriving. Even with the honey. They needed another way to bring in money. And pumpkins are an easy way of doing so."

They're doing corn too.

Dad nods his head. Mom hands him a mug and then drops down on the sofa next to me but remains silent.

"The thing is, Lula, there isn't anything we can do about the Finleys expanding their farm. There's no law saying no other farm in Juniper Ridge can open a pumpkin patch."

But we've been the only one for eighty years.

"It's not like we called dibs, and that's that. This is real life, not a Kelsey Ballerini song," Dad says, chuckling to himself.

There is nothing I find funny about this situation. The Coleman Family Farm operates year-round. But pumpkin season is what not only keeps them afloat but keeps them thriving. If the farm has competition, there's no telling what it will do to them.

> But what will happen to the farm?

Mom sees my message to Dad before I can turn and face the screen toward him, and she harrumphs beside me. "Now you care what happens to the farm?"

"Judy," Dad says and shakes his head at her. He sets his mug down on the coffee table and scoots to the edge of the chair, looking intently at me. "You want the truth?"

I nod. But I'm not sure I do. I wait, fidgeting with the hem of my sweater.

"We don't know. But since there's nothing we can do about it, we just have to wait and see what happens."

> Your solution is to wait and see?

"And pray that those eighty years of being the only pumpkin patch in Juniper Ridge will be enough to bring our loyal customers back."

I lean into the sofa, pressing my head into the worn fabric. My parents are trusting their livelihood to prayer and loyalty. That does not seem like enough in my mind. I drop my phone on my lap and press my hands to the sides of my forehead, the earlier pounding resuming.

After a moment, Dad takes my hand, and I straighten, fixing my attention on him. His new-to-me wrinkles creasing his face and his receding head of graying hair are both signs of the hard work he's put into this farm for the last fifty years. The skin on his hands is rough as they hold mine. My chest tightens from the touch as old memories flood my mind. My dad, this home, this farm, at one point, was all I ever needed or desired in life.

"That's why we're glad you're home."

I knit my brows together in confusion.

What can I do?

"Besides being extra hands around the farm, I have a feeling that you're here for a reason."

And I have a feeling he's going to tell me next that it was God who wrecked my vocal cords and sent me here. And I'm in no mood to hear that today. I'm still livid at Kade and the entire Finley Farm for doing this to my family. And I'm still mad at my parents and Emmaline and especially Garrison for not telling me.

I tap a message on my screen and stand, facing my phone toward Dad.

I'm here because Mick and Leslie sent me here. That's it.

Bending, I press a kiss on his rough, scruffy cheek. I force a smile toward Mom before shuffling to the stairs.

"Lula?" Mom calls when I've reached the bottom step.

I turn, glancing over my shoulder at her.

"If Kade forgot to tell you last night, he's getting married. In three months. Please don't interfere with his plans. I could never forgive myself if you did."

"Judy," Dad says sternly.

Kade did not tell me. Though, the news doesn't bother me. Not really. What bothers me is that Mom felt the need to warn me not to screw up his plans. What about when he screwed up *my* plans?

But I don't give her the negative reaction she wants. Instead, I smile and turn back around, continuing up the stairs.

# Chapter Nine
## AXEL

Today is Friday, and thanks to Lula Coleman returning home, I apparently have been given the day off. I drive Sadie to preschool anyway because I have to pay the tuition regardless if she attends or not. And Sadie loves school.

I walk her to the front door and kiss her goodbye, then watch as she runs to the playground with her friends. Back out in the truck, I flip through every programmed station on the radio, skipping commercials and local news before landing on a country song I recognize. *What's Your Name* by Chase Rice.

Since I never get a weekday off, I have no clue what to do. I turn down the road that will take me back to the farm and stop in front of the small house. I consider going to find Garrison, but he's extra busy with pumpkin season right around the corner. Plus, there's been an uproar around the farm since the Finley Farm announced last year that they'd be growing pumpkins and corn and opening a pumpkin patch this fall.

After being the only one in the entire area for close to eighty years, the farm has every right to worry. Fall is the Colemans' biggest money-making season. Having competition could severely affect their livelihood.

Not to mention mine.

I spend a good two hours cleaning the house and doing laundry, including stripping the sheets off our beds and washing them. Probably a good choice considering Lula slept in my bed last night. And I can't get her scent out of my damn mind. She smells like she's been swimming in a field of fresh wildflowers.

The small house was built by John Coleman and his father back when he and Judy got married. The plan had always been for John and Judy to take over the farm one day, but since Judy Coleman didn't want to live in the big farmhouse with her in-laws, they built this house on the property. When John's parents moved into a retirement facility about twenty years back, the younger Coleman family moved into the big farmhouse.

It's hard to imagine John and Judy Coleman, along with four children, living in this small two-bedroom, one-bathroom house. Some days the quarters feel too tight for just Sadie and I. Learning from Lula that the house is referred to as the *newlywed house* is strange, and I'm probably gonna see the place differently now.

It's still early when I finish cleaning and remaking the beds. I try not to picture Lula sprawled out and wrapped in the sheets, sleepy-eyed, and looking sexy. It's been a long time since I've had a woman in my bed.

Which is exactly how I'd like to keep it. It's better this way for Sadie and I. Less confusion. We've been fine on our own for three years, and I don't need some woman changing all that. Even if she is the most beautiful thing I've ever seen stroll onto this farm.

I shake these thoughts away as I head outside into the late

afternoon warmth with a basket to pick some apples from the modest orchard on the Colemans' property. Free apples are another perk to this job. I want to surprise Sadie when she gets home. I've been promising her an apple cobbler, and she's been wanting to make it with me.

Some quiet time in the orchard will do me good. I can clear my head from Lula's surprise drunken visit last night. And Joanie. And inconceivable tea parties.

But when I reach the orchard, I discover I'm not alone. Lula is perched on the top rung of a ladder, looking fine as hell dressed in fitted jeans and a blue Coleman Family Farm T-shirt with a burlap sack slung over her shoulder and across her chest.

I clear my throat, and she cranes her neck to see who has interrupted her. She rolls her eyes at me and returns to her apple picking. I'm not exactly sure what I've done to deserve the eye roll when I was the one who helped her out of a jam last night. *Her* jam, which then became mine when Sadie saw her this morning. Trying to explain to my five-year-old why I was sleeping on the sofa and there was a woman in my bed was new territory for both of us.

If anyone should be rolling their eyes at the other, it should be me. "You put me in a tough spot this morning," I call up at her, tugging the brim of my hat down further to shield my eyes from the sun.

Lula smirks while she drops an apple into her sack.

It gets my blood pumping. "Look, there's something you should know about me, I don't like people knowing my business. I don't like trouble, either. And from the looks of things, you, Lula Coleman, are the epitome of trouble," I mutter.

She shoots me a devilish grin before reaching for an apple from a high branch. It's nearly out of her grasp, so she stretches farther, and I'm too late with my warning.

"Be careful!" I shout.

The ladder wobbles and topples over, sending Lula tumbling toward me. She releases a strangled scream, and apples fly every which way. I do my best to break her fall, catching her and clinging to her when her body comes in contact with mine. I pinch my eyes tight, wincing before we hit the ground together.

It isn't as hard as I suspected it would be. But Lula's weight on top of me sends shooting pain down my back. I cough and open my eyes. Lula's icy-blue, wide eyes gaze at me. I recognize something in those eyes. A familiarity to them.

"You okay?" I press my fingers into her back, holding her tighter.

She wriggles from my grip, climbing off me and scooting backward on the ground. I sit up, and my back complains from the movement. We stare at one another.

"Are you okay?" I repeat the question.

She nods.

"For some reason, the universe keeps throwing us together," I growl.

She slides her phone from her back pocket, taps on it, and then holds the screen out toward me.

Literally.

Maybe you should stop stalking me.

She grins.

I quirk my brows, setting a palm against my chest. "Me? And who was it who showed up at *my* place last night? Needing *my* help?"

Fine. You're right.

I give her a satisfied nod, as if I've won some sort of an

award for winning this argument. I can't help but wish the award was a chance to kiss her again. If given the opportunity, I'd be more prepared. And I'd make sure she hadn't come straight from Kade Finley's or been drinking.

We sit in awkward silence for too long. Not talking about the fact that our bodies were just pressed close together or about the kiss we shared the night before. I'm not sure she even remembers the kiss. Which means my hope of it happening again are slim to none.

I push my thumb and finger into my closed eyes and groan. The last thing I should be thinking about is kissing this woman.

She kicks her foot into my cowboy boot, and I cautiously pry my eyes open. "What?" I grunt.

I can tell you're a good dad.

"Yeah?"

But you also look like you could use a little trouble in your life.

Our eyes lock and for just a moment, I allow myself to imagine a world in which I could let a woman into my life and heart again. A woman like Lula. I imagine what it would feel like to draw her into my arms, glide my hands against her bare skin, and kiss that tempting mouth of hers.

My mind shifts to an image of the two of us sitting on the porch, watching the sunset sink into the cornfield after a long day on the farm. Sadie near us, coloring pictures of her new family. A family that includes Lula. And maybe a dog too.

But fantasizing about a future with a woman is a luxury I don't have. Sadie is my number one priority. So I clear my thoughts and ignore her last comment.

"What are you doing here? I thought you were taking over my responsibilities today since Emmaline gave me the day off?"

Wiley and Garrison handling it. Emmaline sent me to pick the apples.

What are you doing here?

I search the ground around me until I find my basket and hold it up. "Came to pick a few apples too."

Isn't this your day off?

"I've been promising Sadie that we'll bake an apple cobbler together but I'm usually so busy." I wipe my hands over my thighs, brushing away some dirt. "Oh, and thanks, by the way."

For what?

"For allowing me to have a day off."

And yet you're here, picking apples. On your day off.

I chuckle. "Yeah, I suppose I am."

She slips the empty burlap sack off her shoulder and sets it on the ground beside her before leaning back on her palms.

"I haven't had a weekday off from work in a long time. Guess I don't really know what to do with myself."

Lula has her head tilted toward the sunny sky with her eyes pinched shut. I study her facial features, her upturned nose with a few freckles sprinkled across it. I move my gaze down the length of her without meaning to, and I jerk my attention away when she opens her eyes.

I clear my throat. "Kinda pathetic, huh?" I take off my baseball hat and push my hair back before resituating it on my head.

Lula glances at me, crossing her legs at the ankles before typing a message on her phone.

It's sweet.

I lift my brows. "Sweet?"

You picking apples for your daughter.

My face heats, and I don't know why. "Well, thank you, I guess."

That was a compliment. Women find single dads who care about their children to be a turn-on.

Single Daddies is a popular trope in romance novels.

I can feel my face contort into a scowl. Women get turned on by guys who take care of their kids? As strange as that is, a bit of pride fills me, and I sit up a little straighter. And by the way Lula is looking at me, I'd say she's one of those women she was referring to, who find single dads attractive. Her gaze causes the heat from my face to travel through the rest of my body.

I swallow the lump in my throat. "Okay then." I stand abruptly, my shoulder blade protesting. "I should go."

Lula smiles wide at me, like she knows exactly what she's doing to me. I reach for her hand to help her to her feet. She slips her hands into mine, and it sends a bolt of electricity zinging through me. Once she's safely on her feet, I drop her hands and rub my own down the back of my jeans.

She holds her phone out to me.

What about your apples?

"Right." I pick up the ladder and lean it against a tree.

Once I've climbed up, I pick a few good-looking apples, and place them into the bottom of my shirt, all the while I feel Lula's watchful gaze on me. I clear my throat. "Hey," I call down to her. "You mentioned last night that if your parents caught you coming home in that condition, they'd tell Mick. Who's Mick?"

I pick two more apples and then climb back down and join her on the ground. I set all the apples carefully into the basket. She holds her phone out to me again.

Let's just say Mick calls the shots. The less
he knows the better.

"So, you and Mick? Are . . ." I pause, hesitating on my question and hoping she'll give me the answer without me having to ask it, but she doesn't. "Are the two of you dating? Married?"

She busts up laughing.

I rub the back of my neck. "Okay, I'll take that as a no."

She finally recovers and shakes her head at me.

"That's a big no. Okay, got it." I pick up the basket. "I should get going. I'll see you around."

She smiles and I stand there gazing at her for a beat too long, her long, dark hair and confident blue eyes that I could get lost in for hours if given the opportunity. But it's not her appearance alone that has seemingly awoken my hormones; she's easy to talk to. I feel like she's someone I could confide all my deepest darkest secrets to. My hopes and dreams and fears. About Sadie, about Joanie returning one day.

The feeling is new, and it downright scares me. The idea of

being vulnerable with someone causes my heartbeat to quicken. And if I'm being honest, this woman scares me. She's a Coleman. As tempting as she is, the last thing I need is to get wrapped up in something with my employer's daughter.

Lula waves, and I raise a palm at her in return before I spin around and walk in the direction of the house, not turning back.

Nope. Lula Coleman is definitely trouble. And most definitely off limits.

AFTER I PICK Sadie up from school, I bring her home. It doesn't take her long to spot the apples on the kitchen counter, along with brown sugar, cinnamon, and oats. She kicks her shoes off and runs into the kitchen while I hang her backpack on a hook next to the door.

"We're making apple cobbler?" she squeals.

She's a smart one, never misses a beat. Her quick wit will surely give me trouble one day. Most likely when she's a teenager.

"Yep." I grin.

She claps her hands together. "Oh, Daddy, I'm so excited. I wanna start now."

I chuckle. "Okay, but wash up first."

She drags the stool in front of the kitchen sink and climbs on it to reach the faucet. While she does that, I find a small casserole dish in the cupboard and set it on the counter. Since it's just the two of us, I've had to learn how to modify recipes so food doesn't go to waste. Our apple cobbler will be no exception.

"Daddy," Sadie grumbles at me, stuffing her tiny fists onto her hips. "You have to wash your hands."

I chuckle. "Yes, ma'am." I wash up and then set my phone out on the kitchen counter, opened up to the recipe.

Sadie is just now beginning to read. She doesn't know much yet, but I encourage her to try, and I teach her along the way.

"I'll peel and slice the apples while you put the other ingredients into this bowl." I set a glass bowl in front of her. "How much oats do we need?"

She hovers over the screen and scrunches her forehead. "I don't know. Which one says oats?"

"Look for the *o*."

"I found it," she says, a big smile stretching her face. "There's a number one in front of it."

"Okay, good." I point at the screen. "The word next to it says cup. One cup of oats. But since we're going to cut the recipe in half, we're only going to add half a cup of oats."

"Daddy," she groans. "Don't make me do math too."

I laugh again. This kid always keeps me entertained. "Don't worry, I'll do the math. You just worry about filling up the measuring cups." I hand her the correct one, and she grins, seeming pleased by this deal.

After I've peeled and sliced the apples, I toss them in the bowl with the cinnamon and brown sugar. A knock comes from the front door, so I hand Sadie the one-fourth cup measuring cup and tell her to fill it with flour while I hurry to the door.

I swing it open, and I'm surprised to find Lula standing there.

"Lula? What are you doing here?" I glance over my shoulder at Sadie and then back at her.

I have a plan.

I pinch my brows together, unsure of what she's referring to. "Um, a plan for what?"

For saving the Coleman Family Farm.

# Chapter Ten

## LULA

I AM WELL AWARE OF THE FACT THAT AXEL IS NOT A Coleman. But if he has truly won over my parents' approval like Garrison says he has, then they'll listen to his ideas before they'll listen to mine. And he'll be the one who's here to see it through for years to come after I'm long gone.

"That's great, Lula. But shouldn't you be talking to your parents about this? Or to Emmaline and Garrison?"

They won't listen to me. But they'll listen to you.

"I'm not so sure about that. Because last time I checked, I'm not a Coleman."

But they respect you.

He rubs at the back of his neck. "Look, I'm glad you wanna help, but this really isn't my problem."

I push open the door.

He throws his hands up in the air and grunts at me.

But I know she IS your problem.

He turns and gazes at Sadie, standing on a stool and leaning against the kitchen counter with flour dusted on her cheeks.

She glances our way and waves. "Hi, Lula. You wanna eat some apple cobbler? It's not done cooking yet. Daddy won't let me use the oven. But when it's all done, you wanna help us eat it?"

I smile at Sadie and look pointedly at Axel. He's shifting his feet side to side, and it's obvious he's uncomfortable.

Good.

I don't want to impose.

"No?" he whispers in a hiss, shooting me a glare. "Could've fooled me."

I'm desperate for his help so I don't back down and simply hunch my shoulders.

He exhales so dramatically like he wants the world to know he's not okay with this. "I guess it's fine if Sadie says so."

Sadie claps her hands together. "Yay! Daddy is making spaghetti for dinner."

Somehow the invitation for dessert has also granted me an invite from Sadie for dinner, and I don't think Axel nor I are ready for that. He seems nice and all, and he did help me out, but regardless, I can't let this man's generosity cloud my judgment.

Even if he does have the finest backside in a pair of jeans I've ever seen.

And that's saying something. I've been on tour to all the southern states where the cowboys and farm boys are an endless supply. He tops them all.

Axel clears his throat, and I jump, caught in my scandalous thoughts.

"I asked if you wanted to stay for dinner?" he grumbles.

I chew on my bottom lip and glance back and forth between a grumpy Axel and a hopeful Sadie. Fine. One dinner. There can't be much harm in that.

Fine. Thanks.

"She said she'd love to," Axel calls over his shoulder to his daughter, animation in his voice I haven't been privy to hearing, and it does something weird to my lady parts.

"Yay!" Sadie pumps both small fists into the air.

Axel chuckles. I smile but quickly suck my bottom lip between my teeth, a bit of uneasiness coursing through me that this little girl's personality is already chipping away at my heart.

"C'mon," he says, waving me inside. "You can help with dinner."

Great. I slip my shoes off and set them by the door, then follow Axel into the kitchen. The house already carries the aroma of cinnamon and sugar, and the cobbler has yet to be baked.

This looks great.

"Thanks, but it's all Sadie."

I raise my eyebrows in question. I'm impressed.

"I'm teaching her how to follow a recipe."

The fact that a guy can cook or bake is definitely a turn-on. But he's also teaching his daughter how to cook, and now my ovaries feel as if they're exploding.

And I'm not even sure I want to have kids.

That's really sweet.

Axel's cheeks blush a soft pink tint, and it causes my stomach to clench. I'm not sure if he's flattered by the compliment or embarrassed. He takes an apron off a hook in the kitchen and puts it over my head before gesturing for me to turn around and raise my arms.

I do so slowly. And as he wraps the apron around my waist, I suck in a breath, feeling the heat radiating off his body at our close proximity. He ties it and clears his throat.

I spin around.

Thank you.

He nods. "Okay, wash up."

I wash my hands and return to the kitchen counter. My phone has a million germs on it, so I can't use it to type out messages to Axel. I worry we won't be able to communicate without it.

"Let me toss this cobbler into the oven, and then you can help me with the sauce." Axel picks up the glass casserole dish and slides it into the oven. "Good job following the recipe, Sadie." He puts up a palm, and Sadie jumps to smack her little hand against his. "Why don't you go grab a coloring book or a puzzle and bring it to the table while Lula and I work on making dinner?"

"Okay, be right back." Sadie zooms out of the room.

"I should warn you," Axel begins after she's left the room, "I'm not a great cook."

Something tells me he's being modest.

"But I had to learn. I didn't really have a choice." His tone is growly again. He may think he's coming across as hostile, but

I find it enticing. I'm always rooting for the grumpy hero to get the girl in my romance novels.

Axel pulls out a large can of tomato sauce and takes several canisters of seasoning out of a drawer. He hands me a can opener and gestures for me to open the tomato sauce. I do, and then he sets an empty pot on the stovetop. I pour the contents from the can into the pot. Axel measures different seasonings and adds them to the sauce.

Sadie enters the room with a coloring book and a box of crayons. She's quiet as she sets up a spot at the kitchen table.

"Here." Axel hands me a measuring spoon and the garlic powder. "We need a quarter teaspoon."

I measure it out and dump it in.

"And a teaspoon of salt." He nudges the canister toward me.

I add it to the sauce.

"Okay, we've added all the ingredients. Now we just need to let it simmer. In the meantime, why don't you get started on telling me about your plan, and I can decide if I'm even able to help. Or want to." He glowers at me, but I shrug it off.

I glance at Sadie, who's still flipping through the pages of her coloring book, trying to choose the right page. I wipe my hands on the apron before picking up my phone.

It's less of a plan and more ideas.

He gives me a blank look, as if to say he's not impressed and I am completely wasting his time.

But he surprises me when he says, "Okay then, what are your *ideas*?"

A themed corn maze.

He raises a skeptical brow at me. "Okay," he stretches out the word. "But doesn't that usually require growing the corn into the design? Or require someone cutting it into the correct design, at the very least? You'll probably need a photographer to take a few pictures from a small plane for advertising purposes. You know, to put on the farm's website."

You know a lot about this stuff.

Axel shrugs as he submerges dry spaghetti noodles into a pot of boiling water. "What else you got?"

We've got horses. Why not use them and do hayrides?

"Usually we do train rides with the small carts your granddad built years ago. They're getting old and probably should be retired along with Granddad."

There's a pinch in my gut at the thought of Axel knowing Granddad. That he most likely has a relationship with him.

"The hayrides could work, but that might require hiring more employees. You'll need someone to drive the horses."

Food trucks?

"That's a great idea. Though, sounds like these are similar ideas the Finley Farm is already using."

The hope and excitement I've been feeling all day dissipates. I stare down at my phone, my last few ideas remaining there without being shared. Axel is right. I've completely ripped off Kade's ideas.

"I'm not saying we can't do the same things. But you'll need to prepare for some backlash from the Finleys. When Kade finds out, he isn't gonna let this go easily."

He's right again. But upsetting Kade Finley isn't something that worries me. In fact, the idea of a little competition has a flutter of excitement returning in my chest.

"Let's eat," Axel announces.

Dinner is oddly satisfying. As I suspected, Axel was being modest regarding his cooking skills. And the easy conversation and interactions between Axel and Sadie are comforting. The idea that two people can spend each night together sharing meals without running out of conversation or growing sick of one another is a mystery. Growing up as a Coleman, you had to practically yell and fight to speak or you'd never be heard.

After dinner, Axel hands me a cup of coffee, and we sit across from one another at the table. He bribed Sadie with a show on Netflix so the two of us could finish our conversation we put on pause while we ate dinner.

Thanks again for dinner. And dessert.

His eyes darken before he glances down at his mug and wraps his hand around it. "No problem. I'm glad I had enough. It's been a while since we've cooked for three."

There's a heaviness in my chest at his words. My attention flicks to the apple cobbler I've been pushing around with my fork on the plate.

"So, do you have other ideas? Or do you at least have ideas on how you're gonna see the ones through that you want to pursue? Because doing the things you mentioned sounds great, but they all cost money. And I'm gonna take a wild guess that it's money the farm doesn't have."

I realize, in this moment, that I have no clue what the farm's current financial status is. That's never been my department. Besides, I've been gone a long time.

He's quiet, and I stare down at the dark coffee in the mug in front of me. And then it hits me. I've got it. Something I haven't heard of the Finleys doing.

Coffee!

"What?"

Coffee. We sell coffee. Espresso. Mochas, lattes, cappuccinos. All of it.

He appears as if he's considering this. "That's actually not a bad idea. It's typically cold here by the time the pumpkin patch opens. You'll need a machine, and those aren't cheap. Or you'll need a coffee business with their own cart or one who's willing to set up shop in one of the buildings."

A local coffee business. They can give a percentage of their profits to the farm.

He pinches his lips together, nodding methodically. "That could work. No money upfront."

My phone dings and a text from Jax appears on my screen.

JAX

So how's our hometown? Have they sucked you back in yet? Or do you need The Broken Halos to come rescue you?

I suddenly have an epiphany, the idea coming to me fully formed and in a matter of only seconds. My stomach flutters, and adrenaline courses through my veins. I jump to my feet and fling my arms around Axel's neck.

"Whoa, what's that for?" he chokes out.

He doesn't shrug off my touch, but he's stiff and gives me a friendly pat on my shoulder. I rear back, and mouth *sorry* before stepping away from him. I type a message on my phone.

> Gotta go. Thanks again for dinner and dessert.

I hurry and slip my feet into my shoes, and I wave at Sadie before I'm out the door in a flash. Axel doesn't even have time to holler goodbye before I shut the door behind me. While I make the walk to the farmhouse, I respond to Jax.

> I just may need you guys to rescue me after all.

I compose a text and send the same one to Mick, Leslie, and the band before stuffing the phone in my back pocket and stepping into the office. Emmaline is seated behind the old mahogany desk, and the sight takes me by surprise. I freeze just inside the door. Not seeing Dad's serious expression there, in the place I'm used to, causes uneasiness to rack my bones.

"Lula? Is everything okay?" Emmaline clasps her hands together and rests them on the top of the desk.

I glance around as I tentatively step farther into the office. The same bookcases line both outside walls of the office, but some of the pictures on display have changed. Now, there are more photos of Emmaline's children and family than of the Coleman children. Stick figure drawings are hung on the wall behind the desk. Dust-collecting trinkets have been randomly placed on the bookshelves. When I think there's hardly anything left that's familiar, I see a single photo of the four Coleman siblings taken before Riley left on deployment.

Emmaline presses her hands against the desk and stands, her pregnant belly now noticeable. "Lula?"

I pull my phone.

> Where's Dad?

"He's chatting with the guys in the pumpkin field. It's almost time. Have you been out there to look at them yet?" She moves to the window and peers out. You can hardly see the pumpkin field as it's nearly dark, but that doesn't stop her from continuing to face the window. "It's a really good crop this year. We've been really blessed." She spins around to face me.

> When did you take over for Dad?

"I haven't yet. Not officially, anyway. He's been preparing me for years but only just started training me last year. This will be my second pumpkin season where I call the shots." She presses her lips in a flat line.

> You've gotten what you always wanted.

Emmaline drops her head, smoothing a hand over her belly. "Not without a cost." She's silent for a few seconds, and my mind is reeling. I'm not sure what she means. When she glances up, her eyes are watering. "Lula, you've been here two days, and you haven't even asked where my husband is."

She's right. I tuck my hair behind my ears. My cheeks burn with embarrassment. I noticed Jackson's absence when I first arrived, but it quickly slipped my mind. How did I not think to ask Emmaline about his whereabouts? My sister has probably needed me, and I've been ignorantly oblivious. Is the press right? Am I really that selfish?

> Where's Jackson?

Tears fill her eyes, but she swipes them away so quickly I think I imagined them completely. "We're taking a break. The stress of the farm and probably living under the same roof as the in-laws got to him. Got to us." She shrugs. "He's staying at his parents' for a while. Maybe all the way through pumpkin season. He says I get a little too intense during the pumpkin season. Can you imagine?" She forces a laugh.

But you're having a baby. He wants you to have the baby alone?

"I'm not alone." She sits back in her chair. "I have Ariel and Caleb. Mom and Daddy. Garrison. We have a good team this year, Axel most importantly. We're gonna be fine."

But will YOU be fine?

"It's not about me. It's never been about me. And if you had stuck around after high school and been here these last nine years, you'd remember that."

Then why did you want me to ask about Jackson?

She wipes under her eyes again before powering her laptop to life. "I was merely using that as an example."

An example of what?

"Of your selfishness."

Clearly, I was wrong. My sister doesn't need me. I shake my head and whirl around, stomping toward the door.

"Lula?"

I cringe, sucking in a breath and holding it while I spin around.

"What did you need? From Daddy? Maybe I can help you. You know, since I'm in charge and all."

I hesitate to share my ideas with Emmaline. Especially the

big one. But if she's in charge, I suppose I'll have to. I approach the desk again.

> I have ideas to bring in business this pumpkin season. To help save the farm.

Emmaline laughs bitterly. "Are you serious? You came up with some ideas to save the farm?" She throws her head back dramatically. "All you've done is complain for the last two days, and suddenly you care what happens to the farm? You haven't cared in nine years. Why now?"

Her words pierce through my chest like an arrow, and tears burn at the corners of my eyes. I shouldn't be hurt or upset; it was my choice to leave the farm and not return. But just because I left doesn't mean I don't care about the farm, or my family.

"Good luck," she hollers as I storm out of the office. "All decisions regarding the pumpkin patch go through me."

I brush off her words as I stomp across the field again, but this time I head toward the pumpkin field. It's no wonder Jackson wanted to take a break. Emmaline has always been intense during pumpkin season, but this year, I think she's taken it to a whole new level.

It's nearly dark when I reach the pumpkin crop. I find Dad and Wiley on the outskirts of the field, examining the pumpkins closely. Dad smiles warmly when he sees me approaching.

"Hey, there, Lula. Come to check out the pumpkins, have you?"

I return the smile and decide I better ease into this conversation before I just spring it on him.

"Wiley, would you look at our girl, Lula? She's all grown up now."

I shake Wiley's hand.

"I'd say you better start referring to her as woman," he says around the toothpick poking out of the corner of his mouth. "How are you, Lula?" He tips his cowboy hat at me.

"Poor thing still can't talk. About another week or two," Dad explains my silence.

"That's a shame. I've been following you on the Instagram thing and boy do you still have a lovely voice."

I mouth *thank you.*

"The voice of an angel," Dad says.

His comment surprises me. The last I heard from Mom, she and Dad don't listen to The Broken Halos music.

Me: The crop looks really good this year.

Dad hugs me to his side. "It really does, doesn't it? The good Lord has blessed us for sure."

"Amen," Wiley agrees with a nod.

"Emmaline did real well with the soil this year and choosing the right time to plant. She's very proud."

"Rightfully so."

I fight back an eye roll.

I wanted to talk to you about something.

"Sure, honey. What's going on?"

It's about the farm.

He frowns, rubbing his forehead like he's attempting to rub away his exhaustion. He pulls his arm away from me. "What about it?"

I'm about to tap out a long message describing my ideas for helping out the farm when a lifted Ford truck flies into the field, nearly reaching the pumpkin patch. It comes to an abrupt stop, just before the door flings open. A woman, dressed in cowboy boots and a pair of Wranglers so tight it's a miracle she can even move in them, climbs out of the truck and stomps toward us.

Dad whispers in my ear. "That's Kade Finley's fiancée."

I feel the color drain from my face. *Craaaaap.*

"McKayla, you know Finleys are always welcome at the Coleman Farm, but if you drive through my pumpkin patch, I may have to retract that invitation," Dad teases, though there's a firmness in his tone.

She stops in front of me, stuffs her fists on her hips, and narrows her eyes. "I heard you were back in town, but I couldn't believe it until I saw with my own two eyes."

I open my mouth to speak and then suddenly remember.

"McKayla Sanders, this is Lula Coleman. Lula, McKayla." Bless Dad's heart, he's trying to intervene.

"I'm Kade Finley's fiancée. We're getting married this Christmas."

"Her mama and I have already told her the good news," Dad says.

She keeps her glare razor focused on me. "So you knew Kade was engaged, and you went and saw him anyway? And you thought it was appropriate to get drunk with him?"

Dad glances back and forth between us, and he seems to have lost his words after this new information. So I jump into action, ignoring her questions.

Super happy for the two of you. And nice to finally meet you.

She leans in close to me, ignoring my text. "You can cut the nice act with me. I know all about you and your past with Kade." She wiggles a finger around in the air. "Don't think that you rollin' into town with that little singing career and reputation of you two being each other's lobsters is enough to win him back. You had your chance, and he's my lobster now. Stay away from him and the Finley farm or you and I are gonna have a problem."

Then she turns around, whipping her hair in my face before stomping back to her truck.

"Hey, McKayla?" Dad calls.

She spins around, hand resting on a jutted hip.

"On second thought, you threatened my daughter, so I've officially retracted your invitation. You step foot on Coleman property again, I'll have you charged with trespassing."

"Ugh," she shrieks. "Have all you Colemans lost your damn minds?"

She climbs back into the truck and puts it into reverse before tearing up the gravel on her way back to the back road toward the Finley Farm.

I want to hug Dad and thank him for sticking up for me, but when I turn and look at him, his expression is stony and serious.

"I don't care what happened last night. I don't want to know. My only advice to you is, stay away from Kade Finley. The farm doesn't need any more trouble this year." He brushes past me and heads toward the farmhouse, leaving a chill in his wake.

So much for sharing my ideas of saving the farm.

# Chapter Eleven

## AXEL

It's been two days since I've seen a trace of either a news van or a reporter on the Coleman Family Farm property. I assume they must have their story by now. I also assume it's none of my business. If it were, Emmaline would let me know. I also haven't seen Lula for the past two days.

I step out of the barn and into the unusual warmth of the fall afternoon. Even the wind is warmer than normal. But I welcome it because in only a few weeks, we could be hit with snow. Sadie is perpetually anxious for winter. As most kids are.

When I was a kid, though, growing up near Seattle, we were lucky to get half an inch after one snowfall, and school would be canceled. In Juniper Ridge, we could have ten inches dump in one night, and school will not only be in session but on time. It's something I'm still trying to get used to.

As I head to the pumpkin field to meet Emmaline, Garrison cuts off my path, jogging to catch up and walk along with me.

"Hey, buddy. Where you headed?"

"Meeting Emmaline in the pumpkin field. Where've you

been?" I sweep my eyes over him, head to toe, and find he's not dressed in work clothes.

"Oh, you know, sleeping in after my late night." He waggles his mischievous brows at me. He's waiting for me to ask.

*Oh what the hell.*

"Late night? With who this time?"

"You know that woman I told you about that I met last week when I made the apple delivery down south?"

I nod and keep walking.

"I met up with her at a bar. One thing led to another, it got late, I stayed over."

"You stayed at her place?" I'm a little shocked. Garrison has a habit of one-night stands, and he has a rule of never staying the night.

"I was tired. And a little tipsy. I couldn't make the hour drive back to the farm."

"So what now? You guys a couple or something?"

He runs his thumb and finger over his lips. "I sure hope not. Mostly because I can't date someone who lives an hour away. That'll really cut into my social life and hunting."

"Not to mention your work," I say, side-eyeing him.

"Right. Exactly. See, you get it."

Emmaline is standing on the outskirts of the pumpkin patch with her palms pressed to her belly.

"But I don't know how I'll break things off with her." He leans closer to me. "I can't risk pissing her off and having her drive over here and threaten to tear up the pumpkin patch. One psycho woman is enough, am I right?" He elbows me, but I'm not sure what he's referring to.

"Garrison, so help me, if you've pissed off a girl that bad and she so much as sets foot on Coleman property, I will have you taken out of the will so fast you won't even have time to zip your pants," Emmaline expels in one breath of air.

I snort. I'm not even sure if what she just said makes much sense, but I think she's made her point clear.

"Oh, c'mon, sis. Why do you always gotta be so serious?" He puts her in a headlock, and she swats him away. "It's no wonder Lula's been MIA for the last two days, you've probably been riding her."

I thought I'd been the only one who had noticed her disappearing act.

"The reason why Lula has been hiding is that she's gone and pissed off the wrong woman. And rightfully so. You can't just go over to your ex's place, get drunk, and then stay the night with him and expect no consequences."

I stuff my hands in my front pockets and bounce on the balls of my feet, restraining myself from correcting Emmaline. Because Lula didn't stay at Kade's, she stayed at mine.

Garrison crouches, studying the vines on a few pumpkins. "You know nothing happened between Lula and Kade. Lula would never do that."

"Oh no? And how can you be so sure? Have you and Lula been BFFs for the last nine years?" Emmaline bends, checking the same pumpkins.

"No, but you know Lula."

"What I know is, she's gone and crossed the wrong woman." She shakes her head. "And here I always thought it would be you who brought trouble to the farm first."

"You're welcome." He grins.

I tap the toe of my cowboy boot into his butt. "I don't think that was a compliment."

Emmaline grunts as she straightens. "Axel gets it." She smiles. "Why can't you be more like him? A hard-working employee who doesn't cause a ruckus every time I turn around."

Garrison stands. "Thankfully, I've got Lula, who seems to be taking much of the focus off me now."

She sighs. "You're not wrong about that."

I clear my throat, tired of wasting working hours listening to these two bicker. Or maybe I'm tired of them dragging Lula down when she's not even here to defend herself. "What's your plan with the pumpkins? We can get the delivery schedule all planned as soon as you give the go-ahead on when they're ready."

She swipes the back of her hand against her flushed forehead and gazes out over the field. "They're close. But they need a little more time."

"You sure, sis? It's gonna be a warm week, but night temps are dropping."

She turns to him, narrowing her eyes. "I'm well aware of the weather," she snaps.

He puts up his palms. "Easy. Just trying to be helpful."

"You wanna be helpful? Go do some actual work today."

He backs away. "Fine. Got it, boss." He salutes her. "Good luck with those pregnancy hormones, Axel."

Emmaline glares so hard at his back that I worry she's working on putting a hex on him. But when she turns toward me, she smiles. "What do you think, Axel?"

"Um, about the pumpkins?" I cross my arms, the breeze too warm under her pressing gaze.

"Do you think the temps will be too high this week?"

"Maybe," I draw out the word. "But Mr. Coleman trusts you to handle it this year. You'll make the right decision."

She smiles, but it's sad and sorta pitiful. "I hope so."

We stay quiet for a few moments as we both stare at the field.

I clear my throat finally. "Hey, did Lula ever tell you her ideas for the pumpkin patch?"

Emmaline turns to me and rolls her eyes. "Not yet. She may have told Daddy, but neither of them has said anything to me about it. Knowing Lula, it was a fleeting thought, and she's long since forgotten about it."

I consider this. But it's hard for me to believe. Lula seemed pretty excited when she left my place two days ago. "Maybe."

"There's something about my sister you should know. She's not here because she wants to be. It was Mick's bright idea, and quite honestly, I don't think he wanted to deal with her given her condition."

I scratch at the scruff on my jaw, my mind spinning. "Her condition?"

"You know, her injured vocal cords? That's the only reason why she's here. Mick had to send her somewhere. I guess why not home, where she can be someone else's problem?" She waves me off. "Anyway, it's pumpkin season. That's the Colemans' main focus. Even if Daddy believes Jesus sent Lula here for a reason."

"And Mick is . . . ?"

"The Broken Halos's manager." She knits her dark eyebrows together and frowns. "You didn't know Lula is the lead singer of the band?"

My chest tightens while my brain tries to play catch up. *Lula Coleman is the lead singer of The Broken Halos?* The bits and pieces I know about the band are few. I don't follow much music, never mind that indie-Portland-hipster music.

I can't help but feel like I was deceived. My face heats and my fingers tremble—even though my reaction may not be merited. Over the past week, I've grown closer to Lula than I have any other woman since Joanie left.

And then it hits me hard. When Lula's voice heals, she's going to leave. Just like Joanie.

"Shoot. I think she wanted this to be some covert mission,

but Mick convinced her that their fans would have more empathy if she came home and helped on the farm this fall." She sighs. "That's probably why she's coming up with ideas to *save the farm*." She uses air quotes. "Sorry, Axel. I assumed you knew." She shrugs.

"Uh, it's okay. No big deal," I lie through my gritted teeth and readjust the baseball hat on my head. "Listen, if we're done here, I still have about an hour of work to do before I begin on the end-of-the-day chores."

"Oh, absolutely. Go." She steps back and waves me off. "Thanks for your input. I really value your opinion."

I nod and watch my boots as they stamp the ground on my way toward the barn. My mind whirls with about a million questions for Lula. But one spins back around repeatedly. Why didn't Lula tell me?

AFTER EVERY HORSE has been brought into the barn and tucked in for the night, I step outside, where the glowing sun hangs low and the air has cooled. I untie the flannel from my waist and stuff my arms back into the sleeves. I take my time walking to the old farmhouse tonight. The last person I want to run into is Lula. The lie is still sitting in the pit of my stomach like indigestion.

I have no right being mad. But it doesn't take away the fact that I am. It just makes no absolute sense why she didn't tell me.

After I knock on the back door, it swings open, and Lula's standing there, her face bright. Her blue eyes sparkle as she smiles at me. It's alluring and tempting me to draw her into me and kiss her.

But I don't have permission. And even if I did, I don't have the freedom to mess around with women who lie. I have a daughter. I have a job and a life that I can't risk screwing up.

I force myself not to react to seeing her beautiful, smiling face. "I'm just here to pick up Sadie."

Lula reads my blank expression. Because she's not a young, naive farm girl. She's an experienced, successful city woman.

Her smile dims and she steps aside so I can enter the house.

The children are seated at the table playing a game while Emmaline and Mrs. Coleman bustle around the kitchen. Sadie spots me right away.

"Daddy!" she squeals and runs over to hug me.

"Hey, baby." I bend and squeeze her small body tight.

"Axel, I haven't seen you this week. How are you?" Mrs. Coleman asks before dipping a wooden spoon into a large pot on the stove.

"I'm doing just fine, thank you. And you?"

"Staying busy."

Sadie pulls away. "Can I stay and finish the game?"

"Um." I scratch at the scruff on my neck. I don't want to be here any longer than I need to be. But Sadie is giving me her pouty face, blinking her wide brown eyes at me. "Fine. But only this one game."

She grins and races back to the table.

"Say, Axel, you and Sadie want to stay for dinner?" A timer dings and Mrs. Coleman reaches into the oven, removing a pan of cornbread. "As always, I made way too much chili."

Mr. Coleman saunters into the kitchen. "Stay. We'll talk about pumpkins."

He plasters on a persistent smile I'm unable to back down from. After all, he offered me the job here in the first place.

I glance at Lula who's tossing a salad in a large bowl and is trying extra hard not to peek in my direction.

"Uh, sure. That sounds great. Thank you." My shoulders slump. "What can I do to help?"

Mrs. Coleman waves me off. "Nonsense. You head into the living room with John and chat until dinner is ready."

"You sure?"

Mrs. Coleman takes my shoulders from behind and leads me out of the kitchen and into the living room. "Sit," she demands.

I chuckle. "All right." I sit on the edge of the sofa, bouncing my knee up and down.

Mr. Coleman sits on his recliner. "Hey, Judy? How about a couple beers for us?"

She raises both eyebrows at him in question, and he gives her a wink.

I usually don't drink around Sadie, but I don't want to offend my hosts. I accept the bottle when Emmaline hands me one with a smile on her face. I nod at her, and when we make eye contact, I realize why Lula's eyes looked familiar to me. They nearly have the same shade of blue. Lula's are brighter—a stunning, icy blue. The kind you want to jump into and get lost in.

Mr. Coleman clears his throat, and I whip my head in his direction. "You doing all right, Axel?"

"Just fine, sir."

"When are we gonna get you to call us by name? We're practically family by now."

"Sorry"—I breathe out a laugh—"John."

"So, Emmaline tells me you think the pumpkins will be fine another week?"

"What?" I straighten. Had I said that? I don't think I did. I rub at the back of my neck. "I'm sorry, I don't think—"

"Until the end of the week. Friday, maybe?"

"Um, sir, Mr. Coleman. John," I correct and stumble, "what I said was, you trust her, and I believe she'll make the right decision."

"I see." He rubs his chin, considering, though, what I'm not sure. "I appreciate your support of Emmaline. You've helped make the transition easier on her, and well, on me too."

"You're welcome."

"I also appreciate your loyalty to the farm. And the family. You don't know what that's meant to us."

He relaxes in his chair and takes a sip of his beer, so I do the same. Taking a long pull, I hope the liquid will wet my dry throat and cool my nerves.

Garrison comes tumbling down the stairs like he's having a race against himself. "Hey, Mama, supper almost ready?" He must see me from the corner of his eye because he stops abruptly. "Oh, hey, Axel. What's going on?"

Though it seems like he's asking his dad and not me. He joins us in the living room and sets his hands on his hips, eyeing the beer bottles in our hands.

"Hey, son. We're just chatting. Nothing serious."

"Over beer? Daddy, you never drink. Unless you're discussing business." He glances over his shoulder. "Where's my beer?"

"You're no guest in this house, get your own," Emmaline snaps.

"Fine." Garrison leaves the room in a huff.

After he's gone, Mr. Coleman leans forward and sets his bottle on the coffee table. "This was perfect timing, you coming by to pick up Sadie and agreeing to stay for dinner."

I'm confused. "Perfect timing for what, sir? John?"

"I've been meaning to talk to you about something. But you and I are both busy men." He chuckles. "I'm gonna get right to it because, obviously, I'm not a guy who has time to beat around the bush."

The bottle's condensation drips down my fingers, and I wipe my hand across the thigh of my jeans.

"How would you feel about teaming up with Emmaline in running pumpkin season?"

Garrison enters the room, freezing in the entryway. I glance up at him and find he's slack-jawed. Worry courses through my gut that he's going to get mad and cause a scene.

"I'm flattered, sir. But what about Garrison?"

Garrison shuffles in and drops onto the sofa next to me. "Bro, you and I both know I'm not management material. Daddy knows too." He salutes Mr. Coleman with his raised beer bottle.

"I've already spoken to both Garrison and Emmaline."

"I don't know, I don't think I have enough experience for something like that."

"You're being modest. Of course you do. This is your third pumpkin season with us, and I've never had another employee pick up on the business as fast as you have. We've been really impressed with your work ethic. And I think the Coleman Family Farm would benefit from having you in charge. With Emmaline as your partner, of course. This fall would be a trial basis, but if by some miracle we survive, you and Emmaline would take over pumpkin season permanently."

To say I'm not flattered would be complete BS. This could be the promotion I need to make a better life for Sadie. Maybe even move out of the honeymoon house.

"Dinner," Mrs. Coleman calls.

Mr. Coleman scoots to the edge of his chair. "Just say you'll at least think about it?"

I nod. "Yes, sir."

"Good." Mr. Coleman stands and slaps me on the back. "Now, let's have a nice family dinner."

Family.

A warmth fills my chest and twists in my gut. I take a seat next to Garrison and Lula slides onto the bench across from me. Sadie sits at the end of the table with the other kids.

Lula glances up at me and we make eye contact. She gives me a pitiful smile. Like she knows that I've finally discovered her identity. But she doesn't look guilty or afflicted. Instead, she looks sad and maybe disappointed.

The conversation during dinner is lighthearted. The sound of Sadie's giggling is comforting. As soon as we finish, I jump up and offer to do the dishes while Mrs. Coleman and Emmaline finish the card game with the kids. Lula shuffles toward me while I stand at the sink.

Without speaking, I rinse the dishes and Lula takes them from me and loads them into the dishwasher. A strange feeling snakes through my gut. It's almost as if we're having a conversation without actually talking to one another. In a way, this monotonous activity is therapeutic.

"Thanks," I say after we're done, not expecting a response.

"You know?" her voice comes out in a hoarse whisper.

It's so shocking to hear her speak, I can't help but stare at her for a long moment.

Finally, I nod. Because I don't even need to ask what she's referring to. "I know. Emmaline let it slip."

She shakes her head up and down slowly.

"The question is, why didn't you tell me?"

Lula retrieves her phone from her back pocket and types me a message.

> Because I didn't want you to look at me
> differently.

I pinch my brows. "Different how?"

> Like I'm some kind of a rock star. Like I'm famous. Like I'm conceited or selfish.

> And exactly how you looked at me all through dinner.

I flick my gaze toward the floor and rub at the back of the neck. Guilt pinches in my gut. She's right. Ever since I learned of Lula's true identity, I've thought of her as someone different than the woman I met a few days ago.

Swallowing the lump in my throat, I say, "I'm sorry."

> I'm sorry too. I guess I just liked how you looked at me before you knew. Like I was someone special.

As she backs away from me, she flashes me another small, sad smile. She spins around and crosses the kitchen. When she reaches the bottom of the stairs, she doesn't glance my way before rushing up the steps.

"You *are* someone special," I whisper.

Only it's too late. She's already gone.

# Chapter Twelve

## LULA

I AWAKE TO THE HEAVENLY SCENT OF ROBUST COFFEE flooding my mind with memories of home. Before I open my eyes, I allow myself to imagine I'm back in Portland and Olive has surprised me with coffee and macarons from Ink Café. It's something she does on occasion.

Having a roommate who's an early riser can have its perks. She'll sneak out of the apartment early, go for a run on the Washington River Trail and stop at Ink Café. Then we'll snuggle under blankets, drink coffee, eat macarons, talk about men and bad dates, and collaborate on new lyrics.

Gosh, I miss her.

But when my eyes finally flutter open, it's not coffee from Ink Café dangling in front of my face, and it's not my mother's coffee either. Instead, it's a Starbucks cup. My fingers go to it without even thinking, and I shift to sitting.

My eyes are momentarily in shock as they adjust to the figure in my room, blinking through the sunlight streaming through the open curtains. The figure is not alone. A woman stands next to my bed, holding her own Starbucks cup, a man behind her hoists a video camera over his shoulder, and another man behind him holds a giant light above his head. Just beyond him in the doorway, I spot Garrison. And I swear, if he had anything to do with this, I will kill him.

"Good morning, Lula," the woman towering over my bed says, a bright smile stretching wide with a fake-ness that's not hard to miss. "I am so thrilled to have the chance for this exclusive face-to-face interview with you. First of all, thank you for agreeing to this. And second, I know your time is precious and you're in an extremely vulnerable state at the moment, so I don't take this lightly. Let's get right to it, shall we?"

I throw a palm in the reporter's face and shake my head.

She ping-pongs her gaze between me and Garrison. "I don't understand," she mutters. "You did agree to the interview, didn't you?"

I narrow my eyes at Garrison, who's still lurking in the doorway. *Such a coward.* I fumble around on the nightstand for my phone and type out a message.

> How could I agree to an interview when I don't even have a voice?

She smooths her skirt. "I'm sorry, but your brother said you had agreed."

Garrison finally pokes his head into my bedroom. "I thought you'd agree, considering your *big idea*?" His eyebrows raise in insinuation.

Right. My big idea.

If I could get this woman to announce my idea to save the Coleman Family Farm, maybe it would not only bring in more business, but it could also grant me and the band more empathy. There have been wavering opinions on social media as of late, and this could squash all of that.

Fine. I'll do the interview. But no camera.

She glances at her cameraman and lighting guy before returning her attention back to me. "Okay, agreed." She motions for them to both put down their equipment.

Obviously no audio either. Strictly on paper.

She snorts and rolls her eyes. "Fine. But I'll have to include some shots of the pumpkin patch and the old farmhouse. And maybe some old footage of you and the band."

Fine. But all media gets approved by me first.

She groans. "Fine."

I yank the covers up to my chest, trying to hide the fact that I'm not wearing a bra under this old T-shirt. Before I take a sip from my cup, I prepare myself for a lukewarm coffee. The nearest Starbucks is about twenty miles away. But what I'm not prepared for is the intense explosion of pumpkin and nutmeg on my taste buds.

I gag and cough and shove the coffee into the reporter's chest.

"Something wrong? I know it might be a little cool, even though I asked them to make it extra hot."

Garrison chuckles at the doorway. "Let me guess, pumpkin spice latte?"

"Yes, that's right." The reporter looks genuinely confused.

"Yeah, she hates anything pumpkin. Especially in her coffee."

She quickly taps on her iPad. "Interesting."

I glare at Garrison. Great. I can see the story headline

already: *Lula Coleman hates pumpkins despite her family owning the largest pumpkin farm in the entire PNW.*

"I'll go grab you a cup of coffee, sis," Garrison offers and hustles out of the room and down the stairs.

> You don't need to include that.

"Since you've already agreed to the terms, everything is on the record." She smiles the fake smile again.

Of course it is.

> Your crew can sit in the window seat or wait downstairs.

They both head to the window seat and sit.

"So, tell me, Lula, how long has it been since you left?"

I fidget with the covers in one hand while the other remains available to tap on my phone.

> Nine years.

"And why have you never come back? I mean, Portland isn't that far away."

> At first—busy working. Writing lyrics. Practicing with the band. I didn't have a lot of time. Lack of funds. It's not cheap living in Portland. Life got busier after the band signed with Boss Records. Rehearsals. Recording albums. Preparing for tours. Tours.

"During all that time, you couldn't squeeze in time to make a quick trip to see your family?"

Her tone is accusing. And I know I don't have to answer any of her questions.

> They came to Portland a few times to
> visit me.

"But not your sister"—she glances at her iPad before peering back up at me—"Emmaline? In fact, she has two children you'd never even met. Isn't that right?"

I groan inwardly and wish Emmaline would've used the four plane tickets I sent her two years ago as a Christmas gift. But she made up some dumb excuse. I also wish I had a voice so this interview would go more smoothly than it is.

> That's right. I invited her to come several
> times. Gave her entire family airline tickets to
> come to Portland for Christmas. Her kid got
> sick. They had to cancel their trip. Guess she
> never got around to rescheduling.

"What about your brother, Garrison? Did he visit you?"

> Yes. Garrison has come to Portland many
> times. Crashed at my place. Been to the
> studio and quite a few concerts.

"Interesting."

Garrison pops his head into my room, knocking on the open door. "Knock, knock. Here's your coffee, sis."

I take the cup and mouth *thank you.*

"So, would you agree and say you and your brother are close? Say, closer than you and your sister?"

We look at one another, blank-faced. I type out the following words and leave it at that.

> Garrison and I have always been close.

"What about your brother, Riley?"

I stiffen at the mention of his name, and my gaze shoots to Garrison again. He opens his mouth, but I shake my head at him.

Since my brother Riley is no longer with us, anything pertaining to him is off-limits. Show a little respect.

"But you didn't even come home for his funeral," she argues.

I said he's off-limits.

"Fine," she huffs, reading over her screen and crossing her leg.

I watch as Garrison's attention grazes over the reporter's bare legs, and I roll my eyes.

"So, how does it feel being home, after all these years?"

Great. Happy to be home with my family. In the home where I grew up and was shown nothing but love and taught a strong work ethic.

"So do you believe growing up on the farm helped teach you a strong work ethic?"

I do.

"But when things got tough, when your voice got injured, you ditched your band, and you came running back home. I hear they've all been practicing and keeping up with rehearsals. And yet you're here, your brother's bringing you coffee in bed, and your family welcomed you home. Sort of like the prodigal son story, I'm sure your parents would agree."

"Hey." Garrison pushes away from the wall. "Maybe I wouldn't have had to bring her coffee if you'd been a better reporter and brought her one she actually liked."

My entire body heats. This is the worst thing about having any kind of celebrity status. Your personal life is not your own. Everything and anything is up for grabs for anyone to use to their advantage and to take you down if they want.

My band is exceptionally loyal to The Broken Halos. When my vocal cords became injured, we could've parted ways. But they wanted to continue rehearsing so when my voice is healed, we can get back in the studio again as if we didn't miss a beat.

"Sounds like they're loyal to *you*."

We're loyal to each other. We're a band. We're family.

"So then just like you're loyal to your own family?"
"That's enough," Garrison interjects.
I put out a palm at him.

Exactly. Because while I have been home— allowing my voice to heal, along with writing new lyrics—I've come up with a plan to help my family's farm.

"Really?" She raises her thick-lined brows. "Because that was the next topic I wanted to address with you."

Good. Let's talk about that.

"The Coleman Family Farm has been the only pumpkin patch in Juniper Ridge for nearly eighty years, but there's a rumor the Finley Farm just down the road is going to give you a little competition this year. How does your family feel about that?"

> We've been aware of the Finley Farm's plans for a while. The Finleys and the Colemans have been friends for years. But the Colemans are prepared for the competition.

"I bet the two families have been close. Especially since you and Kade Finley were high school sweethearts. In fact, didn't the two of you have plans to get married?"

I choke on my coffee. Though I'm not sure why I'm surprised she dug up this dirt. She is, after all, a reporter. And somehow weaseled her way into my bedroom for an exclusive interview. If I had to guess, she promised Garrison a date. At the very least.

"That's really irrelevant, don't you think?" Garrison asks.

> It's fine. Yes. We dated in HS. I will always treasure Kade's friendship. But as far as marriage, no, we were never engaged.

> How about we get back on topic?

"Sounds good." She takes a drink from her Starbucks cup, and I feel like snatching the coffee from her hands and dumping it on her head, ruining her expensive sleek blonde hair. "Rumor has it the Finley Farm is planning on having a Star-Wars-themed corn maze this year, along with food trucks parked on their property. How do you plan to top that?"

> Glad you finally asked. Not only are we planning on a themed corn maze and hayrides—both new to the Coleman Family Pumpkin Patch—we're also having a coffee vendor. A local café has agreed to partner with us.

The reporter nods, seeming impressed. "But no pumpkin spice for you, right?" she sneers. But then rearranges her expression to serious. "So, that's it? That's your plan? Because Garrison made it sound like you had something big. And while coffee is a great idea, it's not huge. I mean, I don't see it drawing in much more business."

"Oh, she's just warming you up and saving the best for last." He grins at me.

During the last weekend the Coleman Family Pumpkin Patch is open, The Broken Halos will be here. We'll perform two live, intimate concerts. Tickets will be limited and decently priced, with the option to donate additional funds in an effort to keep the Coleman Family Farm operating for years to come.

Her thickly-lined brows are in her hairline, and her mouth is hanging open. I think I've finally given her information she didn't already have. Besides me not liking pumpkin flavored anything.

That one will most likely come back to bite me in the ass.

"You're not kidding?" she finally asks after she's recovered from her shock.

I shake my head.

"See, I told you it was big." Garrison waggles his eyebrows at her, grinning.

"Your band has agreed to this? And your family?"

I nod.

"What about your voice?"

I'm not surprised by the question. It's valid. And quite honestly, it's the same one that's been on repeat in my head and haunting my dreams for the last two days. But by the last weekend of the pumpkin patch, it will be two months since I injured my vocal cords. The doctor said no talking for two weeks. That leaves six weeks for practicing.

I'm holding onto hope that my voice will be ready by then. It has to be. My band is counting on me. My family is counting on me.

The last eighty years of a family business is relying on my voice.

I hold my head high, and peer at the reporter with the most confidence I can muster.

It will be ready.

# Chapter Thirteen

## AXEL

News vans are scattered on the Coleman property again today, but this time I don't think twice about it. They've been here all week. Ever since Lula Coleman announced to one local reporter in an exclusive interview that The Broken Halos will be performing a concert at the pumpkin patch. If she'd asked me, I would've told her the coffee idea was enough.

But she didn't.

I attach the flatbed trailer to the end of the tractor and drive it out of the barn. Emmaline wants me to load it with hay bales and arrange them so they're ready for the hayrides. Garrison is supposed to come give me a hand with it, but I haven't seen him all day.

Maybe deep-down he's upset with me that his dad offered me the promotion instead of him. I never even gave Mr. Coleman my answer, Emmaline just started treating me as if I had said yes. All week she's been giving me responsibilities that are usually hers.

I don't mind though.

After loading and arranging the hay bales on the flatbed trailer, I leave it parked outside the barn for Emmaline to inspect later. I head over to the empty field to help prepare the wood crates for the pumpkin displays. Wiley is explaining to a high school worker how to organize the produce we're planning to sell when the pumpkin patch opens next week.

"Hey, Axel."

"Wiley." I shake his hand. "Emmaline said you might need help with the crates?"

"We sure do. All the crates need to be built and arranged exactly like Emmaline has planned out on this map." He hands me a sheet of paper.

Skimming the page, I shrug. "Looks similar to last year. I'll take care of it."

"Thanks. And say"—he plucks the toothpick from his mouth—"I haven't got a chance to tell you congratulations."

"Oh." I scratch at the scruff on my jaw. "I haven't verbally accepted the position, but thanks."

"I know it must be strange. What with you not being a true Coleman and all. But even if Garrison wanted the responsibility, his daddy made the right choice for the farm."

"I hope you're right."

"Emmaline is busy with reporters today so I told her I would fill you in on what needs gettin' done. Would you mind coming with me for a minute?" Wiley doesn't wait for me to reply, just shoves the toothpick back into his mouth and takes off shuffling in the opposite direction.

I jog to catch up to him, and he hands me another sheet of paper.

"This a rough design Emmaline and I came up with for the stage."

"You mean the band isn't setting up their own?"

He looks at me like I have two heads. "No, don't be silly. Don't you know anything about live music?"

I shrug. "Guess I don't."

"The venue provides the stage. Plus, Lula is hopin' with having a permanent stage on the farm that next fall, they can get a local band to come out. It won't bring in nearly the amount of money or customers as Lula's band, but it will be somethin'."

I suppose that's a good idea. Long after Lula Coleman is gone, at least she'll leave the family farm with something. Though I'm not sure why no one is asking the obvious question; how will the band perform when Lula's voice doesn't work?

"So?" Wiley says expectantly.

I scan the page again. "Does the stage really need to be this big?"

"It's a decent sized band." He counts on his fingers as he continues. "Six members, five instruments, I'm guessin' some lighting, amps, and so on." He swivels the toothpick from one side of his mouth to the other.

"You sure know a lot about The Broken Halos."

Wiley takes off his cowboy hat and rubs his handkerchief over his sweaty bald head. "Do you know how long I've been workin' for the Colemans?"

I stare out over the field. "Not sure."

"Thirty-five years. So I've been here before Lula was even born. She's been sort of like a daughter to me. Plus, I stand by what I said, that girl has a voice of an angel." He returns his cowboy hat to his head and stuffs the old handkerchief into his back pocket. "Did you know she started singing in church? That was the highlight of my week, listening to that girl's pretty voice every Sunday. I just knew, she had a bright future."

"Not sure Mr. and Mrs. Coleman see it that way."

He grunts and gives a dismissive wave. "They'll come around. Just you wait." He smiles, his eyes glassy. "Anyway, I gotta get back to that high school boy before he mixes up the Cinderella pumpkins with the sugar pie pumpkins." He chuckles, shaking his head. "Just be sure to measure it all out first before you start buildin' it."

I stare at his back as he heads across the field.

There's a rustling behind me, and when I turn around, I suck in a breath, surprised to see Lula standing there. She holds up a hand in a wave. The sight of her easy smile and blue eyes nearly cause me to forget our conversation in the Coleman kitchen the night before.

I clear my throat. "Man, someone sure is smitten over you."

She gives me a confused look.

I hike a thumb over my shoulder. "Wiley," I blurt out, clearing things up real quick so she doesn't think I'm referring to myself.

She nods slowly and smiles.

There's obvious tension between us. Keeping her identity a secret from me was like her telling me she didn't trust me. And me looking at her differently once I found out, hurt her. I'm not really sure where we stand now. Or even how to act around her.

So I revert back to my usual tactics.

"Looks like I have a lot of work to get to." I shake the paper with the stage design in the air. "So I guess I'll see you around." I pluck the measuring tape off my belt.

She tugs on the sleeve of my flannel shirt.

I'm sorry I didn't tell you.

"Hey, you don't gotta apologize to me. I guess I should've put the two together." I glance at the paper and then walk to where it looks like Emmaline intends for one edge of the stage to begin. Lula follows behind me, and I ignore the screen she's trying to hold in my line of vision.

> Ever since I became Lula Coleman, lead singer of The Broken Halos, people only care about my voice. They only pay attention to me because of my voice.
>
> Everyone except for you.

I rub the back of my neck.

> You were kind when you didn't even know who I was. Even before you knew I was a Coleman.

"Yeah, well what was I supposed to do? Leave a helpless woman stranded?"

> Just to clear things up—I wasn't helpless. I could've asked a family member for a ride to the farm. I could've paid for an Uber. But I wanted to get to the farm myself.

"Fine. You're right, you seemed to have it all under control. Squeezing out that window and nearly getting mobbed in the parking lot at Sal's." I hand her the end of the measuring tape. "Hold this and don't move," I growl.

I don't want to be a jerk. But my old tendencies of putting up a wall between me and women and having feelings for them is comfortable. I don't know how I thought I could do this. Have a relationship with someone.

Pulling the tape along with me as I walk, I stop when it reads forty-six feet and I mark the spot with a loose rock I find on the ground. "Okay," I holler, "let it go but don't move."

I find another rock and pick it up, carrying it over to where

Lula's standing. "All right, thanks. You can go ahead and move now." Crouching, I wait for her to shuffle her feet away so I can set the rock there, but she doesn't budge. I glance up at her, flipping my hat backwards. "I said, you can move now." Still she doesn't. Standing, I study her and frown.

You treated me like a person. Not just a voice. That hasn't happened in a long time. Not since The Broken Halos.

She shifts so she's standing with the toes of her boots touching mine, and she doesn't tear her eyes away from mine. She has me transfixed, and it's a lost cause. Because even though I didn't know who she was, her hypnotic blue eyes drew me in that very first day. They're the same eyes I want to peer into for the rest of eternity while the world just slips us by. And that thought scares the hell out of me.

"You're definitely more than a voice. You're special." I rub at the back of my neck. "But I don't like being lied to. Joanie . . ." But I let my words die in my throat.

Lula goes on tiptoe, grips the collar of my flannel in each hand, and brings her mouth near my ear. Her lips brush my cheek, and her breath tickles my neck, causing a shiver to travel south.

"Thank you," she whispers, and it comes out sounding more clear than the night before.

Hearing her voice is like the sweet glorious sound of ocean waves crashing onto the beach. And I think maybe, Wiley might be right. She just might have the voice of an angel. Selfishly I crave to hear it again. I crave to have an actual conversation with her.

She loosens the grip on my collar and slides down the length of me. When she's sturdy on her feet again, I exhale a shaky breath. *Oh hell.*

I clear my throat. "You're welcome."

Lula saunters away, and I'm so captivated by her and the moment we just shared that it takes a second before my eyes focus, and zone in on a person holding a camera about thirty feet across the field.

THE NEXT MORNING when Sadie and I are climbing into the truck, Emmaline waddles across the field toward me with a newspaper tucked under her arm. By the time she reaches us, she's nearly out of breath. Her face is flushed, and a sliver of worry slides through me. She looks pissed. Sadie waves at her, but I close the passenger door on her, thinking this discussion is about to get heated.

"Morning, Emmaline." I nod at her.

She holds the paper out to me. "What's the meaning of this?" she spews.

On the front page of the local newspaper is the caption: *Trouble in Paradise for Local Ross and Rachel?* Beneath the caption is a picture of Lula's body pressed against mine and her lips touching my ear. I glance over the top of the page at Emmaline. Her eyes are crinkled with concern.

I groan and dig the toe of my cowboy boot into the dry dirt.

"She's only been here for a few weeks. Are you two really dating?"

"What? No. No," I say, though I don't even sound convincing to my own ears. "She was just thanking me, that's all."

"This"—she taps at the picture—"looks like more than a thank you," she hisses.

"Look, truthfully?" I stare at my boots as they shuffle back and forth, stamping down some unruly weeds. "I think Lula is great. She's easy to talk to, and she's kind. But I know she's leaving soon. So don't worry, whatever this is"—I gesture at the newspaper with my chin—"it's not gonna get in the way of my job."

Emmaline shoves the paper into my chest. "It better not."

She glares at me but gives Sadie a smile and friendly wave before she stomps away. She gives off a little Jekyll and Hyde vibe, and I shiver.

I roll up the paper and stuff it in the back pocket of my jeans before climbing into the truck.

"Miss Emma looked mad. Are you in trouble?" Sadie asks, her lips pushed into an adorable pout.

"Oh, you know Miss Emmaline looks mad most of the time." I chuckle.

"Daddy," Sadie whines, stretching out my name.

"Don't worry, Daddy's not in trouble. Miss Emmaline and I have a lot of work to do, that's all."

I put the truck in drive, and we pass the area that's still being set up for the pumpkin weigh-in station.

"Where are all the pumpkins?" Sadie asks, peering out the passenger window. "The crates are empty."

"They'll probably be filled by the time you get home from school today. Don't you worry, your dad is on it."

"So they'll be ready when my class comes here for our field trip? Mrs. Diaz says we each get to pick one small pumpkin from the dollar bin to bring home."

"They'll be ready. There will be lots of pumpkins for your classmates to choose from," I assure her, pulling the truck onto the main road.

The entire way to school, my phone vibrates in my front pocket. I ignore it until after I've walked Sadie onto the playground and she's hugged me goodbye. After hopping back into the truck, I slide my phone out of my jeans pocket and find several missed calls from a phone number with an out-of-state area code I don't recognize, a few more with a local area code, and a text from Garrison.

GARRISON

Saw the paper. We should talk.

*Great.*

If I had to guess, he saw the newspaper and now he wants to have a chat with me about dating Lula.

After I'm back in the truck, I remove the newspaper from my pocket and study it. The moment Lula and I shared out there in the field felt intimate, but seeing it captured in a photo appears even more so. The two of us are close, and her lips are touching my ear. My hands are on her back, fingertips digging into her while she grips the collar of my flannel and she's on tiptoes. If I was an outsider studying this photo, the sexual tension would be difficult to miss.

My phone dings again.

GARRISON

Let me know when you're back from dropping off Sadie.

I shove my phone into the cup holder and toss the newspaper onto the passenger seat. But before I can even process my thoughts regarding my upcoming conversation with Garrison or the newspaper or Emmaline's reaction to the newspaper, my phone rings.

I pick it up and check the caller ID. *Unknown.* Groaning, I answer anyway. I don't typically get sales calls on my cell phone, so I worry it might have something to do with Sadie.

"Hello?"

"Axel?"

I don't need to ask who it is. Joanie's high-pitched is easily recognizable. But even still, the sound of it steals my breath away. My words jumble in my mind and get lodged somewhere between my throat and mouth.

*Why now?*—Is the only thought that seems to solidify.

# Chapter Fourteen

## LULA

As I sit in my childhood twin bed with the bedspread covered in yellow sunflowers pulled up to my chest, I scroll through Instagram on my phone. I try to mentally prepare myself to ignore any negative comments—the ones still calling me selfish for not returning home for Riley's funeral. Or the bullying ones regarding my terrible performance or even the harassing ones for canceling the last shows on our tour.

But what I'm not prepared for is a photo of Axel and me plastered on every social media and gossip site. My chest tightens as I suck in a breath. He's going to be pissed when he finds out about this. But maybe he won't ever see it. The guy doesn't have a single social media account which is baffling. I mean, who is this guy, Paul Rudd?

Since my interview with the local reporter, the announcement of The Broken Halos concert at the Coleman Family Pumpkin Patch has spread like wildfire. Juniper Ridge may be small, but social media has spread the news far and wide. Fans from out of state have been reaching out on The Broken Halos website and social media pages asking how to get tickets to our intimate show.

Leslie has been drowning in the publicity. The band has been overly supportive and is anxious to get here and perform. I've even received a few encouraging texts from Cody. Maybe having Jax in the band, who also grew up in Juniper Ridge, is helping to get the rest on board.

The worst part of the concert is having to limit the number of tickets we can sell. We haven't even officially gone live with sales, and already I think we may have a problem. Tickets will sell out fast. I don't like the idea of leaving out any local family and friends who might want to come. But at the same time, I don't have any control over that side of the business. Mick and Leslie are in charge, and I need to let them do their job so I can focus on mine.

Getting my voice back.

The second worst thing since the announcement went live is how little I've seen Axel. While I'm used to seeing myself in the media, Axel is not. He prefers to keep his life private. Figuring he's either seen or heard about the leaked picture, I assume the worst and have an achingly strong desire to go and check on him.

My phone pings with an incoming text, and my chest flutters with expectancy. But when I glance at my screen, it's Jax's name I see there.

JAX

Who's the mystery man? Because without even reading the article, I can tell he ain't no local.

Your hometown intuition is strong.

JAX

Just like the saying goes. You can take the guy out of the town but can't take the town out of the guy.

I snort out a laugh. During the last nine years, Jax has been my rock. Having someone from home who understands how I grew up and knows my family has been lifesaving.

He works on the farm. Co-operating things during pumpkin season with Emmaline. He's from the Seattle area.

JAX

Knew it!

Too bad he's already been ruined by joining forces with the dark side.

I think you're mistaking real life with Star Wars again.

JAX

Would you rather I refer to her as the devil?

I laugh again. Only Jax understands my complicated relationship with Emmaline and can get away with making fun of it.

He is pretty much the sweetest and doesn't deserve this.

JAX

I will be the judge on whether or not he deserves you.

I was referring to the media coverage.

JAX

Don't get too serious. At least not until I have a chance to approve. See you in four weeks.

Four weeks feels like a long way away. But at the same time, it feels extremely too short.

Can't wait!

Axel should be back from taking Sadie to school, and I plan on catching him before he starts work. In the bathroom, I stare at my reflection in the mirror and open my mouth to try a vocal warm-up, but fear jabs me in the throat, and I swallow. I've been saying a few words here and there, mostly when I'm by myself. The doctor said I could begin speaking one to two weeks following the surgery. It's been three. So it's safe to assume I'll be fine. But what if my singing voice no longer sounds like it once did?

I force the fears aside. My top priority right now is to see Axel. I don't even bother showering, just wash my face, brush my teeth, and comb my fingers through my long, wavy hair. I shimmy on a pair of designer jeans that have seen better days since being back on the farm, slide my feet into my Timberland boots, and throw on a navy-blue Coleman Family Farm hooded sweatshirt.

The weather has been warm, for it being the first week of October. Though I'm reminded that this is typical for fall in Juniper Ridge. It's not unusual for a high of sixty-eight during the day and thirty-eight at night.

Mom is downstairs in the kitchen, already fixing a stew in the crockpot for tonight's dinner. She's got a mug of coffee in her hand, one of Nonna's aprons tied around her waist, and flour dusted across a prominent cheekbone. I spot the newspaper sitting on the table, and my face is front and center.

"Hey, Mama." The words slide out of my throat, and a shimmer of melodious glee bubbles inside me. I glide into the kitchen and use a hand towel lying on the counter to brush the flour off her cheek.

She eyes me skeptically. "Well, isn't someone in a good mood."

I shrug and smile limply.

"But I have to say, it's so good to hear that sweet voice of yours." She kisses me on my temple.

"I gotta go. But leave the coffee on, will you?" I toss the kitchen towel to her and race out the back door, ignoring her comments. Though I catch a few words: *Newspaper. Axel. Dating. Inappropriate. Family. Kade.*

It's cooler than I anticipated. The chilly early morning air breezes through the threads of my sweatshirt. Besides the higher-than-usual traffic on the farm today, I'm relieved not to see any news vans. After the reporter snapped that intimate photo of Axel and me, it wound up on the front cover of the newspaper and all over social media, prompting Leslie to get involved. She set up restrictions on the presence of media on the farm until the week of the concert. They'll be slapped with a hefty fine if they ignore it.

Axel's truck is parked outside the newlywed house, and a rhapsodic feeling dances through me. But after I knock twice and there's no answer, the elation fades. I head toward the tractor barn first because it's the closest to the house.

The barn door is wide open when I approach, and I walk inside, glancing around at the farm tools hanging on the wall to the right and the old John Deere tractor on the left. Axel is climbing down from the tractor and chew my bottom lip as I admire his backside.

He jumps down and sucks in a breath when he sees me. "Hell," he breaths out, "Lula, you scared me."

I can't help myself, I grin wickedly at him.

He takes off his baseball hat and shoves his fingers through his dark waves before returning the hat backwards on his head. My body tingles at the sight. It's sexy, the way he wears his hat. As if he's a hero from one of my romance novels popping straight off the page.

"Is everything okay?" He strides toward me, and my eyes drink him in fully from his work boots, fitted jeans, and worn flannel shirt, all the way to his head, where his hair is curling out from beneath the hat.

And now I forget why I'm here. Because his whole hot farm boy thing he's got going on is distracting as hell. But as he stands before me, my mind takes me back to my past. To Kade. And I'm reminded that farm boys and I do not go together. Our hopes and dreams always clash, causing us to go in separate directions. My heart isn't strong enough to withstand that again.

"Is this about the newspaper?" He moves closer to me but crosses his arms, and I exhale a breath of relief.

I want to use my voice to speak to him. But I also don't want to push my luck. I'm afraid if I start speaking, I won't ever want to stop. I feel like I've been waiting years to have an actual conversation with him.

I trust the doctor and take the risk.

"Yeah, I just saw it. I wanted to check if you're okay."

He gasps. "You're talking?"

"I'm trying to." My cheeks warm. "So, you're okay?"

"Me? I've been wondering how you're doing?" He moves his hands to his hips.

And I realize I am way too aware of where his hands are going.

"I'm fine. I'm used to it. But you're not. I know how you like your privacy."

He rubs the back of his neck and looks down. "Yeah. For Sadie mostly."

Right. Sadie. I worry about what this will mean for her. Exposing her connection to not only the farm but to me. What will happen with her classmates? Her teachers?

I tug on his sleeve, and he slowly moves his eyes to meet mine. When our gazes lock, warmth travels through me all the way to my depths. Darn it.

"How is she?"

"She's fine. Though when I dropped her off for school, she hadn't seen the article yet. Good thing she's too young for the internet or social media." He chuckles half-heartedly.

"That's good. Do you want me to be there when you explain it to her?"

"Explain what?" He tilts his head and arches one dark brow at me.

Oh good, he's gonna make me say it. "Us."

"Us . . . right." He nods slowly. "And how would you explain *us* to a five-year-old? Because when you have that figured out, maybe you could explain it to a thirty-year-old." He grins.

My cheeks heat, and I'm fairly certain that I was not mistaking the electricity between us. There's something here. Something real. And if I'm truly being honest with myself, it's terrifying.

"You're right, explaining it to a child would probably be easier." I smile, and he stuffs his hands into the front pockets of his jeans where they're safe.

"So what now?" he asks.

"I don't know." I chew my lip. "But what I do know is, I really like spending time with you."

His lips spread into a wide sexy grin. "Yeah?"

I nod, and my fingers tremble at my sides, itching to touch him, to grab a hold of him.

"Because I really like spending time with you." He takes a

tentative step closer to me, finally tugging his hands from his pockets and setting them firmly on my hips. And dammit if it doesn't feel amazing. "Really, really." He rests his forehead against mine, and it feels as though all the air is being sucked from my lungs. "I haven't let a woman in for a long time."

His words are real and raw, and I feel them all the way to my core. I don't want to ruin this dulcet moment between us, but after the lie by omission, I don't want to hurt him again.

"It's just that, I'm only here for a few more weeks."

He yanks my hips closer, causing my phone to slip from my grasp, but I ignore it. Resting my open palms on his face, I feel the scruff underneath my fingertips and pull him into me. I want to tell him exactly how I feel about him—that I think he is the sweetest person, kind and gentle, who really listens and has a big heart.

"Then I guess we better make the best of the time we have together," he whispers as our lips barely graze one another's.

His confession sends me over the edge, and I can't stand it another second. I press my mouth against his. My feelings for him soar as our lips move and our tongues dance. My desire to be closer to him only deepens the longer our kiss lasts.

He thrusts into me, forcing my body to stumble backward until my back presses against the barn's wall. He adjusts his knee between my legs and grips my backside. I knock his hat off and tether my fingers through the waves of his hair, winding and tugging while a moan escapes against his lips.

"So it's true?"

Our lips break apart at the jolting interruption, and we turn our attention to Garrison, who is standing in the doorway of the barn, his face stony. Axel backs away from me, though gently and hesitantly. Like the very last thing he wants to do is stop touching me.

I don't want him to stop either.

"Oh, hey, Garrison," Axel stutters.

Garrison stabs his fingers through his dark hair. "I can't believe this."

Axel picks his hat up off the ground and pulls it back onto his head, tugging on the brim. "What? That I like your sister?"

"Yeah? What's so hard to believe?" I snap.

"It's not hard to believe, but why didn't y'all tell me?"

Axel and I make eye contact and I chew on my lip.

"You're my best friend. And you're my little sister. If you guys are dating, you should've told me." Garrison crosses his arms.

"You're right, sorry, Garr," I say.

Axel shuffles his feet. "So, you're not mad?"

"Mad?"

I hold my breath as I wait for his response. I've always valued his opinion even though he's my younger brother.

"As long as you promise you're not gonna hurt her, how can I be mad? My best friend and my sister," he says happily. He swings an arm around each of us, hugging us close, and I'm reminded of the scene from *Friends* where Ross finds out about Monica and Chandler's relationship.

"I'm pumped," he says.

And I'm relieved. I think Axel is too.

# *Chapter Fifteen*

## AXEL

It's Monday, and no one has seen Garrison for two days. He's probably hunting or fishing and forgot to tell us. Wouldn't be the first time. But the pumpkin patch opens in forty-eight hours. There's more work to prepare for opening day than normal, and now we're down an employee.

With Lula's ideas to expand the pumpkin patch's activities this year, I could really use Garrison's help. Though my new apprentice isn't terrible on the eyes. Lula has been instrumental in helping in any area she's physically able. Not only did she come up with the theme for the corn maze, she designed it herself. The Finleys and their *Star Wars* theme aren't gonna know what hit them when our *Stranger Things* maze opens.

Lula has asked me to accompany her during her meeting with the coffee vendor later today. I feel unequipped for the position as I'm no coffee expert. I'll drink anything as long as there are a few heaping teaspoons of sugar in it. I knew enough about coffee to get by in the corporate world, but the terms for fancy espresso drinks are especially foreign to me. Yet I'll jump at any excuse to hang out with Lula. Alone time with her this week has been impervious with the amount of work that needs to be done. I can only cling to the hope that we'll have more time after the pumpkin patch opens, but I think I'm kidding myself.

I drive Sadie to school, and she insists we listen to the local country station. A song comes on she not only recognizes but has some of the lyrics memorized too. She sings along, and her sweet voice is enough to momentarily distract me from everything happening back at the farm. I join in at the chorus, singing along, and Sadie's smile brightens her face. She giggles when it ends. I'm not entirely sure if it's because she's happy or if she's laughing at my singing voice—I'm no Lula Coleman, that's for sure.

I pull up in front of the school and put the truck into park. When the radio commentators begin speaking, I reach for the dial to turn it down. But at the mention of Lula Coleman, I freeze midway.

"Turn it up, Daddy," Sadie instructs, halfway unbuckled.

I turn the dial, and my interest piques.

"I just don't know," one DJ says to another, "if you ask me, fans are taking a risk buying tickets for a concert they don't even know is gonna happen. Lula Coleman just had surgery on her vocal cords. Who's to say her voice will be ready in three weeks?"

My body heats, and defensiveness sits in my gut, permeating.

"Yeah, I can see your concern, Blake," the woman DJ says, "but I think The Broken Halos's fans have faith she'll be recovered by then. If nothing else, they're showing their support of Lula Coleman."

"Why are they talking about Lula?" Sadie asks.

"Shh," I say, pressing a finger to my lips.

"If you ask me, I think they're taking advantage of the people of Juniper Ridge, that's what I think."

"Oh, Blake, always a cynic." She laughs. "Why don't we let the people of Juniper Ridge be the judge of that? How about we open up our lines for fans to call in and give us their opinion?"

"Sounds good to me, Kelly. Okay, callers, we want to know, do you think Lula Coleman will be ready to sing live with The Broken Halos in just three weeks? Or do you think she's taking advantage of her fans by scheduling a concert she has no clue if she will be prepared for?"

The intro to a song begins, and one DJ says over the music, "Hey, maybe her vocal cords are fine, and she's just using it as an excuse to spend more time with her local farm boy toy—"

*Don't say it, don't say it.*

"Mr. Axel James."

I squeeze my eyes shut while the song begins and drowns out further talking from the radio commentators.

"Hey, Daddy, that's you." Sadie squeals, jumping out of her booster seat. "They said your name on the radio."

But I'm unable to look at her. My eyes remain pinched together, and I want to erase the last five minutes. From Sadie's ears. From mine. Hell, maybe from existence altogether.

She reaches for me and takes my face in between her hands. "Did you hear it?"

I open my eyes and stare into the deep brown eyes of my daughter. They're glimmering and full of hope and excitement, so I force a smile.

"I heard, baby girl. Do you wanna talk about it? About Lula and me?"

She pinches her brows.

Maybe she didn't hear anything more than my name.

She drops her hands from my cheeks and clasps them in

front of her. "Are you gonna sing with Lula's band? I know her band is coming to the farm. If you do, will I get to sing on the stage too? Will we have to leave the farm?"

Her questions zip out of her mouth like she's an auctioneer. I have some serious explaining to do. Something the preschool drop-off line won't permit time for.

"How about we talk about this when you get home?"

I open the truck door and hop out, meeting her on the other side. Disappointment takes over her expression, but the distraction of being at school, her second favorite place, is enough to alter her mood to excitement. She slips her small hand into mine and forces me into a skip as we make our way toward the playground.

Back at the farm, Emmaline is waiting for me in front of my house. Instantly, different scenarios pop into my mind of what could have prompted the visit. Something wrong with the tractor, the scheduling, or worse, something happened to Mr. or Mrs. Coleman.

"What's up?" I ask once I'm out of the truck, my stomach twisted in knots.

"I wanted to see how you're holding up?"

"Oh." Relief undoes the knots. "You mean with this whole local farm boy facade I've been labeled with?"

She laughs. "Yeah, that. I know you don't like your and Sadie's business being out there for everyone. I'm sorry about that."

I unbutton my flannel shirt and take it off, the warm morning confusing the fall season and, along with it, my body. "It's fine. Could be worse, I guess."

"Look, Axel, I love my sister. But are you sure you're ready for all that will change in your life by dating her? Your personal life will be gone. Everything you do from here on out will be public knowledge. Are you and Sadie prepared for that? Is it really fair to Sadie?"

I'm not sure if she's asking because she cares about Sadie's well-being or mine, but I decide to nip this in the bud now. "Listen, I appreciate you looking out for me and Sadie." I rub at the back of my neck. "But the last person I wanted to find us already has. So at this point, it really doesn't matter what they post about me on Twitter or any of those other godforsaken social media sites."

Emmaline's mouth hangs open, and she cups her hand over it.

"I know it may be awkward between you and me working together now that I'm dating your sister, but I hope it isn't. We're all adults. I don't plan on letting my feelings for Lula get in the way of my job."

Emmaline finally recovers and sets a gentle hand on my arm. "Oh, Axel. I'm so sorry. Were you referring to Sadie's mother?"

I nod. It's no secret. Though I haven't told Sadie or Lula yet. So far, it hasn't come up. And so far, it doesn't feel all that important with everything else going on.

"Is Sadie okay?"

"Actually . . ." I scratch at the scruff on my chin. "I haven't told her yet."

"Well, what did her mother want?"

Over the past three years, Emmaline has been someone I've grown to trust. I mean, I trust her with watching Sadie. But this isn't her business. And I shouldn't tell her before I've even told Sadie.

"If you don't mind, Emmaline, I'd rather not discuss this right now. It's just that, I haven't even had a chance to talk to Sadie. And we have a lot of work to do over the next few days. This can wait."

She hunches her stiffened shoulders to her ears and presses her lips in a flat line. Shit. I've hurt her feelings.

"You're totally right. I'm sorry." She takes a few steps backward. "If you change your mind, you know where to find me."

I nod once. "Thank you. I appreciate that."

"We're partners, remember?"

"Right."

She gives me a small smile before turning around, taking her time to shuffle to the middle of the field where the tent has been set up. All the wooden crates are nearly full of various pumpkins, squashes, and corn.

I glance at my feet, shake my head, and take off toward the barn, relieved I dodged that bullet. At least for now.

As soon as I step inside the barn, Lula bombards me, lunging herself into my arms. I catch her, and she wraps her legs tight around my waist.

"Whoa," I say breathlessly. "What if I hadn't caught you? Then what?"

She giggles into my neck.

"Then you'd have another injury besides those vocal cords to worry about," I tease, tethering my fingers in her long hair.

She winds her arms around my neck and presses her lips against mine. I trail my hands down her back and grip her thighs while I spin us around. The hunger for her increases, and I deepen the kiss. I have the urge to carry her the few feet to my house. But responsibility wins out.

I regretfully withdraw from her sensual lips and enticing kisses. "Okay, we've got work to do," I breathe out the words against her mouth.

She mocks a pout, and I playfully bite her lower lip. She giggles and agrees by releasing the hold on my waist and sliding down my body. It takes all my willpower not to pick her right back up again and take charge of her mouth. It's unclear where this willpower has come from because it wasn't there while I was in my twenties.

My guess is Sadie and being a dad has something to do with it. When you're a dad, especially a single dad, you don't have the luxury of being careless with your choices.

"I've missed you." Lula adjusts her Coleman Family Farm T-shirt.

The sound of her voice is still new to me, and it sends goose bumps dancing down my arms.

"Lucky for us, we get to work together today," she says.

I'd almost forgotten. Between the radio commentators, my encounter with Emmaline, and this surprise make-out session, I forgot about our meeting with the coffee vendor this afternoon.

"Right. The coffee vendor. I remember."

"And I'm helping you with the stage."

"You're helping me?"

She nudges her fist lightly into my arm.

I put my hand on the spot and chuckle. "Sorry, I just thought Wiley was helping me."

"Too much to do with the maze."

"Well, I guess we better get started before our meeting with the coffee vendor." I lean over and press a kiss to her cheek before waving her on to follow me.

I attach a tool belt to my waist and drop in a hammer, tape measure, and nails. Together we load the bed of a Coleman Family Farm pickup truck with sheets of plywood, 2x4s, and cement blocks. We climb in the truck, and I drive to the spot in the field near the farmhouse designated for the stage.

Lula helps me unload the materials, and her strength and lack of complaining are a breath of fresh air after spending the past few years working alongside Garrison. I'm not sure how Lula has got a bad rap for not putting in the work around the farm when it's Garrison who's been slacking.

Lula helps me measure out the stage, and I spray paint an outline on the grass. Her phone distracts her and steals her attention, so I get busy setting the concrete blocks in place. I prop 2x4 studs on my shoulder and carry each one to its place. All the while, she taps away on her phone.

Based on legal requirements that Wiley researched, the stage can't be any taller than thirty inches without a railing. It won't give the band much height, but I suppose it will be better than being on the ground. I attach braces to the concrete blocks and screw the studs to the braces, giving the stage a sturdy base.

Swiping at the sweat gathering on my forehead with the back of my gloved hand, I glance over my shoulder. Lula is pacing the dry terrain, her face focused on her phone screen. Part of me is jealous that whoever she's texting has captivated her attention so fully that she's completely neglecting me. The other part of me is annoyed that I'm doing this job on my own. Might as well have had Garrison here with me today.

By the time Lula shoves her phone into her back pocket, I've already got the entire base of the stage built. She chews on her bottom lip once we make eye contact.

"It's fine," I say, letting her off the hook. "I know you're busy." I open a bottle of water and chug half of it before I return the lid.

She smiles at me, her cheeks full and blushing. "Okay, how can I help?"

I lean in close and give her a kiss before handing her a hammer. She saunters away and I can't help but check her out as she does. I let out a whistle and she shoots me a mischievous smirk over her shoulder.

"I didn't think it was possible for you to look any

Out of the corner of my eye, I spot a truck speeding down the gravel road heading toward us. As it gets closer, the words Finley Farm plastered to the side of it become clearer.

*Oh hell, what now?*

Kade Finley stops the truck and jumps out, slamming the door behind him. He stomps toward us in his worn cowboy boots.

I rest my hands on my hips and wait, mumbling to Lula, "This should be good."

"I can't believe you, Lula," he hollers.

"Hey, Kade." I tug the brim of my baseball hat in the form of a nod.

He points at me. "Stay out of this, Axel. This doesn't have anything to do with you." Kade shoulders past me and stops in front of Lula.

"You couldn't just leave and stay away, could you?"

# Chapter Sixteen

## LULA

I'M NOT SURE IF KADE IS MORE UPSET THAT I LEFT ALL those years ago or that I returned. But either way, a heaviness sits in the pit of my stomach.

"What's wrong? Why are you so mad?"

"You don't know why I'm mad? You're kidding, right? Lula," he spits out my name. "You stole my ideas."

"What ideas?" I play dumb.

"My ideas. For our pumpkin patch. I told you those in private."

"No, you told me those ideas when you were drunk. You would've blabbed to anyone who would've listened that night."

"And what's with you making this announcement about your band performing here? You know that will kill the business at the farm."

Axel clears his throat. "All right, you said what you wanted to say, now how about you get on your way."

"Oh, I'm just getting started."

Kade's face is red and scrunched. I've never seen him this

angry. Back in the day, I knew all his faces. But mostly only the lovely ones.

Kade used to be sweet. An oversized kid in a tall, lanky body who filled out a pair of tight, worn Wranglers so perfectly. His dreams were small, but his heart was big. I knew from the get-go our relationship would eventually come to a fork in the road. Because Kade had always planned on staying here and taking over his family farm, and I had always planned on leaving as soon as I turned eighteen.

The Coleman roots may run deep, but I could no longer be planted with them. My dreams had wings. And I needed to fly.

"It wasn't bad enough you left and destroyed our future, but now you have to destroy my business?"

His blame hits me straight in the center of my heart like a bullet. I wasn't entirely at fault for our failed relationship, and yet here he is, after nine years accusing me of exactly that.

"I didn't intend on destroying your business. I only wanted to save mine."

"Newsflash, Lula, it's not your business to save," he hollers.

I swear, the next person who says that to me, I'm gonna punch them straight in the nose. Because where does he get off saying the farm isn't my business? Like it or not, last time I checked, my name is Lula Coleman.

"I'm a Coleman. This place will always be a part of me."

"Does Emmaline feel that way? Or your parents? Last I heard, they put *this guy* in charge, not you." He points at Axel.

"What was I supposed to do? Sit back and watch the Finley Farm run our business into the ground?

"You know just by having you here, working at the pumpkin patch this year, will be enough to bring in extra business. But no, you had to go and make a big announcement about a concert. How is the Finley Farm supposed to compete with that? Huh?"

A smidge of guilt slices through me. My plan had only been to save my family farm, not hurt the Finleys' in the process. But had the Finleys even thought about what their farm expansion and opening up a pumpkin patch would do to the Colemans when they made their decision? My guess is no. I force the guilt away and straighten.

"What about you feeding that reporter all the details of our past?"

Affliction smears his face before he can recover. And he doesn't deny it.

I shrug. "You had to do what you had to do. I had to do what I had to do."

He tugs down the brim of his cowboy hat. "So that's that?"

"Guess so."

There's so much more I want to say but I'm using my voice more than I have since my surgery and it's making me nervous.

"Fine." He examines me up and down, and my body heats under his scrutiny. He backs away slowly. "You know, after everything we've been through, I guess I expected more from you."

He has no right to stare at me that way, to remember what I look like beneath these clothes, to bring up our past and insinuate what it sounds like he is.

"How dare you."

He smirks and shakes his head, moving back in front of me and stepping into my personal space. "You're still the same girl. Scared, lonely, and searching for something you're never gonna find. Because I'm right here, baby. And I'm no longer a free man."

Hot anger seeps into my veins like lead.

"Hey, that's enough," Axel warns.

Kade leans close to my ear. "You may have everyone else here fooled, including him, but as soon as your voice heals, you're gonna be out of here so fast and back to your regular life," he whispers, causing the hairs on my neck to stand at attention.

Axel slaps Kade on the shoulder. "Time for you to go, man."

"Yeah, yeah, I'm leaving." He backs up toward his truck. "Have you asked her what's gonna happen when she gets her voice back? What's gonna happen between the two of you? Because I hate to break it to you, boss, but if her own family and the person who loves her most can't keep her here, you sure as hell won't be able to either." His glare doesn't leave me the entire time he climbs back into his truck.

Axel and I stand in silence, watching until Kade pulls his truck onto the back road.

"The person who loves you the most, huh?" Axel questions.

It's hard to decipher his intention behind the question.

"Obviously he was referring to nine years ago. Not now. He's engaged."

"I'm not so sure." Axel rubs at the back of his neck. "That guy looks like he's still very much in love with you."

I gasp. "And what gave you that impression? His cruel words and accusations?"

"He's doing a pretty good job trying to convince us it's a bad idea we start a relationship. I mean, he's not wrong. Your home is in Portland and on the road. Mine is here. Maybe we're just kidding ourselves." He picks up his water bottle and finishes it off before tossing it into the grass.

I knew beginning something with Axel would be complicated. I knew from the start it was a bad idea. But I also knew from the second our eyes met that there was electricity neither of us could deny. So why fight it? Why not see where this could go?

"Hey." I tug his arm until he makes eye contact with me. I

smile and trace my fingers up his bare arm. The corner of his mouth tips up. He sets his hands on my arms and glides them up to my shoulders, causing goose bumps to dance across my skin. His hands stop on my neck.

Axel peers into my eyes. "I guess it's no surprise he'd still be into you or bitter over you leaving. You were the one, after all, who decided to leave. He's probably never gotten over that. Being left sucks. Believe me, I know all about that." He kisses me on the forehead before dropping his hands. "And I don't know if I can go through that again." He spins around, and yanks the hammer from his tool belt.

My heart slides into my throat. This whole time I've only felt bad for Sadie. Having your mom decide she doesn't want to be a mother anymore, ultimately deciding she doesn't want you anymore, has to be a tough reality to grasp. Because moms aren't supposed to leave.

But I gave very little thought to how that would make Axel feel. He had built a life with Sadie's mom. So when Joanie left Sadie, she left Axel too.

I'm not prepared to discuss our relationship. I'm also not prepared to leave Axel in a few weeks, even though those were our terms. In such a short time, he's become an important part of my life. He's someone I can trust. He's someone I feel comfortable with. I don't have to be Lula, the voice of The Broken Halos or Lula, the daughter of the Colemans.

I can just be me.

So I do the only thing I can, allow my heart to decide. I stand behind Axel and wrap my arms around the front of his chest, resting my cheek on his back. I feel the weight of the hammer returning to his tool belt, and he grasps my hands in his, pressing our joined hands against his heart. It's more intimate than I'm prepared for, standing there with our bodies pressed together and my heart pounding against his back, our fingers intertwined.

"I'm sorry," I whisper.

He releases my hands and spins in my arms. He pulls me against him and smiles. "You don't need to apologize, you didn't do anything wrong."

I nod and rest my palms on his rough face, ready to tug him close and kiss him stupid. Kiss him until the pain of being left leaves him for good.

"Will you sing something for me," he whispers as he gazes at me, the sun shimmering in his brown eyes.

I've only been using my voice to speak for a few days. I haven't attempted to sing yet. I'm scared. I *want* to sing. But the concert is the most important thing right now and possibly the only chance at saving the farm. So I can't risk it. Not yet.

"My voice isn't quite ready for singing. But you need to know, there's no one else I'd rather sing for than you."

Then I kiss him stupid.

It's Ariel who wakes me early on the pumpkin patch's opening day, jumping up and down on my bed as if it's Christmas morning. Though to her, whose entire life has revolved around pumpkin season, it's probably just as exciting. Memories of being a little girl myself, waking up on that first day with anticipation bubbling in my chest, come rushing into my mind.

"Whoa." I reach out and still her before grabbing and tugging her onto the bed with me. She tumbles, and I tickle her until we're both giggling.

When she recovers, pushing herself up to sitting, she says, "you gotta get up. It's pumpkin day!"

I stretch and exhale a yawn.

"Mommy and Grandpa are already up. C'mon." She hops off my bed and tugs on my arm.

I find my phone on the nightstand, and when the screen lights up, several texts from Leslie, Mick, and the rest of the band grace the screen.

"Coffee first," I mutter.

"Fine. But hurry," she whines.

"Wait, Ariel? Have you seen Uncle Garrison?"

She frowns and shakes her head.

I bite my lower lip. "I'm sure he'll be here today. Who can miss the first day of pumpkin season?"

She pumps both fists into the air and squeals. "Yes! I'm gonna go put my boots on. I don't want to miss the first customers." She runs out of my room in a flourish.

I throw on a pair of distressed designer jeans, a Coleman Family Farm T-shirt, and my Timberlands before trudging downstairs and straight to the coffee pot. Scrolling through the texts on my phone, I pour a generous amount of coffee into an oversized mug. I head out front, where I'm more likely to get some peace, rather than going out back, where I have to pass the office.

It's a chilly fall morning without the sun up yet, so I grab a Coleman Family Farm jacket off the coat rack in the entryway. I sit on the porch swing while cradling the hot mug between both hands. The old, weathered wood of the swing creaks under my weight. The layers of white paint are chipping, and it surprises me that Dad or Garrison hasn't given it a fresh coat.

I sip the steamy mug of bitter heaven while I reply to my missed texts, starting with Leslie, who would like me to prepare some kind of a statement for the press before our concert. I know what she's really asking for. She wants me to give them some kind of guarantee that I'll be ready in three weeks. A guarantee that my voice will be ready. But I can't give anyone that.

I reply with a simple response along the lines of, *I'll work on it.* There's a text from Jax letting me know he and Olive are planning to travel together and are coming a day earlier than the rest of the band. The text from Mick is only to inform me that the band is planning on arriving the Thursday night before the last weekend of the pumpkin patch. They'll be traveling by tour bus and will bring all of the band's instruments and equipment. His follow-up text gets the knots of anxiety in my stomach twisting.

Mick: Just in case your voice isn't ready for the concert, do we have a backup plan?

I stare at the text, reading the words over and over. I spent two weeks planning the concert and meeting with Wiley, discussing the size of the stage and the electrical requirements. It was a good distraction so I didn't have to think about the big thing. The one thing that could be standing in the way of my idea being a total success.

All I can do is focus on the farm, pumpkin season, and the upcoming concert. And trust my voice will be ready. With the limited amount I've been speaking in the last few weeks, I have hope it will be.

The sounds of the farm waking up send familiar vibes through my core. The tractors coming to life, the roosters crowing, the horses neighing. These are the sounds of my childhood. The memories race back as if no time has passed at all and I haven't missed the last nine years of pumpkin seasons.

I'm twelve years old, and it's the first day of pumpkin season. I race downstairs, nearly tripping over my feet, eyes still bleary, and stuffing my hat on my head. I hop to grab my jacket from the coat rack and pull open the front door. Daddy has already beaten me and is sitting on the porch swing sipping his coffee, gazing out over the yard and at the goat pen.

It's cold this year. There've been rumors of early snow. Mostly by Mama, Daddy, and Emmaline. They've been worried about the pumpkins. But they survived the few freezing nights. Daddy says it's thanks to the Lord for saving the pumpkins. I want that to be true. But what about the Finley Farm, whose corn crop was ruined before they could harvest it? I'm pretty sure they pray over their crops too.

When Daddy smiles at me over the brim of his coffee mug, the steam curling into his mustache, I'm just happy we get to have another pumpkin season. I sit next to him and try hard not to swing my legs since my feet don't reach the porch. Daddy keeps gazing out at the farm and breathes in deeply through his nose.

I copy him, staring at the goats and sucking in a breath through my nose too. The air is so cold it feels like the tiny hairs in my nostrils are freezing. He chuckles next to me. The darn rooster crows, probably waking up the rest of the house with his annoying calling. I cringe. Riley has always been an early riser, and now he'll for sure be coming out here interrupting my time with Daddy.

"That dumb rooster," I pout.

"What? You don't like Colonel Sanders?" Daddy nudges my arm, teasing me with the name I gave him last year.

Garrison had threatened to kill him and cook him up for Thanksgiving supper for waking him up too many days in a row. So I decided to name him. Once an animal on the farm is named, Garrison no longer has the heart to hurt them.

"He's fine, I guess." I cross my arms for warmth.

Daddy puts an arm around me and gestures at the farm with his coffee mug. "You wanna know a secret?" he whispers.

I nod.

"Colonel Sanders's crowing, the horses neighing, even Garrison's complaining are all sounds of the farm waking up. And they're my favorite."

"Is that why you like coming out here on the first morning of pumpkin season?"

"It's one of the reasons. The sounds, the smells, the view. They're reminders that as hard as I may work, as much time or money I put into the farm, I don't have any control over it. God has control over it. I just need to keep coming back to the soil and keep trusting we'll survive another year."

It's scary that Daddy could put so much time and work into the farm and that the weather could take it all away in an instant. But that's all I've ever known. That's all Daddy has ever known. He grew up on this very farm. He's spent season after season worrying about the weather and the soil.

I sit quiet for a moment, tucked under Daddy's arm where it's safe and warm. Looking at the farm and the goat pen and smelling the hay while the cool wind bites at my cheeks, I wonder who will take over the farm one day. Riley is the oldest, so maybe it will be him. But Emmaline is the bossiest, so she seems like the best choice. Garrison is the baby of the family and the laziest.

For as long as I can remember, I've always loved the farm. But Daddy has always said that making decisions based on the heart is careless. And lately, my heart has been going in another direction. No one knows about my dreams of leaving the farm one day to be a famous singer other than my best friend, Jax. Growing up as a Coleman on the farm means not being allowed to have dreams.

Here I am, over fifteen years later, hearing those once familiar sounds, inhaling the familiar scents, and overlooking the same view but as a different person. A person, some days, I don't even recognize anymore. There was a time this porch, this farm, these acres were all I needed or wanted. But that was a long time ago.

And why couldn't I have had both?

New lyrics for a song begin buzzing in my mind, bouncing around like a ball in a pinball machine. I close my eyes and only focus on the rhythmic sounds and the smells. The old memories flitter through my mind.

When my brain repeats enough words that actually make sense, I open a new note on my phone and tap fast, so the lyrics don't fly out of my mind.

Dad pops his head outside. "Hey, sweetie. It's time."

I glance away from my phone screen and find him grinning. Besides additional wrinkles and gray hair, he's the same as I remember on each first day of the pumpkin season. It causes an ache of sadness and regret that weighs down my chest along with a stirring of excitement and happiness in my stomach.

I stand and gulp what's left of my coffee before I return the smile. I follow him through the house, setting my mug in the sink on the way to the back door. Dad waves inside the office to Emmaline, gesturing it's time. She moves faster than I've seen her since I've been home, her round pregnant belly suddenly not slowing her down.

Outside, Mom, Ariel, and Caleb are already there waiting. Axel is hurrying across the field, hauling Sadie along with him. Wiley stands, holding his cowboy hat in his hands. Dad, Emmaline, and I join the others. I glance around, hoping and nearly praying Garrison has magically returned. Disappointment slides through me when I make eye contact with Mom, who is undoubtedly hoping the same thing.

"All right, it looks like we're all here," Dad says, hands on his hips and glancing around.

Except we're all not here.

Besides Garrison not being here, Jackson isn't here either. And Riley. The last time I was here on the first day of pumpkin season, Riley was still here. His absence now hits me hard, and I gulp in deep breaths to hold in the tears. It was much easier to deal with his death being away from the farm and the farmhouse and this town.

Here and now, everywhere I turn is a reminder of him.

Axel and Sadie reach us, and he stands next to me, giving my shoulder a squeeze. Sadie forces her small body in between me and Ariel. We reach our hands out, taking hold of the ones next to us. Axel's rough hand holds mine with a grip that makes me feel safe and cared for. My arm hairs stand on attention at his touch. On my other side, Sadie puts her tiny hand in mine. It's soft and a little clammy. Axel and I share a look, and I smile at him.

"Let's pray," Dad says.

Axel winks at me before bowing his head. While Dad begins his prayer, I glance around at everyone with their heads bowed and eyes closed. Every year it's the same. The family and the farmhands gather together early on the first day of pumpkin season, and Dad leads us in a prayer, thanking God for the blessings of the year.

This year, he says something similar, but unlike that last year when I was here and couldn't wait to get away from this mundane, predictable life, I want to freeze this moment in time. I want to hold onto it and stuff it in my pocket and take it with me when I leave. I'm hit with the realization of how much harder it will be to leave home this time around.

# Chapter Seventeen

## AXEL

THE FIRST DAY OF PUMPKIN SEASON GOES DOWN IN THE books as the busiest in all the years the Coleman Family Farm has been in operation. Emmaline can hardly believe the numbers and makes me recount them three times. When she asks me to do it a fourth, I refuse.

Slouched in the rickety wooden chair across from the desk in the main office, I close my eyes and pinch the bridge of my nose, letting my head fall back. "Emmaline, I'm tired. I was up early. I did all my regular work, along with managing the pumpkin launcher part of the day and the pumpkin scale for several hours. And then I've been in here counting people that aren't going to magically disappear or increase."

"Fine." She rolls her eyes. "You're right. You should go. I'm sure Sadie is ready to go home by now too."

I push off the chair handles, and my body complains, as if it's sixty years older than its true age. "You should be ready to call it quits for the night, too. Overworking yourself in your condition can't be good."

"My condition?" She raises her dark eyebrows, challenging me.

Hell. I've been around the block enough times with women to recognize what's going on here. I'm no idiot. "You're pregnant. And nearly full-term. If you want that baby to stay put until pumpkin season is over, and I know that you do, you better take it easy."

She drops her head and waves me off. "Yeah, yeah, I know." She stands, though not easily. "It was the first day. It won't be like this every day. I can't let either of us burn out already."

"I think you forget this is my third pumpkin season working here." I pick up my hat from the desk and stuff it backwards on my head.

"Yeah, but this is your first season of being in charge. As you discovered today, it's not always easy." She ushers me out of the office. On her way out, she shuts off the light and closes the door behind us.

"It probably wouldn't have been as much work for either of us if Garrison had been here." I don't realize how inconsiderate my words sound until they're out there in the open. "Sorry," I mutter.

Emmaline puts up a hand. "No, no, you're right." She groans. "As much as I hate to admit it, things definitely run more smoothly when he's here."

We round the corner into the kitchen. "Has anyone heard from him?"

"Not that I know of. Though if anyone is gonna hear from him, it will probably be Lula."

The kids are piled on the couch watching the newest Disney Pixar movie with bowls of popcorn in their laps. Sadie is so fascinated by the animated characters on the screen she doesn't even notice I've entered the room. It's a comforting sight. Seeing her happy and not so reliant on me.

"Hey, kids."

Sadie glances in my direction but only long enough to say hello, then her attention is back on the movie. I glance around the room, searching for Lula. My shoulders drop at the realization that she's probably upstairs. That's a part of the Coleman farmhouse where I have yet to venture. Just being down in the main area of the house feels too personal. Though despite trying to keep a professional relationship with the Colemans, they will have none of it.

Emmaline stands behind the couch and bends, pressing a kiss on the top of each of her kid's heads. "As soon as the movie is over, then it's bath and bedtime."

"Okay, Mama," Ariel says.

"Can I stay and watch?" Sadie asks without looking at me.

I hate when she puts me in this situation. It makes it impossible to keep the professional line drawn. But I also hate tearing her away from the connections she's formed with the Colemans. As sad as it may sound, they're the closest thing to family that Sadie has.

Neither my parents nor Joanie's parents have much of a relationship with her. Joanie's parents only met Sadie once when we went back to Seattle for her first Christmas. My mom has been here a few times, usually making the trip for Sadie's birthday. But since my dad was diagnosed with Parkinson's about two years ago, they don't travel much. And the farm keeps me busy, so we don't get to Seattle often.

"Fine. But then it's straight to a bath and bed. No negotiations. Got it."

"Got it."

So much for talking to Sadie tonight about Joanie's phone call. By the time we get home, it will be much too late. And that conversation can't be a rushed one. I know Sadie, and she will have a million questions. Most I probably won't even have answers to.

Emmaline waves me into the kitchen. I follow, though hesitantly. She fills a kettle with water and puts it on the stove before picking up a worn metal tin.

"Tea?"

"No thanks."

"Sit down, relax," she insists.

I consider it. What else am I gonna do? Go home for a few minutes and then have to turn around and come back here? Go upstairs in search of Lula, probably crossing some invisible line?

"So, have you had a chance to talk to Sadie yet?" She asks in a low voice. "You know, about her mom?"

I shuffle my feet and scratch at my chin, glancing over my shoulder. "Not yet, as you know, things have been a bit busy."

"Would you like me to be there with you when you talk to her?"

Her intentions are genuine, but I decide that her and I sitting here having tea and discussing Joanie is not how I want to spend my evening. "You know, I'm gonna head outside and just double-check all the pens are locked up."

"I'm sure they are, Axel."

"I'd feel better if I double-checked. Besides, I got the time. The movie won't be done for a little while yet."

She sighs, leaning against the counter and bracing her hands behind her back. "Okay. I think Lula is outside somewhere."

I turn and don't bother telling Sadie where I'm going. No sense interrupting her movie again. The backdoor slams behind me loudly, and I head to the chicken coop first. Sure enough, the gate is locked. I make my way around the back of the house and toward the side where the pig pen is. I whistle to the noisy animals and check the gate. It's locked as well.

As I move on to the goat pen, I hear a single phrase being sung quietly. The tone is clear, and the words are sweet. I recognize the voice as Lula's. I move swiftly around to the front of the house and up the walk. She's sitting on the porch swing, her legs tucked underneath a blanket, writing in a notebook.

She spots me right before I reach the porch. A wide smile spreads on her face, creating a warm fluttering in my chest. It's a feeling of coming home. A feeling of the world aligning itself. It's scary and exhilarating all at once.

I've never wanted to date because that would mean having to introduce them to Sadie. And what if that woman didn't stick around? What if Sadie thought it was her fault if we broke up? I couldn't let Sadie feel at fault or feel abandoned again.

But this woman, Lula, would've been around Sadie regardless if the two of us had started anything. Sadie is an honorary Coleman. Probably to some of them, she's more of a Coleman than Lula is. Something about that doesn't sit well with me. Sadness aches in my chest for Lula.

"Hey, stranger," I say, taking the baseball hat off my head.

She pats next to her on the porch swing encouragingly. I should decline. After a twelve-hour shift, I can't be the cleanest person. But she doesn't seem to mind, so I sit and press a kiss to her forehead. She covers my lap with her stocking-covered feet and the blanket while I set my hat down on the other side of me. I decide right now might be a good time to tell her about Joanie's phone call.

"So, I've been working on something," she says.

I raise my eyebrows. "Yeah? Was it what I just heard you singing?"

She smiles so big I'm afraid it hurts her face.

"I thought you weren't supposed to be singing yet."

"I couldn't help myself."

"Well, I'm not complaining. Believe me. Wiley wasn't kidding. I'm pretty sure an angel descended from heaven and overtook your body. And that ain't no line. You've got some voice."

Her face blushes, and it's so adorable I have to tear my attention away so I don't yank her straight on top of me. I nudge my foot against the porch, and the swing starts to sway.

She nudges my thigh with her toes, and I glance at her.

"You've hardly heard me sing. Maybe four or five words."

"I've heard enough to know. It's probably a good thing I haven't heard an entire song. It might just kill me dead." I mock grabbing at my heart.

She shoves her foot into me, snorting a laugh.

"For real, though." I finally gaze at her. "How can you still blush at compliments on your singing when you've been out there"—I spread my arm into the air—"singing to thousands from a huge stage?"

Her facial features shift when she pinches her dark brows together and presses her lips in a tight line. I worry for a moment I said something wrong. That maybe I somehow hurt her feelings.

"Compliments from people who really know me are what mean the most."

I hadn't thought of that. For years she's been trying to impress strangers. She's been vulnerable, putting herself out there. Her art. Herself. Spending all that time trying to be liked by people you don't even know has to be exhausting.

I lean closer to her and massage her neck. Something about her blushing cheeks and her vulnerability with me gets my body humming. I give her a sensual kiss on her parted lips before withdrawing slowly and regretfully.

"You want to see what I've been working on?"

I sigh dramatically. "Fine. If I must. What has the genius been working on?"

She swats at me and then hands me the worn leather notebook that's been resting in her lap.

Right away, I recognize the four to five words I overheard Lula singing. These appear to be lyrics for what I'm guessing is a new song for The Broken Halos. I hadn't been aware until this moment that Lula's talents range far and wide. Not only is she the lead singer, she's the songwriter too. It's impressive.

"Lyrics? For a new song?"

She nods, confirming my assumption.

The song is about being back on the farm after being away for so long. She talks about her family roots, the familiarity of the house she grew up in, the sounds and smells of the farm. I read over the lyrics more slowly this time, taking my time to put myself in Lula's shoes and feel what it might be like coming back to the farm after being gone for so many years.

Part of my brain goes to Joanie. Her leaving Sadie. Her home. Me. I don't know why my brain goes there, but it does. When I reach the end of the song, my mind travels back to Lula.

I hand her back the notebook. Her face is open, and she's anticipating my reaction. But my feelings are conflicted. Because her song is all about coming home. Of redemption. Of making amends. The exact things I feel when I spend time with her. But nothing in the song mentions her sticking around.

"It's really good. Really, really good."

She grins, dipping her head to study the lyrics again.

Since I'm slightly uncomfortable complimenting her any further, I make light of the moment instead. "It's almost as if you've done this before."

She smiles, and if I succeed in nothing else, that smile is gift enough.

"I'm gonna send it to the band and see what they think. I really want to sing it at the concert."

"That's just about three weeks away. Is that enough time for your band to create the music for it?"

"I hope so."

"And do you think your voice will be ready?" It's something I haven't really asked her. I know she's worried about it enough on her own. Besides getting crap from her band, Mick, and her publicist. But if she's gonna make the band practice a new song, I hope she'll be ready to sing it.

She chews her bottom lip. "I'm already able to talk. And as you heard . . . even sing a bit. Hopefully another week or so, and maybe I'll be able to talk normally, and maybe a week after that, sing."

"That will leave you with one week to practice the song."

"The band and I can practice on FaceTime. And they'll be here the night before. Hopefully that will be enough time to practice together."

"That's an awful lot of hoping."

She shrugs. "It's all I got right now. Hope. And faith."

I draw her in close, tucking her underneath my arm. She rests her head on my dirty flannelled shoulder, not even caring. Out loud, I say, "I'm here for whatever you need." But inside, I'm selfishly saying, *maybe if your vocal cords don't fully heal, you'll stay.*

And I try to ignore the pinch of guilt in my gut.

# Chapter Eighteen

## LULA

By Saturday night, no one has heard from Garrison. I send him a few texts each day with no response in return. It's not completely out of character for him, but he at least keeps in contact with me when he goes MIA.

The door to the office is open, but I knock on it anyway, not wanting to startle Emmaline, who has her attention completely transfixed on her laptop screen. She glances up and an expression of surprise passes over her face. She closes her laptop when I enter the office.

"It's Saturday night. Thought you and Axel would be out on a date or something." She leans back in her chair, her round belly appearing even rounder in this position.

"I think Axel has a shortage of babysitters."

"Ah, I guess because he spends the majority of his time at the farm and with Sadie. That makes it difficult to meet people. And in his case, trust people."

"It's fine. I'm heading over there now to spend the evening with them."

"He could've asked me to babysit. Or Mom. We're always happy to do it."

"I don't think anyone wants to ask you to do anything more than what you're already doing."

She crosses her arms, and they wind up resting on her stomach. "Speaking of, I'm just finishing up some work stuff before I get the kids in the bath. Did you need something?"

"Just checking again to see if you've heard from Garrison?"

She shakes her head. "Nope. Believe me, when I've heard from him, everyone will know."

I fidget with the hem of my sweater. "This isn't like him. I'm getting really worried."

"You can't be serious." Her brows shoot up. "He takes off all the time. One of his hunting buddies calls, and he goes running. Why do you think Daddy picked Axel over him to be my partner? Garrison can't be trusted with that much responsibility."

Defensiveness slides into my gut and sits there, permeating. "But he's never just not responded to my texts."

"Well, aren't you lucky. Because the rest of us don't get the same courtesy."

Coming in here to talk to Emmaline was clearly a mistake.

"Can you just give me some of the names and numbers of some of his hunting buddies?"

"Lula," she breathes out, annoyance in her tone, "let it go. If he doesn't make an appearance in another few days, then we'll send out the search party. For now, we keep our focus on the farm. More importantly, you keep focused on your part. If you don't hold up your end of the bargain, our customers are gonna feel ripped off. So your voice better be ready."

*Ugh.* Clearly, a huge mistake. Talking to Emmaline always feels like a mistake. It's gotten me nowhere with Garrison. Even worse, our conversation has left me with a heavy weight of pressure sitting on my chest. I'm well aware of where my focus should be. I'm also well aware of what will happen if my voice isn't ready.

"I'm working on it."

"How? How are you working on your voice if you can't even use it yet? The concert is in less than three weeks."

I fidget with the sleeves of my sweater. "Trust me. I'll be ready," I say.

"You better be."

I turn around and walk out of the office, finished with our conversation.

"Hey, Lula?" she calls.

I peek my head back through the open doorway.

"I haven't wanted to say anything, but . . ." She pauses, sucking her lips in and pressing them together. "I see the way Axel looks at you. He hasn't looked at another woman like that since I've known him." She sets her hands out flat on the wooden desk, and I wonder where she's going with this. Emmaline studies me with sharp eye contact. "Everyone knows you're leaving at the end of the season. I know he knows it too. And yet, for some reason, he's willing to get involved with you. I just think you need to know, he's one of the good ones."

What she said is true. All of it. Axel has willingly started a relationship with me, knowing it can't last. My life is in Portland and on the road. His life is here, with Sadie. I could never ask him to uproot their life to come with me. Not that the thought hasn't crossed my mind. But I can't do that.

It's a little disheartening that Emmaline seems to be more worried about Axel's heart than her own sister's. But this is where our relationship is now after the two of us have been separated for so many years. Since Emmaline thinks I was selfish in choosing my dreams over the farm and family loyalties. The unfairness of it is that Emmaline's dream was to stay and work at the farm. It's all she's ever wanted. But since my dreams changed and didn't include the farm any longer, I'm the bad guy?

There's nothing further I want to say to Emmaline, so I simply smile and nod and slip out the back door.

Axel opens the door of the newlywed house and welcomes me inside. The sight of his handsome face and come-hither eyes is all I need to wipe away Emmaline's speech. Because what I said to Axel was real and honest. And I meant it. I may miss the band, miss my early morning chats over coffee with Olive, miss the banter with Jax, miss singing. But right now, in these few weeks that I've been home, there's nowhere else I'd rather be than here at the farm with him.

"Welcome." He ushers me inside with a firm hand pressed to my lower back. The gesture is friendly, yet that low on my back says we are more than just friends. And I like the feeling it gives me, an electric current zipping all the way to my toes.

"Lula!" Sadie rushes toward me and takes my hand, dragging me along. "Come see my room. Last time you were here, I forgot to show you. And now I have new curtains. Purple curtains!"

I go with Sadie into her room. Despite the newlywed house being small and only having two bedrooms, the rooms are spacious. It's strange being back in a space where I lived my first few years of life. As a child, the four of us Coleman kids shared this room. It wasn't for too long. By the time Garrison was two, Nonna and Granddad had moved into the retirement facility and we moved into the farmhouse. Since I was only four, my memories of our time in the newlywed house are sporadic and probably mostly revolve around stories Mom and Dad have shared over the years.

"Look at my curtains." Sadie points to her window. "Miss Emma gave them to me for my birthday."

I smile brightly and graze the sheer fabric of the curtains with my fingers.

"Aren't they pretty?"

I nod enthusiastically.

Axel pokes his head into the room. "Sadie, did you know that a long time ago, this used to be Lula's room?"

Sadie's brown eyes go huge. "Really?"

"It's true."

Her face scrunches. "But this used to be Miss Emma's room."

"That's right. Remember, Miss Emma and Lula are sisters? They shared this room together," Axel explains.

The corner of her lip quirks up. "I wish I had a sister."

I want to tell her that having a sister isn't all that it seems to be. But then again, Emmaline and I did play together a lot when we were children. When the two of us played dolls together, she always let me use her favorite. We also played on the farm, hide and go seek in the cornstalks, a form of hopscotch over the pumpkins, riding the horses in the acres in the back of the property.

Emmaline was the one I told when I got my period, not Mom. And when Kade broke up with me after senior prom, it was Emmaline who egged his lifted Chevy truck. Of course, it was Riley who took the blame for that and ended up paying for Kade's new paint job. He'd been home on leave from the marines that summer. And even though Garrison was my little brother, at sixteen, he had already towered over me. He was the one who punched Kade so hard it broke his nose. I suppose growing up with siblings wasn't such a terrible thing.

Axel clears his throat, running his palms down the sides of his jeans. "On that note, let's have dessert. Then it's bath and bedtime for a certain little person."

"But you promised I could stay up thirty minutes later tonight. It's Saturday night."

"You're right. I did promise. Fine—dessert, one show on Netflix, bath, then bed." Axel picks Sadie up, throwing her over his shoulder and carrying her out of the room while she giggles.

After we finish dessert, an apple pie Sadie helped Mama make, we squeeze together on the small sofa, Axel between Sadie and me. Being crammed close with these two feels warm and cozy. But I can't shake Emmaline's words from earlier. The thought of leaving Axel, leaving Sadie, causes my chest to tighten with panic. They've been left before.

While Axel bathes Sadie and puts her to bed, I text Jax to find out where the band is with the new song.

> How's the band coming along with the new song? Has any of the music been written yet?

JAX

We love the new song.

Oscar and Cody are working out some of the kinks.

> Think it will be ready?

JAX

It will be ready.

Question is will you be ready?

> Hope so.

JAX

If we can pull this off it's gonna be huge.

> What's gonna be huge?

JAX

This song. It's gold. You've really outdone yourself.

Butterflies dance in my stomach, and anticipation whirls, spreading through my veins to my fingertips. Having someone else validate your talents is the best thing in the world.

That means a lot.

JAX

You know I wouldn't lie to you. I've never stroked your ego. I'm not that kinda guy.

Have I told you thank you lately?

JAX

Thank me by having that beautiful voice of yours ready when we get there.

Working on it.

Axel enters the room and joins me on the couch, setting his hand on my knee. He rests his head on the back cushion and sighs. "Since the Netflix show was only twenty-three minutes, I, of course, owed her seven minutes. Which meant I had to read her a story as well."

I snort a laugh, and he looks at me, clearly not amused by the way his jaw is hanging open. "You're not very good at bargaining, are you?" I give him a teasing smile.

"You try bargaining with a five-year-old and tell me how it goes."

Besides the last few weeks spent with Ariel and Caleb and now Sadie, I haven't spent much time with children.

He leans close to me and cups my cheek with his rough hand. My skin tingles in response.

"If we're really quiet," he whispers, "she might fall asleep without even asking for a drink of water. Because, as you probably guessed, I am a sucker for the after-bedtime-I'm-thirsty call."

I've witnessed this move from Caleb already, so I smile at his comment. I reach my arm around him and caress his back.

"I wonder what we can do, that requires us to be really quiet?" He smiles against my lips, teasing.

But my willpower isn't strong enough, and my craving to be closer to him is nearly painful. I devour his mouth, deepening the kiss almost instantly. He doesn't object, and his tongue battles with mine as if he's trying to win. But I have no idea what. Soon, our tongues find a tantalizing rhythm, and my desire for him radiates through my entire body.

He pulls me on top of him so I'm straddling him. I slide my fingers through his soft curls while he spreads hot, wet kisses down my neck. When he arches into me, I tug his hair and he gasps. He maneuvers my body so my back is pressed against the couch and he hovers over me, sliding his hand inside my sweater. When he finally brings his lips back to mine, they're needy, and I whine for more of him. For all of him.

"Daddy!" Sadie calls.

The sound of her voice puts an instant halt to our hot and heavy make-out session. He shifts to his knees and runs a hand over his mouth, his chest heaving.

"Yeah?" he grunts, nearly out of breath.

"I'm thirsty," Sadie says.

Axel sighs, stabbing both hands through his hair before climbing off the couch. "What did I tell you, like clockwork." He chuckles half-heartedly. "Sorry. I'll be right back."

But I wish he wouldn't apologize. Not for taking care of his daughter. For putting her needs first. If anything, I like him even more.

He returns a few minutes later, dropping on the couch next to me. "What did I tell you?"

"It's fine," I whisper.

He places his palms on my cheeks and searches my face

with his brown eyes, almost as if he's studying it. "You're something else, you know that?"

He pulls me toward him and gives me a soft sensual kiss on my already swollen lips. For some reason, this gentle kiss is more intense than all the passionate ones we've ever shared. It's intimate and feels as if there's more behind it than lust. A pang of worry slides through me. We agreed on a short-term relationship—a fling. But this feels like more than that.

Axel presses his forehead against mine, his hands gripping my neck. "Lula?" His whisper comes out sounding rough.

I nod against his forehead.

"I don't know how this is possible, but—"

My phone dings, causing both of us to jump. I grab it off the coffee table, feeling awful I forgot to turn the sound off so it wouldn't wake Sadie. It's something I've never had to think about before, waking sleeping children.

I switch it to vibrate and whisper, "Sorry." But can't help from glancing at the screen as I return it to the coffee table ready to ignore it.

KADE

Saw your Instagram story. Promising your autograph for every customer who buys a pumpkin from you? Really?

This is an all time low for you. Better watch your back.

# Chapter Nineteen

## AXEL

Sadie and I are up early for a Sunday. While the Colemans head to church, I'm left in charge of running the pumpkin patch for the morning. Lula's family somehow managed to guilt her into attending with them. Maybe she's trying to make up for lost time—the nine years she hasn't been able to go.

I help Sadie into her cowgirl boots. They're light brown with a small heel and a smidge big so that she can grow into them and they can last longer. I bought them for her birthday. She wanted a pair like Ariel, though Ariel's were pink, and Sadie specifically said if she couldn't get them in purple, she'd take them in brown, just like Caleb's.

"Ready?" I ask her once I've gotten them on her feet.

"Why can't we go to church with the Colemans?" Sadie asks as we slip out the front door of the house.

I lock it and double-check it with a jiggle of the handle. "I already told you, we gotta run the show this morning."

She's sulking, I can tell. Her shoulders are slumped, and she doesn't seem all that excited to have her new boots on.

Sometimes we attend the same small church in town that the Colemans do, but not often. Usually only when Sadie asks me. She likes Sunday school with the singing and the Goldfish snacks. For me, though, I could take it or leave it.

"Hey, wanna help me bring all the wheelbarrows out of the barn? We can race?"

Sadie's face lights up. She never turns down a race. This girl was born with competition in her blood. "I'll race you to the barn."

She takes off running, and I jog behind her.

Once we've pushed all the wheelbarrows near the edge of the parking lot where the customers enter, Sadie and I stop at the coffee truck. I order a hot chocolate for her and some fancy, extra-sweet espresso drink that would make my friends back home in Seattle proud. Growing up so close to Starbucks's birthplace makes everyone from back home a coffee snob.

We reach the pumpkin weigh station just as Wiley unlocks the gate to a long line of cars waiting to enter the parking lot. If our opening day this past Wednesday was record-breaking, I'm gonna guess today will be as well. Sundays are always our busiest. But with the prospect of a certain famous Lula Coleman roaming around the farm, the crowd coming through the gate is astronomical.

When I spot two news vans pulling into the parking lot, I lean close to Sadie and say, "You stick close to me, you hear?"

"Okay, Daddy," she says, running up and down on the pumpkin scale and weighing herself over and over.

The reporters and cameramen from the local news wait around for a few hours, ordering drinks from the coffee cart and wandering around the shop set up inside the largest barn. Only one of the reporters recognized me from my six seconds of fame, but I told her she better not even think twice about recording me while my daughter is around.

My stomach stirs with anxiety while I wait for Lula to return to the farm. And it's not only because I want to see her, but also mostly so I can get these reporters off my back and they can bother her instead.

When she finally does return, they all navigate toward her like moths to a bug zapper. And I finally breathe normally again.

Lula spends the next two hours with the reporters and cameramen while her fans swarm around her. For some reason, the sight of it burrows under my skin and irritates me. I don't care that she's famous. Or known by the locals. What bothers me is that a few weeks ago, before the pumpkin patch opened, she wanted to help the farm. She wanted to help drive the profits, work on the farm, sell pumpkins. But instead, she's been doing a whole lot of nothing to help out.

Unless you can call smiling pretty at a camera work? Because it's not like she can do much talking. I can only imagine how her interviews are going. Only occasionally does she glance my way and shoot me a wink and a sexy smile. Each time, it nearly steals my breath away. Then I curse. Because her glance and smile have too much damn power over me.

"Daddy," Sadie hisses, scolding me with a look. "That's a naughty word."

"Sorry, you're right, baby." Part of me forgot she was standing opposite me at the scale.

"Ariel says that sometimes she hears Miss Emma say that word," Sadie whispers while we wait for the next customer to push the wheelbarrow weighted down by pumpkins onto the scale.

"Is that so?"

"But Miss Emma says she's just meaning that awful place. You know, down there"—she points to the ground—"where you burn forever."

I chuckle and decide we'll need to have a discussion about heaven and hell and all things associated with the afterlife. "Okay, that's something we should probably talk about later." It's not something I'm planning to put on the agenda for tonight. Instead, I have a seat on my porch reserved for Lula and I.

WHEN THE LAST car merges onto the main road and I lock the gate to the parking lot, it's 6:15 and I'm exhausted. Even the walk across the back field to the Coleman farmhouse to pick up Sadie makes me tired. But since she's only five, it's not as if I can very well expect her to walk the several hundred feet home on her own. I reach the back of the house and find Lula sitting on the top step. She stands when she sees me approaching, her expression expectant.

"Hey," I say by way of a greeting. But mostly because I can't think of anything else to say. It's not as if I'm angry with her. Guess I'm just frustrated.

Standing at the bottom step with her on the top, she's slightly taller than me now, and she tethers her arms around my neck. I'm tired and sweaty and probably smelly too. Her eyes glint with that glimmer of trouble, and she gives me that sexy grin, showing all her teeth, and some of the irritation slips away.

I kiss her, slow at first, but darn it if I can't help myself and deepen it until we're practically making out on the back stoop like we're a couple of teenagers.

"I've missed you," I finally say when we break apart.

She smiles but knits her brows together in confusion. Probably because she doesn't understand how I could possibly miss her when she was in the same vicinity as me for the last six hours.

"You seemed pretty distracted today," I finally elaborate, sliding my hands off her hips.

"Yeah, I'm sorry about that."

"It's fine."

"I'm just trying to keep everyone interested in the pumpkin patch and the farm. It takes a little sweet talking."

"I guess." I shrug and climb the remaining step, reaching around her for the door handle.

She tugs on my arm. "Hey, I said I was sorry," her voice is soft.

I can hardly resist it. It's a melody that could easily lock me in a trance. "And I said it's fine. I'm just tired and I need to get Sadie."

"You're going home?" She appears genuinely hurt. Her eyes droop right along with her lips at the corners.

Now I'm frustrated with myself. She's wasting her voice apologizing to me. I take her in my arms, if only to reassure her that things between us are okay. Or at least, they will be. Feeling jealous that the media gets time with her when our time together is already limited is my own issue I need to deal with. I squeeze her and breathe in her cherry-blossom-scented hair. Before I release her, I press a kiss on top of her head.

"We're okay," I say to reinforce it.

Her lips scrunch this way and that, but she finally settles on a smile, and I almost give in and invite her over so we can live out my earlier fantasy of sitting on the porch with her. But the muscles across my shoulders ache.

"I'll see you in the morning." I go in through the back door, and she follows.

I wince when I find Sadie sitting at the kitchen table with Mrs. Coleman and her grandchildren, worried they've invited us to stay for dinner again and wondering how I'm going to decline.

"Hey, Axel," Mrs. Coleman says, glancing up from the puzzle she and the children are working on. "How'd today go?"

"Hi, Daddy," Sadie says, jumping up and running to the coat rack for her jacket.

I stuff my hands into the front pockets of my jeans, all too aware of Lula hovering behind me. "It was busy," I say on an exhale.

"Busier than Wednesday?"

"I'm guessing so. Emmaline was in charge of counting the numbers today, and I was in charge of locking up after the entire parking lot was empty."

"Well, good. I'll be anxious to see the numbers," Mrs. Coleman says,

"Me too."

She stands and notices Lula boiling water on the stove. "Say, if you want Sadie to stay over, she's more than welcome to. Then maybe you two can go out on a proper date?"

Her invitation both surprises me and puts me in a predicament. "I truly appreciate the offer, Mrs. Coleman, I really do. But I'm beat. All I'm looking forward to is laying my head on my pillow just as soon as Sadie is asleep."

"I bet. You go get some sleep. The farm needs you in tip-top shape in the morning."

Sadie hugs Mrs. Coleman and says goodbye to the children. When she gives Lula's waist a tight hug, my chest feels as if it's tightening right along with it. Lula doesn't look at me.

"I'll definitely take a rain check on that offer, though, thank you," I say, and then I take Sadie by the shoulders and usher her out of the kitchen, shooting Lula a quick wink while I head to the backdoor.

# Chapter Twenty

## LULA

I start Monday off right by getting up early with a plan to make up for the discord yesterday between me and Axel. I fix two cups of coffee along with a cup of hot chocolate, even finding the little marshmallows Emmaline has hidden in the pantry, and make the trek across the field toward the newlywed house.

Maneuvering the uneven terrain of grass and weeds, I grip the three travel mugs while the cold wind whips through my thin sweater. The change in weather is a clear sign fall is finally hitting our small high-desert town.

By the time I reach the newlywed house, my teeth are chattering, partly from the cool air and partly from nerves. I have to sort of kick the front door because my hands are full, so when Axel greets me with a look of annoyance, I shouldn't be surprised. He recovers quickly, smiling and taking the mugs from my hands.

"Morning. You're up early."

I give him a hesitant smile. With the way we left things last night, I'm not sure what's going on between us. I've been in enough relationships to know a thing or two about how conflict and arguments go. But things with Axel are so new and also so incredible that I'm afraid to mess this up.

"Please, come in." He steps aside, and my tense shoulders drop with ease. "What do we have here?" He eyes the mugs.

"Coffee, you." I point at one of them and then point at another. "Hot chocolate, Sadie."

"Wow, this is . . . great. Unexpected, but great."

I reach for the third mug for myself.

"Hey, Sadie? Lula is here, and she's got a surprise for you," Axel calls over his shoulder.

It doesn't take her long to race into the living room. "Lula!" She hugs me like it's been years since she's seen me. My heart shifts in my chest. Already this girl is becoming important to me.

"Here." Axel hands Sadie the mug. "Lula brought you hot cocoa."

She smiles wide and bright, her chubby cheeks growing fuller. "I love hot cocoa. Thank you."

"Marshmallows too," I whisper.

"Yummy!"

"Go drink it at the table. I'll bring your breakfast in a sec." Axel watches her skip to the table and climb up on the bench.

I fidget with the release button on the spout of my travel mug.

"You know you have a best friend for life now," Axel says, smiling at me like I am his favorite person in the world. And even though I know that isn't true, Sadie is his entire world, I allow myself this fantasy. He presses a kiss to my cheek. "This is great, thank you."

"Hope I put enough sugar in there for you. I know how sweet you like it."

"I don't like everything in my life sweet." He grins playfully at me. "Some things I like spicy."

My cheeks heat.

"So, it's early. Everything okay? Emmaline okay? And Garrison?"

It strikes me in this moment just how connected he is with my family. He's been here for three years, living and working alongside my siblings and parents. Years I've missed. It's possible he knows them better than I do. I don't know if it feels good to know he's been here or if it hurts.

"Everyone is fine."

He exhales a breath.

"Guess I'm just anxious to get the day started. And I also want a do-over of yesterday."

He drops his head, his focus on his work boots. "Sorry about that. I told you it was me, not you. And I just needed some time to think."

When someone says they've been thinking, the outcome is never good.

Axel peers up, his gaze flicking to Sadie. "This is all new to me, you know?"

I don't answer, just wait for him to hopefully elaborate.

"Not just a relationship, but a relationship while being a dad. And a relationship with someone famous."

"Pft," I breathe out. "I'm not famous."

"You're definitely not not famous. You're not only well-known by the media, but you're well-known by everyone in this town and around this farm. That's just something I need to get used to."

"You sure that's all that's bothering you?

I watch as the hesitation plays out on his face.

"Look," he finally says, "when you came to me with all these ideas to save the farm, I found your determination inspiring, not to mention sexy." He lowers his voice with the last word.

I keep my expression stony, awaiting the *but*.

"For the past few weeks, I watched you work hard around here. I watched you get dirty and sacrifice your sleep and time for your family. But since we opened, and especially yesterday . . . you were distracted."

My stomach plummets to my feet at his words.

"You were so busy talking to reporters, you hardly did anything around the farm."

"Talking to reporters is a part of my life. It comes with the job."

"I get that."

"Do you?" I say too loudly. My voice nearly cracks, and it sends a shiver of worry down my spine.

He rubs the back of his neck. "Look"—he lowers his voice—"you wanted to start over, so that's what I'm trying to do."

"Bringing up yesterday isn't starting over."

"You asked."

"You're right. I did. But if you expect me to apologize for doing my job, I won't."

"I don't expect that."

"Daddy?" Sadie calls from the table, interrupting us, and we both glance at her. "I still need my breakfast."

Axel exhales loudly. "Okay, I'll be right there."

"I should go."

He grabs my hand. "Please don't."

His eyes portray sincerity, and I feel myself caving. Because I understand what he's meaning. All this is new to me too. Working on the farm while being Lula Coleman lead singer of the Broken Halos. If I'm not used to it, I can't expect him to be either.

"Can we finish this conversation after I get back from dropping Sadie off at school?"

I shake my head and let myself out. The cold air rips through my thin sweater and I shiver. "I get it, Axel. And it's okay. We're okay." I rise on my toes and give him a quick kiss. "I'm gonna get to work."

THE HARDER I WORK, the faster the day passes. I should've figured the distraction of work would do that. It's the same when I'm in the studio with the band rehearsing. The hours will fly by, and if it weren't for Mick, we'd forget to eat. Besides being slightly naggy, Mick is an exceptional manager. He takes care of us like we're his children, even though he's only about ten years older than most of the band members.

I'm assisting a young couple with five small children out to their car, pushing the overfilled wheelbarrow with pumpkins. The woman has a baby in a carrier strapped to her chest and a child in each hand. The guy has one child on his back and another crying in his arms. While the mother straps the children into their car seats, the father opens the back door of their Chevy Suburban, and together, we load the pumpkins into the back.

"Thanks for your help, but I can take it from here," the guy says.

But if I leave now, one of them will have to return the empty wheelbarrow to the check-in station. I wave him off and wait. The mother comes around to the back, smiling wide at me, and I realize she knows my identity.

"It's fine, I don't mind."

"I hope you don't mind me saying, but I just think how the media treated you after your vocal cord injury was just terrible."

"Thank you."

"All right, sweetie. You saw her, you got to talk to her, now leave the poor girl alone," the guy says, slamming the back door shut on the Suburban.

The woman's face blushes, and I realize this family might have made the trip here just to see me. I don't know if I should be flattered or irritated.

"Have you been to the Coleman Family Farm before?"

The woman shakes her head. "This is our first time."

"I'm honestly not trying to be conceited, but I'm just wondering, did you only come because you thought you might meet me?"

The woman bites her lower lip. Guilty.

"But we're new to the area. Moved here less than a year ago. And we loved your family's pumpkin patch. We'll definitely be back."

"We almost went to the Finley Farm," the husband admits. "They have a food truck that serves the best Philly cheesesteaks without having to go all the way to Philly."

The wife smacks the husband in the gut with the back of her hand. "We're recommending the Coleman Family Farm over the Finley's to everyone we know and on my mommy blog Instagram account."

I nod and force a smile. "Thanks, we appreciate it."

"And we love the Broken Halos. Fingers crossed we get tickets," she says as she gets into her vehicle.

I take a hold of the wheelbarrow's handles and push it over the bumpy ground of smashed weed-filled grass. In this moment, I realize that if I want the farm to be sustainable for years to come, I need a better plan.

# Chapter Twenty-One

## AXEL

LULA DOESN'T TRY TO COMMUNICATE WITH ME THE entire day, despite the two of us working alongside one another. What I said to her about her not pulling her weight around here is bothering me. I was just tired. And irritated. She's doing the best she can.

Today she must be trying to prove me wrong. She's been pushing wheelbarrows full of pumpkins across the bumpy terrain to customers' cars in the parking lot, selling tickets for the maze, and working in the store in the barn. She talks to the locals as if they're friends, because I figure, at one point, they probably were.

I hate that the harder she works, the more attractive she becomes. There's something about her putting in the effort for something bigger than herself that turns me on. I've also seen her vulnerable side when she showed me the new lyrics she wrote about what it has felt like coming home. Each part of her has been another piece of the puzzle that makes her special and unique. But her here, on the farm, putting in the work, not giving up, makes her sexy as hell.

After the last customers leave and Wiley locks the gate, Lula is already gone. I have to check in with Emmaline, who is probably still crunching numbers in the office, before I can pick up Sadie. I'm tempted to text Lula and have her meet me outside before I go in and handle my responsibilities, but it's late, and Sadie will be hungry.

I open the back door of the Coleman farmhouse and make a beeline for the office. Emmaline is alone, sitting on the other side of the desk. When I walk in, she glances up, and I see her mascara-streaked cheeks.

"Oh, hey . . . sorry. I can come back if you want?" I back up.

"No, no." She sniffs. "It's fine. Come in."

I take a few hesitant steps inside, my body itching to get the hell out of here. "You okay?"

Emmaline tears a Kleenex from the box on a shelf behind the desk and wipes at her smeared cheeks. "Not really." She gives me a halfhearted smile. "I just got off the phone with Jackson. The kids have been asking if he'll come and take them through the new cool maze that Auntie Lula designed. But he's making every excuse in the book not to come. Because he knows if he does, he'll have to see me. In my element. Taking charge and being stressed and all that."

"I'm sorry." Mostly sorry I asked. But I guess I do know a little something about being a single parent. Though I can't imagine what she's going through, two kids and another on the way.

She hunches a shoulder.

I clear my throat and take a seat in the chair across from her. "Let me help with the numbers?"

"Already done."

I raise my brows. "Really?"

"Yep. I counted them twice. And the revenue for the day. The money has already been put in the safe."

"And you don't want me to recount?"

She shakes her head and wipes the Kleenex underneath her nose. "Nah, you should get Sadie and go home. I know she really misses you during pumpkin season."

I rub my sweaty palms down the thighs of my Carhartt pants, anxious to bolt but unsure if I should leave Emmaline like this. "Okay, but only if you're sure."

She dismisses me with a flip of her wrist as if I'm her peasant servant, and that's enough to prompt me to stand. "Go, Axel. Good night." She opens her laptop, already focusing on something on the screen.

"Night." I exit the office and hope Sadie is ready to go.

I find her standing on a stool at the kitchen counter, Mrs. Coleman helping her knead dough.

"Hey, baby, ready to go?"

"Oh." Mrs. Coleman puts a floured hand to her chest. "Axel, you startled me."

"Sorry about that," I apologize.

"Almost ready, Daddy."

"Sadie here is a natural at kneading dough for bread."

"Oh, yeah?"

"For a five-year-old, she has some strong little hands."

Sadie grins at Mrs. Coleman, and it sends a pang through my chest. The older Sadie gets, the more she resembles Joanie. And then I'm reminded of the pressing conversation I need to have with her regarding her mother that I've been putting off.

I shift in my work boots, glancing around and peering into the living room and up the stairs. There's no sign of Lula, and disappointment lands in my stomach. I need to apologize for our earlier fight. She's not wrong. Being somewhat famous is a part of her and her life. So if I want to be included, at least for the next few weeks, it's something I need to get used to.

"Okay, Sadie, wash up. We need to get home for dinner."

She wipes her hands on the oversized apron tied around her waist. "Next time, can I help you make cinnamon rolls? Your cinnamon rolls are my favorite."

Mrs. Coleman giggles. "I think that can be arranged. Thanks for your help." She unties Sadie's apron and moves the stool to the sink so she can wash her hands.

"As always, thanks for watching Sadie," I say.

"And as always, it's my pleasure. Sadie is a big help around here. She's a good mediator between Ariel and Caleb."

"Good, glad to hear it."

Sadie finishes at the sink, and we manage to say our good-byes and sneak out the back door without interrupting Emmaline's crying again. I make us one of Sadie's favorite meals; grilled cheese and tomato soup. She's extra tired tonight, which makes her extra whiny.

I spend the entire evening through dinner, bath time, and story time debating how to tell her about Joanie's phone call. But any intro into a conversation doesn't sound right. Any way I word it will most definitely get Sadie's hopes up. And the last thing I want to do is give her false hope. And the probability of Joanie making good on her promise of returning is slim.

After Sadie falls asleep in the middle of a Curious George book, I stretch out on the sofa. Flipping through Netflix, I debate heading to bed early myself. Pumpkin season is typically busy, but it hasn't even been a full week and I'm already exhausted.

My phone rumbles across the wood surface of the coffee table, the vibration startling me. I pick it up, relieved I put it on silent after Sadie went to bed. I'm surprised when I see Emmaline's name and catapult to sitting.

**EMMALINE**

Thanks for listening tonight. I know that isn't in the job description. So I truly appreciate it.

My fingers hover over the keypad, considering how to respond. And contemplating if I even need to. But I figure women always appreciate a reply.

Not a problem.

**EMMALINE**

It's not easy discussing my failing marriage with my mom. Or Lula for that matter. Not all of us Colemans can be successful.

I really don't want to get into this. Not in the middle of two sisters, one who basically employs me and the other I'm in a relationship with.

Maybe Lula is the perfect person for you to talk to.

**EMMALINE**

Why's that?

Because maybe she thinks you're the successful one.

**EMMALINE**

Did she say that to you?

I curse under my breath and run a hand down my face. Not even enough hours of sleep or a shit ton of alcohol could be enough for this conversation. This is really not my element. I like my life simple. Just work and Sadie. That's it. But suddenly I'm in a relationship, I'm the middle-man of a sister feud, and I've got my baby's mama calling me.

*I have got to shut this down.*

This isn't my business and I'm exhausted. I'll see you in the morning.

EMMALINE

Okay. Goodnight, Axel.

I ignore the text and drop my phone onto the coffee table before slumping back onto the couch. After I finally settle on reruns of *The Office*, my eyes fight to stay open. But my phone skittering across the table jolts me upright again.

*You've got to be kidding me.* I groan. But this time, it's Garrison. If it hadn't been days since I've heard from him, I'd probably curse at every single Coleman and shove my phone under the couch cushion until morning.

GARRISON

Hey! I'm in a jam. Need your help.

Where have you been?

GARRISON

Sorry. Last minute hiking trip. I had no cell service.

So you gonna help me or not?

EMMALINE AGREES to come to the house so I don't have to wake Sadie. In exchange, I had to fill her in on what I know. But all I know is, Lula is with Garrison, they've both had a beer or two, and they're at a bar in town listening to a local singer. They're hoping to get her to agree to come sing at the pumpkin patch. They want my help in convincing this girl and also to be their designated driver. Emmaline isn't thrilled by any of it, but she drags herself over to my place anyway.

The bar is twenty miles north of the farm. The parking lot is packed with zero signs of anyone leaving soon. I have to park my truck on the side of the road along with a row of about a dozen vehicles. I jog up to the door and swing it open, and it's standing room only. There's a girl on the stage, and she's alone. Just her and a microphone, strumming a guitar and sitting on the edge of a black metal stool.

I weave through the swaying crowd and make my way to the bar.

"What can I get for ya?" The bartender is sporting a thick head of slick black hair resembling Ross Gellar from *Friends*.

"Just a Coke, please."

He raises a dark brow but fills a glass from the fountain and sets it on the shiny mahogany bar. "That'll be two bucks."

I already have my wallet out and ready. I hand him a five-dollar bill and mumble my thanks.

"Hey, you're that guy." He points a finger at me. "You're Lula Coleman's new guy."

My lips twitch. "Yeah, I guess that's me."

He gives me a knowing smile, nodding his approval but remaining quiet.

After shoving my wallet in my back pocket, I search the crowd for Lula and Garrison. It doesn't take long to spot them off toward the right-hand side and nearly in the front row. There's a good crowd around them.

It takes several long seconds to make my way to them. The people are less than enthused that I'm interrupting their deep connection with the singer on the stage. I mumble my excuse mes and sorries until I finally reach the Coleman siblings, scaring off a few fans waiting for Lula's autograph. The annoyance of the bright lights, too many people, and the stuffy atmosphere are almost enough to put me in a bad mood. But when my eyes take in Lula, it all melts away. She's dressed in fitted black pants, a light blue short-sleeved sweater hanging off one shoulder, and black heels. The sweater not only makes her icy-blue eyes appear bluer, but it's showing off her smooth shoulder. Have her shoulders always been this sexy?

The sight of her is a vision to remember, and I take a picture with my mind so I don't ever forget. But what makes the moment sweeter is when she takes notice of me. She tucks her short wavy hair behind her ear, and when she smiles at me, even her eyes smile. Pink tints her cheeks, and I don't even let myself wonder if the hot room is the cause.

"Hey," I say, my voice coming out in a growl without fully intending it to.

"Well, it's about damn time." Garrison punches me lightly in the shoulder, but it's enough for the Coke in my glass to nearly spill over the edge.

"I came as fast as I could. Your sister is not the easiest to get away from."

"No kidding." Garrison takes a swig from the beer bottle in his hand.

Lula isn't drinking so I'm relieved one of them is at least trying to be responsible. She opens her palm to me. I think it's an invitation, but it's been a long time since I've been in a relationship. One where you hold hands in public. One where you want to be touching when you're together. This isn't a real relationship—we decided on a fling—but it's the closest I've had to a real relationship since Joanie.

I take my chances and slip my free hand into hers. Her smile is confirmation, and I exhale. I rub my thumb against the back of her hand.

"So, is this the girl? The singer?" I nod at the stage.

"This is her. Isn't she something? Her voice is like nothing I've ever heard before. It's smoky and raw." Garrison gazes at the singer on the stage.

"What do you think?" I look at Lula.

She taps a message on her phone using only one hand. I assume she doesn't want to risk her voice by yelling.

LULA

She's definitely talented. A little rough in some areas. Her uniqueness is her strong quality.

"And do you think she'll agree to sing at the pumpkin patch?"

LULA

She said to talk to her again at the end of her set. It sounds promising.

I glance around at the crowd drawn in by the girl's voice and lyrics. They're hanging onto every word. If she can draw in a crowd like this, hell, it may just work at the pumpkin patch as well.

"Do you think she can really help bring in more business?"

Lula nods.

"She's got my business," Garrison says.

Lula swats him in the chest. He hunches over and exhales a breath.

"Hey," he protests.

LULA

You can't hit on her," she says. "We can't have you going and scaring her off."

"Fine, fine, whatever."

"Besides," I say, scratching my jaw, "she looks super young. How old is she?"

"Eighteen. She's legal."

Now *I* want to punch him. Sure, age is just a number and all that, but now that I'm a father, I can't turn that part of my brain off. When Sadie is eighteen, the last thing I'll want is a twenty-five-year-old guy coming around her.

The song ends, and the crowd hollers, whistles, and claps as if this girl has just solved the answer to the climate change problem. Garrison may be the loudest of all. When the girl strums her guitar, going into her next song, the crowd quiets down. It's a slow song. A love song.

Lula drops my hand and, instead, hooks her arm around my waist, resting her thumb on the top of my belt. I reach my arm around her and run my hand down her back. She rests her head on my shoulder, and everything between us feels right and like whatever may have caused a rift between us doesn't matter. I slip my hand inside her sweater, and my fingers trace lines down the smooth skin of her back. My breathing hitches, and the more I touch her, the closer I want to be.

When she glances at me, I press a kiss to her temple. My lips linger there, and I grip my hand tighter around her waist. She tugs my belt, bringing me in closer against her.

For a moment, I allow myself to push away the crowd and Garrison and my fatherhood responsibilities. I slide my hand up to her neck and bring my lips down on the hot skin of her bare shoulder. She inhales a sharp breath, and then a round of applause sounds out around us. Like a cymbal crashing, I'm brought back to reality.

We are not alone. And I'm not a young kid anymore.

I release her, regretfully. I clap along with the rest of the crowd and let out a few hoots. Lula's face is flushed as she claps. She smiles at the young singer, hope shining in her eyes.

After the crowd dwindles and the singer's already growing fan base disperses, Garrison, Lula, and I pounce. We take the stage without invitation.

"Wow, Macie, that was incredible," Garrison gushes, taking Macie's hand in his.

"Thanks." She blushes, and it's an indication she doesn't know how good she is.

Garrison introduces me. "Axel here is the co-leader at the Coleman Family Farm pumpkin patch."

"Nice to meet you." She shakes my hand.

"You were good. Real good."

Garrison's jaw hangs open at me. "Oh, c'mon, I think you can do better than that."

"Sorry, I'm not familiar with your genre of music. Or really any genre of music. I just know what I like. And what you just did up there was impressive."

"I appreciate that. And while we're being honest, I have no idea what my genre is either. I just know what I like to sing."

"And she writes her own songs too," Garrison adds.

"Is that right?" I glance at Lula, who is biting her lower lip. She's clearly saving her voice for only the most important words. "Lula here also writes all the songs for The Broken Halos."

"I've heard that. I'm a huge fan of you and your band."

"And now I'm a fan of yours," Lula finally says, smiling.

Macie blushes again and stares at her shuffling feet.

"So what do you say? Do we have a deal?" Lula asks.

Macie looks at Lula, presses her lips together, and glances at me and then Garrison. "One set, next weekend. No pay, but my family gets free tickets for the maze. Then one set next year, I pick the date. You give my demo to your record label."

Lula peers at me, and I suppose since I'm in charge of the pumpkin patch I do have a say. But this feels like something she and Garrison need to handle on their own. I smile and nod before she looks at Garrison, who, no surprise, is grinning ear to ear like an idiot.

Lula stretches out her hand. "You've got yourself a deal."

# *Chapter Twenty-Two*

## LULA

EVERYTHING HURTS. WHEN I SIT UP IN BED AND THROW my legs over the edge of the mattress, they ache. Even my fingertips throb. The only thing that doesn't seem to hurt is my voice which is too ironic to even think about.

My head pounds, and my breath smells like death. I didn't drink much, but I wish I hadn't drunk at all, much like responsible Axel. I knew I had another busy day with hard work ahead of me.

It's still dark outside, and I'm tempted to reset my alarm and go back to sleep. But my stubbornness to prove something to Axel outweighs my need for sleep. Regardless of the obvious connection last night between us, my guess is there's still a conversation needing to be had.

I drag myself to standing and pick out a pair of jeans I've ruined since returning home and a Coleman Family Farm sweatshirt and trudge across the hall into the bathroom. I'm too tired to even do anything with my hair or face today. So mascara and a beanie hat are going to have to do. Downstairs, I find the coffee pot already half-empty and glance around for Dad. The porch light is on, so I fill my mug and take it with me out front.

"Hey, Dad," the words exhale easily.

He's sitting on the front step, coffee mug in hand. I plop down next to him and curl my fingers around my mug.

"Morning." He eyes me skeptically before he returns his attention to the fields. "You're up early."

"There's a lot of work to do."

My eyes follow his gaze.

He shrugs. "No different from any other day."

"Maybe not."

"I'm glad you joined me this morning. I've been meaning to tell you, I'm grateful you've been able to help keep our business thriving."

I smile and nod.

"It's also been nice to have you home."

The air suddenly feels thick with tension. Sometimes it's like that with Dad and me. "It's been nice to be home."

He clears his throat, and I'm not sure if he's getting emotional or if he's just got something to say. "I know it was hard for you to return, you know, after we lost Riley. It was hard for all of us to be here. But in a way, I think being here is what helped me get through it. Working kept my mind off things."

My eyes burn, and it doesn't take long for tears to build in the corners. "Dad, it wasn't just Riley that kept me away," I whisper.

He glances at me, his own eyes watering. Which only makes me more emotional.

"It was . . . a lot of things. I needed to be on my own. I needed to follow my dreams."

He wraps an arm around me, and just like that, I'm twelve again. Except this time, I'm not promising him I'll devote my life to the farm. I'm telling him the honest truth.

"I know you did, sweetie. And I'm darn proud of you for doing so. God blessed you with a beautiful set of pipes, you should be showing them off to the world."

I smile and rest my head on his shoulder, noticing the sharper edges to his bones that used to have more muscle covering them. The nine years I've been gone aren't only evident in his wrinkled facial features and graying hair. It's in the way he feels and the words we exchange. It's been a long time since Dad and I have had a conversation about my singing career, my choice to leave, Riley, really a conversation about anything.

"I'm proud of you, always have been. And what you're doing for the farm, for the family, rallying your band together is something we'll never be able to repay you for."

"While we're on the subject, I want to be able to help the farm after I'm gone. As in, next year and the years to come."

He gives me a squeeze. "Oh, sweetie, we'll figure it out."

I lift my head to gaze at his face. "Not if the Finley Farm is still running a pumpkin patch. I'm gonna ask the band to agree to play here next year. We'll plan it around a tour. And there's a singer who went on tour with us last time. He's new and leans toward more country, but I think by next year, he's really gonna be something. Also we talked to a local singer. We saw her perform last night. She's really good. We asked her to sing here next weekend. We offered to give her demo to my record company in exchange.

"Who's we?"

I suck in my lower lip.

"Garrison and Axel and me."

"I see. And when were you gonna tell me you heard from Garrison?"

I wince. "Today."

He gazes back at the goats, his brows furrowed. It's his thinking expression. "So the three of you convinced this girl to sing at our farm, for free?"

"Actually it was Axel who really did the convincing."

He raises his wiry brows. "Really?"

I nod.

"I'm impressed. That Axel is something else."

He really is.

We sit in silence for a few moments, both of us gazing at the farm and the goat pen, breathing in the scent of hay and everything I loved at one time before despising it. This morning, I welcome it. The rooster crows, and his timing is nearly comical.

Dad tucks me in tighter when a cold breeze hits us. "This is gonna be the best pumpkin season yet." He inhales a long breath. "I can just feel it."

"Dad?" I whisper into his neck. "You know my heart never left?"

GARRISON not only shows up to the farm for work, but he's early. Even Wiley makes a joke in regard to Garrison being early. He looks good. He looks ready to work.

"I'm glad you're back," Emmaline says, crossing her arms over her pregnant belly.

"What can I say, I missed working alongside my best friend."

Axel chokes. "Best friend?"

"You know I couldn't be away from you for long," Garrison teases.

"Well, whatever the reason, we're happy you're back. We need all the help we can get." Wiley adjusts the toothpick in his mouth. "Now speaking of, enough with the sappy reunion, we got work to do." He turns around. "C'mon, Garrison, you're with me today. Apparently the pumpkin cannon is malfunctioning."

Garrison groans but takes off in a jog to catch up to Wiley.

"So?" Emmaline glances back and forth between Axel and me. "Is one of you gonna tell me what's going on?"

I peer up at Axel, and he sets his hands on his hips.

"What do you mean?"

"I'm talking about last night. With the mystery singer." Emmaline glares at me impatiently. "Since it was late when Axel returned last night, he said we'd discuss it today."

Axel takes his hat off his head. "Lula can fill you in. I'm gonna go unlock the gate." He takes a few tentative steps away from us, and I glare at him, wishing he wouldn't leave me alone with Emmaline. He just snickers at me, which looks adorable.

"Her name is Macie. She sings solo and sounds indie folk with a little Celtic. She's agreed to play here for free next weekend and one weekend next year.

"In exchange for?"

"Free maze tickets, and I have to send her demo to my record company."

She nods dramatically. "Okay, if you all think this is a good idea, I suppose I'll get on board."

"Why wouldn't it be a good idea?"

"I just don't like the idea of owing someone something. It never goes well."

"This time it will."

Her pinched expression tells me she doesn't believe me, or trust me."

"For once in your life, just trust me," I say louder.

"Okay." She smiles. "Okay."

"Thanks." I nod before spinning around and heading toward the large barn to get the store ready to open.

THE DAY FLIES BY, and I do my best to stay focused, once again, and not get distracted by my band, my phone, social media, and reporters. For the most part, the locals are accepting and sympathetic to my condition. Several longtime customers have even voiced their loyalty to the Coleman Family Farm pumpkin patch.

But today has felt less busy than it normally does. Not by a lot, but enough for me to notice. By late afternoon, when we still have two hours before closing, the parking lot is only three-quarters full. A high school employee relieves me at the pumpkin weigh-in station. I'm about to check on the store to see if they need help when I notice a Finley Farm truck in the parking lot.

It doesn't take long to spot Kade Finley, oversized cowboy hat and long legs in tight Wranglers striding across the back field toward Axel and Garrison, who have been working on the broken pumpkin launcher for hours. I'm afraid to find out the reason for his visit, but my curiosity gets the better of me. I take off in a jog toward them.

"Oh, well, if it isn't sweet, innocent, Lula Coleman," Kade spits out.

I raise my brows, glancing around at the men who all appear angry. "What's going on?"

"You know what!" he shouts. "You've been telling everyone they'll get your autograph if they buy their pumpkins from the Coleman Farm."

I chew on my lower lip. *Guilty.*

"You didn't, did you?" Axel asks me, disappointment sounding in his voice.

"I may have." I wince.

"This is cold. Even for you," Kade bites out. "I thought I'd give you the benefit of the doubt. But you wanted to play dirty." He tosses what looks like a metal part of some kind onto the ground. "You might need this to get your pumpkin cannon working again."

Garrison picks up the part. "Did you take this off our cannon? On purpose? To sabotage it?"

"I may have," Kade says, mirroring my words with a sly grin.

Garrison rushes at him, and Axel hauls him back after he's got a good punch across Kade's jaw. I wedge myself in between them. Kade cradles his jaw in his hand.

"You better get on out of here," Axel hollers.

Kade backs away, stumbling at first. "Just remember, you started this." He's glaring at me with fire in his eyes.

"I can't believe he intentionally broke our pumpkin cannon," Garrison grumbles.

"That's illegal. He trespassed and vandalized our property," I say.

"You don't have any proof. Besides, he didn't vandalize it. We have the part now." Axel holds the part in his hand. "I just can't believe we've been wasting all day trying to fix it and didn't even realize a part was missing."

"Exactly, we've been wasting the entire day, and the

pumpkin cannon has been down all day. Both are causing us to lose money."

"He's right," I say.

Axel turns on me. "How can you not see your fault in this?"

"What? I didn't do anything wrong."

"You used your popularity to get more business."

I throw my hand in the air. "That's exactly what I'm doing with the concert, isn't it? You didn't have a problem with that."

"That's different." He whips off his baseball hat, adjusting the brim before stuffing it back on his head.

"How?"

"You knew if you told people that, they'd choose to come here instead of the Finley Farm. That's worse."

"Fine, whatever. When you figure out what's okay and what's not okay, why don't you let me know." I back up.

He pinches the bridge of his nose. "I'm in charge here. When things go wrong, I'm gonna be at fault. Not you."

"Thanks for the reminder. Of how little importance I have around here. At my own family's farm."

I stomp toward the barn and dodge Axel for the remainder of the day.

After we close, I see Axel make his way to the gate for the pumpkin patch parking lot. Assuming he's still not ready to talk, I head toward the farmhouse, ready for a shower. What I could really go for is a massage. Maybe an entire spa day. A soak in a hot tub. But I'll have to settle for a bath in the old farmhouse clawfoot tub that probably should've been replaced years ago.

The office door is closed when I pass, so I tiptoe by, hoping Emmaline doesn't open it. I can only imagine how upset she is about Kade and the pumpkin cannon fiasco. I find Mom, Garrison, and the three children watching TV in the living room. I sneak up the stairs, forgetting the creak in the fourth step, and wince.

"Hey, Lula? Wanna join us?" Mom calls out.

I shake my head. "No, thanks."

"You sure? We're watching that one movie with the talking snowman."

"Please?" Sadie begs.

I bite my lip. The bath is calling me from just a few feet away. "I'm really tired. But I'll see you tomorrow."

"Awww," Sadie whines.

"Okay, honey. And you be sure to rest that voice of yours."

*Then maybe she should stop asking me questions.*

I nod and drag myself up the stairs.

Inside the bathroom, I strip off all my dirty clothes, feeling like I'm also stripping off the day, and step into the tub while it fills. The water is so hot it nearly scalds my skin. But it's the closest thing to a hot tub I'm gonna get so I tell my body to shut up and take it. I ease into the tub and groan. Nothing has felt this good since I've been here. I stretch my foot up to the faucet and allow the hot water to pour over my toes.

Once it's full, I close my eyes and sink further underneath the bubbles. I long for the water to swallow me up and ease my tense muscles, releasing me from this exhaustion. My phone pings, interrupting my relaxation. I prepare myself for a text from Kade or Axel so I'm surprised when it's Jax.

JAX

We listened to Macie's YouTube videos.

I dry my hands on the towel.

Who's we?

JAX

The entire band. Mick. Leslie.

Why everyone? I asked you to have a listen and if you agreed she was credible, to send her info to the record label.

JAX

You're right. She's got something there. We all think she's solid.

Okay. Great.

JAX

So much so the band has an idea.

My stomach stirs. I can already feel things shift, and I know I'm not going to like it.

What's up?

JAX

What if she was the backup plan?

I sit up fully in the tub, drawing my knees to my chest.

What do you mean?

JAX

If your voice isn't ready in time. She fills in for you.

My chest feels as if it caves in on itself, crushing my lungs, and I find it difficult to catch my breath. The band wants to replace me? My head pounds, and I resist the urge to chuck my phone across the bathroom.

You want to replace me?

JAX

Of course not. Don't get all freaked out. This is why the band wanted me to talk to you.

> How else would you describe it?

JAX

It's called being prepared. Having a plan. Just
in case.

> You don't have faith I'll be ready?

JAX

Stop making this personal. Sometimes it has
to be about the band. Not just you.

*Wow.*

My heart rate accelerates, and I suck in several quick
breaths.

> Is that what you think? That I'm selfish?

JAX

Sometimes. Yeah.

I pause, thinking over the words to text back. What do you
say to your best friend after they call you selfish?

> Fine. If that's what the band wants. Then
> I'm out.

JAX

What are you talking about?

> If you all want me out of the band then fine.
> I'm out.

JAX

No one is saying that. Now you're just being
irrational.

Now I'm irrational? I throw my phone, and it hits the tile
and skitters across the floor. I don't bother checking to see if it
survives. Anger seethes through me, and I have nowhere to

direct it. My chest heaves, and tears spring to my eyes. As my head pounds, I pull my knees to my chest and hug them close while sobs wrack my body.

Things in my life finally seemed to be aligning themselves, returning home and reconnecting with my family and my band, helping out the farm, beating Kade Finley, even my relationship with Axel. All of it, in a matter of hours, has blown up in my face.

# Chapter Twenty-Three

## AXEL

THE NEXT TWO DAYS, I STAY FOCUSED ON WORK AND MAKE sure I'm doing my part in running the pumpkin patch smoothly. I need to talk to Lula. But more so, I *want* to talk to her. I want to work things out with her. Our time together is already limited. She's leaving in a few weeks, and I don't want to argue until then. But at the same time, for the last five years, my priorities have been Sadie and staying employed. I haven't had room for a woman.

By Friday morning, our business is back up. Even though I worry about what Kade is planning next to sabotage, I'm relieved. For now, things are calm. Emmaline is more than satisfied with our business. Both Garrison and Lula are working harder than ever, and it doesn't go unnoticed. Even Mr. Coleman has been out on the property paying close attention.

When school ends for the day, it's my turn to pick up Sadie along with Emmaline's two kids. They're extra hyped up today because it's the weekend and all three of them love spending it around the pumpkin patch.

"Mrs. Coleman promised us caramel apples," Sadie squeals after she fastens her seatbelt.

"Is that so?" I raise a brow, smirking while I latch Caleb's belt on his car seat.

"I wuv caramel apples," he says, grinning.

"Don't we all?" I play along even though I haven't had a caramel apple since I was a kid when I visited the Western Washington Fair, and it ripped a filling out.

I bring the kids into the back door of the Coleman farmhouse, and they all zoom past me. The office is empty; Emmaline is covering for me at the store in the barn. Mrs. Coleman is waiting in the kitchen for the kids, arms open wide, and all three rush into them. My chest squeezes. If this is the closest thing to a grandma my daughter gets, I'd say she's damn lucky.

"How was school today?" she asks.

At once, all three kids spout off about their day with random information.

When Mrs. Coleman can finally get in a word, she says, "All right, quick water and bathroom breaks, and then we're gonna go outside and get caramel apples."

All three kids cheer.

I give Sadie a hug and kiss on the cheek. "I'll see you around six."

"Okay, bye, Daddy!" She kicks off her boots and runs up the stairs for the bathroom.

"Hey, Mrs. Coleman?" I rub at the back of my neck. "I was wondering if I might take you up on that offer? You know, of having Sadie sleepover?"

Mrs. Coleman is on her knees, helping Caleb with his boots. "Absolutely. You know I'd love to have her anytime. When were you thinking?"

"Uh, tonight. If that's okay?"

"Definitely. Ariel will be thrilled."

"Thank you. I'll bring her stuff by after we close. Say around 6:30?"

"Sounds great." She stands. "You finally asking my daughter out on a proper date?"

There's an edge to her voice I've never heard before. I clear my throat. "Um, yes, ma'am. That's the plan. Hopefully she'll accept."

"Good. I hope she will too." She walks to the coat rack and stuffs her arms into a jacket. "It will give her an excuse to stay," she mumbles.

I decide to ignore her words. "Well, I better get back to work. Thanks again."

I leave the house in a rush, hoping our conversation was over. Mrs. Coleman's reaction makes me think she cares about Lula's well-being more than Lula thinks she does. But that's a conversation I don't want to get stuck having.

I return to the barn to relieve Emmaline at the store. My mind spins with the possibility that Lula might actually turn me down. Four days ago at the bar, I wouldn't have second-guessed her answer. But after the encounter with Kade, I'm not sure how she will respond. The only way I'll know is if I ask.

"Finally," Emmaline breathes out. "I've had to pee for fifteen minutes. Do you know what that's like for a pregnant woman?"

I wince. "Sorry, got here as fast as I could."

"How are the kids?" She turns sideways and shuffles out from behind the counter and cash register.

"Fine. Going with your mom to get caramel apples."

She rubs at her temples, pinching her eyes closed. "Lovely. Their next dentist visits should be fun."

I chuckle but don't bring up my experience with caramel apples.

"Call me if you need anything. Wiley should be here in

about an hour to relieve you so you can handle the wheelbarrows and the parking lot." She waddles away without waiting
for me to respond.

In between running the cash register, I compose a text to
Lula, weighing my words carefully. I type a few and then
delete them. I try again and delete them again. It takes me a
good twenty minutes before I'm satisfied and hit send.

> Was hoping you would accompany me on an official date tonight?

After an agonizing thirty minutes, my phone vibrates in my
front pocket.

LULA

What about Sadie?

> Your mom offered to babysit. All night.

I realize too late how my text might sound and what it
might imply. So I type a text to recover, but Lula responds
before I can hit send.

LULA

What time should I be ready?

Relief floods my chest, along with an explosion of
excitement.

> 7:30.

LULA

I'll be ready.

The rest of the day drags on. Garrison gets on my nerves,
cracking dirty jokes while we bring the horses from the pen and
into the stables. But at least he's here. Lula has been working

the pumpkin launcher most of the day. I'm not sure if it's because that's really where Emmaline assigned her or if she's guarding it in case Kade Finley decides to pay us another visit.

"So, listen," Garrison says as he shuts the last horse stable. "What's this thing with my sister?"

His question takes me off guard.

"I'm not sure."

Garrison takes his Coleman Family Farm hat off his head and swipes his sleeve across his forehead. "In the three years I've known you, I have never heard of you dating anyone."

I give the horse a pat before shutting the stable. "What's your point?"

"You must really like Lula."

"I do," I admit.

"And nothing about her being here temporarily bothers you?"

"I mean, of course it bothers me, but we both agreed we wouldn't think about that. We're living in the moment and just seeing what happens." I can't very well tell him that his sister and I decided on a fling.

We leave the barn, stopping at the door while I close and lock it.

"You're not really the live-in-the-moment kind of guy."

I grunt and roll my eyes at him.

"Look," he says, patting me on the back, "all I'm saying is, I've seen this play out before. With Lula and Kade. And obviously, that didn't end well."

"This is different."

"How?"

"For starters, I'm not using Lula. I'm also going into this knowing she's leaving and I'm staying. There's no other option for us."

"So why even start something?"

"Because. The heart wants what the heart wants." I shrug. "I gotta go pack up Sadie's stuff. She's staying the night at the farmhouse. Lula and I have a date."

Garrison shoves his hat back on his head and stares at the ground shaking his head.

I scratch at my jaw. "What?"

"I love you both. Lula is my sister and you're my friend. I don't want to see either of you get hurt. But that's exactly what's gonna happen. How can you not see that?"

I grit my teeth. "We'll figure it out."

"Fine, fine. But listen, I may not be around to pick up the pieces when it's over."

I tilt my head and pinch my brows together. "What's that supposed to mean?"

"I've applied for a job. And there's a good chance I'm gonna get it."

"What kind of a job?"

"A hunting guide. It's here, in Juniper Ridge."

I'm not necessarily shocked. But I am a bit surprised. Mostly because I never thought he'd have the guts to leave this place. "Have you told Emmaline? Or Lula? Your parents?"

He shakes his head. "You're the first person. It's not for sure, so I'd appreciate if you didn't tell anyone."

"When will you know?"

"A few weeks. Maybe by the end of pumpkin season."

"I know the family will be sad to see you go. *I'll* be sad to see you go. But this is something you're passionate about. Something you'll be good at."

"Yeah, have you met my parents?" He laughs bitterly. "They aren't big on us Colemans going after what we're passionate about."

I nod. I can imagine Mr. and Mrs. Coleman will be less than thrilled. But maybe a small part of them knew Garrison wasn't gonna stick around the farm forever. It makes sense they would put me in charge of pumpkin season. I've proven to be not only a reliable employee but permanent. The thought of that sends an aching feeling in the pit of my stomach.

*Permanent.*

Garrison's not wrong. In just over two weeks, Lula and I are going our separate ways. It's a conflicting feeling as I prepare to take Lula out on our first date.

"Well, good luck. You'll be great at that job."

"Thanks, man." He reaches out for a handshake, and when I take it, he brings me in for a hug.

"I gotta go. See ya tomorrow." I smack him on the back and head home.

I pack up Sadie's things, pushing my conversation with Garrison to the back of my mind. Lula and I will be fine. It's not like I love her. I don't even know her that well. I mean, I was with Joanie for three years, we had a baby together, and I don't even think I loved her. But do I have feelings for Lula? Of course. And since she's the first girl my heart has warmed up to since Joanie left, I'm letting it have its fun. Then it will say goodbye, and it can close back up for however long it needs to.

Maybe until Sadie goes to college.

COMING to the farmhouse to pick up Lula for a date feels different from any other time I've entered the house. My palms are sweaty while I debate if I should knock. Or go to the front door. I'm not really sure what the protocol is here. But since I've got Sadie's sleeping bag and backpack in my hands, I figure I'm still allowed to come to the back. After a quick rap on the door, I push it open and go inside. The office door is closed when I pass, and I frown, considering if Emmaline is still working.

Sadie, Caleb, and Ariel are sitting at the dining table drinking hot chocolate and playing Go Fish, her favorite game. She sees me and waves with a big grin but doesn't get up. She takes the game seriously and won't take the chance of missing her turn.

"Hey, kids. Where is everyone else?" I set Sadie's things down at the bottom of the stairs and glance around with no sign of Lula.

"Grandpa and Grandma are outside on the porch," Ariel says, focus still on the cards in her hands.

"And what about your mama?"

"Office," Ariel says. Then she asks, "Sadie, do you have any twos?"

"And your Aunt Lula?"

"There!" Caleb grins and points.

I whip around and see Lula and her long, bare legs making their way down the stairs. My eyes drift over her body, from her legs to her face. She's wearing a tight black skirt and a loose, low-cut black sweater, and her long, dark hair is in waves. I feel underdressed in my only pair of good jeans, cowboy boots, and gray T-shirt with a leather jacket over top.

She reaches the bottom step and tucks a strand of hair behind her ear while peering up at me. When her blue eyes make contact with mine, my entire body heats. I crave to be near her. Touching her. I'm regretting the jacket now.

"You look amazing," I say on an exhaled breath.

She smiles when she reaches me and dances her fingertips up my chest until they reach the collar of my T-shirt. She grips it in her fist. My insides tighten, and I forget the young audience behind us until I hear a giggle.

Lula lets go and backs away, her cheeks blushing.

"You wanna kiss him," Ariel teases.

Lula rushes to Ariel and tickles her. "Actually, I want to go eat because I'm starving."

Ariel giggles hysterically, and I use this as my chance to tell Sadie goodnight. I kneel, and she wraps her arms tight around my neck.

I give her a kiss on the top of her head. "Night, baby. I love you."

"Love you, Daddy."

"You be good, and I'll see you in the morning."

"Okay, you be good too."

Lula and I make eye contact and she snorts into her hand.

No guarantees on that. Being good is the last thing on my mind. All I want to do is skip dinner and take Lula back to my place and do all kinds of filthy things with her.

We wave goodnight to the kids and go out the front door.

"Oh, hey, you're leaving?" Mrs. Coleman says.

"Yes, thanks again for agreeing to keep Sadie."

"Not a problem. Honestly, any time."

Mr. Coleman shakes my hand. "You two have fun," he says.

It's friendly enough but still somehow feels threatening. As if I'm not the same guy that's been working for him for the past three years. The same one who he's entrusted pumpkin season with.

"Night," Lula says.

We take the steps and walk side by side, but I keep my hands stuffed in the pockets of my leather jacket. It feels oddly like high school again. Yet, I'm fully aware of having adult experiences and responsibilities waiting for me after this date.

I open the passenger door of the truck for Lula. Before she climbs in, she grips the collar of my jacket with both hands and yanks me toward her. She presses not only her lips against mine but her body as well. My hands find their way to her hips and then slide up her back, nearly making their way into her hair before she lets go and un-suctions her lips from mine.

"There. Now we've got the awkward end-of-the-night kiss out of the way," she whispers.

Then she climbs into the truck, leaving my body on fire, and I shut the door before shuffling around to the drivers side.

Behind the wheel, I flip on the radio and leave it on the country station Sadie likes. The song "Black" by Dierks Bentley plays, and Lula turns it up. The lyrics to this song aren't helping the fact that I'm already so completely turned on. And something tells me this was her plan all along.

At the restaurant, it's not as secluded as I originally thought it would be. All kinds of eyes are on us. I realize too late that going to a restaurant with Lula Coleman is different from going to a restaurant with anyone else.

After our server brings us each a glass of pinot noir, a young man dressed like a Portland hipster at a nearby table has the nerve to shimmy over to us.

He clears his throat. "Excuse me, but aren't you Lula Coleman?"

The muscles in my shoulders tense.

Lula, being used to this obviously, smiles and nods. "Yes I am."

"Your voice is incredible."

"Thank you," she says.

I grind my jaw, and heat travels through my veins.

"No, I mean, it's like sexy as all get out. It's like a kitten purring."

Lula gives him a tight smile and opens her mouth to speak again, but I cut her off.

"Hey, buddy? Why don't you let us get back to our evening, will you?"

He barely gives me a glance before he rests his palms on the table and leans in close to Lula. "Sometimes, when I'm alone, I put your music on and—"

I shove back my chair, standing abruptly, the metal screeching against the tiled floor loudly. "That's enough." I slap my hand on his back.

He puts his palms in the air and slinks away. "All right, all right, easy. Just thought I'd pay her a compliment."

After he returns to his table, I sit back down. I can feel the eyes on us from all directions in the restaurant.

I lean across the table. "Maybe this was a bad idea? Coming here, I mean."

She shrugs. "I'm used to it."

I sigh and glance over both shoulders. "So you're saying I should get used to it too?"

"I'm saying *I'm* used to it. I'm not saying you should be."

"Do you want to get out of here?"

"And go where? Anywhere we go will be like this." She tucks a wave of hair behind her ear.

My mind works quickly, and I have an idea. I pluck a couple of bills from my wallet and drop them on the table, then stand, shrugging into my jacket.

"C'mon, let's go." I put out my palm for her, and she takes it, sliding out of her seat, but gives me a quizzical look. "Trust me."

We make our way out of the restaurant, hand in hand, in a hurry, and a few people call to her before we make it out the door. Back inside my truck, my shoulders release their pent-up tension. I drive us to my favorite place.

When I put the truck in park, Lula peeks out the windshield at the sign: *High Desert Drive-In.*

"Have you ever been here?"

"No. This is new since I left."

"I know it's not fancy and probably different from what you're used to, but this is mine and Sadie's favorite place."

Lula smiles. "You do realize I've been mostly eating casseroles and cleaning up horse poop for the past month?"

I chuckle.

"I don't need fancy. I just need you."

Her voice is like honey. Her words are like fireworks. And I feel like I'm never going to get used to hearing her talk.

I unbuckle my seat belt and cup her face in my palm, running my thumb across her cheekbone and then onto her smooth lips. She holds my hand there and kisses the pad of my thumb, and my depths groan approvingly. I cup her other cheek and bring her face toward mine, kissing her longingly, memorizing the feel and taste of her.

There's a knock on my window, and we both jump. The drive-in worker is standing on the other side, seemingly annoyed, waving her order pad and pencil in the air. Lula snorts a laugh.

I place our order: two cheeseburgers, one curly fry, one order of onion rings, and two Cokes. While we wait for our food to arrive, we continue our make-out session in the truck. Both of our jackets are yanked off, and our hands graze skin. Our tongues touch places they've never touched before. It's the first time I've not only felt alone with Lula but free to explore her body. Though, there is the pressing issue of being in a public place to keep in mind. At least here, inside my truck, we can share a kiss and a meal without being on display for family, reporters, and fans.

My phone vibrates in my pocket, interrupting our kiss this time. I release a long groan. Since I'm a dad, I don't have the luxury of ignoring it.

"One sec." I hold up a finger, and Lula readjusts in her seat.

I slide my phone out of my pocket and am relieved it's not

Mrs. Coleman or Emmaline until I see the same unknown phone number I received when Joanie called. Oh hell. I hit the ignore button and do just that, shoving it back into my pocket.

"Everything okay? Is it Sadie?"

"No, no, everything's fine. It's . . ." I pause, considering if I should tell her about Joanie now or wait. "Garrison," I lie. Well, not lie completely. I plan to tell her. At least I have every intention of telling her.

# Chapter Twenty-Four

## LULA

I'm not even exaggerating. From now on, when someone asks me where's the best place I've ever eaten? I will answer without hesitation, *High Desert Drive-In*. The cheeseburger was packed with greasy, oniony flavor, the curly fries were curly, the onion rings were crispy, and the Coke was sweet. So maybe my date added extra icing on the cake. It's an evening I'm never going to forget.

Axel and I reach into the basket at the same time and find only one onion ring left.

"You can have it," he says.

I shake my head and shove the basket in his direction.

"No, really, take it. I can eat here all the time. You eat it."

"Split it?" I offer.

He furrows his dark brows, considering this before a mysterious, sexy grin forms on his lips. Butterflies dance around in my stomach, and I'm almost afraid to know what he's thinking.

He turns in his seat to face me, propping a knee on the seat, and holds both palms out flat. "C'mon, let's play for it."

I laugh.

"The slap-hands game, you know it?"

Of course I know it. I grew up with two brothers and my best friend was Jax, who was king of the game. But it's been years since I've played.

Fine. Why not play his game? I turn in my seat, sitting crisscross applesauce, and hold my open palms facedown over his.

"Ah." He nods approvingly. "You do know it."

He begins without giving me a warning and slaps the backs of my hands before I have a chance to move them.

"Hey," I say too loudly. And shake my hands out.

"Sorry, I thought you were ready."

He does it again, and I'm too slow.

We both laugh.

"Are you ready now?"

He almost gets me a third time, but I am finally ready and rear back my hands in time, so he swipes at the air.

"Nice, now you've got it. But I'm already two ahead so—"

While he's talking, I slap his hands, and he winces but laughs. "Okay, okay, two against one."

I get him again, this time, even harder than the last. I laugh but actually feel bad because my palms are stinging.

"Two for two. This is for the tiebreaker."

He goes in for the slap, and despite my laughing, I manage to move my hands in time, so he smacks the air. I try but hit nothing except air as well. We do this over and over until he finally gets me before I have a chance to yank my hands out of the way. Regardless of the stinging hands, we're laughing, and Axel is punching the air and hollering in victory.

"I win, I win! In your face," he says. But as the laughter dies down and I'm rubbing my hands together, Axel takes the last onion ring out of the basket, breaks it in half, and gives me a piece. "I think we both deserve to win."

We eat in silence, and my silly brain thinks over the evening. I never want it to end. As much as I love to sing and be on stage with my band, I think I love spending time with Axel just as much. Maybe even more. With him, I don't have to be anyone but myself. He doesn't expect anything from me. Not even my voice.

On the drive back to the farm, Axel turns the radio down and clears his throat. "So, I just wanted to talk about the argument we had. About you and your life at the farm and your life in the music industry. And I realize those are both a part of you. Those things are what make you, you. I don't want you to think I want to change you, because I don't. I want all of you."

He stops talking, and I'm silent. My mind replays his words: *I want all of you.* My heart allows the meaning of his words to wiggle their way inside. Regardless of the reasons I've given to myself and to everyone on why my relationships over the last nine years have ended, I know it's because of me. Because I wouldn't let them into my heart. After Kade had broken it, I put a trench around it, a straitjacket over it, and attached a padlock to it, tossing away the key. Somehow, in these short weeks, Axel James has managed to cross the trench, take off the straitjacket, and find the key for the padlock.

"Oh, man." Axel rubs at the back of his neck. "Did that freak you out? Should I not have said that?"

I put my hand on his thigh and give him a confident smile. "It's good."

"You sure?"

I nod.

When Axel turns into the Coleman Family Farm entrance, he heads toward the farmhouse. I reach for the steering wheel and direct it toward the newlywed house. He eases his foot on the brake, studying me.

I shrug. "It's early."

"It *is* early, isn't it?" I smirk.

We get out of the truck, and part of me feels like my parents are in the farmhouse watching me. I want to hurry and get inside with Axel so they don't see us. Axel unlocks the door and waits for me to enter first. I glance around, and everything looks the same as I remember.

"Bathroom?" I mumble.

"Oh, right. Yeah, just down the hall to the left. But you already knew that." He chuckles, and I realize he's nervous.

It's adorably attractive. Especially considering he's thirty and besides his dry spell after Joanie, he's told me he's had multiple relationships.

I hurry to the bathroom and shut the door, checking myself in the mirror. I check my teeth and find a breath mint in my purse. Threading my fingers through my hair, I try to pouf it up a bit. After I pee and wash my hands, I swipe my fingertips underneath my eyes.

When I come out of the bathroom, Axel is standing in the living room holding a beer bottle in each hand. His jacket is off and it's lying on the back of the sofa. The soft fabric of his shirt is just tight enough to cling to his muscular chest.

I pull my lip in between my teeth.

He shrugs. "Sorry, this is all I have. I don't usually have company so there really isn't much reason to keep wine on hand."

I smile and accept the bottle, but I don't drink it. Instead, I set it on the coffee table, and he watches me, closely, his head tilted in confusion. I move toward him slowly, pressing my palms against that tempting chest of his once I reach him. I nuzzle his neck, and his lips hover over mine while my hands trail down his chest and slip inside his shirt. He cradles the back of my head in his hands, and our lips finally graze one another's. It's passionate nearly instantly, our mouths taking on a quick rhythm and his fingers tangle in my hair-sprayed hair.

He breaks the kiss and sets his bottle down before capturing my mouth again with his. My fingers drag over his muscular chest, his abs, until they reach his belt. His sharp inhale of breath is visible. My fingers linger there, teasing. He forces me backward against the wall, shoving a knee between my legs, not once tearing his lips from mine. When I undo his belt, he moans and spreads hot kisses down my neck.

I give him a playful push in the chest with my pointer finger, and he pulls back, swollen lips and a trace of apprehension smearing his expression. I step out of my shoes and take him by the hand while persuading him with a suggestive smile. He comes willingly as I saunter backward, leading him toward his bedroom.

When we reach Axel's room, I let go of his hand and tug my sweater over my head. Axel's eyes darken as he watches me slowly undress in front of him.

I shove my pants down over my thighs, and kick out of them. My heartbeat accelerates. For a moment I stand in front of him, and while his gaze sweeps over me, I chew on my bottom lip.

"You're beautiful."

My skin heats at his compliment. I unhook my bra and let it fall to the floor. And as soon as it does, Axel groans.

I take a step toward him, my fingers eager to touch him. I slip my hands inside his shirt and his sharp inhale of breath is audible. He grabs my hips and squeezes them as he yanks me against him. His longing for me can be felt against my stomach as he presses into me.

I lift his shirt up his torso and rise on my tiptoes to pull it over his head. My fingers have a mind of their own, and take an extra moment to rake down his chiseled abs.

Tilting down his chin, he crushes my mouth with his. He thrusts his tongue into my mouth and kisses me long and hard.

Axel glides his hand up my bare side, causing me to shiver, and stops when he reaches my breast. A tiny moan escapes my throat.

"I need you, Axel," I breathe against his lips. "Now."

He grips my hips and guides me backwards until I reach the mattress. He lowers me onto it and drags my underwear down my legs.

"Patience, woman. I'm gonna take my time with you. I want to learn every dip and every curve of your body. And then I'm gonna memorize it."

Chills travel down my spine. *This man.* "As hot as that sounds, could you hurry up?"

"Not a chance. I've been waiting to find out what makes your body hum. It might take me all night. But I promise it will be worth your while." He shoots me a devious grin and my core tightens.

"It's hot when you get bossy."

"Yeah? You like that, do you?" He runs his hands up the insides of my thighs, leaving a sizzle in their wake.

Axel makes good on his promise. He takes care of me. He plays my body like a fiddle. After he relishes in pleasuring me in more ways than I thought possible, we finally join together, and my body molds to his like it was made for him.

We move together, so completely in sync with one another. As an unrestrained thrill racks through me, he holds me against him as he thrusts into me.

At last, Axel presses a lingering kiss to my lips, his heart pounding fast and hard against my chest.

"Was that long enough for you?" I ask, breathlessly.

"Not even a little. Let's go again." He grins and I laugh into his neck.

I AWAKE to a dreadful loud string of beeps. Axel flings his arm across me and punches off his alarm. He relaxes in the bed next to me and assails my bare arm with kisses. I face him and nuzzle my face in his neck, breathing in his pine scent.

"Morning," he whispers and nudges some wayward strands of hair off my forehead.

I smile and kiss his neck before resting my head on his shoulder. The sky outside is just beginning to wake up, causing a thin stream of light to fill the room. Even though his bed is cozy and warm, and I want to stay here all day, I know I need to get up and head across the field to the farmhouse.

"I need to go," I whisper, pushing onto my elbows.

"Not yet." He yanks me back down and rises over me, peering into my eyes and threading his fingers through my hair, splayed out across the pillow. "I just want to remember this moment. Remember exactly how you look."

I'm sure I look awful, makeup smeared on my face and messy hair. Not to mention, my breath must be stagnant. But he peers down at me as if I'm a sight to behold, memorizing every part of me. I suck my lower lip between my teeth, and he runs his thumb over it before releasing it. He gives me one kiss before he props himself up and swings his legs over the side of the bed.

"Okay, now we can go."

I squeeze my eyes tight for a second, smiling and allowing myself to also revel in the moment. But only for a second. Because the day that stretches out ahead of us is long and busy. For most people, a Saturday is a weekend, a day off from work. But at the pumpkin patch, Saturday is one of our busiest.

I dress in a hurry, and we agree I'll sneak back over to the farmhouse before he comes over to get Sadie.

Inside the farmhouse, it's quiet, and I exhale a sigh of relief while I tiptoe up the stairs. The fourth step expels a moan against the pressure of my weight, and I pause there, waiting.

"You're getting home late," Dad says through the mostly darkened house.

I suck in a breath and turn, slowly. He's coming in from the porch, closing the front door behind him.

"Coffee's on and ready."

When the back door closes, I jog up the remaining steps to hop in the shower as a sort of restart to my day. My phone is full of unanswered texts I don't care to respond to yet. It's been three days since I texted Jax and told him I wanted out of the band. Of course, I didn't actually mean it. But to think he and the rest of the band don't have faith in me, and my voice, hurts deep into my bones. It feels like a betrayal. Even if it wasn't intended that way.

Out on the farm, I inhale a breath of fresh fall air. Its crispness enters my lungs and wakes up my entire body as if it has been sleeping for years. I feel light on my feet as I make the long trek toward the tent, hoping to find Emmaline there so she can give me my assignment for the day. When an out of town news van pulls into the parking lot, it doesn't even faze me.

But it does give me the push I need to text Jax, apologize, and tell him I agree. Not only is the band counting on me, but so is my family. Having a backup plan is smart. And Macie is a solid choice. I tell Jax to forward our set list to Macie and make sure she agrees and will be ready to rehearse next Thursday night. Jax's response comes quickly.

JAX

That's my girl. Knew you'd come around.
Love you!

Love you!

I reach the tent and am pleasantly surprised to find Axel, not Emmaline.

"Hey, stranger." He stares at me like I'm a hot fudge sundae with cherries on top, which is fine because I'm probably looking at him the same way.

It's hard not to check him out in his worn-in, perfectly low-slung jeans paired with a thick brown corduroy jacket with wool on the collar. His red Coleman Family Farm baseball hat is turned backward, and his dark hair flips out beneath the edges. His arms are full of pumpkins, enhancing his muscled forearms, and he's already got a thin sheen of sweat on his fore-head. He winks and grins at me, and a thrilling shiver shoots through my body straight to my core.

I give him a quick kiss, wiping at the sweat above his lip afterward. "Gotta get to work. Maybe see you later?"

"Absolutely."

I leave and can feel his intense eyes on me as I do. My body heats, and I'm tempted to give my hips an extra shimmy until I spot Wiley, so I decide against it. Emmaline is in the barn, managing the cash register, and Garrison is replacing all the empty spots on the displays with more miniature pumpkins and bags of candy corn and caramel popcorn.

"Oh, good. Lula." Emmaline waves me over. "You can work the register until lunch."

I'd rather be outside. Or wherever Axel is working today. But I don't have the option to be picky. I wait for Emmaline to shuffle out from behind the counter before I slide in. She runs her palms over her belly, and her eye appears twitchier than usual.

"You okay?"

Emmaline seems like she's having a battle with her own mind, chewing her lip and rubbing at her arms. "It's Jackson. He's finally agreed to come."

"That's great."

"It is great."

But her face is saying something entirely different. Her lips droop at the corners, and her eyebrows are raised so high they're nearly hidden in her hairline.

"What's the problem?"

"He's coming today. I haven't seen him since I dropped the kids off for the weekend two weeks ago. I've only got bigger since then."

I raise one quizzical brow at her. "You know you're supposed to get bigger, right? You're pregnant."

"Of course I know that. I've been pregnant before." She wipes the back of her arm across her forehead. "I just want to look good when he sees me."

"You look great."

"I'm huge and I'm sweating. It's cold out, and I'm sweating."

"You're just nervous."

She inhales dramatically and releases it. "You're right. I just need to calm down."

"He's gonna take one look at you and realize what an idiot he's been."

She presses her lips together and gives me a half-hearted smile. "Thanks."

"Now go. Put on some perfume and lipstick and take off that Coleman Family Farm T-shirt."

She chuckles and leaves, waving over her shoulder. "Thanks, Lula."

Garrison saunters over and rests a hip on the counter while I help an older woman with her purchase. I hand the woman her change, and after she's out of ear shot, Garrison says, "Twenty bucks says Emmaline drives Jackson so crazy he doesn't last two hours."

I swat at his arm.

"You know it's true. That girl doesn't know the definition of playing it cool. She's got that maternity underwear yanked so high and tight I'm not sure how they'll get them off when it comes time for her to have the baby." He laughs.

I don't join in, though I can't help but smirk. Garrison always makes the best jokes.

"You're terrible," I mutter instead.

"Seriously though, I hope he comes to his senses and comes home. At least when he's around, he somewhat balances her out. I don't think I can put up with it much longer."

I haven't seen Jackson in nine years. Back when the two of them were both just college kids and had only been dating for a few months. I didn't get the vibe he was very serious about Emmaline. But I suppose a lot can change in that many years.

Garrison is still leaning against the counter, fidgeting with the open box resting on his hip while I help two more customers. I eye him curiously. After the customers are out of ear shot, I shove him in the back.

"What's up?"

He shrugs. "Nothing."

"I hate to break it to you, little bro, but I know you too well."

He slides the empty box onto the end of the counter and sighs. "Okay, fine. You're right."

I wait impatiently.

"There's something I've been meaning to talk to you about." He tips the brim of his cowboy hat further over his forehead. "I've applied for a job."

My chest tightens. "What kind of job? And when would you start?"

"It's a hunting guide position. And . . . uh, soon. But not until after pumpkin season."

I nod my head, considering. He wouldn't be telling me if he didn't need my support. So even though I think the family and the farm will miss him, it's something he needs to do. "I think that will be perfect for you."

"Yeah?" His face is open and vulnerable.

"Of course. It's been obvious to everyone that you've been way more passionate about hunting than working at the pumpkin patch."

"I suppose it has." He chuckles and shoves his hands into the front pockets of his Carhartt's. "Just do me a favor and don't mention any of this to Dad or Emmaline yet."

"What are you waiting for?"

"Pumpkin season to end. I don't want to give Emmaline anymore stress. She's already dealing with the pumpkin patch and Jackson and she's pregnant. I couldn't do that to her."

I nod. "That's probably a good idea."

"But I wanted to tell you." He shrugs.

I smile, warmth spreading in my chest.

"All right." He shoves off the counter, picking up the empty box. "Back to work. See ya, sis."

I wave to Garrison, and at the same time, Axel strolls inside the barn. He smiles, and it heats my entire body.

"Hey, you wanna go to the fair tonight?"

With all the busyness around the farm, the pumpkin patch, the concert, I'd nearly forgotten the fair was in town this weekend. I also hadn't planned on attending. Screaming on rides is not an option for my vocal cords. "Not sure that's a good idea for my voice."

"Sadie is coming, so we'll only be hitting the kiddie rides. No Super Loop or Zipper that will make you scream."

"Then count me in. Sounds fun."

"Good. You have made a little girl very happy." He grins.

I quirk a brow. "Just a little girl?"

"And me, of course." He rests his elbows on the wooden countertop.

I lean across, meeting him halfway. I reach up and snatch the baseball hat off his head and stick it on my own, flipping it backward. He laughs, and the sound vibrates in my chest. He kisses me, and before he pulls away, someone enters the barn and clears their throat. I expect to see Garrison or Emmaline. But when Axel and I break apart and I glance in the direction of the barn entrance, Kade is standing there.

"What are you doing here?"

"So the rumors are true? Your voice is back," he says, driving the toe of his cowboy boot into the dirt.

"It's getting there."

He nods slowly, glancing around the barn and pursing his lips.

I move away from Axel, coming out from behind the counter cautiously. "What do you want?"

Kade glares at Axel, giving him a look that asks, *can we be alone?* But that's the very last thing I want. Whatever he's got to say, he can say in front of Axel.

"I wanted you to know"—he pauses, sucks in a deep breath, and rolls his eyes—"what I mean is . . . I apologize for sabotaging your pumpkin cannon."

My vision slides to Axel, and we share a stunned look. I'm not really sure what to say to that. Tell him it's okay or I forgive him? So I remain quiet and fidget with the hem of my flannel shirt.

"Annnnnd," he stretches out the word and finally gazes at me, with intention this time. "If our parents don't have bad blood between each other . . . neither should we. So, I'm sorry . . . for everything."

*Everything?* The word is a loaded one.

"Everything," he answers my silent question aloud.

My heart screams for the past trauma it suffered as a result of Kade's actions, his decisions, our breakup. I know him coming here like this is huge. I thought I had long since recovered from the heartache caused by our relationship, but maybe this, right here, is all I've been waiting for.

"I'm sorry too," I find myself saying. "For using my name and fame to get more business. And possibly hurting the Finley farm in the process." My apology isn't completely genuine, and we both know it. But maybe one day, it will be.

He nods and backs up. "And Lu—whatever you're searching for out there . . . I hope you find it."

Before I can respond, he spins around on his heel and walks right back out the way he came in.

My cheeks are damp with tears I hadn't expected. And I don't know why I have a difficult time making eye contact with Axel.

# Chapter Twenty-Five
### AXEL

THE WORKDAY DRAGS TO AN UNIMPRESSIVE END. SADIE IS amped to go to the fair. The last two hours we were open, Sadie stayed at my side, helping at the pumpkin scale. Some of our repeat customers recognize her now and ask her questions about her cowboy boots and comment on how much she's grown.

After I lock the gate to the parking lot, Sadie and I race back home so I can shower before Lula comes over and we head to the fair. I dress in layers for the cool fall evening, including my cowboy boots and Sherpa-lined corduroy jacket. I have to practically bribe Sadie to change out of her dress and into jeans. And when she puts up a fight about the fleece jacket, I do bribe her. I promise her cotton candy. So what if her teeth get full of cavities. They're just baby teeth, they're gonna fall out eventually anyway.

There's a knock on the door. I open it and discover a gorgeous Lula on the other side. She's dressed in a cropped red sweater, fitted black pants, boots, and an oversized fleece jacket.

"Ready?" she asks, tucking a curl behind her ear.

"Almost. Sadie's going to the bathroom real quick." I grab my beanie and stuff it on my head, and Lula grins at me. "What?"

"Nothing. It's just, you look good in that hat." Her cheeks blush.

I grab a hold of her, clasping my hands together behind her back. "Well, you look good in just about anything." I kiss her neck, and she giggles. "But even better in nothing at all."

"Ready!" Sadie yells, racing into the room.

When we arrive at the fair, we wait for Emmaline at the gate entrance we told her to meet us at. After only five minutes, Sadie is already impatient.

Lula crouches next to her. "Do you know how to play the hand slap game?"

"Does she know how?" I chuckle. "Who do you think taught me?"

Sadie grins. "I'm good at this game."

The two begin, and Lula beats Sadie the first round, but Sadie wins the next two. When they start a fourth round, I spot Emmaline with her two kids trailing behind her.

"It's about time," I call.

"Sorry," Emmaline pants. "This one needed to go to the bathroom . . . again." She hikes a thumb in Caleb's direction.

Sadie hugs Ariel and Caleb, and the three of them squeal and jump around like they got ants in their pants.

Lula sidles up next to Emmaline. "How'd it go with Jackson?" she asks quietly.

Emmaline arranges a fake smile on her face, her rosy cheeks defined. I know it's fake because I know Emmaline. "I think we made progress."

What I can't figure out, is why she's lying to Lula?

"Oh, good." Lula elbows Emmaline in the side. "See, told

you he wouldn't be able to resist you. I'll bet he comes tomorrow with his bags packed, begging you to take him back."

"We'll see." Emmaline takes a hold of Caleb's hand.

Sadie runs up alongside me and Lula and squeezes herself in between us. She takes a hold of both our hands, and Lula peers at me, curiously but with a smile spread across her lips. It's a sort of strange feeling, my daughter holding my hand and another woman's hand who isn't Joanie. But at the same time, it's the best feeling. The ache in my chest hits me out of nowhere.

I've put off meeting anyone new or growing close to another woman so Sadie wouldn't get hurt. But maybe I've been hindering her from having a relationship with a motherly figure. From not having that bond that kids have every right to.

The first thing Sadie wants to do is buy cotton candy. Emmaline rolls her eyes at me because now she feels obligated to buy her kids some of the sugary cotton as well. I wince but hunch my shoulders. We buy tickets for games, and Sadie plays one where she has to try to pick up a rubber duck floating in a spinning circle with a hook on the end of a stick. No surprise, after ten tickets, she still doesn't win the rubber duck.

She pouts next to me, and my chest gives a gentle heave.

"What about darts?" Lula asks me. "Are you any good?"

"Am I any good at darts?" I scoff, mockingly. I haven't played darts in a while. When I was in my twenties and was frequenting the bars, I was pretty good. "Let's just see, shall we?"

We walk up to the carnival game, where a board is full of blown-up balloons, and I hand the guy working behind the counter three tickets in exchange for three darts. Emmaline huffs beside me, and next thing I know, she's shoving her own tickets in the guy's hand. She gives me a devious grin.

"Oh, I see how it is. You gonna try to show me up in front of my daughter, Miss Emma?"

"Maybe." She throws her first dart off to the side, in my line of aim but misses, the tip of the dart bouncing off a balloon. Before she has a chance to wind up again, I throw a dart. It does the same thing, bouncing off a balloon before landing on the ground. I'm positive this thing is rigged, but I have two more darts.

"Go, Daddy!" Sadie yells, jumping up and down next to me.

Emmaline and I alternate throwing our next darts. Both missing. Emmaline bows to me, allowing me to throw my last dart first. I do, and no surprise, it misses the balloons altogether, hitting and sticking into the board.

Emmaline throws hers, and a loud *pop* sounds out. Her kids jump and shout. Popping the one balloon only warrants her a medium-sized stuffed animal, but it's enough to satisfy Ariel. She squeezes it into her chest.

Emmaline shoots me a sly smile. "Better luck next time."

"Yeah, yeah." I wave her off.

Lula tugs on my hand. She points to a game with fishbowls crammed together where live fish are swimming in the bowls, and people are tossing ping pong balls into them.

"How were you at beer pong?" Lula whispers.

I smirk. "Very good." Not that I should be proud of this, but if it wins Sadie something, a tiny stuffed animal even, this may be my only chance. "Hey," I call to Emmaline. "We're gonna play a few more games. Mind if we catch up with you over at the kiddie rides in about thirty minutes?"

"Okay, see you over there," Emmaline says.

"Daddy, I want to go with them," Sadie pouts.

Lula crouches in front of her. "Do you wanna watch your dad play another game?"

"Will you win me something?"

"That's the plan," I say.

I wait in line, watching two other dads in front of me fail. When it's my turn, I step up to the front and am less confident now. The young kid working the game gives me three ping pong balls.

"One ball in a bowl wins," he mutters.

Sadie is mostly distracted by the live fish swimming inside their bowls. Lula is biting her lower lip, watching intently.

My first ball hits the rim of one of the glass fishbowls and bounces off, landing on the ground in the "out of bounds" area. My second ball hits the rim of another bowl and pings against the glass of a few more before splashing into a bowl. Sadie shouts and jumps up and down. Lula pumps her fist in the air and picks Sadie up, twirling her around.

"You did it, Daddy." Sadie smiles wide.

"I knew you'd win this one," Lula says.

The kid working the game hands me one of the bowls with a fish swimming inside.

"What's this?" I ask him, genuinely confused.

Deadpanned, he answers, "Your prize. One ball in a bowl wins."

"Yeah, but I thought I'd win like a stuffed animal or something. You know, something my daughter can carry around the fair with her." I hold the bowl outstretched, unsure of what to do with it. And a little worried Sadie is gonna be disappointed.

"She can carry that around." He gestures with his eyes.

"Is that my prize?" Sadie's eyes go wide. "I get to keep him?"

"Ehh," I gape at Lula as if she can help me out of this.

I've told Sadie no pets until we can move out of the newlywed house. I don't have time to take care of pets.

"Yes," Lula answers for me. She takes the glass bowl from

my hands and bends, holding it out for Sadie. "What are ya gonna name him?"

"Next," the kid working the game calls, and that's our cue to step aside.

I run a hand down my face.

"Hmmm." Sadie scrunches her face, considering. "Pumpkin."

I frown. "Pumpkin?"

Lula smacks me in the gut, and I exhale a breath.

"I think that's a great name."

"He's orange."

"Well, I'll give you that. He is orange." I gaze at my daughter while she holds the bowl, watching the goldfish in awe. While I know this isn't gonna end well—I mean, how long can a fair goldfish live?—she's happy in this moment. "C'mon, let's start making our way toward the rides."

Sadie walks proudly, the bowl outstretched in her hands, the water sloshing back and forth. The chances of that fish even surviving the evening are getting less the further we walk.

"You want help carrying that?"

"No," Sadie says. "I can do it."

We finally reach the kiddie rides and find Emmaline sitting on a bench by herself. Sadie tries to run with the bowl to reach her.

"Miss Emma, Miss Emma, look!" She holds the bowl out, water spilling over the edge. "Daddy won me a fish. His name is Pumpkin."

"Wow." Emmaline's face is animated, but when she glances at me, she snickers. "Isn't he cute?"

"Where are the kids?" Lula glances around.

Emmaline points to the merry-go-round. "I decided to sit this one out. Those make me nauseous even when I'm not pregnant."

"I wanna go on the merry-go-round," Sadie says.

"I can watch Pumpkin if you all wanna go?"

"Are you sure?" I ask her.

She gestures at her stomach. "Where else am I gonna go? Ditch you all to hop on the Super Loop?" She laughs to herself.

"Okay, thanks." I take the bowl from Sadie and set it carefully on the bench next to Emmaline.

"Bye, Pumpkin." Sadie waves to the fish and then takes a hold of my hand. Lula takes my other hand.

We ride the merry-go-round, the tilt-a-whirl, and the mini roller coaster, taking turns watching Pumpkin. When we pass booths selling roasted corn on the cob and giant fair cookies, Emmaline offers to keep Sadie and Pumpkin so Lula and I can have a few minutes to ourselves.

A few weeks ago, I would've passed on her offer. But now, I'm craving to be alone with Lula any chance I get. We take one another's hands and slip into the crowd like we're a couple of teenagers. And maybe that's one of the things I like most about my relationship with Lula. It's new and exciting.

We walk hand in hand, my thumb grazing over the slightly calloused skin of her knuckles. She's lagging behind a bit, complaining about her feet hurting from standing on them all day at the pumpkin patch. I spot the Ferris wheel and waggle my brows at her. She winces before rolling her eyes.

"Fine," she says on an exhale. "I know you just wanna ride it so you can make out with me," she teases.

"Is that so wrong?" I drag her along faster toward the towering ride.

"It's just such a cliché."

"How so?" We get in line.

"Oh, I don't know. Maybe all the romcoms I've watched. Everyone rides the Ferris wheel, and they either have their first kiss, or they get into a big fight and realize they aren't meant to be together after all."

We reach the front of the line, and I hand the guy running the ride our tickets, and we slide into a seat. I pull the bar across us and latch it closed.

"Well, we've already had our first kiss so we don't need to worry about that. And if we don't talk, we can't get into an argument." I grin.

One of the ride workers comes along and double-checks that the latch is locked and secure. After a moment, the seat rises, and our feet dangle in the air. Each seat is checked, raising us higher and higher before the ride finally begins. It's slow and perfect. From the top, you can see the entire fairgrounds. You can see as far as the parking lots and the surrounding town. If it weren't dark, you'd be able to see the mountain range from way up here.

I inhale a deep breath of clean, crisp air, not able to smell the fair scents this high. Lula turns toward me and rests her palm on my face, cupping my cheek. She's got my attention in an instant. She stares deep into my eyes as her thumb traces along my jawline.

"What?" I ask.

"Shh," she says. "Remember? No talking."

"Oh, right."

I cradle her head with one hand, moving my other to her back. I draw her toward me slowly, not taking my eyes off her. We kiss like this for several moments, our eyes staring deeply into each other. Instead of being off-putting and weird, it's more intimate than any other kiss we've shared. I want to devour her. All of her. Right here and right now.

My neediness causes me to push too forcefully into her until she's against the other side of the seat. I release her lips, and she gasps for a breath of air. I kiss her lightly again, closing my eyes. Then I kiss the tip of her nose before pulling away.

As the ride comes to an end, it stops in intervals, emptying and filling each seat again. When we're at the very top, Lula grips my coat collar in each hand, pressing a lingering kiss to my jaw. I press my lips to her cheek and her forehead and her nose. My mind is racing now, fearing a timeline that's ending. I don't want to ever get off this ride. I don't want to ever let her go.

"Stay," I whisper against her forehead. Then instantly regret it.

She freezes but is still clinging to my jacket.

"Let's not get off. Let's ride it again."

"We can't," she says quietly, nuzzling my neck. "And"—she pauses—"I can't."

And I know what she means. Not, *I can't stay on the ride.* She means, *I can't stay here, in Juniper Ridge, on the farm, with you.* My heart aches and pounds against her chest. I press slow, purposeful kisses against her forehead. I'm unable to take back my plea, and suddenly, I don't want to.

"Lula," I whisper in between my kisses, "I love you."

She loosens her grip on my collar, and her eyes fly open. They sweep up to meet mine. "You promised."

Technically I didn't promise we wouldn't talk. Or get into an argument. But since we only have a week left together, I don't want to argue either.

"You're right. No talking. No arguing."

I kiss her on the tip of her nose and then tuck her underneath my arm. I lean my head against the top of hers, and she runs her hand over my chest. It feels right, but at the same time, it feels awkward. Like my confession has ruined everything between us. Everything that was perfect only moments before.

Lula's shoulders lift and drop shakily, and I sense she may

be crying. I rest my hand on her thigh and console her, though I'm not sure why. It's my heart hanging out there on the line and getting trampled on. She runs her hand inside the collar of my jacket and then slips it inside my T-shirt. The smooth skin of her hot palm running along my bare chest is enticing. But I'm relieved when we reach the bottom, and the worker unlatches the bar across us so we can get off the ride.

When we go to find Emmaline and the kids, Lula trails behind me. I'm not angry at her. But I'm angry at our situation. At our expiration date. Was it not bad enough that Joanie left me? Now Lula will leave me. Where's the justice? Where's my break?

I reach my hand out to her, still not speaking, and she hesitates before accepting. But she does. And that small gesture jumps leaps and bounds in my mind. I smile purposefully at her. She smiles back, and we walk hand in hand, her still trailing a bit behind me.

The crowd among us is buzzing. Brightly colored lights blare around us. Whirling and beeping sounds surround us. The scent of freshly baked scones and deep-fried Twinkies wafts through the air. There are crying kids and loud conversations. Teenagers in love. Somehow all of it is comforting rather than overwhelming. Maybe it's the distraction I appreciate.

We come upon one of those photo booths where you get a slide of four different poses. I tug on her hand and gesture with my head. I'm almost expecting her to say no. But she doesn't. She grins and nods, and we step inside the booth. I tug the curtain closed behind us and feed the money into the slot. I sit on the small, worn bench, and she sits on my lap. She threads her arm around my neck, and I hold in a moan. She can't possibly know what she's doing to me. I cling tight to her middle, and we allow the camera to capture us in a picture-perfect pose with smiles on our faces.

The second picture, Lula kisses me on the cheek. The sense of her warm mouth lingers there. For the third pose, she nuzzles into my neck. It seems to be her favorite place, and I'm not complaining. I kiss her temple. On the fourth, we kiss. But after the photos are done, she doesn't stop kissing me. My craving for her is at an all-time high, and I knead my fingers into her back. There's an impatient kid outside the booth, huffing and complaining about how long we're taking. Lula stands abruptly, and I fight to hold onto her. But she presses her finger to her lips and plucks money out of her back pocket. She quickly feeds it into the machine.

For this round of pictures, we start in the same position, her sitting on my lap. I hook my arm around her neck, and we laugh. The second one, she turns into me, puffing her cheeks full of air as she plants a mock kiss on my lips. For the third, she surprises me when she straddles me and stabs her fingers through my hair, kissing me on the forehead. My hormones skyrocket. And on the last one, she bends backward, shutting her eyes. I lean forward, kissing the bare skin on her chest. I raise her back up, and she returns her fingers to my hair, twisting and pulling. She teases me with her lips on my forehead, rocking her hips into me.

The kid outside flings open the curtain and shouts at us. We both laugh, and she climbs off me. I resituate my jeans as Lula takes the two sets of slides out of the side of the photo booth. She hands one to me—the first set. She doesn't have to say anything. I assume she's saying, *to remember me by.*

"Your feet still hurting?" I ask as she stays at least a stride length behind me.

"Yes," she groans.

I stop and spin around. "Okay, hop on."

"Really?"

"We gotta meet Emmaline and the kids. At the rate you're going, it's gonna take us all night."

"Thank you," she exhales and hops onto my back.

I give Lula a piggy-back ride, weaving through the crowded fair until I spot Emmaline up ahead. The kids are sprawled on the grass. They're eating what appears to be deep-fried Twinkies. I can only imagine what kind of bellyache Sadie will have tonight. Emmaline has her phone pressed to her ear and looks as if she's been crying.

"Hey," I say, and Lula hops off my back.

Emmaline stuffs her phone into her pocket before swiping her fingers over her wet cheeks.

"What's going on?" Lula asks.

"Nothing," Emmaline mutters.

Lula presses her hands to her hips. "It doesn't look like nothing."

Emmaline squares her shoulders, her jaw set in a tight line. "Well, I said it is, so just drop it."

Lula holds up her palms and spins around. "Fine."

But she misses the sadness streaked across Emmaline's expression.

# Chapter Twenty-Six

## LULA

THE NEXT FEW DAYS FLY PAST, CONSUMED BY BUSYNESS and work and stealing moments of kissing here and there. While these last few days spent with Axel feel sacred, I can tell a shift has taken place between us. I'm not positive if it's the result of his confession on the Ferris wheel or the private minutes spent in the photo booth. Or maybe it's the realization that our time together is coming to an end.

When Axel told me he loved me, it wasn't fully unexpected. Because I've felt the love from him. In the way he kisses me, in the way he gazes at me, in the way we share a conversation without exchanging any words at all.

And if I'm being honest, I love him too. In the weeks we've spent together, I've shared more with Axel than any other man. The two of us have clung to every minute and every second as the precious gift that it is.

Selfishly I want more seconds. More minutes. More days. But that was never the plan. We never intended to fall in love with one another. We never intended on staying together. This was supposed to be a fall fling.

It's Wednesday, and Jax and Olive will arrive tomorrow, followed by the rest of the band on Friday. When I meet up with Axel in the barn as promised, there's a heaviness in the air. He's leaning against the barn's wall, hat turned backward, and a foot propped flat. His facial expression softens when he sees me, as if relieved I showed up.

"You act surprised to see me," I tease to try and lighten the mood.

"Not surprised. Happy." He smiles.

And I'm happy too. I lean into him, kissing him and pressing my body firmly against his. Heat radiates through my chest. He's gentle with his touches, meaningful. Maybe even careful. It's new and strange, and I know he can feel the shift in our relationship as well.

"You okay?"

"Fine." He stares at me, his brown eyes darkening.

"I know we don't have much time. I know you have to pick up Sadie soon, so I was wondering if I could come by later?" I dance my fingertips up his chest suggestively. "Say, after Sadie's bedtime?"

He grins and clamps his hand around my fingers, stilling them. "I think that would be a good idea."

"Good." I slide my hand from his grasp and back away. "I'll see you in a few hours then."

Before I get ready for our date, there's something I've been meaning to do since I've been back home but have been putting off. I take the keys with the apple keychain off the holder in the office and slide behind the steering wheel in the Coleman Farm delivery truck. The drive to the cemetery isn't long, only a few miles up the road. Mom and Dad decided on the small one nearby rather than the one in the next town over. It makes for easy access for them to swing by and pay Riley's grave a visit, but it's not maintained as well.

I park on the street and slam the truck's door after I climb out. Closing my eyes, I inhale a deep breath of the wheaty country air. I take my time as I mosey across the street and enter the open gate of the cemetery. It's welcoming, with thick green grass and pine trees for shade scattered around. But it takes all my strength to force my feet to propel forward. All I really want to do is turn back around and run.

Perspiration forms at my hairline where the collar of my denim jacket rubs, and my heart races about a million beats per second. I shouldn't be nervous or scared. But I doubt it's either of those things getting to me now. What sits front and center in my brain, causing not only an unforgiving ache in my heart but threatens to escape . . . is the guilt.

So much guilt.

It takes me several minutes to locate his headstone. When I do, the remorse is instant, slamming into my chest with an invisible thud. I read over his name carved into the stone, *Riley Peter Coleman*, and drop to my knees, tears already sliding down my face.

"Oh, Ry." I sob silently.

Why have I taken so long to come here? My regret burrows a hollow cavity deep into my chest. Growing up the way I did, I know Riley isn't here. I believe he's in heaven. But I still feel his presence here. It's alive and pulsating through me. I drop my head and spread open my fingers, running my hands through the grass and tugging the blades.

"I'm sorry. I'm so sorry." I sniff and rub my nose with the sleeve of my jacket. "I wanted to come. I swear. I just couldn't. I missed you too much." I pop onto my knees. "Ry, I'm trying here. But this place . . . it only reminds me of you. And I don't know how to be here without you. I need you. I need you."

A cool breeze swirls around me and ruffles my clothing. Pushing my fingers through my hair, I tilt my head toward the sun and close my eyes. I swallow and try to catch my breath. Voices fill the background, and I check over my shoulder, spotting a couple with a young child visiting a gravesite a few yards away.

I glance back at the stone and shove my hands into my pockets. When I do, my fingers find something. A lot of somethings. I cup the smooth seeds in my fist and remove them from my pocket. Opening it, I find several pumpkin seeds. An overwhelming calmness envelopes me, and I can't help myself. I laugh out loud, marveling at the seeds in my palm.

I open my hand and spread the seeds onto the stone, burying Riley's carved name. At the same time, a sense of peace washes over me. My lips pull into a smile, and the trusty seeds that represent love in our family give me the comfort I've been longing for.

"Thanks, Ry," I whisper.

Back at the farmhouse, I take a long shower, spending extra time shaving everything that needs shaving. I moisturize and spray on perfume, and even though it's silly, I slip into a dress and shove my feet into cowboy boots. I picked them up on a quick shopping trip in town at the used clothing shop.

I wrestle on a jean jacket before checking myself out in the narrow full-length mirror in my bedroom. In a way, it looks as if I've gone back in time, and I'm eighteen years old again, dressed as a cowgirl. I shudder, and it's enough to prompt me to take the jean jacket off and put on an oversized, cozy cardigan. I leave my hair down and finger through the long waves.

Tiptoeing down the stairs, I'm careful this time and skip the fourth step. I don't want to give my parents an explanation of where I'm going and why I'm going so late. But I think it's safe to say, by now, they know exactly what Axel and I are up to. When I sneak past the office, I'm not surprised Emmaline is sitting at the desk working on her computer.

I pop my head in through the open doorway. "You okay?"

She lifts her chin and gives me the once over but doesn't say anything about my appearance, thankfully.

"I'm okay. Or I will be. I hope."

"You will be," I say, and mean it. Next to Mama, Emmaline is the strongest woman I know. "If Jackson doesn't come around, then he's an idiot."

She laughs so I find it safe to laugh as well.

"Thanks."

"You wanna talk about it?"

Emmaline chews on her bottom lip and for a split second, possibly for the first time ever, I see part of myself when I look at her.

"Jackson sent me an email." She laughs bitterly. "That's what our marriage has come to. Emails."

I take a few hesitant steps inside the office and stop when I reach the desk, propping a hip against the wooden edge. "What it say?"

Her eyes glide over the screen for a moment before she spins the laptop around to face me. I read the words silently.

*I love you, Emm. But I can't go back there. That old farmhouse, your parents always lurking, your brother. That house is too crowded. And you're on hyper-mode every second of every day trying to keep that place afloat. I can't stand back and watch you work yourself into the ground just to save that place. I love you too much.*

Quiet sobs rack Emmaline's body.

Not wanting to hurt my sister further, but also not knowing if I'll get another chance to say this, I don't think long before speaking. "He may have gone about things wrong, leaving you without much of an explanation, but his confession is . . . he still loves you. And too much to sit back and watch you work yourself to death to save the farm."

She shifts away from the desk and stands shakily. "And what do you suppose I do? Give up on the farm? On Mom and Dad? On our livelihood?"

"I know you, Emmaline. You're not a quitter." I fold my lips between my teeth before saying what needs to be said. "And I know you won't quit on your marriage either."

She collapses back into the chair.

"Give Axel more of the responsibilities. You know that was Dad's plan anyway. He saw what needed fixing and knew you wouldn't do it on your own." I rest my hand over hers. "You're not alone."

She peers at me, her chin quivering, and she nods.

After a moment, she wipes her cheeks and whispers, "Thank you, Lu."

I give her a pained smile because it doesn't feel like we're done here, and yet, I can feel the dismissal. "You should go to bed soon. It's late."

She turns the laptop back around. "I was just reading over some social media stuff. Like stuff about The Broken Halos."

I quirk a brow. "Oh, yeah? What now? Or do I not want to know?"

"I have to say, you have some of the most loyal fans I've ever seen. I thought people were loyal to the Coleman Family Farm, but it's nothing compared to how loyal they are to you and your band."

My heart warms, and I feel like how maybe the Grinch felt in *How the Grinch Stole Christmas* when his heart grew. Emmaline has never given my band, much less me, a compliment before.

"Not only is this Saturday's concert sold out, but people are planning on coming out here tomorrow just to support that girl you got to agree to sing. People without tickets are talking about parking up and down the side of the main road just so they can hear you all."

"Wow, you sure we've hired enough people for security?" I'm only sort of teasing.

"I'm never gonna be able to repay you for saving us, Lula. Not just for this year. But for years to come. We never could've afforded to build that stage and pay for bands to play here."

I shrug. "Just don't ever go under on account of the Finley Farm, promise?"

Emmaline grins, her eyes swimming with tears. "Deal."

"I gotta go."

"Have a good time."

And it seems like she genuinely means it.

"Oh, and Lu?" Emmaline calls.

I peek my head back into the office.

"It's really good to hear your voice again." She smiles, and I feel my face blush. "It's been missed around here."

My heart races, and my skin tingles as I walk across the field toward the newlywed house. That had to have been one of the best conversations Emmaline and I have ever had.

I knock quietly on the front door, and I'm not even standing there for more than a second when it opens. Axel scoops me up in his arms. I squeal, and he throws me over his shoulder. I fight to keep my dress from flipping up to my head.

"It's about time."

"What's going on?" I ask shakily.

"I've got a little outdoor date planned."

"What about Sadie?"

"She's already sleeping. And Garrison has agreed to hang out for a bit inside and listen for her."

He carries me into the barn, and my mind races back to that night. The one spent in a barn. With Kade Finley. My fingertips thrum as the anxiety courses through my veins.

But when Axel sets me down on my feet, I see he's got his truck parked in the barn. The bed is piled with blankets and pillows, and a white sheet is pinned to the barn's wall.

"What's all this?" I spin around.

He shuts the barn's big doors and then sets out an open palm to me. "My lady?" He waggles his dark brows.

I eye him skeptically, but I'm so overcome with delight that I don't hesitate. I set my hand in his, and he helps me into the truck bed. While my feet dangle off the edge, he tugs off my cowboy boots before taking off his own. We crawl over the mounds of blankets and pillows, and Axel sets his phone on the roof of the truck. He has a projection adapter attached to his phone, and just when I get settled in, propping a few pillows behind my back, the white sheet turns into a movie screen.

"This is amazing."

Axel cuddles in next to me, tucking me underneath his arm. I kiss him on his rough jaw, gliding down to his neck, before I rest my head on his shoulder. He kisses me on the top of my head. We stay like this, wrapped in one another's arms while the movie plays. But when I slip my hand inside Axel's shirt, it's as if I've pressed *play* on his hormones that were previously on *pause*.

He lays me down against the blankets and pillows and kisses me while running his confident hands all over my body. I can't keep from touching him either, and I feel needy and desperate. The moment feels as if we're clinging to it, both knowing it could very well be our last evening together. Our last chance to explore one another's bodies. He slides my dress up my body, and I shimmy out of it as he slips it over my head. Hot kisses down my chest and stomach cause me to shiver under his lips.

Axel shifts onto his knees and yanks his shirt off. When he

presses his bare chest against mine, it clouds my mind with longing for a connection, a forever commitment. But I know it isn't a possibility for us. It never was. And nothing has changed. Yet, I have a strong desire to never be without him. In the last few weeks with Axel, I've learned more about myself. I'm more than just my voice. I can be useful and still function without it. Axel was drawn to me without even knowing who I was or hearing my voice.

While he spreads kisses down my stomach and inner thighs, I breathlessly say, "Axel, I love you."

He stops kissing me and hovers over me, meeting my eyes. He drags his fingertips over my arm. "Are you sure? Because I don't want you to say it just because I did."

"I wouldn't do that."

He grins and kisses my lips, smiling against them. Cradling my head and holding me tight with his other hand wrapped around my back, he kisses me hard and passionately. The craving for him deepens, and I dig my fingernails into his back, clinging to him. He stares at me purposely, as if studying my features, like I may disappear at any moment.

"So, what now?"

"I don't know." I bite my lower lip.

"I know we're on expired time, but what if we resist the expiration date?" Axel shoves my hair out of my face with his thumb.

"How? Because nothing has changed. I have to go, and you have to stay."

"Then we figure out a way to make it work. Portland isn't that far away. Sadie and I will come to visit. And you can come here." He holds me closer, kissing my forehead before running the tip of his nose down the length of my face until we're nose to nose. "All I know is, I don't want this to end. What we started here doesn't feel over."

"I don't want this to be over either," I whisper. "But things could get complicated."

"Only if we let them." He gently kisses the tip of my nose and my lips, sliding down my neck.

I thread my fingers through his soft hair as he continues south. I rise and climb into his lap, straddling him while he continues to kiss the delicate skin of my chest.

"Let's try it," I say on an exhale.

He stops kissing me, his eyes going wide. He takes my cheeks in his hands, a big smile breaking on his lips and an expression of hope radiating on his face. And even though there's a bit of anxiety sitting in the pit of my stomach that this may be a huge mistake, at this moment, wrapped tightly in Axel's arms, it feels right.

# Chapter Twenty-Seven

## AXEL

THERE'S A SHIFT IN THE WEATHER ON THURSDAY. TODAY, Jax, the lead guitarist of The Broken Halos, will be here. My anxiety over meeting him has nothing to do with being starstruck. I've never cared about famous people. But he's Lula's best friend. I'd be lying to myself if I said I didn't want to make a good first impression.

I drive Sadie to school, and while I'm content to leave the radio off, she wants to listen, so I flip it on. After only one song, the DJs begin talking about The Broken Halos and their concert Saturday night at the Coleman Family Farm pumpkin patch. Sadie asks me to turn it up so she can hear. I'm sure she's only half following along, but based on her worried expression, I'd say she's picking up on enough.

"Daddy? Why do they think Lula can't sing?"

"Um, remember when Lula first arrived at the farm and she couldn't talk?"

She nods.

"Well, it's because her voice was hurt. But now it's all better."

"I've heard her sing. At the farmhouse. She sings pretty."

"Yes, she does." I smile, and my heart reacts to her words.

It makes me happy that Lula's been practicing some at the house. I haven't worried too much about whether she'll be able to sing with the band. I have faith in her. Even if her hometown doesn't.

I pull the truck in front of the school, and Sadie slips her hand into mine while I walk her toward the preschool's front doors.

"Excuse me?"

I turn around and see a woman I recognize as the mother of another child in Sadie's class. She's rushing to catch up to me, dragging along a distracted child.

"You're Sadie's dad?"

I glance at Sadie and back at the woman and nod.

"Are you Axel James?"

I nod again.

"You're dating Lula Coleman? Lead singer of The Broken Halos?"

"Um." I pause, tugging down the brim of my baseball hat. "Yeah, I suppose that's right."

"Wow. What's that like?"

"Uh . . . excuse me?"

"I mean, dating a rock star, that has to be pretty amazing." She's smiling.

I decide not to correct her on the rock star term. I'm fairly certain Lula wouldn't refer to herself as a rock star. "It definitely has its moments." Sadie is getting impatient next to me. "It was nice to meet you . . ." I pause, realizing I never got her name.

"Hey, so listen. By the time I tried to get tickets for the concert, they were sold out. I was wondering if you had any extras?"

A few other parents form a crowd around the mom, and the cost of dating a well-known singer is strange and new. It's something I'm not sure I'll ever get used to, but I suppose I better.

"Un, no, sorry."

"Not even when you're dating the lead singer of the band?"

"Sorry," I mutter again and tug Sadie into the school.

Back at the farm, I find Lula at the coffee stand getting her caffeine fix before the pumpkin patch opens. She's been let off the hook of doing any farm work from here on out. It's strange not seeing her dressed in her usual dirty jeans and Coleman Family Farm sweatshirt and work boots. I'm not complaining. She looks hot dressed in black fitted jeans, fancy heeled boots, and a light blue sweater.

"Coffee?" she asks when she sees me.

"Nah, thanks. I'm good. Had two cups already this morning."

Lula picks up her drink from the counter and links her arm around mine. I lead her toward the tent. Emmaline wants me to start my shift at the pumpkin weigh-in station. Lula's phone dings, and she has to unhook her arm from mine to slide it out of her back pocket.

"Jax and Olive just landed."

"Yeah? I thought he wasn't coming until later."

"Jax's mom will pick them up from the airport and then take them by his house first. His family wants to see him before he comes over here. Because most likely, once he gets here, he won't be leaving." She shoves her phone back into her pocket and takes a sip of her coffee.

"So, you nervous about rehearsing with the band?"

"A little."

I take hold of her hand and give it a squeeze. "You're gonna be great. You've been singing for the last week. You got nothing to worry about."

We stop near the edge of the pumpkin crates underneath the tent.

She gazes at me and smiles. "Thank you."

I kiss her softly. "You think your friends are gonna like me?"

"What? Of course. They're gonna love you."

"What about after they find out you and I are gonna try the whole long-distance relationship thing?"

"Why would they care about that?"

"Maybe they'll be worried I'll be a distraction?"

She drops my hand and grabs my jacket collar, leaning into me. "You'd be a distraction regardless if we stayed together or not." She smiles and presses a sensual kiss to my lips.

Something about that doesn't sit well in my gut. Like, we could try this long-distance relationship or not, and it wouldn't make a difference to her. Or, like I'm gonna be a distraction either way and possibly affect all she's worked so hard to accomplish.

We have thirty minutes before we open, and already, cars are lining up and down the street. A few news vans are in the lineup, including some from out of state. The entire band isn't even supposed to arrive until tomorrow. Someone must've leaked about a few members arriving today. And since they figured it would be good for The Broken Halo's publicity, Mick and Leslie have allowed the media to be here.

"I better go." I resituate the hat on my head.

"Okay." She kisses me one more time. "I'll see you later."

A few wheelbarrows are parked under the tent where they shouldn't be, so I take them one by one, pushing them near the edge of the parking lot. Wiley is sitting in the golf cart, waiting to open the gate.

"Gonna be a mob today," he calls, a toothpick poking out of the corner of his mouth.

I glance at the street, the line of cars growing. "Looks that way."

Wiley hikes a thumb over his shoulder. "I thought we wouldn't see those kiss-butt's until tomorrow?" I must give him a confused look because he explains further. "You know, the reporters."

"Guess they wanted to get a jump on the story."

"We may need extra security to get all these guys back out of here tonight."

"Let's hope not. You be careful out here." I turn to make my way back to the tent to take my post before we open.

We're short-handed for part of the day because of Lula and our high school employees, who can't make it here until later in the afternoon. If everyone sticks to manning their post, we should be fine. And as long as Kade Finley doesn't break anything again.

After Wiley opens the gate, the cars file in and the parking lot attendants direct them where to park. My post is fairly slow. Most people who come to the pumpkin patch plan to make a day of it. Or at least several hours. They take their time going through the maze and the petting farm and take their turn using the pumpkin cannon. Typically the weigh-in post is their last stop before they leave.

A school bus parks in the lot and several small children pile out. It's the local kindergarten class on a field trip this morning. Emmaline has appointed Garrison to take them on a hayride before ending their visit by choosing a pumpkin from the one dollar bins at the weigh-in station. I unload boxes of mini, sugar, and Cinderella pumpkins into the designated bins while waiting for customers ready to weigh their pumpkins and pay.

I check the time on my phone and see the class won't be headed my way for about two more hours. A few older women peruse the bins of pumpkins, choosing a couple for each of them. They pay, and I exhale a sigh of relief they didn't recognize me. Every day at least a couple dozen people say they heard my name on the radio, saw me in the newspaper, or now even on social media. For the most part, I've kept Sadie out of the media. I wish my personal life was still private too, but it's a sacrifice I'm willing to make if it means being a part of Lula's life.

My line doesn't take long to grow. Soon I've got several people digging through the bins, choosing cornstalks and hay bales. Some parents with young children are already done at the patch for the day after less than two hours. Toddlers whine and babies cry, and the parents appear worn out.

A guy pushes a wheelbarrow holding three large pumpkins onto the scale. His three children appear to be triplets and around two years old. His wife is distracted by one child as well as the coffee cup in her hand.

"All right, that will be $15.00."

The guy's mouth drops open. "For pumpkins? What are these, magic pumpkins?"

"We at the Coleman Family Farm believe our pumpkins are magic. They've been growing in this soil for eighty years." This is something Emmaline has taught me to say when customers complain about the cost of our pumpkins.

"Just pay the man, will you?" The woman takes a sip of her coffee.

The transaction is almost complete when the woman gasps. Both her husband and I fix our attention on her.

"Are you the guy who's dating Lula Coleman?"

I hesitate to respond.

"OMG! I grew up in the next town over. I didn't know Lula personally, but I knew of her. The Ross and Rachel relationship between her and Kade Finley was legendary. People still talk about them." Her eyes are wide. "When the Finley Farm announced they were opening up a pumpkin patch, everyone knew it would be some sort of a feud. And then, when word got out that she was returning, everyone thought it was fate and they were gonna get back together. Like Ross and Rachel found their way back to one another. Lula was Kade's lobster."

The woman's romanticized version of Kade and Lula's high school relationship is disturbing. So far, everyone has been accepting of me. But after hearing this woman tell that story, I assume she can't be the only one disappointed that I entered the equation and messed that all up.

"Well, I guess . . . I'm sorry," I say, thinking apologizing may at least shut her up.

"Oh, don't be silly. I heard what Kade did to your pumpkin cannon. That's why we chose to come here and not the Finley Farm. I wouldn't dare give them my business after that stunt."

"And the Colemans appreciate that."

One of their triplets plops onto the grass and starts crying.

"Okay," the woman says, "time to go. But please tell Lula that Becky Thompson says hello, and I'll be in the crowd Saturday night showing my support."

I nod. "Becky Thompson. Will do. Thanks again."

They shuffle away, and I glance at the clipboard in my hand. My next customer steps onto the scale without a wheelbarrow. I groan, preparing to tell them the scale is only for wheelbarrows with pumpkins. But when I glimpse at the scale, I can't find words. Or my voice.

"Hello, Axel."

My head jerks to attention. "Joanie?"

# Chapter Twenty-Eight

## LULA

A KNOCK ON THE FARMHOUSE'S FRONT DOOR CAUSES ME TO fly down the stairs in a flurry. My heart nearly bursts when I see Jax and Olive standing on the front porch. Olive and I squeal with excitement. Jax wraps me up in his arms, lifting me off the ground and squeezing me. Everything feels right again. My childhood friend, my bandmate, is here.

"I'm so glad you're here," I say after he puts me back on my feet.

"And I'm so glad to hear your voice."

I hug Olive and pick up a duffel bag and small suitcase from the porch and usher them into the house where it's warm. They follow me inside. Olive carries another bag on her shoulder, and Jax has a backpack strapped to his back.

"Oh, honey, your hair." Olive pinches one of my curls in between her fingers, inspecting it.

"I know. I don't have time to go to a salon to get it back to my natural color."

Jax studies me up and down. "Or time to . . . change your clothes? Or at least . . . wash them?"

I smack him in the chest.

"Don't worry, we'll pick up a bottle of bleach at the drugstore and I'll get you fixed up."

Jax spins around, taking in the space around him. "I swear nothing has changed."

I hunch a shoulder. "What'd you expect? My parents are allergic to change."

"I love it." Olive's fingers graze the afghan folded on the back of the sofa. "It has such a homey feel. Unlike my folks' place."

I take the stairs two at a time, talking over my shoulder. "Jax, you're staying in Garrison's room. Olive, you're with me."

"You weren't kidding. They really haven't changed. We're twenty-seven years old, and we can't share a room?"

"You know them."

"Yeah, I do. But they also know me. And they should know that I've never been interested in you."

I shove an elbow into his side at the top of the stairs. I set his bag in Garrison's room, where a cot is set up along the wall underneath the window. We all go into my room, where another cot is set up, complete with blankets and pillows.

"Lots of pillows, just how you like it." I set the suitcase on the floor.

"It's perfect, thank you." Olive squeezes me into her side. "But you know what we're really here to see." Her thick, dark-lined brows are raised.

"Axel?"

"You guessed it," Jax says.

Olive sits on my bed, taking my hand and tugging me down with her. "We gotta meet this guy who has stolen your heart."

"I wouldn't say, stolen. I mean, that would imply I didn't give it to him willingly."

"Wow." Jax crosses his arms. "This is serious then?" he says it like a question.

My fingers fidget in my lap. "It is. We talked last night, and we're gonna try the whole long-distance thing."

"Seriously?" His light brows shoot up. "You know those never work."

"We won't know unless we try."

"I think it's super sweet," Olive says.

"Thank you." I give her a thankful smile.

"Oh, no, not sweet that you're gonna try to stay together, but sweet that you actually think it will work," she corrects herself. "Oh, my sweet summer child," she says in sing-song.

I shove her in the shoulder and stand. "Thanks," I mutter.

Out of all the members in the band, I expected Jax and Olive to be the most supportive. But maybe after they meet him and get to know him a bit. And meet Sadie.

While Jax came prepared for the Central Oregon weather, dressed in a thinner Patagonia jacket and his hipster boots, Olive did not. We wait for her to change out of her strappy high heels and into ankle boots. She throws on a jacket over her cardigan.

I take them by the office first, but it's empty. Outside, I inhale a breath of fresh, crisp air. Before taking them to meet Axel, I take them on a tour of the farm, starting at the chicken coop and working our way around the house where the goat pens are. We pass the petting farm area, stopping to see the pigs. At the food truck area, I introduce them to the different owners and rave about their food. Jax knows a few of the local vendors. The three of us order coffee, and Olive is only somewhat satisfied. She's been in Portland and has grown used to the bitter taste of burnt coffee. She doesn't know what good coffee is.

We walk across the field toward the horse stables. I point

out the newlywed house to Olive. I tell her the story of Mom not wanting to live in the farmhouse so when I was a kid, four of us were crammed into one room. Olive nearly gasps since she grew up with well-off parents, in a gigantic home, with a bazillion bedrooms and a live-in nanny.

"Did you know her then, Jax?" Olive asks.

"Nah, not yet. We met in kindergarten but didn't become friends until, I think, fifth grade?"

"Yeah, that's right." We pass the newlywed house and head toward the horse stables. "This kid bullied me every day at recess until Jax finally stepped in. Threatened the kid that he'd tell everyone about how he played with his sister's Barbies if he didn't leave me alone. Then Jax and I discovered we both loved music. Particularly The Black Eyed Peas and Fall Out Boy."

Jax chuckles. "We were a bit obsessed."

I show them the horse stables, though Jax has been here probably a thousand times. The horses are in the pen where everyone can see them. Toby, one of our quarter horses, is near the edge of the fence. Olive reaches out and pets his neck.

"This is Toby," I say. "She's my dad's favorite horse."

"Speaking of." Jax nods his chin.

Dad is heading toward us, his gait slow. He has on a camouflage hat that sits low on his head.

"Jax Garcia," he says.

"It's good to see you, Mr. Coleman." The two shake hands before dad brings Jax in for a hug.

"Dad, this is Olive King."

"Nice to meet you." She shakes Dad's hand. "Thank you for allowing me to crash at your place."

"Friends of Lula's are welcome here anytime. Especially ones who are trying to help save this place."

"It doesn't need saving. It just needed a little boost."

Dad squeezes my shoulder. "I like that. A little boost," he repeats.

"I'm just giving Olive a tour of the farm and showing Jax all the improvements we've made."

"It's very impressive, sir," Jax says, flipping on the charm easily.

"Again, that's all thanks to Lula."

"Oh, stop. Emmaline, Garrison, and Axel have been doing most of the work. And Wiley."

"That's true, they've been a huge asset. This girl's beau has been instrumental in assuring pumpkin season is running smoothly."

Jax mouths *beau* with a smirk on his face.

"You better take them to meet Axel. I believe he's working under the tent this morning."

"Thanks, we're heading that way soon. Gotta take them to where the magic happens first."

"I'll see you kids around then." He waves and continues into the barn.

The three of us pass the back of the tent, the food trucks again, and the corn maze entrance.

"I'd love to go through the corn maze," Olive says.

"Yeah, that picture online looks amazing. I don't know how they didn't think of doing a themed corn maze before now." Jax admires the cornfield before we pass.

"We'll definitely go through it. But first, you gotta see where the magic happens and how the Coleman Family Farm began."

We step onto the soil, and a burst of pride explodes inside my chest. The field is crowded with children perusing the pumpkins while parents with wheelbarrows wait. The spots of orange are more sporadic than a week before when I stood here last. We've been busy, and Emmaline couldn't possibly have accounted for us to have attracted as much business as we've had. Especially with the Finley Farm opening its patch this year.

I gaze out over the field. "Just over eighty years ago, this is where the magic began. Granddad and Nonna took a risk and planted their first pumpkin seeds."

"Wow, Lula. What a legacy they've built."

"I remember Lula taking me here when I was a kid and telling me the same exact thing. I was impressed, even at that young of an age. But then her mom gave me a pumpkin seed and said, *love starts with a simple, tiny pumpkin seed.* She closed my hand around it and gestured at Lula, who was playing leapfrog with the pumpkins. I opened my hand and threw the seed and said *ick.*"

We laugh, even though I've heard this story a hundred times. Told both by Jax and also Mom.

"I got lucky my mom didn't scare him away after that," I say.

"Well, I think it's sweet. Your mom was already trying to find you a husband when you were just a kid," Olive says.

"It wasn't sweet. She was just trying to find someone with local roots who wouldn't take me away from this place."

Olive looks me in the eye. "Well, Axel may not have local roots, but he sounds pretty grounded here."

I consider this. She's not wrong. Axel and Sadie are doing well here. He'd never consider leaving. No matter how much he says he loves me.

"He definitely has wiggled his way into the hearts of my family, that's for sure." I start walking toward the tent, and Olive and Jax follow. "My dad chose him over Garrison to help run the pumpkin season, Garrison refers to him as his best friend, and Emmaline raves about his work ethic. She gives him the credit for the farm thriving the last three years."

"He sounds like a superhero. Or better yet, Prince Charming," Olive gushes.

"He sounds too good to be true," Jax mumbles.

My eyes scan the people under the tent. An employee is manning the pumpkin scale but it's not Axel. My feet freeze when my gaze finally lands on him, and my heart slides into my throat. It feels as if I'm back on that stage, the bright, hot lights glowing down on me and my voice cracking before breaking and then going completely silent. My body feels as if it's splintering into tiny pieces and crumbling to the ground below.

Axel is kissing another woman.

It takes a moment before Jax and Olive recognize him, zoning in after following my line of vision.

"What did I tell you? Too good to be true," Jax mutters.

I force my feet to move, and then it's as if they're floating or flying over the ground. By the time I reach him, the two have already broken apart.

Axel sees me before I can get any words out. There's already remorse sketched on his face.

"What the hell is this?" My heart beats fast and hard in my chest.

"Lula, it's not what it looks like." He reaches out a hand to touch my arm, but I flinch.

"That's what everyone says when it's exactly what it looks like. Because to me, it looked like you were just kissing another woman."

"Okay, you're right. But it's not what you think." He wipes the back of his hand over his lips.

The action rips through me. As if another reminder of what he's done. As if he thinks he can wipe it all away.

"Lula," he sighs, "this is Joanie."

The sound of the name *Joanie* feels hollow in my chest but, at the same time, monumental. And now that she's standing before me, it feels even bigger. And significant.

She limply raises a palm at me. "Hello."

I swallow the lump of anguish in my throat. "That still doesn't explain why you were kissing her."

"*She* kissed me."

"I've heard that excuse before," Olive mutters under her breath.

"Guilty," Joanie says.

"From where I stood, you didn't look like you hated it."

"She took me by surprise. And if you were paying that close attention, you should've also seen that I pushed her away."

Replaying it back in my mind, I did see that. I also saw the anger etched on his face. This woman hurt him, badly. But worse, she hurt Sadie.

"I'm sorry," Joanie finally says, though her expression looks anything but. "I got caught up in the moment. I shouldn't have kissed him." She shrugs. "Old habits and all, I guess."

As if this saying will be enough for me to forgive her. It's not.

"Well, old habits better die now." It sounds like a threat.

And even though Joanie is beautiful, towering over me with a perfect creamy complexion and long black hair, I mean it as exactly that. I didn't make a promise to Axel to work on a long-distance relationship to have someone swoop in and mess it up already. I haven't even left town yet.

"Okay, let's everyone calm down," Jax says in a low voice.

I follow his vision and notice several reporters lurking. My face blanches, and tears prick the corners of my eyes. Axel kissing Joanie will surely be all over social media in a matter of seconds, if it isn't already.

"This is just great," I mutter, covering my face in my hands but quickly realizing, this will be used against me as well. In a photograph, it will appear as if I'm devastated and crying.

"This is not going to be good for publicity. Or our concert," Olive says. Her phone dings in her hand at the same time Jax's does, and mine vibrates in my back pocket. I'm too afraid to look, so I stare at Olive while she reads the text. "Just as I suspected. Leslie is pissed."

I decide to take ownership of this entire situation and force my feelings and my shattered heart aside. For the sake of the band, I put on a brave face, complete with a wide, bright smile. I stick my hand out to Joanie. "It's nice to finally meet you. I'm Lula Coleman."

Stunned, Joanie takes my hand. "And you. Axel has told me very little about you."

"Axel has told me *enough* about you." I finally stand next to Axel, placing my palm on his chest as if this is natural for us, even though my legs are shaking and my fingers are trembling. He seems relieved. "Axel James, this is Olive King and Jax Garcia."

The two are so used to publicity now that they play right into the show. They shake Axel's hand and smile and play nice. Though I know Jax well enough that I'm sure he wants to tear into Axel. Olive compliments Joanie on her boots. And hopefully, now, to the camera, we are one big happy family. There will be speculation, but hopefully, the kiss will be covered up before too long.

I wrap my arm around Axel's waist and lean into him. "We need to go somewhere private to talk. Now."

He nods. "Let's go to my place."

"Fine." I kiss him on the cheek, but my lips feel as if they touch fire. "Hey, do you two mind going through the corn maze without me? I'll meet you back at the farmhouse when you're done."

Jax grabs hold of my arm and leans into me. "Are you sure?" he whispers.

I nod.

"Okay, we've both got our phones." Olive waves hers in the air. "And we'll handle Leslie."

"Thanks." I watch them walk away before taking Axel by the hand. We step inside the newlywed house, and Joanie follows in behind us. I'm not sure I intended on her being here, but maybe I'll get the full story.

As soon as the door closes and the three of us are alone, I pace the old hardwood floors and drill off questions and accusations. "Do you have any idea what this is going to do to the band? To the farm? And right before the concert." I press my fingertips into my eyes, attempting to keep my tears in check.

"Is that all you're worried about? The band? You?" Axel shoots back.

At first, his anger is off-putting. I expected him to be remorseful. Instead, he's on the defensive.

I take a deep breath so I don't lose my cool. "Once again, this is bigger than you and I. As long as I'm connected to the band, it's gotta be about them too. And now that we're performing a concert here, it's about the farm as well."

"I get that, I do." He pinches the bridge of his nose. "But for just this once, can you please think about how this affects me? And Sadie?"

Joanie clears her throat, and I narrow my eyes at her. I'm not sure I'm prepared for what she has to say. I already didn't think too highly of her, and now she's come here at the worst possible time.

"I just want to say again, I'm sorry. I knew Axel was seeing someone, and I kissed him anyway. It's been so long since I've seen him, I couldn't help myself." She hunches a shoulder.

"Wait." I halt my pacing, and my chest tightens. "You knew

Axel was seeing someone? How if you haven't talked to him in like three years?"

Joanie glances at Axel, and he drops his head, his boots suddenly interesting.

"Axel?"

He peers up at me, his eyes glistening. "Joanie saw our picture in the paper. She called me. I wanted to tell you, but I couldn't find the right time. And then, I thought I should tell Sadie first. But when I never heard anything more, I assumed I'd heard the last from her."

Disappointment bubbles in my chest. "You had plenty of chances to tell me. And Sadie. That's bull. You just didn't want to tell us."

"You're right, I didn't. Sadie has been hurt enough. I couldn't get her hopes up that her mom might be returning and then have her not show up."

Something about his confession sticks in my mind and twists. "Sadie has been hurt enough, or *you've* been hurt enough? You didn't want to get Sadie's hopes up or your own?"

"What? You know it's always been about Sadie."

"I know Sadie is number one in your life, yes. But Joanie didn't just leave Sadie. She left you too. Regardless if you think you loved her or not, when Joanie left, you felt abandoned."

Joanie presses her lips together, staying quiet, and I feel like she already knows she doesn't need to say anything. Because deep down, we both know she's already won.

"Did you get your hopes up?"

He grunts. "What? No, that's crazy. I've already told you that Joanie staying far away from Sadie is the best thing."

"Not for Sadie. For you? When you thought Joanie might return, did you think you might get back together with her?" My voice cracks.

A pang of worry shoots through me. Over my voice and his answer. Because I'm afraid I already know what it is.

"No." He rushes toward me, reaching for my hands, but I tear them from his grip. "I've told you. I never loved her."

Joanie clears her throat. "During our last phone conversation, I told him I wanted to see Sadie. And not just for a visit. I want to come back and be a part of her life permanently. I also told him I wanted to try to work things out between the two of us."

The remaining shards of my heart burst, and I'm no longer able to force the tears back.

"But I told her I wasn't interested. I told her that I was seeing you and that what we have is special."

I can tell he's trying to control his hands from reaching for me again; they're trembling at his sides.

"It's true," Joanie confirms. "But I decided I needed to come here and at least give us a fair shot. We have a child together. My family deserves a fighting chance at being together. I owe them that much, at least."

I realize what this is all about now. Joanie isn't just here to fight for her chance to mother Sadie again, but she's here to fight for Axel and their family. And I'm not sure how I can compete with that.

"But I've already told you, Joanie, I'm not interested. I love Lula." His words vibrate against the walls of the small house and hang there like the vulnerable confession that it is.

But what is love? What can love do? Is it enough to overcome history and a bond connected through a child?

I'm beginning to doubt it.

# Chapter Twenty-Nine
## AXEL

There's so much more I want to say to Lula. And to Joanie. But my unofficial break is over. I need to get back to work. Joanie has agreed to go to her hotel, get settled, and return once Sadie is home from school. Lula will be busy with Jax and Olive most of the day.

While returning to work is nearly the last thing I feel like doing, it will at least help distract me from what has now become my complicated life. First, Lula interrupted my routine, and now Joanie. The last thing I want is to get back together with Joanie. But Sadie will want nothing more than for us to be a family again.

I arrive under the tent just in time for Garrison to escort the kindergarten class on their field trip toward the pumpkin bins. I greet them with a big, fake smile.

"Hey, kids. Each of you can pick one pumpkin from any of these three bins."

Garrison appears to be extra chummy with the kindergarten teacher. He's whispering near her ear, and she's blushing and covering a giggle with her hand. Two children argue over a pumpkin, so the teacher tears herself away from Garrison to play referee.

Garrison strides over to me. "Well." He places his hands on his hips. "Better fill me in."

I don't need to ask what he's referring to. "You saw?"

"Not firsthand, but it's all over Instagram already."

"What?" I run a hand down my face, realizing too late the repercussions of that kiss and why Lula had every right to be upset. I'm not sure why I'd been so naive about it. Of course the reporters or Lula's fans would catch the kiss on camera. "How bad is it?"

He sucks in an exaggerated breath and releases it. "It's pretty bad. That woman had your lips locked tight and her claws digging into your neck."

I subconsciously rub there, groaning.

"I know there has to be some explanation . . . but what, I have no idea. Who was that woman?"

"Joanie. Sadie's mother."

"Okay, okay, now I see the resemblance."

The children surround the bins like vultures, and Garrison and I take a few steps back.

"So, Sadie's mom is back, huh?"

"I guess. She says she wants to stay. For good."

Garrison studies me, quirking a brow. "For good?"

"And she wants to get back together. She wants us to be a family again."

"Whoa. And what do you want?"

I shake my head as if I can dislodge the confusion swimming around in there. "I don't know."

"Gotta admit, not the answer I want to hear. You told me you loved my sister."

"I know. And I do. But all Sadie has ever hoped for is for her mom to come home and for the three of us to be a family.

How can I stand in the way of that?" I watch the children and only see Sadie on their faces. The innocence. "Everything I ever do is for Sadie. She's my world."

Garrison leans in closer to me. "Just maybe it's about time you do something for yourself." He presses his pointer finger into my chest. "And for your heart." He leaves, meeting the teacher on the other side of the bins.

Who would've thought it would be Garrison to speak such truth and have it make so much sense?

"All right, class," the teacher says, "it looks like you have all chosen your pumpkin. Why don't you thank Mr. Axel and Mr. Garrison and buddy up and get in line."

There's a slew of thank yous, and in a matter of seconds, the class is walking two by two out toward the parking lot. Garrison hangs back, accompanying the teacher. I take my place at the pumpkin scale, relieving another employee. My mind has a difficult time focusing on anything other than Sadie, Joanie, and Lula.

EMMALINE HAS GRACIOUSLY OFFERED to pick Sadie up from school today. While I take a quick break, cleaning out my truck and thinking over what I'm going to say to Sadie, Joanie shows up.

"I know you said to wait until Sadie was home, but I was bored at the hotel, and I really just wanted to see you. I thought it would be a good idea to talk before she came home."

Emmaline's truck pulls into the Coleman farmhouse driveway. My heartbeat accelerates and thrums all the way through to my fingertips.

"There's Sadie now. Just let me do the talking first. We don't want to frighten her."

Emmaline parks, and Sadie, Ariel, and Caleb climb out first. Emmaline opens her door, but it takes a few extra seconds for her to maneuver from behind the steering wheel.

"Daddy!" Sadie rushes at me, flinging her arms around my waist.

I bring her in, holding her extra tight and kissing her on the top of her head. She has that distinct outdoor smell that typically causes me to flinch, but today, I breathe it in.

"Hey, baby girl. How was your day?"

"Good. Some man came and taught us how to draw with oil pastels. I get to bring my picture home tomorrow. Can I have some oil pastels?"

"Let's add it to your Christmas list."

Joanie clears her throat, her hands clasped together in front of her. "Or, maybe I could get them for you?"

I glance back and forth between Joanie and Sadie, watching the frown form on Sadie's face.

"Who are you?"

I crouch and press my trembling hand to Sadie's back. "Sadie, this is Joanie—"

"I'm your mama," Joanie interrupts, bending so she's eye to eye with Sadie.

So much for letting me do the talking. "Right, this is Joanie, and she's your mom."

Sadie's face brightens, her eyebrows raised as she looks at me for confirmation. I nod, and she smiles, fidgeting with the zipper on her coat. "Really?"

"That's right. And my, have you gotten so big and so beautiful."

"Thank you. Daddy says I look a lot like you."

My face heats, and Joanie gives me adoring eyes. "Is that so?"

Sadie nods.

"I've missed you so much." Joanie takes hold of Sadie's hand, stilling her fidgeting.

"I have been hoping and hoping you would come home. And praying. Miss Emma told me I can pray too. Look, Miss Emma." Sadie points to Joanie. "My praying worked. My mama is home!" Sadie rushes toward Joanie and wraps her arms around her.

"I see that," Emmaline mumbles.

I can already read her thoughts. She's worried about me. She's concerned for Sadie. She's wondering what this will mean for the farm. But I'm right there with her, anxious over all of the above.

"Daddy, Mamma is home, and now we can be a family. We can all live in the newlywed house and get a dog. Just like my friend, Lily."

"Whoa, let's just focus on today. Joanie, your mom, is here to see you, get to know you. For now, she's staying in a hotel in town."

Sadie pouts. "She's not gonna sleep in the newlywed house?"

I shake my head.

"I'd love it if you showed me your room," Joanie says.

"Okay," Sadie says brightly.

"Maybe she'd also love it if you showed her around the pumpkin patch," Emmaline says.

"Oh yes, can I, Daddy?"

"Um, sure. You could probably do that. I gotta get back to work, so I suppose that would be all right." Even though I say the words aloud, my insides are a jumbled mess. Trusting Joanie has never come easy.

"Hi, and you are?" Joanie sticks her hand out for Emmaline.

"Emmaline Coleman."

"Oh, so your family owns the farm?"

Emmaline fakes a smile. "That's right."

"It's nice to meet you. And so nice of you to give Axel a job here."

Emmaline presses her lips together, placing her hands on her hips. "Well, he's a valuable employee here at the farm. He and I are in charge of the pumpkin patch this season."

"Wow, that's great."

"Mommy," Caleb says, tugging on Emmaline's sleeve. "We wanna go home."

"Okay, you two go and get a snack, and I'll be right there."

Caleb takes off running. Ariel follows behind him, waving to Sadie. "Bye, Sadie. See you later."

"So, you're also Lula Coleman's sister?"

"I am. It's been a while since people have linked the two of us together," Emmaline says.

"I've heard some of her music. She's pretty good." Joanie smiles at her, but when she glances back at me, she drags her gaze over my body, head to toe, before sucking her bottom lip between her teeth. It's familiar, and yet, at the same time, a shiver runs through me.

"She better be. We have a lot of people showing up here tomorrow night just to listen to her sing."

"Sounds exciting."

"Mommy!" Caleb calls from across the field. "C'mon!"

"I better get going."

I tug the brim of my hat down. "Thanks for picking up Sadie today."

"No problem. You'll get them next time."

"You two have quite the arrangement," Joanie observes.

"Well, Joanie, Axel works a full-time job and takes care of a child. All on his own. I try to help him out because he deserves a break once in a while," Emmaline says in a snarky tone.

Joanie crosses her arms. "I can see Axel's been saying all kinds of nice things about me."

"I gotta go. Axel, are you gonna be okay?"

"I'll be fine, thanks."

She waddles away but glares at Joanie over her shoulder.

"Wow." Joanie blinks. "She really doesn't like me."

"Uh . . ." I rub at the back of my neck. "Yeah, she really doesn't." I take Sadie's hand. "Hey, Sadie, why don't you go put your backpack in the house and grab a snack before you take your mom around the farm."

"Okay. Be right back." She runs into the house.

Joanie surprises me when she slips my hat off my head and pushes her fingers through my hair.

"What'cha doing?"

"You have such nice hair. I don't know why you always cover it with this silly old hat." She bends the bill and shoves it into the back pocket of my pants.

"Joanie." I swat her hands away and snatch the hat from my pocket, stuffing it back on my head. "You gotta stop."

"Why? What's the problem? You're worried about your girlfriend? It's not like she doesn't have a million guys falling all over her." She presses her palm on my chest and leans in closer. "Besides, this is harmless," her voice purrs.

I shove her hand away and take a step back. "According to pictures and reporters and social media, this would not look harmless."

"Why are you so worried about all that anyway? You never used to care what people thought of you." She waves me off, annoyance in her tone.

"I care now. And it matters to Lula. I don't want to do anything that could wreck anything for her."

"You're right. I don't either. But hopefully, she'll come out looking like a hero in all of this."

"What do you mean?"

"If she steps aside so we can be a family again, Lula's fans will respect her."

I pinch the bridge of my nose. "Joanie, I love Lula."

"How is that possible? You've known her for what? A few weeks?"

"It doesn't matter how long."

"And yet you've known me for years and don't love me?" she asks.

Deep down, I know I don't love Joanie. What I told Lula is true; I never did love Joanie. But I think, on some level, I have a sort of love for her. Because she's Sadie's mother. I don't answer with words, only a small shake of my head that I hope reveals my answer.

"Is she good with Sadie?"

"Yeah, she's great. Sadie adores her."

"But I think Sadie would prefer if we were a family."

"I don't think you have any clue what Sadie would prefer," I spit out. "She was two when you left. You don't even know her."

"I deserve that." She peers at her shoes before glancing back up. "But I'm also her mom. A mom always has a bond with their child."

"Bond or no bond, that's not exactly what I'm talking about here. I'm talking about the fact that since you haven't been around for over three years, you don't know her. You don't even know what her favorite color is. What her favorite animal is. Which stuffed animal she sleeps with every night. That's the kind of stuff a mother should know."

"Well, it's never too late. I'm here now."

Sadie runs out of the house, slamming the door behind her. "Okay, Mama, I'm ready."

Joanie smiles. She puts her hand out for Sadie, who slips her hand into hers, and they walk away together. Sadie waves over her shoulder at me.

"Bye, Daddy, see you later."

"You keep your phone on at all times, Joanie," I holler.

I wave to Sadie, but my gut is tight. A rush of nausea hits me.

# Chapter Thirty

## LULA

Growing up on the farm, I learned early on that the acoustics in the barn are remarkable. After the pumpkin patch closes, Jax, Olive, and I practice the new song. It will be the first time I've sung with them since the surgery. I'm nervous, but I'm confident my vocals are ready. Just in case, Macie is here. This way, she'll be able to practice with us. I'm not completely prepared to relent and allow her to sing with the band tomorrow night, but I need to put them first.

"You sure you're up for this?" Jax asks.

"Yeah," Olive says, "we can wait until tomorrow when everyone else is here. Save your voice?"

"It's fine. I've been dying to try this new song out."

"As long as you think you're ready."

"Jax, if I'm not ready tonight, I won't be ready tomorrow." I glare at him.

"Okay, fine." He sticks his hands up.

Macie is propped on a bar stool off to the side, listening quietly.

Olive has her phone set up ready to record. "Okay, count us off." She hits record.

"One, two, three," I say, and Jax begins playing.

My voice starts off quiet at the beginning of the song. It sounds good. My tone is clear and nearly sounds the same as it did before the surgery. Gratification spreads through my veins, and my voice grows louder at the chorus where Olive joins in. Our voices meld and harmonize together like a fine aged wine.

<u>Nothing Changes Around Here</u>
These acres of soil and crop fields
They represent generations of blood, sweat, and tears
The chipped paint on the porch swing
Nothing changes around here

Old pictures line the walls
Showing better days when life wasn't so hard
That old crack in the wooden step
Giving me away on late nights of fun
Nothing changes around here

Take me back to those days
When this old farm and dusty house was all I ever needed—or wanted
To the carefree days of tag in corn fields and leapfrog over pumpkins
Nothing changes around here—and I hate it

Waking up to the rooster crowing and the fresh scent of dirt in the air
Of leaves changing and nights growing crisp
Gathering 'round while Dad says a prayer—but all I see is the empty spot where he should be

Take me back to those days
When this old farm and dusty house was all I ever needed—or
wanted
To the carefree days of tag in corn fields and leapfrog over
pumpkins
Nothing changes around here—and I miss it

The song ends, and without intention, tears fill my eyes. Olive turns off the recording and then wraps her arms around me.

"Whoa," Macie mumbles.

"That sounded incredible," Olive says after pulling back and taking both of my hands in hers.

"I'm telling you, this song is gonna take off like wildfire," Jax says.

"He's right," Axel interrupts.

I whip around just as he steps into the barn. My emotions are confused and battling with one another. I'm still angry at him for earlier, but at the same time, I'm elated to see him.

"I knew the first day I overheard you singing some of the lyrics," Axel says.

"Thanks," I say shyly.

Everyone is quiet, and the barn takes on an awkward silence.

"Sorry, I didn't mean to interrupt," Axel says.

"It's fine, you didn't." I turn toward Jax and Olive. "I think we're done, right guys?"

"Yes, you need to save that voice for tomorrow and Saturday." Olive puts her instrument in the case.

"Macie, Olive, and I will head back to the house. I'll send this video to Mick and the rest of the band." Jax snatches Olive's phone.

"They're gonna lose it when they hear your vocals. I mean,

I've been singing them during rehearsals, but this song was clearly written for your voice," Olive says. "Just wait until they hear it."

"I'll meet you back at the house in a bit."

"Nice to see you again, Axel." Olive waves from the open door of the barn.

"Hopefully we'll get a chance to get better acquainted tomorrow." Jax's tone is near threatening as he shakes Axel's hand before meeting Olive at the door.

"Use the back door, it's always unlocked," I call to them.

Axel perches on the edge of a hay bale. "I really didn't make a very good first impression with them."

I hesitate, kicking the toe of my boot into the dirt on the barn floor, but join him on the hay bale. I shove my hands underneath my thighs. "It wasn't your fault."

He rests his elbows on his knees, clasping his hands together. "Yeah, I suppose not. But it could've gone better."

"It could've." I smile at him. "It will go better tomorrow. Especially if Joanie isn't around."

"Let's hope."

"How'd it go today? With Sadie? Is she doing okay?"

"She is doing more than okay." He shakes his head. "She's making all kinds of plans."

"What does that mean?" I watch his facial expression shift.

"She wants Joanie to move into the newlywed house with her and me."

"Ah," I exhale, glancing away and forcing my eyes to stare at the toes of my boots. "*Those* kinds of plans. Ones that not only include Sadie and her mom but the three of you."

"Yeah."

I move my hands from underneath my thighs and push my fingers through my hair, resting my hands on the back of my neck. "And what did you tell her?"

"Sadie?"

"Sadie . . . and Joanie." I'm afraid to hear the answer.

"I haven't really had a chance to explain everything to Sadie yet. She's confused." He scrubs both hands over his face. "But I did tell Joanie that I'm with you. And that I love you. Not her."

My heart softens. "You did?"

"Of course. Joanie popping back into my life hasn't changed my feelings for you." He holds out a palm to me, and I slide my hand into his, clasping it tightly.

"But it's obvious she wants to get back together with you."

He gives a curt nod. "She does."

"What are you gonna do?"

He leans over and presses a sweet kiss to my temple. "I don't know."

But his answer does nothing to comfort me. It doesn't tell me anything at all. "What does that mean?"

"You know I don't love her. I told you the truth when I said I have never loved her." He lets go of my hand and tucks my hair behind my ear, grazing his thumb against my cheek. A shiver runs through me. I know he's willing me to look at him, but I'm not sure I can. Dread rises in me because I sense a *but* coming. "Joanie is Sadie's mom."

It's unusual for him to say that out loud.

I finally lift my attention, my vision dancing back and forth between his eyes and his lips, trying to read his expression. "Yeah, I know. So, just what aren't you saying, Axel?"

"I guess, on some level, I have a form of love for her. But only because she's Sadie's mom. That's it." He runs his hand up my neck. "I just need some time to sort this out. To explain things to Sadie. She's got this perfect picture built in her mind of us being a family again. Letting her down isn't something I'm used to doing."

I turn to him, taking his face in my hands. "I respect you for wanting to do things right by Sadie. And for being honest with me. But the one thing we don't have is time."

He reaches both arms around my back and draws me into him, pressing his forehead against mine. "I know."

"I want to give it to you, but selfishly, I want to keep you all to myself for the next three days." I kiss his lips, softly, repeatedly, breaking to gaze into his eyes each time.

"There's nothing I want more," he says between the kisses.

My tongue darts out to lick my lip before we kiss. It's intense and passionate. So much craving driving our kiss and it deepens. Our tongues entangle and we lose ourselves in the sweet moment.

Regretfully, I finally break apart from him, withdrawing my hands from his chest at last. "I should let you go."

"No," he says breathlessly. "Joanie is with Sadie."

"You should go be with them." I don't know why I'm encouraging him to spend time with Joanie. Only that maybe, he should see what it feels like to be a family. It may be the only way he can truly make a choice. Being a family with Sadie and Joanie. Or me. "Besides, you asked for time. I'm gonna try to give it to you." I stand, though not without reservation. He stands in front of me, pressing his hands against the small of my back. "I have my own obligations as well. Tomorrow will be busy when the rest of the band gets here."

"When will I get to see you tomorrow? Alone?" He raises his brows.

There's a lot insinuated in that look. "I don't know about alone, but I'd love for you to hang out with me during the concert tomorrow night. You can bring Sadie along if you'd like. Or, let Joanie hang out with her instead. Totally your call."

"I'd love to," is all he says.

We kiss again before parting ways, him back to the

newlywed house with Joanie and Sadie, and me back to the farmhouse with Jax and Olive.

FRIDAY MORNING, we awake to phones dinging and buzzing before the sunlight even shines through the window, so I know it's not even seven o'clock. Olive and I sit with a start, moaning and groaning. Jax trudges into my room with his phone in his hand and flops face-first onto my bed.

"Mick is calling," Jax mutters into the mattress. He climbs farther onto my bed, yanking the covers up to his shoulders.

"What for?" I ask on an exhaled yawn.

"Make it stop," Olive groans, lying back down and placing the pillow over her head.

Typically, Olive is a morning person. But after staying up until the early morning hours discussing my predicament, a few hours of sleep is not even enough for her.

"I don't know, I didn't answer." Jax sprawls out, taking up the majority of the twin-sized bed.

I check my phone and find several texts from Mick and Leslie. And a few missed calls from Mick.

> **MICK**
>
> Your voice is back baby!
>
> That song is our ticket back on top!
>
> Pack your bags because The Broken Halos are about to go back on tour!

I can't read anymore after that. *Back on tour?* We don't even have a full album to release. I've written a couple of songs since I've been home, but even combining them with the ones I wrote after the last album was released, there's not enough. And the new ones don't even have music to them—only lyrics.

I set my phone down and rub my eyes. My heart is already beating too fast to fall back asleep now. My mind is jumbling with ideas of what that text could mean.

My phone buzzes in my lap. It's Leslie now. But I don't answer. I need coffee before my brain can even begin to comprehend what is happening.

Jax hits me in the head with a pillow. "Make the buzzing stop."

"Would you rather I turned the ringer back on?" I tease.

"I'd rather you turn it off like I did."

"Well, you might want to turn it back on and check your texts. I got an interesting one from Mick."

Olive lifts the pillow off her head. "Did Mick say it was interesting, or are you saying it's interesting? There's a difference."

"Ugh," Jax groans.

"C'mon." I hit Jax in the head with the same pillow and crawl out of the bed. "We need coffee for this."

WHILE WE WAIT for the rest of the band to arrive, I show Jax and Olive some lyrics I've been toying around with for the last few weeks. They're both impressed. Jax even begins trying to put music to them. But they're concerned about getting back on tour so soon. Rushing another album and its release could be a huge mistake. The last thing The Broken Halos need is another setback.

Jax, Olive, and I are waiting near the parking lot of the pumpkin patch when Mick, Leslie, and the rest of the band arrive. An SUV pulling a trailer parks in the lot. My nerves are on high alert, anticipating my new life and my old life colliding. A black high-heel boot steps out the open door of the white rental SUV. Leslie removes her dark sunglasses after she's out of the vehicle.

"Let's get the show on the road, shall we?" Jax squeezes Olive's and my shoulders and walks in between us. "Nice of the rest of you to finally show up."

"Do you know how long it takes to get out here?" Leslie complains.

"It wasn't that long." Mick takes two bags out of the back of the SUV.

Oscar and Davey greet Jax before making their way over to Olive and me. Davey squeezes me tight. "It's great to see you."

"It will be even better to hear you sing," Cody teases, hugging me.

"You've heard me sing." I swat him in the chest with the back of my hand.

"I've heard you on a video." He taps his fingers to his ears. "I need to hear it with my own ears."

Oscar chucks a bag into Cody's chest. "You'll hear it when we get our bags and equipment all unloaded."

Our small reunion is cut short when reporters fill the parking lot. Within seconds, we're bombarded with microphones and questions. Thank God for Leslie; she steps in like the pro that she is, sidestepping as many questions where the answers might be harmful and telling them only enough to get by.

"The Broken Halos are thrilled to be reunited and that Lula's voice is back to its spectacular sound. They can't wait to rehearse together so they're one hundred percent ready to put on a fantastic show for the great people of Juniper Ridge tomorrow night. So go on and get, and let them start rehearsing."

We take this as our cue to leave, taking as much luggage as we can all carry in one trip. I lead my band to the farmhouse first. We drop off their luggage while Mick and our crew unload our equipment from the trailer and into the barn.

"Thanks for letting us crash here," Davey says.

"You sure your parents won't mind?" Oscar winces.

"Nah." I wave them off. "They're used to accommodating a lot of people."

"The Colemans are the best," Jax says.

We truck across the field toward the barn in a hurry while Leslie is still handling the reporters.

"What's this about us rehearsing in a barn?" Cody asks.

"The acoustics are amazing," Olive says. "You'll see."

Axel and Garrison have moved the tractor out of the barn, leaving us adequate room for our equipment. As our crew brings it inside, we begin setting up for rehearsal. I have questions and obvious concerns about Mick and Leslie's idea to release another album and go out on tour. Axel and I agreed on a long-distance relationship, but that was when I had planned to stay in Portland, where access to travel back and forth would be easier. With me out on the road, that would mean months without seeing one another.

But making sure we're ready for tomorrow night needs to be my priority.

As soon as we're set up, we start off with one of our originals. It's the first single from our first album, and it's also the song that put us on the mark. Starting with something familiar and well-known was Mick's idea, and it feels like a good one.

I inhale the scent of the hay underneath my feet, close my eyes, and count us off. I give myself permission to sing without holding back. Inside the barn, my voice, mixed with the instruments, vibrates against the old wooden walls surrounding us. We sound raw and fresh. Almost like we usually do, but somehow different.

I clutch the mic, my bottom lip resting against it as I sing the final lyrics. The song finishes, and my eyes flutter open. Warmth expands in my chest, and a smile stretches across my face.

Mick claps. "That was unbelievable. Your voice sounded incredible. You're back, baby."

As I glance around at my band, with the excitement fluttering inside the barn, it's obvious they feel it too. We are back. In an instant, the worry over not being able to perform at the concert slips away. My plan to help save the Coleman Family Farm just might work after all.

"Now, are you ready to discuss getting back out on tour?" Leslie asks.

# Chapter Thirty-One

## AXEL

It was too late for Sadie to give Joanie the full tour of the pumpkin patch yesterday so they're back at it today. They're waiting to go through the corn maze until I can join them. Around three o'clock, Garrison relieves me for the rest of the day. I meet Joanie and Sadie at the coffee truck.

"Here." Joanie hands me a paper cup. "I got you a coffee."

I rub at the back of my neck. "Um, thanks." When I take a sip, I'm surprised to discover it's not a fancy espresso drink but a plain old black coffee with lots of sugar. What's most surprising is Joanie remembering how I take my coffee. The gesture causes a tightness in my gut and I hate the way it feels.

"C'mon, Daddy." Sadie takes my hand and yanks me along. "Hurry."

"Whoa, settle down. You've been through the maze before."

"But Mommy hasn't."

Joanie and I make eye contact, and there's a familiar sweetness in her appearance. She smiles and glances away. Hearing Sadie refer to her as Mommy is strange. Before Joanie left,

Sadie said Mommy nearly a hundred times a day. Her vocabulary was small back then. And in three years, not only has it grown, but the word Mommy has been spoken very little.

We buy tickets for the maze, even though Wiley tries not to take my money. It's not much, but I want to do my part to help out the farm. As we go through the entrance of the maze, Sadie walks in between Joanie and me, taking each of our hands. Joanie and I share a look again across the top of Sadie's head, and Joanie smiles before her vision dances away. This is how the two of us will be forever tied together, Sadie in between us.

I hold a map as we make our way through the maze. Joanie and I let Sadie lead us and tell us which way to go next, despite me knowing she's choosing the wrong way. I can't help but wish I had a map for my own life. One that would tell me exactly which path to choose that will ultimately lead me to happiness. Lead Sadie to happiness. Because without a map telling me which way to go, I'm afraid I'll choose the wrong path. Or at least, the wrong path for Sadie. My heart wants to choose Lula. Despite not knowing where our future will lead. But my head wants to choose being a family with Sadie and Joanie. Even though I won't be happy.

After an hour of winding through the maze, my toes are growing cold and Joanie's nose is red. When I notice Sadie's fingers are bright pink, I instruct her to take her gloves out of her coat pockets and put them on. The air is growing colder, and it's going to be dark soon. I insist we take a right, like the map shows. Even though Sadie wants to turn left. Turning left will cause us to go in another circle, adding an additional ten minutes. At least.

"Sadie honey, why don't we go right? I remember passing by here before. That scarecrow looks awfully familiar. If we go left, I'm pretty sure we'll do another circle and pass here again."

Sadie studies Joanie's face and then glances over both

shoulders, deciding which way to turn. "Fine." She reluctantly turns to the right and stomps down the path.

I mouth *thank you* to Joanie. She smiles and follows after Sadie.

It's strange to have someone else's opinion matter to Sadie. For three years, it's only been mine she listens to. My instructions. My directions. My parenting. Is this what it would be like if we were a family? I'd have someone else in my corner? Someone supporting the decisions I make? It doesn't sound like a terrible thing. Though co-parenting with Joanie isn't something I've had to think about for three years.

Another hour later, freezing toes, fingers, and noses, we make our way out of the maze. We survived. I congratulate Sadie on her leadership skills, even if, at times, they were questionable. I'm just happy to be out of the maze and not in such close proximity to Joanie.

"What's going on over there?" Sadie points at the stage.

People are setting up sound equipment on the stage. I recognize Macie and then remember that it's Friday and she's singing tonight. Sort of an opening act for The Broken Halos before their concert tomorrow night.

"Remember that singer I told you about? She's getting ready to perform."

"Can we listen to her? Please," Sadie begs.

I turn to Joanie for help, which came too naturally, and I hate myself a little for it. She shrugs. Right. Because I'm the parent here. Not Joanie. It was silly to think that after a day she would be ready to help make decisions for Sadie. I'm not sure she'll ever be ready. She had a hard enough time knowing how to take care of Sadie before she left.

"Sure. But first, warmer clothes. And dinner."

"Yay." Sadie jumps up and down.

"I should probably head back to the hotel," Joanie says.

"Noooo. You gotta stay and listen to the concert, Mommy," Sadie whines.

Joanie looks to me for confirmation. But if she thinks I'm gonna beg her, she's profoundly mistaken. I glance away.

"You should hang out with your dad and your new friend Lula."

I know what she's doing. She may have been gone for three years, but she hasn't changed. She's still as manipulative as ever.

"You can hang out with us too. Lula is so nice."

"Oh, I don't know."

"Please?" Sadie tugs on Joanie's arm.

"Oh, all right."

"Yes." Sadie pumps a small fist in the air triumphantly.

I groan.

After I fix Sadie a grilled cheese and bundle her up, Joanie returns to her hotel to get warmer shoes and a coat. I stuff Sadie's feet into her boots, paying close attention to the new joy I see on her face. She's typically a happy kid. But this is a new expression, a new demeanor. The last thing I want is to take this new joy away. I debate if now is the right time to talk to her about Joanie and me not being able to work things out and that we won't be a family after all.

Sadie flings her arms around my neck. "I can't wait for Mommy to sleep here every day with us and not at the dumb hotel," she whispers in my ear.

*Oh, hell.* I swallow back my words. I wrap my arms around her and lift her up, giving her a hug. "Okay, let's go see if we can find Lula."

Outside, the clear, dark sky stretches with bright white stars. The temperature has dropped substantially since the sun went down. I get a text from Lula that tells me she is with Macie, hanging out in the makeshift backstage that Garrison and Wiley made with extra-long black curtains and rods. Sadie hops on my back, and I weave through the growing crowd. It's strange to have the pumpkin patch closed but have so many people on the farm after hours.

"Hey, there you are." Lula gifts me and Sadie a warm smile. She gives me a kiss and pats Sadie on a dangling leg. "How was the corn maze?"

"I got us out," Sadie says proudly.

"Good for you." Lula gives her a high five.

"Yeah, only took about two hours," I mumble.

Lula swats my arm but smiles. "I want to introduce you guys to the rest of the band."

She takes my hand, and it feels right. With Sadie on my back and Lula's hand in mine, we feel more like a family than with Joanie. I allow a slight amount of guilt to slide into my gut at this thought but push it away. I've put Sadie first for five years. As much as I want her to be happy, doesn't my happiness account at all?

"Guys, this is Axel James and his daughter Sadie."

The entire band is here now. They all greet me kindly with friendly smiles and handshakes. Even Jax and Olive appear to be in better spirits than yesterday, and I'm grateful. Sadie climbs off my back, and they all high-five her and give her fist bumps. She instantly becomes the life of the conversation, asking questions about their instruments and who plays which one.

Lula loops her arm around my waist and smiles while Sadie chats with the band. I spot two people I don't recognize. The woman is busy on her phone, and the man is chatting with Jax.

I gesture with my chin. "Who are they?"

"Oh, let me introduce you." She takes my hand, grazing her thumb over mine. "Mick, this is Axel James. Axel, Mick Sabotini. He's The Broken Halos's manager."

"Nice to meet you." I shake his hand.

"And you. It's nice to put a voice to the face in the photos." He winks.

"This is Leslie Murphy, The Broken Halos's publicist."

She narrows her eyes at me, holding our handshake longer than necessary. "So you're the guy responsible for making my job harder?"

I wince. "Guilty."

"Just no more kissing face with your baby's mama, m'kay?" She waves a finger in my face.

"Leslie," Lula hisses.

Leslie puts up her palms. "Hey, just looking out for you. And for the rest of the band. We can't afford any bad publicity when you're about to release your next album and go back out on tour."

I gape at Lula, who's scratching at her neck and chewing her bottom lip.

"Tour?" I question.

"That's right. This girl writes lyrics like a magician." Leslie loops an arm around Lula's neck. "And sings like an angel who has smoked a pack of cigarettes a day for twenty years. We gotta take advantage of her healed vocals and get The Broken Halos back out on tour as soon as possible."

My shoulders stiffen. "Soon? How soon?"

"Right after the album releases," Leslie says.

"Leslie," Lula mutters a warning.

"And when is that?" My throat constricts.

"As soon as we get them home. They're back in the recording studio come Sunday."

*Home?*

"Leslie." This time Lula raises her voice.

Leslie finally takes notice of Lula's wide eyes, and she glances back and forth between us. "I'm gonna go make sure they're ready for Macie to get on stage." Leslie leaves in a swish.

I grab Lula's hand and yank her out of earshot of Sadie and the band. "When were you gonna tell me?"

"About what?"

"Don't play around with me. You know what," I bite out. "The tour."

"Nothing is for sure. Nothing's set in stone."

"It sounds pretty set in stone to me."

"It's just something Leslie and Mick have been talking about. The band hasn't agreed."

"So if the rest of the band wants to, will you agree?"

Lula crosses her arms, hugging her chest. "I don't know."

I exhale and try to process what this will mean for our relationship. But I already know. If she goes back out on tour, there won't be the weekend visits back and forth that we were looking forward to. Tours can last several months, she's told me. And before they go on tour, they'll need to get the album ready to be released.

"This doesn't change anything," she announces, her words vibrating.

Because I think she already knows that's a lie.

I lean in close to her. "If you go back out on tour, you and I both know that this"—I motion back and forth between us—"is over."

Her blue eyes water as they peer into mine. "Not necessarily," she says.

"When we agreed to a long-distance relationship, it was on the grounds of us visiting each other on weekends. You've said it before, when you're preparing to release an album, you're in the studio practically 24-7."

"It's true, there isn't much time for breaks. But we'll make it work. I'll come as often as I can. And you can come and hang out in the studio. The band won't mind."

"Even if that worked," I say on an exhaled breath, "once you go out on tour, we won't be able to see each other for months."

"I'll give you the tour dates in advance. I'll pay for you and Sadie to fly and meet me."

"I have work. And Sadie has school. We can't just fly around city to city chasing after you."

"You can't or you won't?"

"I won't."

She swipes at a tear rolling down her cheek and glances at her bandmates.

"It's not fair to Sadie. Or me." I take her hands in mine. "Or you. I'm not an idiot. If you go on tour, the band will need you to focus. I'm not gonna be a distraction for you."

"You wouldn't be."

"It already sounds like you've made your decision."

Sadie runs past us. "Mommy!"

I turn and watch as Sadie wraps her arms around Joanie's legs.

"Hey, some guy out there told me I'd find you in here." She picks Sadie up, propping her on a bony hip. "Sorry, am I interrupting something?"

"No." I drop Lula's hands. "Sadie and I were just leaving. I'll catch up with you after the concert." I join Joanie and Sadie and usher them out with a hand to Joanie's back.

"Axel, wait. Please."

But I keep walking and don't turn around.

# Chapter Thirty-Two

## LULA

Macie sings a three-song set list. The crowd goes wild over her last song. My chest expands with tightness, excitement mixed with a bit of jealousy. As I listen to the crowd cheer for her, I know her future is bright. I also know that if Boss Records can get her to sign with them, she will be our opening act when we go on tour. *If* we go on tour.

My eyes scan the crowd for Axel. I'm itching to speak to him, to see him. But I don't find him until it's too late. Sadie is propped on his shoulders, and Joanie is at his side. As he makes his way out of the crowd, I get a clearer look and see he's got his hand on Joanie's lower back. My face heats as a fit of despair coils up my back and snakes around my entire body as if it's constricting me.

"C'mon, let's go talk to Macie." Jax bumps into me.

I blink back the tears burning my eyes and follow him without looking at Axel again.

Macie is modest in the praise the band gives her. We all stay enthusiastic because if Boss Records decides to sign her, we need her. Mick and Leslie tell Macie they'll be in touch and assure us they'll get her back home safely before they head to their hotel.

The band is staying at the already over-crowded farmhouse. It's a comforting feeling, having us all together. Since things between Axel and me are complicated, I'm relieved I won't be alone tonight. The six of us wind up crashing in my room. I'm grateful Mom and Dad didn't throw a fit about it.

Olive is curled up next to me, and Jax's feet are propped near my head, the three of us squeezing on my childhood twin bed. The others are using the cots on the floor. It feels similar to the all-nighters we pull in the studio. But being back in the bedroom I grew up in, surrounded by all of them, causes warmth to expand in my chest. I realize in this moment that they are my adult version of a childhood security blanket. Being home has been eye-opening and therapeutic as old unhealed wounds resurfaced. But my band is what feels like home to me. Regardless if we're in Portland, at the farmhouse, or touring around the country, they're home.

My band challenges me to improve and take risks. I can talk about my hopes and dreams for our future. We all share the common interest of music and the desire to hit certain goals in our careers. They understand the industry.

As the voices turn to murmurs around me and the light from the moon peers through the gap in the curtains, Olive kisses me on the forehead before her eyes flutter closed. I shut my own and breathe in the mixture of scents of my favorite people—Olive's lavender essential oil and Jax's beard oil and my favorite place. The coarse hay and rich soil stuck to the soles of my boots.

My mind wanders to Axel and Sadie, who have quickly become important people in my life. Axel, with his gentle demeanor and charismatic smile, his lanky body in distressed jeans and a flannel. The dark brown curls that sneak under neath his hat. Sadie and her infectious giggle and her welcoming heart. The two of them make me feel as if I'm more than a singer, more than The Broken Halos. Like I can do anything.

Axel challenges me on a different level than the band does. He stretches my abilities in ways I didn't even know existed. He reminded me that, at one time, the farm had been the most important thing to me. And back then, I would've done anything to save it. When I'm with Axel and Sadie, I feel like a selfless person.

How can two groups of people make me feel as if I'm home when neither of them are a place at all? And how can both groups make me feel like I'm the best version of myself? Despite feeling torn, I force myself to push away the thoughts. I have a job to do before a decision can be made, so I find comfort in Olive's rhythmic deep breaths.

MOM FEEDS us a huge breakfast of eggs, thick bacon, country potatoes, and homemade cinnamon rolls. It's more than The Broken Halos have probably eaten for breakfast, ever. Mick and Leslie come from their hotel and join us. They're all appreciative, and Oscar and Jax even try to clean up. But Mom is having none of it.

"Go on, get." She scoots us out of the kitchen, flapping her dish towel at us.

"I don't mind washing the dishes." Jax resists her demands. "It's the least I can do."

"Oh no you don't, Jax Garcia. You do enough. You make

sure my baby is kept safe on those dark, dangerous streets in the city."

"Mom." I roll my eyes. "It's not dangerous." Though my heart flutters at the endearment. She hasn't called me *baby* since I've been back home.

"And if it is, I think I'm the one who does most of the protecting," Olive interjects.

"Hey," Jax argues.

"It's true and you know it." I give him a slight shove in the back. "Olive may be little but she's scrappy."

"Thank you again, Mrs. Coleman," Mick says, encouraging us out the door with a nod and a look that means business.

It's time to rehearse.

Regardless of the job The Broken Halos has to do, the pumpkin patch is hustling and bustling on the last Saturday we're open. Tomorrow is the official last day until next year. My heart is full of emotions as the unknown future awaits me. As much as I want to be here next year for pumpkin season, my loyalties lie with The Broken Halos. I stupidly think that if we go out on tour after the first of the year, we'll be done and on a break by next October. Leaving my time open to return to the farm and work during the pumpkin season.

Despite my greatest efforts to spot Axel on the farm as I truck across the field toward the barn, I'm unsuccessful. I check my phone, but there's nothing from him. Not even a missed text.

We rehearse in the barn for a few hours, Mick keeping watch by the door and assuring no reporters sweet talk Garrison into giving them access inside. Leslie pacing through the dirt and hay strewn across the ground in the barn in her patent leather stilettos is a picture-worthy sight. She's been interrupting us the entire time while talking to the record label and reporters. It's obvious she wants this next album and tour to happen soon, and she's not gonna give up pushing the record label on the idea.

When we break for lunch, there's finally a text from Axel.

AXEL

What do you want?

The question is small, it's simple. It should have a simple answer. And yet, it doesn't. Because he's not just asking, what do I want for lunch. Which is what Mick is asking all of us. Axel is asking what I want. In other words, do I want the band, or do I want him? But why should I have to choose one or the other? If I simply choose love, isn't that enough? Because if it is, that is what I would choose.

Love.

I'd choose us. But it's not that simple. Too many other people are involved besides us. There's the band and Sadie. And now, unfortunately, Joanie. I won't ignore him. So I reply with a question of my own.

What do you want?

There's no lapse in time before a response comes.

AXEL

You.

His response is exact. It's simple for him. So why can't I do the same?

AXEL

But what do you want?

I reply the only way I can, with honesty.

Love.

> Us.

> The Broken Halos.

> I want it all.

AXEL

You can't have it all.

My heart plummets to the hay under my feet, and panic thrums in my chest, rising in my throat, making it difficult to catch my breath. I instantly regret choosing honesty. I want to respond by saying I only want him, just as he had replied to me. But once it's out there, it can't be taken back. Mick is calling my name, and he sounds as if he's in a tunnel, his voice muffled.

"Lula?" He nudges me. "Lunch?"

"Anything is fine." I wave him off and rush through the barn doors, gulping in the fresh air. I press my back against the outside wall of the barn, ignoring the crowds of people hustling around the pumpkin patch.

> Why not?

AXEL

I'd rather have this conversation in person.

Jax pushes out through the door. "Lula? C'mon, we're ready to begin again."

"Okay. Just give me a sec."

"Fine. But hurry. The rest of the guys don't even want to break for lunch."

I check the time on my phone. "At this rate, we'll be having lunch at dinner time."

"Doesn't seem like anyone cares about food right now. We're on a high. I mean, we've never sounded better." He walks backward. "Hurry," he drags out the word.

I force a smile and hover my thumbs over the keypad on my phone.

> We're still rehearsing. Not sure when we're taking a break.

AXEL
> You rehearse and we'll touch base when the concert is over.

> You sure?

AXEL
> I'm not the one going anywhere.

His text is not only a dig. It's a reminder. That he's staying here, and I'm the one going. I choose not to respond and instead, slide my phone into my back pocket.

THE BAND SCOOCHES CLOSE TOGETHER, standing behind the black curtains as if we are backstage. I draw back the curtain and peek through it. The crowd is ginormous. Growing up, I saw the land around my home filled with strangers, visitors of the farm, and the pumpkin patch. But this is the most I've ever seen crowded onto the Coleman property. And the idea that they are here to see me and the band is perplexing.

Their excitement can be felt all around me, filling the cavity of my chest and thrumming through my bones. It reminds me how much I love this. Singing, performing, entertaining. It brings a sense of joy nothing else ever has. It's a level of fulfillment I never got all those years from working on the farm. In the last few weeks, I've been reminded of the sense of family and accomplishment and taking pride in my work. But I've never stopped working hard for what I want.

Jax takes me by my arms and shakes me. "It's almost time. You ready?"

I smile and nod while he continues shaking me, turning my smile into a giggle.

Together, as a band and with Mick too, we crowd around, wrap our arms around one another in a circle, and get hyped up. It's something we always do before every concert. But tonight's hype session feels more intense; the adrenaline pumping through my veins is like fire. I'm itching to get out on stage and perform for this crowd that sounds equally anxious to hear us.

"Let's do this, kids." Mick slaps us each on the back, gives us fist bumps, and claps his hands together. "There's no do-overs here. It's make it or break it time." He claps me on the shoulder.

"Thanks for the pep talk," I mutter, following Olive onto the stage.

I hear the crowd cheer before I see them and before I take my spot in front of Davey, on the drums, and next to Olive and Jax. As my vision scans the audience, I inhale a deep breath, forcing the cool air into my lungs. I give a few waves high in the air at the fans and smile gratefully. Davey taps on the drums a few times, and I glance back at him before making eye contact with each band member, signaling our readiness with a nod to Jax.

I step up to the mic stand, taking it tentatively in both hands. I close my eyes and drop my chin to my chest, my heart beating fitfully, and I do what I always do in this moment. Before Jax strums the first few chords, I say a silent prayer. This time it feels even more vital than usual. This time it feels as if I need a miracle for this voice of mine to come through. *Everyone is counting on us,* I think, referring to myself and my voice as if we're two different people. In a way, it feels as if we are. And I need them to work together to pull this off.

The chords sound out, and an eerie hush consumes the crowd. When Olive starts on her violin, I raise my head, my eyes fluttering open, and I take in my audience. The nearly full moon glows, ricocheting against the heads and faces of the people in the crowd. The lights surrounding the stage and the outskirts of the field are bright enough to reveal their expressions, but it's dark enough to cut out any eye colors or clothing. It's easier to see them as a mass of gray out there.

I glance at Olive and open my mouth, and the lyrics pour out of me effortlessly. Relief floods through me, and we share a smile. When we reach the chorus, where the tempo picks up, I grip the mic, tugging it free from the stand, and move around the stage. I squeeze Jax's shoulder and lean into him while he strums his guitar. I jump up and down as the song crescendos, and I pump my fist in the air, the crowd going even more wild.

We sing two more songs from our second album, which got rave reviews during our tour. Both are fast-paced, and by the end of the second, sweat trickles down my spine.

Before we move to our newest song, "Nothing Changes Around Here," I hold up a finger to the crowd, and they cheer.

"Thank you!" I yell into the mic and then chug half a bottle of water. "For this next one, we're gonna slow it down a bit."

The audience whistles and claps again.

"But before we get to it, I just want to say thank you, again, to all of you lovely folks for coming out. The Broken Halos have the most supportive and loyal fans, and we're extremely grateful." They cheer again, and I have to raise my hand and ask them to let me finish. "You don't know how much you being here means to The Broken Halos, to me, and to my family, the

Colemans. This place is our livelihood, and we appreciate each and every one of you."

The band claps and hollers their thanks to the fans, which only gets them hyped up again. I realize I won't have a chance to do much more talking. And that's not why they're here anyway. I take my place at the mic stand again, sliding it back into place and choosing to stay in one place for this song. Olive signals the person working the stage lights, and they dim nearly instantly. My presence at the mic stand and the lights dimming, quiets the crowd.

"This song is new. I only wrote it since being back home on the farm. But it has become one of my favorites. This place, this soil you're standing on, is generations, seasons, and hours of hard work. Of blood, sweat, and tears. Of sacrifice, toil, and celebration. So what better place to debut our song, 'Nothing Changes Around Here.'"

After the crowd quiets, Jax begins, and I wait for my chord to come in on.

<u>Nothing Changes Around Here</u>
These acres of soil and crop fields
They represent generations of blood, sweat, and tears
The chipped paint on the porch swing
Nothing changes around here

Old pictures line the walls
Showing better days when life wasn't so hard
That old crack in the wooden step
Giving me away on late nights of fun
Nothing changes around here

Take me back to those days

When this old farm and dusty house was all I ever needed—or
wanted
To the carefree days of tag in corn fields and leapfrog over
pumpkins
Nothing changes around here—and I hate it

Waking up to the rooster crowing and the fresh scent of dirt in
the air
Of leaves changing and nights growing crisp
Gathering around while Dad says a prayer—but all I see is the
empty spot where he should be

Take me back to those days
When this old farm and dusty house was all I ever needed—or
wanted
To the carefree days of tag in corn fields and leapfrog over
pumpkins
Nothing changes around here—and I miss it

By the end, I'm crying. I glance over at the black curtains to
where Mom, Dad, Emmaline, and Garrison are standing and
see them crying too. My heart squeezes, and I smile. It's the first
time I've sung and have ever felt as if they're proud of me. It
feels like, for the first time, Mom and Dad get it. They understand what I'm doing, in Portland, with the band, with my life.
The realization is astonishing, but there's also a finality to it.

# Chapter Thirty-Three

## AXEL

I WOULD BE AN IDIOT IF I DIDN'T NOTICE THE EXUBERANCE exuding from Lula as she performed on that stage tonight. It was the most beautiful thing I've ever witnessed and the most devastating. When she's performing, she comes alive. While I've been fortunate enough to see the real and raw version of Lula Coleman over the last few weeks, I've missed this version. It's a beauty in a completely different dimension.

It makes my decision an even more difficult one.

The past two days, I've been blindfolded. I thought it was Lula who needed to decide what she wants. But I have a decision to make too.

I won't stand in the way of her doing what she just did tonight. She owes it to herself to feel that alive, that rush. It's obvious to everyone that singing and performing are exactly what Lula should be doing with her life. What kind of jerk would I be if I stood in the way of that? If I hindered that talent in any way?

After the concert wraps up, Lula hugs Mr. and Mrs.

Coleman and Garrison. And even Emmaline. She hops off the stage and weaves through the crowd and rushes toward me, a huge smile plastered on her face. I don't hesitate when she reaches me; I wrap her up and hug her tight to my chest, breathing in her cherry-blossom-scented hair.

"What'd you think?" she asks after we break apart.

"It was amazing. You were amazing."

She squeals and crouches so she's eye level with Sadie. "So?"

"It was so good." Sadie jumps up and down before throwing her arms around Lula's neck.

Lula giggles. "Thank you. I am so glad you got to be here."

"Mommy says I have to go now. Daddy told her my bedtime." She frowns at me.

"Hey, if you don't want to stick to your bedtime, then you don't have to go at all," I threaten.

"No, no, no," she whines. "I'm sorry."

"Besides, it's already way past your bedtime."

Joanie picks up Sadie. "Lula, you were real good. I could listen to you sing all day."

"Thank you," Lula says.

"I better get going. I promised I'd get this little monkey to the hotel in a hurry and into bed. I don't want to screw up my privileges," Joanie says.

"Sadie, say goodbye to Lula. She's leaving tomorrow so you won't get to see her," I say, having a difficult time getting the words out.

"Will I see you the next day?"

Lula glances back and forth between me and Sadie. "Um, no sweetie. I have to go back to Portland. So we gotta say goodbye now it looks like. But I'll be back to visit soon. And I'm hoping you and your daddy will come visit me too. Would you like to come to Portland?"

My gut twists.

Sadie grins, nodding. "Yes! But where is Portland?"

"Not too far," Lula exhales the words on a laugh.

"Okay, goodnight, baby." I give Sadie a kiss on the cheek. It's half killing me to let her go with Joanie. But what are my grounds? Joanie is her mother, whether I like it or not. "I love you," I choke out.

"Love you too, Daddy."

"She'll be fine," Joanie tries to reassure me but it doesn't help. "I have your number. And Sadie is old enough to help me out with whatever I don't know." She gives me a forced smile. "Nice to meet you, Lula."

"And you. Bye, Sadie." Lula waves.

"Night, Daddy." Sadie waves and blows me a kiss over Joanie's shoulder.

I catch her kiss and pretend to shove it in my pocket. My chest heaves, and when I turn around, I remember the difficult decisions are just beginning.

"Wow, you let her go with Joanie, huh? I'm surprised."

"What was I supposed to do? She's her mother."

"Right." She stares at her feet. "I'm sorry."

My mind battles with what my heart wants and I'm afraid which one will win. Which one will have the stupid idea or make the stupid decision.

"Will you spend the night with me?" And there it is. Apparently my heart won.

She doesn't hesitate in her response. "Yes."

We spend the night wrapped in one another's arms, relishing in each touch, each kiss, each pleasure. We talk about our days together. We talk about our past.

We don't talk about our future.

In the early morning hour, the light peers through the slats of the blinds. We're tucked underneath the comforter in my bed. Our bodies are entangled like we're a couple of contortionists. We cling to one another as if we need the other for air to breathe. And in a way, I suppose that's true. Just the thought of being without her causes my chest to constrict.

Maybe spending this one last night together was a mistake.

Lula intertwines her fingers in mine while I press my bare chest into the hot skin of her back. I kiss a trail down her neck and her arm before resting my chin on her shoulder.

"Don't let me go," Lula whispers.

"Never." It's a promise I'm not sure I can keep. But it's the one I *want* to keep.

IT'S EARLY when we say goodbye. The band climbs into the rental van. I try to wait patiently while Lula says goodbye to her family. Mrs. Coleman cries but wipes each tear with her hankie before it has a chance to roll down her cheek. Mr. Coleman's eyes are red rimmed, and I wonder if maybe he got all of his crying out already. Garrison holds their hug for a long time. The tears Emmaline sheds are the most surprising. I can tell Lula is thrown off by this as well.

After what feels like forever, it's finally just the two of us standing in the parking lot that's so close to empty it's eerie.

We're awkward.

I open my palms, and she slips her hands into mine. We stare into one another's eyes. Both of us having plenty to say but neither one knowing exactly how to go about it.

Until finally I say, "You need to go on that tour."

Her jaw hangs open. "What?"

"What you do on that stage is incredible. The way you

come alive is breathtaking. I could never ask you not to do that. And I won't."

"But you said if I go on tour, that's it for us."

"I know what I said. And I'm not sure I'm not saying it now. But all I know is, you can't *not* sing. You were born for it." I rub the backs of her hands with my thumbs.

"I don't want this to be over." Tears slide down her cheeks.

"I don't want that either."

"Then what are we gonna do?"

"We do what we can. To try to keep this . . . keep us . . . something."

Her eyes widen. "You sure about this?"

"You leaving, Joanie coming back, none of it matters. You're it for me."

Relief washes across her face and she grips my hands tighter. "We'll make this work."

I swallow the lump in my throat. "I love you, Lu."

She sniffs. "Leaving you is harder than I ever imagined it would be."

"I feel the same way. But I don't think it's meant to be easy. If it were, it wouldn't be worth holding onto."

She nods, still crying.

"You better go." I release my grip, dropping her hands. And I feel as if I just dropped my heart at the same time.

She flings her arms around me and we cling to one another as if our lives depend on it.

"I love you, Axel," she whispers into my ear.

I take her face in my palms and draw her in close. I kiss her earnestly until we're both panting for air. When I release her, I have to physically take a step backward so I'm not tempted to sweep her up into my arms again. She does the same which oddly makes me smile. She turns her back to me, and I watch her walk toward to van. She whips around and mouths *I love you.*

The inaudible words nearly crumple me to the ground like dust. They take me back to our earlier days together. My chest is tight and my vision blurs with tears I've been fighting back for years.

# Chapter Thirty-Four
### AXEL

It's Thanksgiving weekend. Lula has been gone for nearly four weeks. The length of time we've been apart has been wearing on me. She says we'll have to settle for FaceTime as she isn't able to return home for the holiday. The band is rehearsing and spending day in the studio so the new album *Generations* will be ready to release after the first of the year.

Lula has been too busy to get away for a single weekend. I expected her to return after Emmaline had the baby. If even for only a day. But since the baby is already two weeks old, I should quit holding my breath.

Sadie is packing an overnight bag for Joanie's. She's getting better at it now that she's stayed there a handful of times. Joanie found a small apartment to rent in the next town over. She also found a position as a bank teller. Despite Joanie assuring me she's planning on staying in the area, I have my doubts. What happens when she realizes this is it?

"Hurry up with those boots or you're gonna miss the movie." I wait at the door of the newlywed house, Sadie's backpack in my hand.

"I'm coming, I'm coming." She rushes past me, hugging her pillow and Perry, the stuffed polar bear, to her chest.

Sadie is non-stop chatter the entire drive to Joanie's apartment. She's excited, and, at times, I will admit I'm jealous. Handing her off to Joanie isn't always easy. Not after I've been the one raising her for three years on my own. But I keep telling myself that Joanie is Sadie's mother.

And I also hate to admit, Sadie has been the happiest I've ever seen her. Bouncing back and forth between Joanie's apartment and the newlywed house has been easier on her than I expected. She wasn't thrilled by the idea that her mom and I weren't going to live together. But I also don't think she quite understands the logistics of it all anyway. For now, this works.

I knock on Joanie's front door. It's strange to be knocking at my daughter's mother's place, but it is what it is. She opens it in a flurry, a bright smile on her face.

"Come in, come in, it's freezing out there," she says, swooping Sadie into a hug.

She takes the backpack from me and ushers us inside and out of the cold air assaulting my back.

"How are you?" I ask, just trying to be polite.

"I'm good, thanks. Better than good, now that Sadie is here."

"Can we still go to the movie?"

Joanie glances at the time on her phone. "Of course, plenty of time."

"Okay, I'm gonna head out. I'll see you tomorrow before Thanksgiving dinner." I crouch on one knee in front of Sadie and brush the dark hair from her face.

"Okay, Daddy." She loops her arms around my neck and kisses me on the cheek.

"You could come with us if you want? To the movies?"

I rise, rubbing at the back of my neck. "Nah, this feels like more of a mother-daughter movie. I'll sit this one out."

I duck out of the apartment and make my way back to my truck. I push away my worries about leaving my little girl with someone who partially feels like a stranger.

Back at the house, I try to busy myself by packing up a few more boxes. A knock on my door causes me to jump. I open it, and the cold wind swooshes inside while Emmaline stands on my stoop.

"C'mon in." I step aside, allowing her to enter.

"Hey, sorry to just stop by without calling first." She steps inside. She leaves her boots on, which tells me she's not planning to stay long.

"What's up?"

Emmaline plops onto the sofa. I glance around, wondering if maybe I was wrong regarding the quick visit and should offer her something to drink.

"Jackson is coming tomorrow. For Thanksgiving dinner." She blows air out of her puffed-up cheeks.

"Good." This news isn't surprising. Since the baby arrived, Jackson has been to the farmhouse every day.

"It is, isn't it? Then why am I so worried?"

I shrug. This issue, again, is not really my territory.

"Since we've decided to work on our marriage, things have been great between us. But he still won't move back into the farmhouse."

I frown. "How does he expect to work on your marriage if he doesn't want to move back in with you?"

She stands and begins pacing in the small living room. "I've been thinking." She chews on her thumbnail while continuing to pace. "Before you and Sadie moved into the newlywed house, we'd been using it as storage. It was a mess, so I had never considered it as an option. But since we fixed it up, and now you and Sadie are moving out . . . maybe Jackson would agree to move in here."

I raise my brows. "Maybe. Couldn't hurt to ask him."

"It's still on the Coleman property, but at least here, we would have our own space."

"I think it's a reasonable suggestion. I'm closing on my house in three weeks. Which means you could all be in here, together, in time for Christmas."

She smiles at me, the thought of that probably comforting to her.

"I'm sorry, I don't mean to rush you out."

"It's fine. Believe me, three years of living here has been beyond generous. I think I've just about overstayed my welcome."

"Never. You'll always be welcome." She smiles and heads to the door, her chin raised a bit higher than when she first came in. "Joanie still coming for dinner tomorrow?"

"Yeah, that all right?"

"Of course. You and Sadie are family. And, well, since Joanie is Sadie's mother, then I suppose that makes her family too."

Her intentions are kind. But something about calling Joanie family—in relation to the Colemans—doesn't sit well.

"You think Lula will surprise us with a visit?"

It's something I realize I want more than anything else. "Probably shouldn't hold our breath."

She leaves without saying another word. I spend the rest of the evening packing boxes and checking my phone for texts from Lula like a madman.

One comes late, when I'm getting ready for bed and brushing my teeth. Just three simple words.

But it's enough.

THE NEXT DAY, we all crowd around the table in the Coleman farmhouse dining room. The kids are seated at a small table in the kitchen. It's not much different from prior years. Except Joanie is next to me. And I feel as if she's the elephant in the room, despite the Colemans trying to make her feel welcome.

Jackson rests his hand on Emmaline's on the tabletop. Emmaline seems genuinely happy. And calm.

Joanie feels too close to me. I'm far too aware of the heat generating off her body. Her skirt is too short, and her sweater cut too low for a family dinner. Though Joanie never cared much about what was expected of her. I guess that was something I once admired about her.

My phone rings loudly, and I jump. I shift in my seat, yanking it from my jeans' front pocket. "Sorry," I mutter. It's Lula's face on the screen, and I don't overthink how it might come across as rude if I answer. "Hey, Lula." My chest heaves at the sight of her beautiful, happy face smiling back at me.

"Happy Thanksgiving," she says. "Ahh, I miss you."

"Miss you too."

Garrison clears his throat, and I glance up, my cheeks blushing with heat.

"Say hello to your family." I hold the phone out, panning back and forth over all the faces around the table and the kid's table too. "Say happy Thanksgiving to Lula, everyone."

There's a choir of *hellos*, *I miss yous*, and *happy Thanksgivings* from everyone.

Sadie jumps up from the kid's table and rushes toward my phone. "Hi, Lula! I miss you!" she yells as if Lula being on FaceTime makes it harder for her to hear. "When are you coming home?"

The question swirls around in my mind at least a hundred times a day. But having Sadie ask it out loud causes a pause on the other end of the phone as well as a hush at the grown-up table.

"Soon, I hope. I miss you so much, Sadie."

Sadie blows her a kiss and runs back to the kid's table, black olives sticking to the tips of her fingers.

"Say hello to your Auntie Lula, Juliette," Emmaline says, holding up the newborn baby with a head full of dark hair.

I hold the phone out so Lula can get a good view of the baby bundled in a colorful afghan made by Nonna.

"Aww, I can't wait to meet you in person, Juliette," Lula murmurs.

"Hey, perfect timing, Lu," Mr. Coleman says. "We were just gonna say grace." He glances around the table. "Let's all hold hands."

I hold the phone in one hand, almost as if Lula is here with us. Joanie takes my free hand. Garrison is on my other side, and he rests his hand on my arm.

"Nice to have you with us, Sis," Garrison whispers, leaning closer to my phone.

After Mr. Coleman says grace, we all say, "Amen," in unison.

I hardly get another peek at Lula on my screen when she says, "Axel, can I talk to you in private for a moment?"

"Uh . . ." I glance around, standing and tossing my cloth

napkin with an assortment of fall-colored leaves embroidered on it. "Sure. Please excuse me."

I walk through the kitchen and step into the office, hoping for some privacy there. "What's going on? Everything okay?"

"You didn't tell me Joanie would be there for dinner?"

I rub at the back of my neck. "Yeah, sorry. I didn't think I should let her spend Thanksgiving alone."

She's quiet but smiling.

"I didn't think you were the jealous type. It's kinda hot," I tease, leaning against one of the dusty bookcases.

She gasps and grins. "I'm not jealous. But . . ." She bites her lower lip. "I do miss you, and I'm all the way over here, and you're there. And she's showing off enough cleavage you could lose an entire pumpkin pie down her shirt."

I laugh. "You're cute when you're jealous."

She pouts.

"And hey, you could've been here sitting right between Joanie and me and competing with who's showing off the most cleavage. Believe me, I wouldn't be complaining."

She groans. "I know, I wish I could. I wish I could be there."

"Me too." I pace the floor in the office, studying her on my phone and really feeling the distance between us. "But it won't be long now, right?"

"Christmas. If we all work our asses off and get this album done before then."

"Whoever isn't pulling their weight, you let me know." I try to sound threatening but fail. I'm not that guy. Especially not since I started dating Lula.

"Axel," she says my name and her voice causes my nerves to tingle. "I love you."

"Love you too. Happy Thanksgiving, Lu."

# Chapter Thirty-Five

## LULA

THE BURNT AND ROBUST SCENT OF ARABICA COFFEE afflicts my senses, and my brain signals my eyes to flutter open. A giant paper cup with Ink Café scrawled across it floats in my line of vision. My hands go to it without hesitation. I've barely sat up, and Olive is already crawling underneath my covers next to me. I lean against my headboard and find her mirroring my position, her eyes peering into mine.

"Hey," she says, giving me a weak smile.

I smile back. "Hey."

"Thought a bit of Ink might do you some good."

"Thanks." I take a sip, and the strong espresso mixed with vanilla is soothing. "Did you bring any macaroons?"

"Sorry, they were out."

I sigh. "That figures."

"Did you get any sleep?"

"A couple hours. I wanted to make sure Cody and Jax had the bridge just right on 'Generations.'" I exhale a big yawn, rubbing the sleep from my eyes.

"Y'all know I want to perfect that song—I want to perfect all of our songs—but working yourself to death won't help anybody."

"That's not what I'm doing," I say incredulously, leaning forward.

When she doesn't respond, I turn my attention to her and find her with brows raised.

"No? Cause you could've fooled me."

"If we can get these last two songs nailed down, we can get home for Christmas."

She hunches a shoulder. "Hey, I'm not trying to tell you how to process your crap, I'm just here to be a soundboard for you. And provide you with the city's worst coffee."

She tips her cup into mine, and I can't help it, I laugh.

"Are you kidding? Whoever thought to combine espresso and tattoos is a genius. I should've used the idea at the pumpkin patch."

Olive snorts. "Pretty sure promoting tattoos at a pumpkin patch is a business tactic no one else has thought of."

My smile remains, but my heart hurts thinking about the pumpkin patch. The Coleman Family Farm. Axel. I miss seeing his sweaty curls sneak out underneath his backwards baseball hat, miss the feeling of his strong arms wrapped around my body.

Facetime just isn't the same as being with someone in person.

"You sure you don't want to sneak back home? Just for a day? I can cover for you."

Olive's question snaps me out of my Axel-filled trance. I turn to look at her, a pout on my lips. "No. You know that's impossible." I rest my head on her shoulder. "And besides, the faster we bust out these tracks, the faster I can get back to him."

The only thing getting me through our long-distance relationship is focusing on preparing the album for release.

AT THE STUDIO, which is quickly becoming my second home these days, Cody paces the floor, annoyed. Oscar and Jax are still arguing over our song "Generations". I sit in the box, propped on a stool with the mic stand between my legs, waiting. I throw my head back and groan, but thankful I can't hear their bickering in here.

Olive's voice sounds through the speaker. "Y'all just sit tight, Lu."

"Like I have a choice," I mutter.

As the rest of the band argues in the studio, I slide my phone out of my back pocket. I open Instagram and mindlessly scroll past posts of Bon Iver playing at The Vision in Chicago, Vampire Weekend on vacation in Bali, baby Juliette snuggled in an afghan only Nonna could make, and Garrison posing on the top of Misery Ridge Trail. I post a quick comment on Garrison's pic before continuing to scroll.

A photo of Kade and McKayla catches my attention, and my thumb scrolls back to do a double take. It's a reminder of their upcoming wedding. Rather than accelerating, it feels as if my heartbeat slows to practically nonexistent. It's not as if this is news I wasn't aware of. I knew Kade was getting married at Christmas. But for some reason, seeing it now, with the details of the ceremony and the reception—held inside their main barn—makes it real.

The picture, the announcement, it sends my brain reeling. The memories take off, rushing to my mind at warp speed.

Instead of thinking about Kade, I think about my family. How they've been friends with the Finleys for years. And how they're planning on attending the wedding. Mama told me so in our last Sunday phone conversation.

My mind is cruel. Reminding me that even though I'm gone, life back home goes on without me. My thoughts shift to Axel. Missing him causes my chest to ache like a heavy stone is pressing into it.

"All right, Lu." Jax's voice interrupts my thoughts. "You ready to go?"

"Been ready," I mumble.

His shoulders visually collapse. "Thank God for you." He smiles. "Okay, let's rock n' roll."

Accept I'm not ready. My voice is melodious, my tone rhapsodic, but my mind is distracted. It's somewhere else. And it doesn't take Jax long to realize.

The music stops streaming through the tinny speakers inside the booth. Jax presses the button on the soundboard. "What's up? Thought you were ready?"

"I am," I lie.

He groans. "Okay, let's start again."

But on the second go around, it's the same. My heart isn't in it. My headspace is fuzzy.

Jax's voice again. "Lula," he says my name long and on an exhale. "Take five."

It's probably the very last thing he wants to say to me. But if he can tell my heart isn't in it, so will everyone else. He slips into the booth, annoyance smeared across his face. He drags another stool over close to me and sits.

"We all know you miss Axel. But you have a job to do. And we need you to do it."

He's using his tough-love tone with me. I hate it's come to

that. But mostly, I hate that he's right. My chest is tight and my throat thick. But I nod.

It's silly.

Jax pats my leg. "We do this and we all get to go home for Christmas."

That reminder is the boost I need.

# Chapter Thirty-Six

## AXEL

The new house is only six minutes from the farm. Sadie had me time it one day on our drive home. It's convenient being close, but it still gives me and Sadie a bit of our own space.

The transition was rough on Sadie at first. Being so far from Ariel and Caleb was hard. But our new home is in a small housing development, set at the end of a cul-de-sac. A few kids around her age live in the neighborhood, so it has made the transition easier on her.

Since Sadie has been spending time with Joanie, I have found myself with free time of my own. I've gone duck hunting with Garrison a few times. It's not really my thing, but if I don't do something to stay busy, my mind wanders to Lula. I just miss her so damn much.

We've hardly spoken the last two weeks. Our schedules are opposite. I'm busy on the farm, she's busy in the studio. I've got Sadie, and she's got the band. But I can't help from worrying if our relationship will withstand the long distance.

LULA

Have some free time tonight. Up for a risqué
Facetime session?

As exciting as that sounds, I'd rather save our
intimate moments until we can be together in
person.

Remember what happened last time?

LULA

Poor Sadie! I'm not sure she'll ever recover.

My face heats. Already I'm aroused at the memory of our
Facetime escapade. It was a first for me and it took some
convincing. But I love Lula and I think it's clear I'd do just
about anything for her. Except after Sadie barged into my room
during the middle of it, I'm not sure Lula will ever talk me into
it again.

Rain check until we can be together in person
at Christmas?

LULA

About that.

Don't tell me.

LULA

It looks like we're scheduled to be in the
studio until Christmas Eve.

My jaw ticks.

You promised Sadie you'd be home
Christmas morning.

LULA

I'm sorry. I'm doing the best I can. I want to
be there, but the band needs me here.

As disappointed as I am by Lula's confession, it's Sadie's little heart I'm worried about. She's been let down too many times in her short life. This is the reason why I didn't want to get close to a woman, because I didn't want Sadie to get close to her either.

Without a doubt, my heart wants Lula. But this isn't about me. I'm a father and I'll always put Sadie first.

And I won't do this through texting. Call me old school, but a conversation as important as this should be done in person. Since that's not possible, I do the next best thing and call Lula.

"Axel, please. I already feel bad enough," she says into the phone, her voice getting my emotions stirring.

I miss her so much.

"Hey, Lu. I'm sorry too."

"Axel," is all she says on an exhaled breath.

It's as if she knows. And maybe we've been kidding ourselves this whole time. Maybe this was never supposed to work.

But we tried. And I'm not ready for it to be over.

I swallow the lump rising in my throat. "I think it will be best for both of us, and Sadie, if we took a break."

"Don't do this, please. We're so close. I'll be home soon," she pleads.

"With the way things have been going since you left, I'd say, you already are home. There in Portland. There, with the band."

"It's only a few days long than I was originally planning. What's a few days?" She sniffs and my chest tightens. She's crying.

"Those few days make all the difference to a little girl you made a promise to. And I made a promise to her that I'd protect her and not let anyone hurt her."

She's quiet for a moment.

"I love you. So damn much. But I think this relationship is draining us both."

"You're right," she surprises me when she finally speaks into the phone. "As much as I don't want you to be, you're right. I'm sorry."

"Me too."

She sniffs. "I should go."

"Whenever you get here, you better come find me. I miss you."

"Miss you too."

SITTING IN THE DUCK BLIND, freezing my butt off with Garrison and Wiley, Garrison tells me it will get easier. But what does he know? He's never been in love.

"We're just taking a break, that's all."

"Look," Garrison says quietly, ticking off on his fingers, "you're a handsome young guy. You've got a great job. You've got a house." His shotgun is propped against his shoulder. "You're marriage material. All I'm saying is, if it doesn't work out with my sister, you need to have a backup plan. Making your dating profile will be a cinch."

"Yeah, thanks, but no thanks," I mutter, taking a sip of hot coffee from my travel mug.

I was doing just fine before Lula entered my life. I can do it again. Except now, my heart knows what it's like to be in love. And ever since Lula left, it feels as if a part of it is missing. Which feels like a part of me is missing.

"Just say the word, I'm happy to help," Garrison says. "I'm a pro at composing dating app profiles."

"I'm not sure that's something you should be proud of," I tease.

"Garrison," Wiley drawls, a toothpick poking out the corner of his mouth, "leave the man alone."

But Garrison ignores him. "I can see you're still unsure. And that's okay. We'll get you there soon enough."

I'm glad one of us is so confident.

"I'm not so sure."

"It's no surprise you're having a rough go at it," Wiley says. "Letting go of an angel is cruel, trust me."

My chest constricts at his words. I haven't let go of Lula. Not yet. And hopefully, never.

Wiley removes his camo hat and wipes at his brow. "I said goodbye to my Violet twenty years ago. Never could replace her. That's the thing about angels, they're irreplaceable."

This is new information I hadn't known about Wiley. That he once had a wife. Possibly children. I've been so busy keeping to myself the last three years, not wanting to let anyone in. Because when you do, they just leave. Like Joanie. Like Lula. And like Violet.

A lump forms in my throat, and I can't seem to speak. When Wiley glances over his shoulder at me, I give him a nod of understanding.

"But with time, it gets easier." Garrison raises his brows at Wiley, as if he's hoping he'll agree, but Wiley just returns his focus to the pond.

"And what do you know about being in love?" My words come out harsher than I intended.

"Don't do that. Don't try to act like I know nothing about love."

I straighten, my shoulders tight with tension.

"Just because I've never been in love with a woman doesn't mean I don't know about what it feels like to lose someone I love. At least the person you love is still alive," his tone is heavy. "You ever wonder why I date women who aren't looking for anything serious?"

I hadn't given it much thought.

"I loved Riley. And he died." He flicks his attention away from me. "So don't act like you're the only one who knows what it's like to love someone and have them leave you."

My chest throbs with unforgiving anguish as a result of my foolishness.

# Chapter Thirty-Seven

## LULA

It's Christmas Eve, and once again, I'm with the band in the studio. But we've sworn we'll leave early enough not to be here at midnight so we're at least not here on Christmas. This is a dream for most, I realize, but spending Christmas in a studio is depressing.

We sent Mick home hours ago to be with his family. His wife, Ashley, would never forgive us if we occupied him on Christmas Eve like we did on Thanksgiving.

I FaceTimed with Mom and Dad this morning. Emmaline showed off baby Juliette in her Christmas jammies, and I told her I couldn't wait to meet her on the twenty-seventh. Ariel sang Jingle Bells for me. A very nice rendition, but maybe I'll be giving her voice lessons as a Christmas gift next year. I had to catch Garrison by text this morning on his way out to guide a hike on Three Sisters.

I'm distracted tonight. While I stand in the recording booth singing the lyrics for "Nothing Changes Around Here," how can I not think about home?

Back on the Coleman Family Farm, the family will gather around Nonna's old piano. She'll play Christmas carols while the family sings along. Granddad will take out his well-aged Bible next, and he'll read the Christmas story. Mom will make her homemade eggnog that the Coleman kids will likely turn their noses up at but then drink the entire crystal punch bowl to the last drop. Emmaline will hang the ceramic baby Jesus ornament that Nonna made since I'm not there to argue with her that it's my turn.

"No, no, no," Cody says through the speaker inside the booth. "Something is off. You're not off-key, but something is off." He scrubs a hand down his face. "Start again."

I roll my eyes but don't argue because he's right. Something *is* off. My body is here, in the studio, physically. But my heart and mind are home, at the farmhouse. And singing a song about the familiar place I grew up is giving me all kinds of nostalgia.

"C'mon, Lu," Jax says through the speakers. "Get this right, and we can all finally go home."

Home.

I clutch the mic with both hands, close my eyes, and try to focus, pushing away my deep longing to be at the very place I'm singing about. To be with the people that make that place home. I begin the song again, but this time it isn't the nostalgia of homemade eggnog and Christmas carols that distracts me. It's Axel. And Sadie. I know they've been celebrating Christmas with the Colemans for a few years, but thinking about them being there now, when I'm not, is gutting.

"Lula, please," Jax pleads.

My eyes fly open. "Sorry."

Olive nudges Jax out of the way and pushes the speaker button. "Don't listen to him, Lula. This song is going to be our first single, and it needs to be perfect. You can't rush it. Take your time until you feel it's right."

Jax drops his chin to his chest.

I suck in my lower lip, my anxiety bubbling in my chest. The band is tired. They want to go home. They nailed down their instrumental portion days ago. Oscar and Davey have parents nearby they probably want to spend Christmas with. Jax, Olive, and I were planning on going out for Chinese food, sleeping late, and opening presents together in the afternoon. Then Jax would head to Juniper Ridge with me on the 27th.

Jax groans through the speaker. "Olive is right. This can't be rushed. You gotta get it perfect. If you're not feeling it, neither will our fans."

The boost from Jax helps to ease the tension zipping through me. He's right. I take hold of the mic again, shutting my eyes and inhaling deeply. To get this perfect, I need to force away any thoughts of Axel. I need to remember what it felt like to come home after being gone for so many years. What it felt like to grow up on the farm. The fields—plentiful and thriving. The pumpkins in all their orange glory, the smells of hay and animals, and the old farmhouse. All the old creaks and chipped paint.

Without opening my eyes, I say, "Okay, let's go again."

The music begins, introducing "Nothing Changes Around Here," just as I imagined the band would play it. The music they composed, combined with my lyrics, meshed in a way I couldn't dream possible. I keep my eyes closed, my breathing even, while my brain continues sifting through images of the Coleman Family Farm. I see our school photos on the hallway wall upstairs, an old family picture of us in the pumpkin patch, and the one of Riley in his uniform.

My heart lodges in my throat, but only momentarily.

I part my lips and begin singing, my tone smooth and airy, almost sounding like someone else's voice entirely. But it's mine. It's my family I'm singing about. It's my memories, it's my feelings. My voice crescendos at all the correct places, and I feel an out-of-body experience. As if my soul is separating and lifting from my body. I stand, clutch the mic tighter, and sing about Riley and hating change, my soul peering down in anguish.

By the time the song finishes, I don't seem to notice it has ended. I remain in place, frozen, eyes pinched shut. My cheeks are wet with tears, and I don't bother wiping them away. My trembling fingers still cling to the mic.

"That was amazing," Jax says softly through the speakers.

And it felt amazing.

My eyes finally flutter open.

"It was breathtaking." Olive peers through the glass at me, swiping her sleeve underneath her eye.

My heartbeat accelerates because I know I got it right, and that was the one. But in this moment, I don't only feel elated to have finally gotten it right, I feel a sense of urgency. Singing about the place where I grew up and that I found most comforting of all, I realize it's still that place for me. Because that is home.

"That's the one, Lula," Cody says. "Now, c'mon, get outta there so we can all go home."

There's that word again: *Home.*

Images of a typical Christmas Eve on the Coleman Family Farm pop into my mind again. I filter through the memories because some are more painful than others. Riley, who, without fail, wore a Santa hat all Christmas Eve and Christmas Day, even while he did his chores on the farm. The scent of Mom's molasses cookies wafting through the house. It's Nonna's recipe, but Mom had to tweak it because Nonna wouldn't give up any of her secrets. It took years for her to perfect it. The sound of Dad's hearty voice as he *ho, ho, ho'ed* his way through handing out Christmas gifts.

Axel comes to my mind next. And I'm not sure what that looks like—a Christmas with Axel and Sadie at the Colemans farmhouse. Even though he's been there celebrating with them for the past three years, I have not. I imagine Sadie fitting right in, squeezing in between Ariel and Caleb. Knowing Mom and Dad, they treat Sadie as one of their grandchildren, giving her one expensive gift she had on the top of her Christmas wish list, one useful gift, and one gift of their choice, something they think she'd like.

Seeing as Axel and Garrison are besties, I can picture them sidled up next to one another on the sofa, drinking spiked eggnog to get them through the long day. Dad probably asks Axel to cut the ham, and Mom may ask him to say grace before Christmas dinner.

"Lula? You okay?" Olive's soft voice comes through the speaker.

*Am I okay?*

But I know the answer to that. No, I'm not okay. I've spent nearly a decade with the band. We've worked alongside one another, some of us have lived together, we've toured together, we've rehearsed for twenty-four hours non-stop at times. And while the band feels like home, especially after all these years and all we've shared, nothing will quite feel the same as Juniper Ridge.

Nothing will feel quite the same as seeing Axel working in the Coleman fields, toiling the soil. He takes pride in the farm when it isn't even in his blood. He loves that place maybe even more than I do. He respects it. And it only makes me respect him more.

But I don't simply respect him, I love him. I love him for the way he treats the farm, my family, and Sadie. I love him for the way he treats me and the way he loves me. It's an unbridled love. He doesn't leave his heart vulnerable. When Joanie left him and Sadie, he built a wall around himself and, more importantly, his heart. But with me, he let that imaginary wall down. He allowed his heart to be vulnerable and gave it to me. And then I gave it back to him. Willingly.

I have been so stupid.

I rush out of the recording booth and shove past Olive and Jax. I yank my purse and jacket from underneath a sleeping Oscar.

"Hey, Lula? You okay?" Jax sidles up next to me.

"I've gotta go home." I don't realize until I've spoken that tears are still streaming down my face.

"Yeah, we're coming. Just hold on." Olive throws her coat on without taking her eyes off me.

"No, I mean, I've got to go *home*." I enunciate the last word and look pointedly at Jax through my glossy vision.

"Oh," he says flatly. "Oh." Realization sets in. "Tonight?" He glances at his phone. "But it's nearly midnight. On Christmas Eve. I doubt there are any flights."

"We could drive?" Olive suggests.

I whip my attention to her, and she shrugs. "We?" I ask.

"I planned to spend Christmas with you. Do you think I'm gonna just let you ditch me?"

"Same," Jax says."

I stab my arms into my coat. "You guys don't have to do that." I pull up the airline's website and start searching for a flight.

"I'm super thrilled that you wanna get home for Christmas and all, but so do I." Oscar climbs off the couch, stretching while yawning. "So good luck with that. Keep me posted if we're actually doing this whole tour thing. You know, once Lula has come back down to reality."

"Oh no, she's not screwing this up for us. We've worked way too hard to quit now." Cody puts his coat on while he stomps to the door. "We're putting this album out on January 1st and then going on tour," he calls over his shoulder on his way out.

My insides plummet to the floor when I see no flights to Redmond airport until late in the afternoon on Christmas Day. By then, all the morning traditions—my favorite ones—will be over. Christmas dinner will also be finished. I'll get there just in time to find Dad napping on his recliner and Mom cleaning the kitchen.

"There are no flights." Disappointment blooms in my chest.

I consider driving, but with the recently fallen snow in the city, the mountain pass will have substantially more. Without winter tires, I'm not sure I'll make it.

"I'll drive," Jax suggests.

I turn around to face him. "No, I can't let you do that. Besides, you need to stay and get the track done and sent off."

"I'll stay," Davey pipes up. "I'll finish the track and get it to Mick so he can send it to the label."

A pang of regret momentarily slides through me. Davey was in a hurry to get home tonight. But, I suppose by now, it's already Christmas Day.

"One week, Lula. That's it. You have one week," he warns.

"Less than a week," Jax interjects.

"Then you're back here, your mind is focused on The Broken Halos, and we go on tour."

He sounds like Mick. But I don't mind. He's right. We go on tour in one week. The album is set to release on January 1st, and we leave the morning after our interview at two local Portland radio stations. Our first concert is on January 2nd in Denver, Colorado.

"I'll be here," I assure him, giving him a hug. "Thank you," I whisper in his ear.

"Thanks, man." Jax fist bumps Davey.

I throw my purse over my head and across my shoulder. "You guys don't have to do this."

"Are you kidding?" Olive says brightly. "We're family. And family spends the holidays together."

BY THE TIME we pack our bags, fill Jax's gas tank, and I pick up a very important snack at the gas station, it's after one in the morning. We make it over the snowy, though luckily not icy pass, by 3:00 a.m. It takes over another hour before we pull into the long driveway of the Coleman Family Farm. I'm relieved there's less snow blanketing the ground here in town than there was on the mountain pass.

Spotting the bright white and twinkling Christmas lights outlining the peaks of the farmhouse roof, a warm, fuzzy feeling unfurls in my chest. Snow covers the fields, and it makes everything appear as if it's sleeping. Winter used to be one of my favorite seasons growing up here. It was our least busy season, and we had endless snow to play with.

At last, I'm home.

The three of us enter through the back door, using my key, which was surprisingly trusted to me on my last visit. Apparently, I'm finally a Coleman once again. The house is quiet, and the Christmas tree lights have been left on. The sight of it nearly steals the breath from my lungs. It's cozy and inviting and confirms my frantic desire to make it home for Christmas.

I wave to Olive and Jax to follow me up the stairs, motioning for them to skip the creaky fourth step. This time, I take them into Garrison's room, where he's set up two cots.

Garrison stirs in his bed but doesn't fully wake. The three of us take turns in the bathroom brushing our teeth before I whisper goodnight to them and tiptoe back downstairs. I want to be awake when my family comes downstairs in the morning.

The gifts I sent a few weeks ago have been dispersed underneath the Christmas tree. The one wrapped in crinkled Disney princess paper and addressed to Ariel appears as if it's had its fair share of snooping. But there's one gift I still need to wrap. I'm relieved when I spot Mom's gift-wrapping station in the corner of the living room; an old card table with colorful rolls of paper, a basket of bows, tape, and scissors, and a stack of different sized boxes on the floor.

Bleary-eyed and exhausted, I shuffle to the table and rummage through the boxes. I get lucky when I find a small jewelry box, complete with the cotton square still inside. I slip the special, tiny gift inside and wrap it, taking my time to crease every edge just right. I even include ribbon, curling the ends with the flat blade of the scissors and attaching a shiny red bow and a reindeer gift tag. On the tag I address it: *For Axel, Love Lula.*

I curl up on Dad's favorite recliner, using Mom's afghan to cover me and stretching it all the way underneath my chin. Rather than putting the gift with the others underneath the tree, I tuck it into the pocket of my cardigan. Even though it's late, or I suppose early, I send a text to Axel, hoping he has his phone on silent.

I'm home.

With slow blinks, I stare at the lit Christmas tree, the white lights blurring through my tired vision. The cozy feeling of being home, on Christmas, blooms in my chest. For the first

time in a long time, I feel as if I made the right decision. I'll
have to return to Portland in a few days and go out on tour but
doing so without seeing Axel first made me unsettled.

Footsteps on the stairs cause me to jerk. But my heart slides
back down, returning to its home in my chest when I see Dad.

"Hey, baby," he whispers, making his way over to me.
"What are you doing here?"

"Sorry if we scared you."

He leans over, pressing a scruffy kiss to my temple. "We?"
he questions, pulling back.

"Olive and Jax came with me."

"That's nice." He smiles, patting my shoulder. "I'm glad
you're home."

"Me too, thanks, Dad."

"You want me to fix you a bed somewhere? In your old
room?"

"No, I don't want to wake Ariel. I'm fine out here."

"You sure?"

He seems tired, rubbing a hand down his face.

"It's the best place in the house on Christmas Eve." I gaze
up at him, smiling.

"Okay." He takes a few steps away, tapping me on the foot
as he passes. "Just don't spook Santa, or you'll have some very
disappointed kids to deal with."

"I won't." I grin. "Night, Dad."

He glances at the clock on the oven in the kitchen. "Well,
good morning, but since your mother won't let me work on the
farm today, I suppose I better go back to bed for at least another
hour or two."

He shuffles back up the stairs, and I'm left alone, once
again.

I stare at the twinkling lights on the tree for a few more
minutes, trying not to think about the look of surprise on each

face in the morning when they come downstairs. I try not to think about Axel's reaction to me being home. Or if I'm too late. If maybe he, Joanie, and Sadie are already a family unit again. That thought creates a ball of fire to burn in the pit of my stomach. But the weeks of rehearsals and the emotions of the night, combined with the nerve-racking drive over the mountain pass, force my eyes to finally shut.

I startle awake, catapulting in the recliner and sucking in a breath when someone nudges my arm. But when my eyes have a chance to focus and send signals to my brain, Axel is hovering over me. I blink back my surprise, rubbing at my eyes, which are suddenly wide awake.

"Hey, what are you doing here?" My heart wakes up, accelerating at the sight of him, and I have a strong need to touch him. I reach for his hand, and he allows it.

He presses his finger to his lips and says a muffled, "Shh," pointing toward the couch where a sleeping Sadie is curled into a ball. "I could ask you the same thing."

He rubs his thumb over the back of my hand, and the simple gesture sends goose bumps dancing up my arm.

"I've missed you. So much." There's so much more I want to say. But I start with that.

"You traveled through an icy pass on Christmas Eve just to tell me you've missed me?"

I adjust myself in the recliner, making room for him to join me, and yank him down. He doesn't object. He situates himself next to me, our bodies overlapping and our hands still touching.

"And to tell you . . . I hope I'm not too late."

He blinks at me, the reflection of the lights twinkling against his brown eyes. "Too late for what?"

My face heats underneath his gaze. "For us." I drop my chin to my chest, forcing my emotions at bay so I can get out the words I need to. "There's no reason why we can't make this work between us. Every couple has their issues. And me pursuing my dreams shouldn't be one of them. I already know you're supportive of them, and that's usually half the battle in a relationship."

Axel releases my hand and runs his palm across my arm, shoulder, and neck, until he cups my face. "What exactly are you saying?"

"I have to go on this tour. But it's only for a few months. We can keep in contact while I'm gone. If you and Sadie can't come visit me, as soon as the tour is over, I'll come back here. We'll have three months off after the tour."

"Me and Sadie?"

I nod. He grazes my cheek with his thumb, and I stare into his glassy eyes, inhaling a gulp of air. "Of course, you and Sadie. I love you both, you know that."

He nods. "But you pushed me away." He runs his hand down my neck.

"I know." I tuck my chin to my chest. "I'm sorry."

He lifts my chin with his finger so our eyes meet. "What's changed?"

I slide the small box from the pocket of my cardigan and hold it out to him. It feels like a peace offering. But it's more than that. This tiny, inexpensive gift is the grand gesture Axel needs in order to fully believe me and know my intentions are true. It's actually the most expensive thing I can offer: my heart.

He glances at it, at first raising his brows in an excited surprise, but it quickly changes to a frown. "What's this?"

"It's your Christmas gift."

"But you already sent gifts." He nudges his chin in the direction of the gifts adorned around the base of the tree.

"This is something I thought I should hand deliver."

"But I don't have anything for you." He rubs at the back of his neck. "I sent yours. Did they arrive?"

"Yes, now just open it," I whisper.

He hesitates but finally does as I ask, meticulously removing the bow, untying the ribbon, and tearing away the wrapping paper. His eyes flicker to mine before he opens the small box.

"It's not an engagement ring or something, if that's what you're worried about." I swat at his arm.

He doesn't reply, but his exhale of breath is audible. When he removes the lid and peers inside, his expression is confused at first, but then realization sets in. Because I know he's heard my mother's saying before. He removes the small pumpkin seed as if it's the most delicate thing he's ever handled.

I take the seed from him and pinch it between my fingers, holding it out to him. And it suddenly feels a little like I *am* proposing to him. I'm asking him to love me, to start a life with me, to commit to me and us.

He stares into my eyes with a burning I swear I can feel into the depths of my soul.

"My mom always says, love starts with a simple, tiny pumpkin seed. In our case, she's right. In the same way pumpkin seeds need water, sun, and good soil, love needs time, work, and to be nurtured." As corny as it's going to sound, I ask anyway, "So, what do you say? Do you want to help me nurture this pumpkin seed?"

"That's all I've ever wanted for us. Is to just love each other. At our best, and at our worst." He takes the seed from me and squeezes it inside his fist, holding it tight, like he's protecting it.

My heart squeezes in my chest.

"I love you, Lu. I'm pretty sure I fell in love with you the moment I saw you."

A smile tugs at my lips, and I have the urge to squish my face against his and never come up for air. "I love you too. And

I'm never giving up on us again. You, Sadie, you're my family now and you're stuck with me."

"That sounds like the best thing I've ever heard of."

We kiss, and even though it's been a few weeks since we've been together, it feels the same.

It feels familiar, perfect, and comfortable. It feels like home.

# Acknowledgments

First, and foremost, I want to thank God for the ability, drive, and talent to be a writer. I am especially grateful for His grace.

To my husband, Jeremy. Thank you for giving me space to chase my dreams and for being supportive of wherever they might take me. Thank you for being cool with me creating book boyfriends to swoon over. Even though you're my forever boyfriend and my best friend. Thanks for loving me and always making me laugh.

Thanks to my amazing kids, who show their support and tell others about my books. I'm so proud of each of you and I'm so blessed to be your mom.

A big thank you to my ultra intelligent editor, Jeanine Harrell. Your attention to detail and investment in my manuscript is much appreciated. Thank you for being a part of my journey!

To my fabulously talented cover artist Jaidyn, (who also happens to be my daughter) thank you for creating this beautiful cover! You saw my vision and made it your own. And I'm so in love with it! And you!

Thank you to my dad for instilling in me the importance of being a dreamer. Thanks for being my cheerleader and bragging about me to everyone you met. You were so proud of me and I knew that. This release day will be difficult without you, but I know you're still cheering me on. I love you and miss you every day!

To my mom, I'm grateful for your encouragement and support. Thank you for loving me in the best way a mom can. Love you! Thanks to my in-laws, siblings, and extended family, for the support, love, and prayers.

To my ride or die beta reader, Lissa Ruck. Your eagerness to read the worlds I've created is so touching. Thank you for your continued support.

Thank you to my beta readers and CP's for reading this book, and encouraging me, and giving insight: Lissa, Cassie, Bethany, Lauren, Kristine, and Tova.

To my ARC team, a huge thank you for being patient with me. Thank you for your time and willingness to give this book a chance and for the early reviews. Thank you to my online support system, the friends, connections, bookstagrammers—I will be forever grateful for you. Thank you to everyone who pre-ordered, purchased, read, and reviewed this book.

# About the Author

Starla DeKruyf writes caffeinated, comical, and swoony love stories. Her love of romance novels began when she borrowed her friend's copy of Tiger Eyes by Judy Blume and kept it hidden from her mom. When she's not slinging coffee or taxiing her kids around, you can find her jamming out to her book playlists and writing her next swoony romance, usually by hand. She lives in Spring, Texas, with her husband, three children, and a rescue pup.

# Also by Starla DeKruyf

Pineridge series:

Eight Days of Christmas

Tricked in October

A Standalone Romantic Comedy

The Heart Rehab Experiment

The
HEART
REHAB
EXPERIMENT
A hilarious and sexy
romantic comedy
STARLA DEKRUYF

www.ingramcontent.com/pod-product-compliance
Lightning Source LLC
Chambersburg PA
CBHW021806130726

47987CB00010B/3029